Cover Up

JOHN FRANCOME

Cover Up

headline

First published in 2005
by HEADLINE BOOK PUBLISHING

1

Cataloguing in Publication Data is available from the British Library

ISBN 0 7553 2690 3 (hardback)
ISBN 0 7553 2691 1 (trade paperback)

Typeset in Veljovic by Avon DataSet Ltd,
Bidford on Avon, Warwickshire

Printed and bound in Great Britain by
Clays Ltd, St Ives plc

Headline's policy is to use papers that are natural, renewable and
recyclable products and made from wood grown in sustainable
forests. The logging and manufacturing processes are expected to
conform to the environmental regulations of the country of origin.

HEADLINE BOOK PUBLISHING
A division of Hodder Headline
338 Euston Road
London NW1 3BH

www.headline.co.uk
www. hodderheadline.com

Cover Up

The man with the ponytail didn't hate the people around him. They'd done nothing to him and to hate them would be a sin. He envied them though. Envy was also a sin but he couldn't help it. He envied their happy faces and good manners and their well-fed good looks. The English out for a day at the races. He envied their niceness.

Nice was one of the first English words he'd learned. It was very useful. It could mean lots of things. Nice day, nice horse, nice woman.

His life hadn't been very nice so far. He took his share of the blame for that. The world was tougher where he came from and he hadn't always done the right things.

Like the girl he'd loved and lost. Sometimes he'd been nice to her but at other times he'd been hard. He'd known it at the time but he hadn't been able to help himself. He regretted that and he wished he had the chance to make it up to her. To say sorry for the bad things he'd done and ask to make it right.

Then they could be together again.

But he thought he was just kidding himself. She'd gone for good, out of the country and out of his life. They'd never meet again.

Turns out he was wrong about that.

He could see her now, amongst a group of nice English, laughing and drinking in the sunshine. More lovely than ever.

She'd be thrilled to see him again and to know he still loved her.

1

They could make their life with each other in this new place. Back together again – like it was meant to be.

She'd be so happy when he showed himself to her again – he was sure of it.

He waited for his moment.

Part One
Spring

Chapter One

The Two Thousand Guineas at Newmarket is the first Classic of the English Flat-racing season. Run over the Rowley Mile course, the race takes just over ninety-five seconds to complete which, by any standards, is not long. If you mistimed a trip to the Tote or the toilet, it would be easy to miss the whole damn thing. But for Rob Harding, former jockey and now stud farm manager, the race seemed to take an eternity.

The horses were all three-year-olds, still young and raw. Some had only had a couple of previous appearances on a racetrack. But one of their number was about to prove himself a Classic winner and enter the ranks of the immortals. Not to mention winning a purse of over £180,000.

But it didn't do to think about prizes. Not when you were the owner of one of the horses in question. A half-owner, to be precise, but that was more than enough horse to get Rob's blood pumping crazily and bottle the air in his lungs. His friend Steve Armstrong, who owned the other half of Goldeneye, muttered something in his ear but Rob couldn't make it out. Nerves had affected his hearing too.

As the nineteen runners hurtled out of the starting stalls, the knot of bodies around Rob seemed to press as one against the balcony rail, though Rob could not have imagined it was possible for them to be wedged any tighter. He was crushed up against Bella and Kathy, his wife and stepdaughter – 'the heavenly twins' as he sometimes called them – and Bella shot him a quick, concerned glance from beneath her honey-blonde fringe, before turning to face the large screen on the other side of the course. As yet there was no point in them craning their necks to try and discern the line of horses thundering towards the stand, still almost a mile off. They would be in clear sight soon enough.

Rob picked out Goldeneye at once to the left of the picture; his rangy burned-sugar frame and white eyepatch were distinctive, added to the fact that Rob had seen the horse almost every day of his short life. Goldeneye had been bred on Rob's own farm and was as familiar to him as his own face in a shaving mirror.

He'd not thought much of Goldie as a foal and it was a bit of a surprise when he'd turned out to be a flyer. As a yearling he'd been spindly and unpromising, like a seedling that shoots up too fast without the strength to sustain its growth. But he'd filled out as a juvenile – 'grown into himself' as racing folk say. He had taken to life in training without fuss and showed some older horses a clean pair of heels on the gallops. All the same, Rob had been amazed when Goldeneye had walked away with his maiden race at Newbury.

Steve had won plenty with that victory which, being a bookmaker himself, had given him particular pleasure. He couldn't believe it when Rob told him he hadn't had a bet. 'Tough luck, chum,' he'd said. 'You'll never see him at fourteens again.' And Rob, who never bet on horses to whom he was attached, had no doubt his friend was right.

But there'd only been one other race for Goldie as a two-year-old – second in the Dewhurst Stakes on this same course – after a virus had put him out of action for the summer months. Fortunately he'd been sound all winter and put in some sharp work, news of which had somehow leaked out and sent his Guineas price plummeting. Rob's father used to say it was impossible to keep a secret in racing and Rob reckoned he was right. If only the old man were still alive so he could tell him so.

Suddenly the runners were upon them, charging towards the packed stands. Rob could see that Goldeneye was a couple of lengths behind the favourite, Tabouleh, his conqueror in the Dewhurst the previous year. But Tabouleh was at full stretch, his jockey working him hard while Goldeneye was moving easily, still with something in reserve.

'Get after him, Tomas!' bellowed Steve's voice to his left.

The jockey was almost perched on the horse's neck, riding so short it would have been out of the question for most riders. But Tomas was nothing if not flamboyant. Rob had often wondered if all jockeys in the Czech Republic went about their business in the way he did. He was matinee-idol handsome and the flashiest bugger in the saddle Rob had ever seen. But beneath the showmanship Rob knew that Tomas was a skilled performer, not to mention a real worker. He'd started out in England breaking in yearlings and helping out on Rob's stud. Later, when there was a staff crisis at Rushmore, the jockey, had introduced Rob to the curly-haired beauty by the side of trainer Charlie Moorehead: Tomas's sister, Ivana. As far as Rob was concerned, the two Czechs were almost part of the family.

'Go, Tom, go!' roared Steve again, anger and frustration clearly audible in his tone.

There was no way the jockey could have heard Steve's shout in the clamour all around but it seemed as if he did. His whip flashed and his body worked as he drove the horse beneath him towards the line. Goldeneye lengthened his stride.

He's left it too late, Rob thought. Even though Goldie was quickening, there were barely a dozen yards left to the post and Tabouleh showed no signs of flagging. Then, remarkably, the daylight between the two animals vanished. Goldeneye was a caramel-coloured blur, floating alongside his rival as if on wings.

In front of Rob, Bella and Kathy were jumping and squealing, Steve was bellowing but the words were swallowed in the tumult around. Everyone was caught up in the ecstasy of the moment. As in a battle, or a lover's clinch, there are no neutrals in the climax of a Classic horse race.

'I don't believe it,' was the thought in Rob's head as the two horses merged into one, flying over the line like a beast with eight legs. But there was a clear winner: Goldeneye by a neck. It was either brilliant timing or sheer good luck.

'Jesus, Ivana,' said Steve, when the hugging and back-slapping finally stopped. 'For a moment there I was going to kill your brother. Now I'm going to find the little sod and give him a great big kiss.'

Rob reckoned he spoke for all of them.

Geoff Wyatt watched the race on a wide flat-screen TV in the window of Dixon's, ignoring the shoppers trooping up and down the high street around him. No one bothered him; they ambled past his skeletal figure as if he didn't exist. In his hand he still held the betting slip he'd filled out in the bookmaker's shop on the other side of the road. It read: Goldeneye, Newmarket, 3.40, £10 win. A winning ticket. If only.

He didn't get out of the house much these days, not on his own anyway. But he'd planned this trip specially. He didn't have many ambitions left in life. Wishes and dreams maybe – winning the lottery, for example. But not anything that could count as a proper objective, apart from watching the racing programmes on the television. Even they no longer held the charm they once had. It was like pressing his face to the window of a house he had once owned, knowing he was barred from entering. Just as he was barred these days from entering a racecourse or a training yard or a bookmaker's. He'd been 'warned off' all licensed premises until he paid the final fifteen thousand pounds he owed.

Once, fifteen thousand pounds would have been simple to arrange. Not exactly petty cash but a single phone call to the bank would have fixed it. Nowadays it might as well be ten million pounds, it was just as far out of his reach.

To think it was a bookie who'd blown the whistle on him.

A bookie, furthermore, whose pockets he had lined for years. The bookie who owned the shop on the high street.

So the purpose of his little jaunt this afternoon – not that jaunt accurately described his hesitant plod, the bloody pills didn't half slow him up – the minor ambition he set out to accomplish, was to place a bet. Even if it didn't come up, just the placing of it would have given him satisfaction. A glimpse of the old life. A foot back in the door of the house he'd once owned.

He'd felt the stirrings of a familiar excitement as he'd slipped inside the bookie's behind a labourer in dirty overalls and sucked in the familiar atmosphere of stale coffee and nicotine – it might be No Smoking these days but the fug of fags was on every punter's clothes.

He'd always had a flutter on the Guineas. He'd had runners in the race, too, on many occasions though he'd never landed the big prize, more's the pity. He had a good feeling about this Goldeneye. He always set store by the breeding and though the colt's sire was an out-and-out sprinter, there was stamina on the dam's side. He still knew how to read a horse's bloodline.

He'd almost forgotten his changed circumstances as he slid the betting slip and the tenner under the window for the clerk. This was more like life should be. Maybe there were some little pleasures left after all.

The woman behind the counter took the money and looked up at him.

'I'll take the price,' he said.

'No, you bloody won't.' It wasn't the woman speaking but a man standing behind her. He was a youngster, under thirty anyway, which made him just a kid in Geoff's book, wearing an ill-fitting off-the-peg suit and an earring. He acted like he owned the place.

'I saw you sneaking in here, you doddering old fool. You've got a bloody nerve trying to place bets. Don't you realise you're banned?'

Geoff's system seemed to have seized up. He wanted to square his shoulders, to speak in the tones that had once addressed the board and the shop floor, and put this jumped-up car salesman in his place. But no sound came out of his mouth.

Everyone in the small room was staring at him.

'Clear off out of it,' the man said. 'Give him his money back, Shelley. If you ever see him in here again you've got my permission to kick his arse back out into the street.'

Now Geoff looked down at the useless slip in his hand. He would have won all of £60 if they'd accepted his bet. How pathetic. He chucked the crumpled paper into the gutter.

Ivana was in a state of shock but not because of Goldeneye's victory. The race had passed her by in a blur and though she had pantomimed excitement to match the euphoria all around, in truth she had hardly taken it in. Her thoughts had been running on other tracks, playing and replaying scenes from a life she thought she had left behind forever.

The last person she'd expected to see among the crowd here at Newmarket was her ex-lover. Milos Cerny belonged to the world back on Uncle Kamil's horse farm in the Czech Republic, an existence she didn't want to revisit. Any life with Milos in it was a hellhole.

He must have been watching before the racing began as they picnicked in the spring sunshine on the grass by the white picket fence that lined the course. Charlie had gone off to fuss around Goldie but the rest of the group were there, Rob and Steve, Bella and Kathy. Ivana had allowed herself to get a little high on the champagne. After all, why not? This outing was a treat: Newmarket on Guineas weekend. How English. She was determined to enjoy everything about it.

That was when she'd made her big mistake – not that it would have made much difference, but wandering off on her own had made it easy for Milos to approach her. Stupidly, on the pretext of checking out the runners for the first, she'd strolled off. Kathy had been getting on her nerves, the way she'd been laughing too loud at Steve's quips and squirming around in that apology of a skirt. Even

10

though her feelings for Steve were in the past – absolutely – the sight of him flirting with other women turned her stomach. So she'd marched off from the group before it spoiled her mood.

Under the trees by the pre-parade ring, a ghost from the past barred her way.

'*Ahoj, Ivana!*' He spoke to her in Czech. '*Jak to jde?*' How's it going?

He'd done his best to fit in with the race-going crowd, a too-tight blazer stretched across his broad chest and a trilby hat – how laughable – perched on his helmet of black hair. At first she thought he'd cut it – his big features seemed larger than ever – then she noticed the ponytail. She should have known better, he'd always been vain about his hair.

'Aren't you going to say hello?'

She'd been staring, dumbstruck. She wanted to tell him to burn in hell but she said, 'What are you doing here, Milos?'

He smiled, an expansive grin that showed his big white teeth. She might have seen it as friendly if those button-black eyes hadn't been trained on her like searchlights. 'It's a free country, *moje holka.*'

'I'm not your girl.'

'But you used to be, didn't you?'

Indeed she did. It made her uncomfortable to think about it, though she had plenty of excuse. She'd been scarcely seventeen at the time and barely knew her way around a stables. He was older and knew everything; he virtually ran the place when Uncle Kamil was hitting the bottle. Strictly speaking, he wasn't handsome but force of personality made his prow of a nose and hooded eyes seem distinctive, warrior-like, imposing.

He'd serenaded her at night in his attic room with the candles and joss sticks burning. He'd crouch over the guitar, the mane of hair loose to his shoulders, softening his features, as he ran his shovel-like hands over the strings and sang in a haunting, ragged voice. She'd probably have fallen for anyone in those circumstances, friendless and miles from home, with him treating her like someone special, rolling her joints and pouring wine and crooning love songs in fractured English that she only half understood. But that had been in the early days. Before he'd started using her as a punchbag.

He was beaming at her hungrily. She wished she'd not left that second button on her blouse undone.

'You're looking as gorgeous as ever.'

'I have to go.'

'To meet your English friends? They look very nice. Quality people. You're doing well for yourself in this country.'

A few yards away, spectators were milling around flapping racecards and laughing in the sunshine. She resisted the urge to run into their midst and disappear. She had her dignity.

He put his hand on her arm. The one he'd used to grip her by the hair while the other punched her in the ribs.

'I'm based over here too, you know. We should get together.'

'Take your hand off me.'

'Ivanicka.'

It was what he used to call her. It disgusted her that she should have to hear it again from him.

She yanked her arm away and ran for the crowd. To hell with dignity.

He called after her. 'See you soon.'

Milos: the first man she'd ever loved, the only man she'd ever hated. She'd thought she was safe and here she was running from him again.

That's all she could think of, as the celebrations of victory raged around her.

The kids next door were playing football, their shouts shattering the peace of the autumn afternoon. The back gardens of the terrace were long and thin, more suited to games of cricket, in Geoff's opinion, though that would put the windows in jeopardy. Not that breaking a few windows would have bothered those little ruffians. In any case, they had no time for Geoff's opinions. No one did, not these days.

A battered black and white checked football flew over the fence and bounced on the dry scrubby grass that passed for a lawn. A barrage of groans and curses rose from the other side of the fence. Geoff was used to industrial language – he'd made his money in industry, after all – but he preferred not to hear it uttered by those whose voices had yet to break.

All the same, he rose slowly from the stained plastic chair and bent to pick up the ball. It felt good in his hands. A man, whatever his age or state of mind, likes to hold a kid's ball. It reminds him of so much.

With an awkward, long out of practice motion, he tossed the ball back over the fence, silencing for a moment the recriminations that had been taking place. Then came a chorus of 'Thanks, mate' – which was something, the most politeness he'd received from outside his immediate circle for some time. It was followed by a muttered remark that he didn't catch, which sparked an explosion of laughter. They'd identified the thrower and whispered the name they used for him – Zombie Man.

They called him that because he was gaunt and ghostly and moved silently about the world as if he were only half alive. It was an accurate name. Kids weren't stupid.

If he could have been bothered to speak, Geoff would have told them that he liked the nickname. That it reminded him of a horse he'd once owned: Zombie Express, a chestnut chaser who'd enjoyed half a dozen decent years back in the eighties. He'd first raced on the Flat, where it became clear that the first half of his name was more apt than the second. So they'd turned him into a useful jumper and his guts and stamina had kept him plugging away through the mud and over the fences of the most testing National Hunt courses in the land.

Zombie Express had had pluck all right – he never gave up. Geoff could do with some of the old horse's spirit in him right now.

Once he'd run a business which turned over millions a

year, employing three hundred workers. Had it running like clockwork, too, so it gave him time to do what he most enjoyed in life – horseracing. At one point he'd had more than twenty animals in training but he tried to keep it down to a dozen, mostly jumpers but always a few choice Flat runners in the hope of landing the big prizes. He'd nearly won a Derby once – Astrakhan Collar, didn't quite get the trip and finished third – and had cheered home several Group One winners. None of them had gone on to have successful stud careers. That was a regret.

There were many regrets, few of them down to the horses, most of them down to himself. He'd always said he never worried about money but that was when he had plenty. It was a worry, all right, when the money escaped you. The harder he'd tried to hang on to it in these last years, the faster it had gone. Like trying to hold water in your hands, watching it dribble away through your fingers till you were left holding nothing. Except your debts.

He eyed the wooden post that leaned against the remains of a garden shed. It had been used as one end of a clothesline but some previous tenant had botched the foundations and it sagged loose. Jason said he was going to fix it at the weekend, dig a deeper hole and lay down some cement. Then Rose could put up the new clothesline she'd bought.

The post couldn't be that heavy, could it? He could surely manage to get it through the kitchen and up the stairs. So what if it tired him out? He had nothing to save his energy for.

Ivana hadn't been able to get near Tomas since the finish of the Guineas and she was desperate to talk to him. When she'd first joined her brother in England she'd poured her heart out about her unhappy romance back in Czechoslovakia. Tomas would understand her distress at the appearance of Milos. But she couldn't isolate him – he was too busy milking his moment in the spotlight.

She'd waited till after the presentation ceremony, watching anxiously amidst the crowd, keeping her eyes open for Milos. Rob and Steve shook hands on the rostrum, Charlie took a modest bow and then Tomas went up with arms raised in triumph, blowing kisses to the crowd. He got a cheer and a round of applause for his antics, mingled with some disbelieving laughter. Ivana knew that wouldn't bother him. He was determined to make a name for himself.

But even after the journalists had finished with him Tomas remained a centre of attention with race-goers – most of them young and female, Ivana noted – eager for a word, some pressing him to sign their racecards.

When she caught his eye he turned from his fans and held his arms out wide.

'You were fantastic!' she said as she embraced him. 'Brilliant – I'm so proud of you.' It was what was expected. 'I need to talk to you,' she added in Czech.

'Sure,' he said, 'but there's a guy here I've got to see.'

'This is urgent, Tomas.'

'So's this. It's Sammy Swan.'

'Who?'

'The agent. It's like I've been telling you, I need a new agent to get anywhere.'

Ivana could see that Tomas was bubbling over with excitement. He'd been trying to find a decent agent since last season when he'd fallen out with the previous one. She probably wouldn't get any sense out of her brother at the moment. He certainly wouldn't want to talk about her wretched love life back in Czechoslovakia.

Later, she managed to get him on his own. He was still full of the afternoon's events. The meeting with Swan had gone well and she could understand Tomas's ebullience – it had been a long road for him. On the other hand, she had needs too and she couldn't keep her troubles to herself any longer.

'Milos is here,' she told him.

She could see it taking a moment or two for him to register the name. Though he knew the history of her unhappy romance – well, most of it – a lot of water had flowed under the bridge in the three and a half years since she had arrived in England.

'Where?'

'Right here.'

'Jesus.' He put his arms round her and immediately she felt her eyes prick with tears. They'd been there all along but she couldn't hold them in any longer.

'Did he see you?'

She nodded, digging her chin into his shoulder. 'He spoke to me. He said he wanted to see me again.'

'No way is that going to happen. He can't touch you here.'

It was good to hear him say it, even if she didn't believe it. 'What if he comes after me?'

He stared at her, concern in his soft brown eyes.

'But you and him are ancient history now. Why would he bother?'

Because he's obsessed. Because he knows I'm scared of him. Because he can.

But she didn't say any of these things. She didn't want to spoil Tomas's day any more than she had done already.

'Maybe you're right.'

'You bet.' He rubbed the nape of her neck tenderly, as you would caress a cat, she thought. Tomas had a way with animals. 'Anyhow, I'm here to protect you. And there's all your other big tough English friends. Nothing bad is going to happen, I swear.'

'OK.' She wiped her eyes and forced a smile onto her face.

But she was not smiling within.

Kathy was having a great time. Of course, just being here to see Goldie take part in the Guineas would have been enjoyable but for him to win was fantastic. And the way it had happened, with Tomas snatching the race on the line, couldn't have been scripted any better. They'd all gone potty afterwards, champagne had flowed and time had passed in a bit of a blur, though she did remember a man with a plummy voice shoving a microphone into her face at the presentation. She'd been on TV! They all had – it had been incredible!

But that wasn't the end of it. So far, it had been a boring year, now the excitement of Mum and Rob's wedding and the move to Rushmore Stud Farm was in the past. She'd even wondered, though she was damned if she'd admit it to Mum, if she shouldn't have stayed on at school or gone to sixth form college. But the thought of schools and exams just turned her stomach. Even the computer course she'd done over the winter, though it had been reasonably interesting, had depressed her. Sitting in class was not her idea of liberated adult life. Neither was hanging around at home, though she did help out on the stud when she could, giving Mum a hand in the office and doing horse chores. But she was aware she ought to be more independent.

So Steve's offer had come just at the right moment and set the seal on a memorable day.

Till now, she didn't think she'd made much of an impression on Rob's bookmaker friend. He cut such a cool figure in his handmade suit yet there was something casual about him – the open-necked shirt, the hint of designer stubble, the glint of mischief in his ice-blue eyes. To be frank, he was drop-dead gorgeous if you liked that kind of look. Kathy didn't think she did until she found him by her side on the rail of the parade ring before the last race.

'What's your fancy then?'

'I like the look of that one.' Kathy pointed to a small bay horse with white feet on the opposite side of the ring. 'I'm sure he winked at me when he went past so I'd bet on him.'

Steve grinned. 'You're just the kind of punter I like.'

'What kind's that then?'

'The sort who keep me in business.'

Kathy was stung. She prided herself on being able to spot a good horse – she'd inherited the knack from her mother. In fact, her choice had a nice deep chest and shiny coat, points which always appealed to her.

'What odds will you give me then?' she said.

He considered, the grin still in place. He seemed to find her amusing. 'Since it's you, double carpet. If you know what that means.'

Naturally she knew – 33–1 – but she didn't rise to the bait. Instead she pulled a ten-pound note from her purse.

'I'll have a fiver each way, then.'

He waved her money away. 'On the house. If you come and work for me.'

She wondered if she'd heard correctly.

'Rob says you're at a bit of a loose end at the moment and my secretary's just left. Are you interested?'

Unusually for her, Kathy was at a loss for words.

Steve's blue eyes fascinated her. 'I gather you know your way round an office and you can work a computer. Come and give it a try.'

'Are you serious?'

'Absolutely. And, as I said, new employees are allowed a free bet.'

She was tempted to accept his offer there and then. It felt right, it would prove she could do something off her own bat – go for it! But she hesitated. Just then another voice cut into their conversation.

'Hi, Kathy. Mr Armstrong.' It was Gary Moorehead, the son of Goldie's trainer. He was also the boy who'd taken Kathy out the previous weekend and whose calls she'd been ducking ever since. She liked Gary a lot, he was the only friend of her own generation she'd made in her time at Rushmore, but she didn't want him going all serious on her. After all, what was a kiss between friends at a boozy party? Trust him to show up now.

Steve had turned from Kathy and was shaking the trainer's son by the hand. 'Great job with Goldie, son. I can't thank you enough.'

Gary blushed. 'It's kind of you to say so, but I only travelled up in the box with him. I can't claim any credit.'

Though officially assistant trainer, Gary had only recently graduated from college and was still finding his feet at his father's yard. Kathy knew a few noses were out of joint at his appointment and that he felt bad about it, which was a bit silly of him, in her opinion.

'How's it going, Kathy?' Gary's gaze was all over her which, to be honest, wasn't always unwelcome. But not right now. Next to Steve, Gary looked just what he was, an awkward boy-man.

'OK.'

'Kathy's coming to work for me,' Steve said, putting an arm round Kathy's shoulder. 'She's going to be my personal assistant.'

Kathy liked the sound of that – it had a ring to it. She beamed at Gary. 'Isn't that fantastic?'

'Er, yes. Congratulations.'

He might at least sound like he meant it.

The wooden post was heavy all right but Geoff managed to get it up the stairs. Up two steep flights because these old terraces were tall and narrow. The good thing was it fitted between the banister rails on the landing and the other end rested snugly on the box ledge opposite which housed the soil pipe running from the top-floor lavatory.

Geoff took a moment to rest and consider his next step. He didn't have all that much time and he wanted to do it properly.

He spent a good couple of minutes tying one end of Rose's new washing line to the newel post, making sure the knot wouldn't slip. He threw the cord over the wooden post. Then he cut it to what he hoped was the right length, leaving enough to make a noose.

He put on his winter coat and filled his pockets with heavy things. He found a couple of half bricks in the garden and some big stones. That was good. The more weight the better. The kids were still playing. He hoped they'd never find out what was taking place next door on a warm spring afternoon when they were having fun. But he supposed it was inevitable.

No point in thinking along those lines.

Rose was never going to have children. Even now she'd

finally got married, there'd be no grandchildren. She'd told him so. At least Rose would have Jason to look after her when he'd gone. She was such a great girl. He hoped she'd forgive him.

He tested his weight on the line. It held, no matter how hard he tugged.

He was getting tired. Nearly over now.

When the Guineas was finished, they'd interviewed Goldeneye's connections on TV. Geoff had stayed on to watch, transfixed by regret. For all of his life, he'd been part of gatherings like this, a group of insiders celebrating in happy disbelief. But standing there on the pavement of the drab high street, watching through a shop window, these people just looked smug and self-important. Is that how he'd appeared to all those outsiders looking in?

He didn't want to be an outsider.

And there'd been one particular face among that smiling, smirking bunch on the TV screen which had filled him with disgust. The man who'd poisoned all his happiness, looking like he owned the world.

If that was what the world was coming to, Geoff no longer wanted any part of it. He put the noose over his head and kicked himself off the top step out into the void.

In the back garden a football sailed over the fence to a moan of disappointment.

'Oy, mister, chuck us our ball back.'

But he didn't.

Effing stupid Zombie Man.

Chapter Two

Though he was clutching a full glass of champagne Rob hadn't touched a drop – not yet. He could get drunk any old day of the week. Around him in the bar, people were in high spirits. He tuned out the laughter and the loud conversation. This was a moment he wanted to remember.

He'd had good times in racing before but nothing like this. Maybe if he'd ridden the winner of the Gold Cup or the Grand National he'd have had a yardstick to measure Goldeneye's achievement. But he'd never climbed the highest peaks as a jockey. Even if he had, he doubted if winning a Classic as an owner and a breeder could be bettered. And it was just the beginning; the prospect of landing more big races lay ahead. Then, when Goldie's three-year-old season was over, the horse could retire to stud. Already, just by winning the Guineas, the horse had a ticket to a career as a stallion. And if he stood at Rushmore it would boost the entire business – kick it up a division or two at a stroke, so long as he proved as fertile as he was quick.

It was just a possibility, but a delicious one. The kind of dream he'd only dare share with Bella.

His wife was just a few feet away, laughing whole-heartedly at some joke, her hand on the arm of the man next to her for support. Bella didn't do things by halves. As her throaty gurgle died away she glanced in Rob's direction and gave him a look. It was the kind of look that said, I might be having a great time with this guy but I'd rather be alone with you. That was exactly how Rob felt about her too.

Bella was an angel. A woman who had appeared like magic to shine her light into his meaningless existence and transform it. A year ago, he had never even met her; now she was as much part of his life as his right arm. It was incredible to think of it.

He might not have known her before but he knew of her. At one time the whole country, it seemed, had been thrilled by her exploits at the Olympics. She'd been part of a three-day event team that brought home a silver medal. A typical British failure, a few cynics said, they missed out on the big one. But the squad had been bedevilled by injury and bad luck, so no one in the know had fancied their chances. And it had come down to a last day clear round by a slim blonde girl on an enormous grey horse which had shot the team into the frame. Rob had been an apprentice at a West Country yard at the time, just out of school, with no prospect of riding races in anything like the near future. He'd watched the games on the telly in the unrefined atmosphere of the lads' hostel where they rated the female competitors strictly in terms of shagability. When Bella Browning appeared on screen in a skimpy Union Jack T-shirt and little white shorts, rooting for our boys in the rowing, she'd topped the poll by a street.

A few years later, he saw her at a racing dinner next to her husband, a languid drink of water with a laugh like a foghorn. A polo player, he was told. She'd looked even more gorgeous than in her riding days, her golden mop of hair gleaming like a beacon from across the room, commanding his attention throughout the evening. But he'd not spoken to her. What could he have said? I used to really fancy you when you were in the Olympics? And with the slight touch of West Midlands in his voice he'd have sounded like a right prat amidst her polo pals. No thanks.

Fortunately, when he met her properly, there was no time for him to prepare himself in any way, no time to worry about what to wear and have his tongue tie up in knots at the prospect of sounding sensible. Funny how a long-distance adolescent crush could still stop a full-grown man in his tracks.

He'd encountered her at the end of the covering season, when her mare had been sent to mate with Rob's senior stallion. Cape Fear was a vicious-tempered mountain of testosterone-fuelled muscle and sinew who terrorised his handlers and had once attacked a stable girl. But Cape Fear had been quick in his short career as a racehorse and his progeny were renowned for their fleetness of foot. As a consequence, he commanded a decent covering fee, twice that of Rob's other stallion, Curtain Raiser. In the equine hierarchy of Rushmore Stud Farm, Cape Fear ruled the roost because he paid the bills.

That afternoon, even though firmly held on either side, the stallion had been particularly truculent and it had required all of Rob's skill and that of Jacko, his regular helper from the village, to ensure that the object of Cape Fear's momentary affections was not savaged. Not unnaturally the mare was spooked by the whole experience.

After the covering, while Jacko led the temporarily docile stallion away, Rob relaxed and the jittery mare aimed a kick in his direction. Instinct prevented the hoof landing squarely on his thigh but, as he leapt aside, Rob slipped and landed heavily in a pile of droppings. He swore loud and long as he sprawled on the floor, much to the amusement of the lads who were watching.

'Just like a bloody woman,' he muttered as he squatted on his knees, brushing horse muck off his jeans. 'Give her the poke of her life and she dumps you in the shit.'

There was a different note to their laughter this time, throaty and melodious. Rob looked up to see that they'd been joined by a woman in jeans and a primrose-yellow shirt. The mare's owner had finally turned up. The booking had been made by a Mrs de Lisle but, as Rob took in the silky blonde bob and familiar, impish grin, he realised who she really was.

'You're Bella Browning,' he said.

'I used to be.' Her smile faded as she stared at him – God,

what must he look like? – and held out a hand to help him to his feet.

She'd raised him up. The way he looked at it now, the act was symbolic. And things had kept getting better for the pair of them, culminating in Goldie's victory today.

Bella caught his eye and grinned.

When he got home he'd look out the old stud book, the one his dad had bought when he'd first started chasing his dream of breeding horses. The brown leather cover was scuffed and stained but the lettering on the cover – 'Rushmore Stud', embossed in gold – still retained most of its gloss. His father had begun the record back in 1973 with a mare called Smithfield Track – named after the first racecourse in Britain, so his dad used to tell young Rob when he sat on his knee and turned the heavy white pages.

In nearly thirty years his father had bred and raced over sixty horses and never produced the really good one he longed for. Until now, of course.

Rob could trace Goldeneye back five generations. His dam had been bred at Rushmore, raced in his father's colours and then sold to Steve's father who had kept her at the stud. She was dead too, more's the pity.

He was getting sentimental but he didn't care. Other people and other horses had played their part in Golden-eye's triumph and they should be remembered. He'd record Goldie's Guineas triumph in his father's old book because it belonged to his dad as much as it did to him. If the old man were still alive he'd be telling everyone in the bar about his lifetime quest to breed a Classic winner.

Rob lifted his glass to his lips and raised a silent toast.

Ivana had slipped away from the crowd in the bar and returned to the balcony of the stand. She felt safer up here, where there was less chance of running into Milos. She wished she could just go. The day was spoiled.

A hand gripped her elbow.

She pulled away, a gasp of fear in her throat.

'Steady on.'

It was Charlie. His face was flushed and his eyes were twinkling with mischief.

'It's OK, sweetheart, they're all still downstairs. No one has got their beady eyes on us.'

He'd misinterpreted her alarm. His big hand found the curve of her waist, pulling her into his bulk. She softened. She liked the feel of his solid form next to her, even though she knew the security he exuded was just an illusion.

How they'd kept their affair secret for the past six months was a mystery. Were people just unobservant? More likely, they didn't think Charlie would dare cheat on his formidable, horse-faced wife. Or that an attractive woman in her mid-twenties would fall for a middle-aged family man with a blood-pressure problem. More fool them.

All the same, she doubted if they would ever have connected if she hadn't gone to look for her brother at Charlie's yard on the day that Green Stripe, the yard's veteran sprinter, had broken a leg at Warwick and been put down. She'd found the place almost deserted, with only the trainer himself standing as still as a statue in the dead horse's stall. He didn't respond to her greeting and she thought he'd not even been aware of her presence as she retreated. But the next day he sought her out at Rushmore to apologise.

He wasn't like her other boyfriends. He wasn't young or handsome or, strictly speaking, available. But he was funny and knowledgeable and passionate about his horses, not to mention accomplished at his business – his yard regularly produced high-class horses. A man of seniority and standing who shared Ivana's love for horses – how could she not be tempted by a suitor like that?

In the first days of their liaison, she'd dreamed that he might dump Louise for her. He wasn't the philandering type, he'd said so and Ivana believed him when he claimed she was the only woman who'd ever tempted him to stray outside his marriage. So he must love her. Successful man changes wife for a younger, sexier woman – it was a familiar tale the world over. Ivana waited for the narrative to unfold.

Well, she knew better than that now. Charlie was no youthful romantic. He wasn't going to turn his domestic life upside down for her. The English had a phrase for girls in her position. She was Charlie's 'bit on the side'. So at least she'd learned something.

'I'll give you a ride back afterwards.' His breath was hot in her ear, the double entendre obvious.

'Aren't there things you have to do?' He was the winning trainer of the Guineas. If the press and public were all over Tomas, they'd be after Charlie too.

'I'd rather spend the time with you.' He kissed her fiercely.

'What time can we leave?' she murmured into his throat, enjoying his grip on her waist.

Even ten minutes in the security of his arms in the back of his car was better than nothing. It was what she needed to wipe the picture of Milos from her mind.

Bella was watching her booze intake – someone had to be sober enough to get them all home. Winning a Classic with a home-bred horse was an incredible achievement but the party could soon go sour if someone got done for drink-driving on the way back to Warwickshire. Not that she wasn't as thrilled as anybody at the way Goldie had thrust his adorable brown and white head across the finishing line to pip the favourite. But what she felt most was not triumph or ecstasy but good old-fashioned relief. Though she'd not been professionally involved in racing she'd worked with horses all her life and reckoned she knew how to spot a winner. In the wee hours of the morning, with Rob lying awake in a nervous sweat, she'd convinced him Goldie would win. Thank God he had. And, practically speaking, the prize money would come in handy.

Since Bella had married Rob and moved into Rushmore Stud Farm, she'd tried not to upset the apple cart by making too many changes. Rob had inherited the ramshackle old place from his father; it was where he'd grown up and she knew it was filled with memories of a family past. But the

place was a disorganised mess, badly in need of modern-
ising. Rob had begun the process of knocking down old
farm buildings and replacing them with barns and boxes
and other facilities suitable for a twenty-first-century horse-
breeding operation. But things had only gone so far. The
trouble with owning a stud was that there was always
something to spend your money on.

Bella had some ideas of her own how to balance the
Rushmore books. She'd helped her father fight off
bankruptcy when his eventing stable was in trouble five
years ago and she'd learned a lot of lessons about staying
solvent. Unfortunately that sometimes meant making
tough decisions, like now, and she didn't want to appear
insensitive. After today, and this windfall, maybe she could
get her hand more firmly on the tiller and steer their ship
on a steadier course. Right at the moment, however,
surrounded by her raucous and well-lubricated fellow race-
goers, it was not the time to open discussions with her
husband. That could wait.

Bella had always been level-headed. In her short time in
the public eye as a three-day-eventer – she'd been an
Olympic team member at the age of twenty – she'd been
plastered all over the back pages and lauded for her skill
and flair. But, to Bella, the truth seemed less glamorous.
Aside from the luck of being photogenic, in her opinion she
was simply well-organised and self-disciplined, a hard
grafter who made the most of her talents. What other way
was there to be?

She took that commonsense approach into everything
she did. Unfortunately, it didn't always work out as
successfully as her eventing. Her first marriage, for
example, had not survived, for all her best efforts. But then,
in marriage as in horse-riding, it takes two to make a
successful partnership. Johnny de Lisle, despite his
aristocratic breeding and public school education, had
turned out not to have an appetite for any kind of graft at
all. When tough decisions were to be made and hard times
to be endured, Johnny went missing and, increasingly, he

had gone missing with other women. Though she was no quitter, Bella had finally given up on Johnny and divorced him. It had broken her heart at the time, but it was the sensible thing to do.

Marrying Rob, on the other hand, was not sensible at all. It brought an end to the occasional handout from the de Lisle family coffers and thrust her into the ramshackle life of an ex-jump jockey with a reputation for controversy both in and out of the saddle. It was common knowledge he'd fallen out with many trainers and owners for being too frank with his opinions, his best friend was a bookmaker and the fortunes of his stud business were founded on a dangerously unstable stallion who was a menace to all who came in contact with him.

But for once Bella didn't care. She could see a core of integrity in Rob that made him worth ten Johnny de Lisles. And he loved her. Like Troublemaker, the big scruffy grey who'd carried her to eventing glory, Rob gave her the feeling he'd lay down his life for her. That was the kind of partner she needed and she'd do all in her power to make their new union a success. This win with Goldeneye was a bit of a windfall and she was determined it wouldn't go to waste. It was a boost for the pair of them, a chance for them to forge ahead.

'Mum.' Kathy's voice interrupted Bella's thoughts as she pretended to take an interest in the race now finishing on the screen in the bar where the Rushmore party were continuing their celebrations. 'Guess what.' The girl's voice was high-pitched and slurred. 'I've just been offered a job.'

It took a moment for Bella to process the information – it was about the last thing she had expected her daughter to say. But she knew it was important to get her reaction right. Kathy's continuing inactivity had been the cause of several mother/daughter shouting matches.

'Fantastic.' She summoned as much enthusiasm as she could. 'What is it?'

'I'm going to work for Steve.'

'Steve Armstrong?'

'His PA's just left. He says I can give it a trial run, see if I like it.'

Bella told herself to keep cool. 'Are you sure this is a proper job, Kathy?' she said in a neutral tone.

'Yeah. I just said so, didn't I?'

'I mean,' she rephrased quickly, 'are you sure he's not just doing it to be kind?'

'So what's wrong with that? Steve *is* kind. I think he's lovely.'

Quite – though 'lovely' wasn't exactly the adjective Bella would have used. Slick, wickedly handsome, silver-tongued and devil-eyed – these were the phrases that sprang to her mind when she thought of Steve. She'd often felt the effect of those devil eyes herself. When Rob had first introduced them she'd caught herself wondering just what might have been the outcome if she'd met his handsome friend first.

But Steve wasn't interested in Kathy like that, surely? He was a trusted family confidant – and much too old for her little girl.

She pushed her suspicions to one side, recognising her true objections to this scheme for what they were.

'Are you really sure you want to take a job in a book-maker's?'

'For God's sake, Mum, don't be such a snob. I'll just be working in his office, like I've been working in the office at Rushmore. Only this way I'll be out of your hair, like you said you wanted. And I'll be getting paid.'

Bella ignored this well-aimed blow. Kathy's work on the stud had not been formally recompensed on the basis that it was a contribution to her keep.

'Where exactly is this office?'

'In Seymour Street. On the first floor. Steve says I needn't go into the shop at all.'

All the same, Bella's suspicions were confirmed. Her daughter would be working just above some seedy book-maker's on the high street.

Her daughter read the objection in her face and laughed.

'Don't worry, I'll make sure none of your pals see me when I go in and out.'

'Let me talk to Rob,' she said.

'What for? I'm not asking your permission, Mum, I'm telling you. Steve's offered me a job and I'm going to take it. I'm eighteen, remember?'

How could Bella forget? But Kathy wasn't the kind of eighteen who seemed old enough to look out for herself. If she were judged on practical things, like washing a cup or making a bed or boiling an egg, she seemed barely of secondary school age.

'Anyway, Steve's already mentioned it to Rob,' said Kathy with triumph. 'He thinks it's a great idea.'

Bella looked across the bar. Rob and Steve were standing side by side, Steve poking a finger into the centre of his friend's chest as he made a point, Rob holding a champagne bottle by the neck and swaying back on his heels. Her husband was beyond the reach of sensible discussion.

'Rob would think anything's a great idea at the moment,' said Bella.

Kathy shrugged, sending one pencil-thin strap of her peach silk vest skittering down her arm (what, Bella wondered, had the girl done with her jacket?). 'Like I said, I'm doing it and I don't care what you say.' And she marched off, not entirely steady on her heels.

Bella tried to think positively. This was a victorious day, after all.

At least *she* wouldn't have a hangover tomorrow morning.

Steve couldn't put it off forever. As the crowd streamed past him to get their money on for the next race he turned on his mobile. It lit up like a Christmas tree. How many missed calls were there? At least ten, closer to twenty. Most of them were from Jerry, his senior manager, who was keeping an eye on all six shops while Steve played hooky for the afternoon.

Like most independent businessmen Steve spent half his life with a phone welded to his ear. This afternoon had been a deliberate time out. For the occasion of Goldeneye's

Guineas attempt, he'd reckoned he deserved a holiday from the effort of trying to keep his ailing enterprise afloat. He'd intended to check in with Jerry but after the horse had bloody well gone and won he'd thought, sod it, and surrendered to the euphoria of the moment.

At a stroke the victory had lifted a weight of worry from his shoulders. Even in the seconds after the race, in the flurry of backslaps and kisses, his brain had been doing the maths. Between them, he and Rob had just won £185,600. Take away from that the trainer and jockey's share, presents for the stable staff – not to mention the unpaid quarterly training bill – and they'd be left with about £140,000. Half of that – his share – would come to seventy grand or so and it would be a couple of months, no doubt, before it actually turned up. Already, it wasn't quite the fortune it had seemed before the race, when it was just a delicious and unlikely possibility.

All the same, £70,000 was a life-saver. Enough to shut the bank up for a bit and keep him in business while he worked out how to survive the threat of Fairweather's, the national bookmaking chain who were making moves on his patch. They'd tried to buy him out and, after he'd said no, they'd opened up across the road from his head office. Their spanking new premises were air-conditioned, with the latest gaming machines, banks of screens beaming in sporting activity from around the globe, and the complimentary tea and coffee was served up by nubile young things in tight tops. More to the point, their gambling prices were ridiculous. Trying to match the Fairweather odds was giving Steve a big headache.

He should have accepted their offer but it had gone against the grain. He'd been outraged. *This is a family firm – my dad built it from scratch. He'd turn in his grave!*

What a sentimental fool he'd been. Family firm – who cared about that? The old man was gone and his sisters had other lives and other interests, not to mention that these days they thought bookmaking on a par with selling arms or manufacturing cigarettes.

So he'd missed the chance to pocket the Fairweather cash and now the fancy new operation over the road was going out of its way to steal his punters and put him out of business. Nothing personal, of course, but that was the way the big boys played the game.

The bastards.

The phone in his hand came to life. He couldn't put it off any longer.

'All right then, Jerry, what's the news?'

Ivana waited by Charlie's car while the trainer bid a group of men in suits a prolonged and hearty farewell. Charlie was who she needed right now. He was the father figure in her life, she'd decided. The kind of decent, reassuring man who would never in a million years treat her like that bastard Milos. Also, the sooner she got away the better. She'd seen no further sign of Milos. Once she left the racecourse she knew she'd be better able to put the episode behind her.

'Ivana.' The voice startled her. It was Gary Moorehead. 'Sorry,' he said. 'I didn't mean to alarm you.'

God, was it that obvious?

'Hello, Gary.' She injected warmth into her voice. She wanted to be friends with her lover's son but, given the circumstances, it wasn't easy.

'I've just met someone who knows you,' he said. 'Some bloke from Czechoslovakia.'

Her stomach lurched. 'Who?' It came out as a bit of a squeak.

'I didn't get his name.' He was looking at her closely now, interested maybe in her reaction. Perhaps he'd never seen anyone go pale with fear before. 'A big man with a ponytail. He saw me in the ring with Goldie and asked if I knew you.'

Ivana thought hard. Milos had said he'd seen her English friends. He must have made the connection between Rob and Steve and the horse.

'What did you say?'

'Just that you were around somewhere. I thought you'd like to see one of your Czech friends.'

Charlie had finally parted from his group and was walking towards them.

'I gave him your address,' Gary said.

'You what?'

'He said he wanted to get in touch. You don't mind, do you?'

Oh God. She could have slapped him round the face.

Charlie was striding over, pulling the car keys from his pocket. She paid no attention as he had a few words with his son and she said nothing as Gary bade her a puzzled goodbye and headed off.

Charlie winked at her. 'It's his job to go back with the horse. Wouldn't want him playing gooseberry, would we?'

Ivana didn't know what that meant though she could have guessed if she put her mind to it. But her mind was on other matters.

Milos knew where she lived.

An owner who has just seen his horse win the Two Thousand Guineas ought to return home grinning from ear to ear. Particularly when that man drives a luxury car, owns his own home and business, and enjoys the kind of unlimited independence that allows him to make the most of his good fortune. But as Steve Armstrong gunned his Lexus down the road his face was set in stone.

Jerry's news had been bad. For the first big Flat-racing day of the year, footfall across all the shops had been poor. In the Seymour Street branch there'd been scarcely any passing trade at all, only the regular punters – who were beginning to be lured away by the attractions across the road. The bottom line was a few hundred pounds' profit across the board, just about enough to cover the cost of opening for the day.

To think that that very afternoon he'd offered someone a job! He must be mad, adding another name to the payroll. What he ought to do was rescind the offer to Kathy and close down Seymour Street. That way he could reduce his over-heads and concentrate on the other shops which weren't in direct competition to Fairweather's.

But there were eighteen months left on the Seymour Street lease and it wouldn't be easy to offload. And he'd look a fool in the eyes of Rob and Bella if he suddenly reneged on his promise to Kathy.

More important, it would mean he'd given in. Surrendered. And if he did, who was to say Fairweather's wouldn't come gunning for his other premises in the same way? They'd swallowed plenty of little players like him before.

He had to think positive. His offer to Kathy hadn't been frivolous. He badly needed administrative help and he'd seen her in action in the Rushmore office, dealing with computer glitches and juggling the phones. She was a bright kid. He was confident she'd be able to sort out the mess that lazy slut Carol had left behind.

She was more decorative than Carol too. She had a lot of her mother's style, though she wasn't yet as elegant – and she didn't have Bella's sexy smile. He'd never admit it to Rob but there was something about Bella's knowing gaze that Steve found quite a turn-on. He had to acknowledge that his friend had done well for himself. If you had to enter the marriage stakes – a desperate outcome to Steve's way of thinking – you could do worse than pick a woman like Bella. And Kathy was from the same mould, but younger. For the first time on the journey home, Steve's face relaxed and he smiled. He'd settle for a younger model any day.

Not that he had any intention of laying a finger on his best friend's stepdaughter. And for all that Kathy would brighten the office, she wasn't going to help him hold off Fairweather's. Thinking about it without sentiment – *sorry, Dad* – what he needed was an exit strategy. Enough money to get out of bookmaking.

His best hope, it was plain, was not human at all but had four legs and a white patch over one eye. Suppose Goldie landed a couple more big prizes this season? Then he could cut his losses and consider his options at leisure.

It was funny to think that Goldeneye, out of all the foals

produced by his father's old mare, should be the animal to hit the jackpot.

After the Guineas, they'd all been raving about him. Some commentators were even talking him up as a Derby favourite, though that was a laugh as all the connections knew he'd never get the trip. All the same, Goldeneye was suddenly instated as the top three-year-old in the eyes of the racing press and the watching world.

What did they know? Not the truth, that was certain.

And Steve wasn't about to tell them.

Chapter Three

Rose Wyatt insisted on standing outside the church hall despite the squalling wind which drove needles of rain into her face. She didn't feel a thing, though the same could not be said of the mourners who scurried gratefully inside once they had greeted her with their chosen words of condolence.

'Thank you,' she murmured over and over. Thank you for braving this late-spring storm. Thank you for remembering my father. Thank you for not mentioning the fact he took his own life.

The last to greet her was an upright silver-haired gentleman who held on to her hand as if trying to impart some of his ramrod-stiff resolve directly into her veins. As a rule, Rose found her husband's uncle hard to warm to. A churchgoer and a lay preacher, Jim Sidebottom was a man of fixed opinions. In these circumstances, however, Jim's support counted for a lot.

'A reasonable turnout,' he said.

It wasn't and they both knew it. Thirty-odd people drinking tea in a dusty church hall was not the kind of send-off that Geoff Wyatt deserved. Since his fall from grace, the multitude of Geoff's acquaintance had vanished like mayflies in winter.

'You'd think at least the bookmaking fraternity would be sorry to see him go.' Jim chewed on the words then spat them out. 'Your father kept half of them in business for years.'

Rose wondered if this was an attempt at levity. But Jim wasn't known for his sense of humour.

'I'd have sent any bookie packing,' she said.

Jim sighed. 'He's with the Lord now.'

'The Lord did nothing for Dad when he was alive. I don't see why He should bother now Dad's dead.'

'I can understand how you feel but you must not give way to bitterness.'

'Thanks, Jim. It's just that I'd rather have satisfaction in this world than the next.'

The silver-haired man nodded, his face grave. 'Who's to say you won't get it?'

Rose was startled. It was exactly what she had been thinking herself.

She doubted if the bookmaker who had hounded her father to his grave would feel a grain of remorse for his death. And he certainly wouldn't be bothered by the prospect of judgement in an afterlife. A man like that worshipped only one God: the God of Money. If she wanted satisfaction she would have to hit him where it hurt – in his wallet.

Then it dawned on her that of all the rogues and racing wheeler-dealers she had known with her father, only upright God-fearing Jim could be of assistance to her now. But how could she ask him?

Easily, she realised as she stared into his slate-grey eyes.

But not now, Jason was calling them from the door of the hall.

'Come on, Rosie, it's too cold to hang around out here.'

They approached the familiar barrel shape of her husband. He put his arm round her shoulders. 'Fancy a cup of tea, Jim? Old Geoff wouldn't want the pair of you freezing to death at his funeral, now would he?'

She'd talk to Jim later. Surely there was a way he could help her. That was something she could pray for without reservation.

Kathy hadn't expected a palace – after all, Steve's office was over a betting shop – but the reality had come as a shock. The narrow stairwell was uncarpeted and her first-floor room had last seen refurbishment about the time Margaret Thatcher redecorated 10 Downing Street. On one side was a tiny kitchen with furred-up taps and stained work surfaces and, on the other, a toilet with a clanking cistern – both amenities being in frequent use by the shop staff from downstairs.

The office itself was dark and squalid, with bottle-green walls and a collection of broken chairs and battered old filing cabinets in one corner. The desk overflowed with unanswered correspondence and junk mail. The stench of neglect was even more pungent than the smell of the rooms either side.

At least the computer looked like a fairly recent purchase but it took a full ten minutes to boot, then the screen flowered into a display of pop-up ads for gaming sites – and froze. She turned it off at the wall with a groan.

For a moment, on that first morning after Steve had glad-handed her round the shop downstairs and left her on her own 'to settle in', Kathy had thought of heading straight back to Rushmore. Going home to Mum. The impulse lasted about thirty seconds. She was damned if she'd do that.

When Steve returned an hour later he'd discovered her standing on the one usable office chair, grappling with the curtain rail.

'What on earth are you doing?' he asked.

'These curtains are disgusting.' They were brown Habitat hessian and a sight older than she was. 'I thought I'd get them cleaned.'

'Oh, really?' He was grinning at her in an irritating fashion.

The rail gave way, depositing the curtains on the floor in a cloud of dust.

'And I want a new lampshade and a proper desk light. It's like a crypt in here.'

'Anything else you'd like to change?'

Only everything in the room. But she didn't say that. 'It *is* a bit shabby, Steve. It could do with a spring clean.'

She watched as he pulled his wallet from his pocket and

took out some notes. 'Sixty quid. It's all I've got on me.' He dropped them on the desk.

She was taken aback. She hadn't been asking for money, though she supposed it amounted to that.

'Thanks.' He was still smirking at her. She wondered why.

'I'll leave you to get on with it then.' But he'd stopped in the doorway and added, 'I suggest that you find yourself a more appropriate spring-cleaning outfit.'

So that's why he'd been grinning at her. Her titchy new black skirt wasn't the best thing to be wearing when standing on tiptoe on a chair and grappling with the curtains. She blushed to think of the eyeful she'd given him.

But if she'd not wanted to make that kind of impression on Steve why had she worn it in the first place?

All this had taken place over a week a ago. Now she sat in a freshly painted room – apple-white walls decorated with some posters she'd brought from home – with a paper lampshade and a faded terracotta blind she'd found in a charity shop. She'd carried the old chairs downstairs and made sure the dustmen took them by smiling sweetly. The filing cabinets were too big to shift but she'd used some of the drawers to order the mess of papers she'd unearthed. As well as painting, she'd scrubbed and dusted and washed down surfaces. Steve and Jerry from downstairs had enjoyed plenty of fun at her expense but they'd been impressed too. She felt quite proud of herself.

Now she was tackling the computer. She was relieved to find a working internet connection but the virus protection had lapsed and the system was riddled with all sorts of nasties. All the same, she reckoned she could do some successful spring-cleaning here too.

The door sprang open, startling her. She'd not heard any footsteps on the stairs, which was unusual – she could always tell when Jerry or one of the others was approaching. Even Steve, light on his feet though he was, announced his presence in this fashion.

'What's gone on here then?'

The man in the doorway was big; he seemed to fill the entire space. His face was all planes and sharp edges and his eyes were small, like currants in a bun.

He didn't wait for a reply to his question before asking another. 'Where's Carol?'

'She's not here—' She was going to add 'any more' but he cut her off before the words were out.

'I can see that for myself, darling. Who are you then?'

'Kathy de Lisle.' She said her full name without thinking. She wasn't just some stupid office girl.

He stepped into the room, looming over the desk. She could smell the cud of gum he was chewing.

'De what? Am I meant to be impressed? I suppose Stevie boy's giving you one, is he?'

Kathy froze in shock. 'Get out,' she said but her voice sounded shrill.

'Don't get your knickers in a twist, sweetheart.' He smiled at her slowly, obviously delighted he'd got under her skin. 'If you're wearing any, that is.'

Kathy blinked. She'd never been insulted in such a cold-blooded fashion. But she was damned if she was going to show it.

'Have you got any legitimate business here?'

He shrugged. 'Just passing. Tell your lord and master, Len came by.'

He sauntered to the door, gliding softly despite his bulk. She didn't hear him go down the stairs.

Suddenly she didn't feel so secure in her newly painted nest.

Maybe this really wasn't the place for her. There were other options. She could reconsider her mother's idea of going to college, like Gary had done. There were a variety of equine studies courses on offer – Mum had given her a pile of literature to look at. She'd not been overly enthusiastic when she'd flicked through it all. Three years to get some certificate? Perhaps, as promised, it would give her a foothold in the 'equine industry' but she had that already. She was living on a stud farm, for God's sake.

Alternatively, she could go to California and stay with her father – she had a standing invitation to visit Daddy any time. But that would mean putting up with his latest female companion and her fourteen-year-old son.

To be honest, she was better off staying put. Life was pretty easy under her mother's roof. But was that what she really wanted – to be dependent? Taking this job was a step towards standing on her own feet. She was damned if she'd pack it in just because some creep had insulted her.

She'd find out who he was and insist Steve put a lock on the downstairs door.

Where *was* Steve?

His office hours were minimal. He rarely showed up before midday and he spent the afternoons running round his six shops. 'I'll leave it in your capable hands,' he'd said once or twice as she'd begun confronting him over the stack of correspondence. But apart from the fact that she knew nothing about his business, she couldn't write cheques and that's what most people were after.

He finally stuck his head round the door at ten past twelve. She hardly gave him a chance to say hello.

'Some thug called Len was here. He just walked in off the street. I want a lock on that door downstairs.'

Steve took the rickety chair that faced her desk. It would probably mark his pale linen suit but serve him right.

'Don't be upset,' he said. 'Len's harmless.'

'He was so rude to me. Just vile.'

'What did he say, Kathy?'

She shook her head. She wasn't going to repeat what the big man had said.

Steve reached across the desk and took her hand. She snatched it away, as if even a friendly gesture might prove Len's foul accusations. She realised she was on the edge of tears.

'What you need,' said Steve, 'is a change of scene. I'm going racing this afternoon and I think you'd better come with me.'

'But I'm in the middle of sorting out this computer.'

'Sod that, Kathy. Racing takes priority. You're coming to Hampton Waters with me.'

The all-weather course was a recent addition to the Midlands racing scene. She'd not visited it yet but had heard a lot about it from Gary. The Moorehead yard had enjoyed some success there and he was full of praise for the facilities on offer which, he said, were almost as good as Wolverhampton. She was keen to see for herself.

'OK then,' she said. Suddenly she felt a hundred per cent better.

Ivana was weary: she'd had a busy morning on the stud. As she wheeled her bicycle up the path to the cottage she heard the phone ringing inside but didn't quicken her step. She wasn't going to rush to answer it. She supposed it might be Charlie offering to take her to lunch at some out-of the-way inn. They'd done that once or twice and it had been fun, even though he'd rushed her through the eating so he could whisk her off upstairs 'and have his wicked way', as he liked to say. It was a funny expression, Ivana thought, and rather more exciting than the deed itself these days.

The phone stopped as she stepped into the hall. If it was Charlie, he'd call back.

She checked for messages. None. She dialled 1471 but the caller's number had been withheld. Charlie was a cautious man – there was his wife to think of.

She poured herself a cold drink and noted the unwashed dishes in the sink. Today Tomas was riding at Beverley and had left the cottage in a mess – not for the first time. Her brother wasn't exactly handy about the house. He spent all of his free time watching racing videos or reading the form book, scheming how to get ahead.

If only Tomas would take as much interest in what concerned her. He might indeed be going places, with a career that could set him up for life, but it was different for her. She was running out of options. Once she'd thought she could put down proper roots here, get married, raise a family. But that was back in the days when she was in love with Steve and thought he felt the same way about her. Well, she wasn't the first to fall into that trap.

She ran hot water over the dishes in the sink and added soap. Her dirty things were in there too, she noted. Really, she shouldn't let herself be irritated by Tomas's success. They were in this together and they'd share the benefits. She knew why she was feeling resentment: it was that business with Milos. Tomas had been sympathetic but it was plain he didn't take the threat of her old boyfriend seriously. When she'd got back from Newmarket and told him that Gary Moorehead had met Milos too, Tomas had just smoothed her feathers, making her feel like a child fussing about something silly.

What added to her annoyance was the feeling that he was probably right. Nearly two weeks had gone by since she'd run into the long-haired Czech and she'd heard nothing. Thank the saints for that. She'd never been as frightened of anyone as she was of Milos.

In their early days, he'd treated her like precious china. He'd spun out her seduction over a week, helped along by songs and dope and cleverly prepared meals by candlelight. He took her trekking on horseback up into the hills, to a secret lake by a meadow carpeted with wild white daisies and purple feather carnations. They swam in the inky blue pool of a mountain waterfall and he didn't lay a finger on her. By the time he took her in his arms, in the moonlit hayloft above the stables on the seventh night, she was ready to beg for it. And he didn't disappoint her. She wasn't experienced with men back then but she knew that what he did to her was special.

Later in their relationship she thought of this period as their honeymoon. It hadn't lasted more than a couple of months, but the glow remained long after, making it difficult for her to cut herself free.

She didn't notice the tables turning. She wanted to please him as he had pleased her and after she'd moved in with him she happily took over the cooking and cleaning. Not that she was much of a housekeeper at the beginning. So when she oversalted the stew and served him glued-together pasta it was right that he should throw it on the floor and make her clear it up. He'd pushed her face into it too, saying that's how you taught puppies not to shit indoors. It made a kind of sense – she learned to cook spaghetti pretty damn quick after that. She didn't even mind that much when he slapped her. She'd seen her father hit her mother before they split so it wasn't the shock it might have been. Maybe that was how men showed their deepest feelings for the women they loved.

The way Milos treated the horses was another matter.

'It's the only way they learn,' he said when he'd caught the look of disapproval in her eyes after he'd snapped a broom handle across the back of a yearling who was resistant to the bridle. Then he'd grabbed her by the neck with his huge guitar-strumming fist and slammed her head against the wall of the barn. 'Horses and women,' he said. 'You're all the same.'

Of course, she realised that what had once been beautiful was rotting by the day. Dump him, said her friends – she'd made some by now – but she was too soft to just walk out and the good times were still too vivid. 'We fit together,' he'd tell her in their tender moments and she'd agree and things would be great between them – until the next time she did something wrong. Like talking to other men.

When Kamil's young cousin, Jiri, turned up for the summer she did her best to avoid him. But Jiri was open-hearted and funny, not the kind of fellow it was easy to snub. She couldn't help liking him; the fact that he was a good looking lad had nothing to do with it. When Milos caught them together, dangling their feet in the river at the end of a long hot afternoon, it was like watching milk curdle. He couldn't touch Jiri, not if he wanted to stay in Kamil's good books.

He didn't touch Ivana either, not on this occasion. Instead he made her watch while he flogged the horse she loved most, a chestnut mare called Skylark who trusted all human beings without reservation. First Milos took a whip to her and then a baton of wood until her silky brown coat was streaked with blood and her squeals of pain and fear echoed off the wooden beams of the stall. Ivana tried to stop him but he flung her off with ease and laughed as he abused the horse.

'How could you?' she cried through her tears.

'Easy,' he said. 'I just pretend it's you.'

She left in the early hours of the next morning, quietly gathering up her things while Milos slept. She fled back to her mother's and planned her escape to England and Tomas.

As she finished the dishes and dried her hands, the phone rang again. She picked it up without hesitation. Perhaps she was in the mood for Charlie after all. He could take her somewhere nice for lunch – she was hungry. Then she remembered that he, too, was racing at Beverley.

'Ivana?'

It wasn't Charlie, it was Milos.

She felt sick. 'What do you want?'

'I want to see you.'

'But I don't want to see you, Milos. Or talk to you. Leave me alone, please.'

'You don't understand, Ivana. I still love you.'

She'd once thought so but she knew now there was no love in this man. He revolted her.

'Besides,' he went on. 'You owe me for what you did. It was you who tipped off the police, wasn't it?'

She knew what he was referring to. Before she'd left Czechoslovakia she'd shopped him to the district police, letting them know he was dealing in drugs. It was no more than the truth – he kept half the kids in the village high.

'I thought of you every night in prison, Ivanicka.'

'You deserved it,' she spat, her control loosening. 'They should have locked you up forever for what you did to that horse.'

'It was you who made me do it. I was mad for you. I still am.'

'Get lost, you creep.'

He laughed, a high-pitched giggle that she recognised with a lurch of fear.

'I don't think you really mean that,' he said and, mercifully, ended the call.

She slammed down the receiver and held it, pressing so hard her knuckles whitened, as if she could somehow put the evil genie back in his bottle.

Bella put down the phone reflecting that there was nothing like the prospect of an influx of cash into your account to make a conversation with the bank manager more palatable. Not that they called themselves bank managers any more, these days they were personal account executives and all very matey but it amounted to the same thing. If things got bleak they'd pull the plug on you just the same. With a customer-friendly smile, naturally.

The knowledge that a cheque for Goldeneye's Two Thousand Guineas win would soon materialise had cast a warm glow on the finances of Rushmore Stud Farm, giving the cash flow a welcome boost. All the same, in Bella's opinion the money should be put to work.

She had managed to convince Rob that some investment in facilities would add to the stud's pulling power in the market, together with results like the Guineas. The better Cape Fear's offspring performed, the greater his attraction to owners wishing to have their mares covered. Goldeneye's win was a fillip to the stallion's market price. She hoped and believed there would be more to come this season. And Rob's dream – she knew before he confessed sheepishly on the night of their Newmarket triumph – was for Goldeneye to stand at Rushmore as a stallion in his own right.

Tempting though it was to dream, Bella knew they couldn't just sit back and hope it would come true. First they should put the money to use.

That morning, she had outlined a few ideas to Rob that had been germinating in her head; namely, to upgrade the foaling boxes, install a horse-walker and lay down a new surface in the all-weather school.

'Shouldn't we wait?' he'd said. 'It would be nice to have some money in the bank for a change. Let's just sit on it for a bit.'

She'd expected this response. It wasn't that Rob was mean, more that he was resistant to change – quite the opposite to her own impulse and she reckoned she'd remained silent for long enough about the state of the business.

She'd kept her cool, though, and they'd talked it through. He could see the improvements she was advocating made sense. To make him feel better she promised to cost each proposal thoroughly so they could discuss specifics. That way, she reckoned he would have a chance to get used to the idea.

He seemed happy with the outcome. 'I knew I was marrying more than a pretty face,' he'd said. 'Any other reforms on your mind'

She should have said no and put a lid on the whole matter; after all, she'd got what she wanted. But she took the opportunity all the same.

'I think you ought to ask Ivana and Tomas to move out of the cottage.'

The smile froze on his lips. 'But Tom's lived there ever since he worked here.'

'He doesn't work here any longer.'

'But Ivana does. The cottage goes with her job.'

'I still don't see why the pair of them should live there rent free. If they moved out we could do it up and let it as a holiday home. I bet we could earn some decent money.'

His face had hardened; it looked as if the line of his mouth was set in stone. 'And you'll serve the eviction notice, will you?'

'If I have to, but it's your job.'

'You realise it amounts to a pay cut for Ivana?'

'But you pay her way over the odds for what she does anyway, I know that in the old days you and she ran the place together but those days are gone. I'm your business. partner now and she's got a lot less responsibility. I don't think it's unreasonable of you to renegotiate her arrangements.'

He'd looked at her as if she were a stranger. Finally he'd said, in a resolute, don't-push-me voice she'd never heard before, 'Ivana does a good job here and I shan't be doing anything of the kind. I think you've got the wrong end of the stick about her.' And he'd walked out.

That had been this morning and Bella had not seen him since. There was something about the way he'd looked at her that rankled. Was there another reason why he was so touchy about Ivana? Naturally, she'd wondered about Rob's friendship with the Czech girl before she'd met him. Why wouldn't she wonder? The woman was a magnet for male attention. She'd never been short of local admirers. She'd certainly had an affair with Steve and now, according to rumour, was carrying on with Charlie Moorehead, which was a considerable embarrassment, if true. The Czech girl was damned sexy, there was no denying it, and she used her attraction to get what she wanted. So why wouldn't she have used it on Rob? She'd certainly got a good deal out of him.

Rob had accused her of getting hold of the wrong end of the stick. The more she thought about it, the more it seemed she'd picked up the right one.

Though her fancy was well-beaten by the halfway mark, Kathy watched the first race of the afternoon at Hampton Waters in a much happier frame of mind. It had been generous of Steve to excuse her from the office for the afternoon and the moment she had snuggled down into the leather seat of his car her spirits had begun to lift. She'd never been in a Lexus before. It certainly put Gary's Mini to shame.

On the journey, Steve had offered an explanation for the threatening visitor in her office that morning.

'You don't want to be put off by Len's manner,' he'd said. 'It's just an act.' Kathy wasn't convinced but she kept her mouth shut.

'He's very useful to the business,' Steve continued. 'Since Len's been around I've had no bad debts to speak of.'

'Bad debts? I thought people always paid upfront'

'Most do. Little punters buy a ticket with cash. But I've got some regulars with accounts – all bookmakers have. Sometimes they get in arrears and you have to persuade them to settle up.'

Kathy was getting the picture. 'And that's Len's job?'

'He's very good at it.'

The thought made her uncomfortable. 'You mean he menaces people on your say-so?'

Steve laughed. 'Don't be daft. This is a legitimate business, we can't go about assaulting customers.'

'But you can send round someone who looks like a gangster.'

'You've got to realise that gambling debts are not recoverable by law.'

'Aren't they?' She didn't know that.

'People are more likely to settle their debts with a big guy than a little guy. Someone who looks like Len only has to ask.'

Kathy could imagine. She supposed it made sense. After all, bookmaking wasn't meant to be a business for cissies. In a funny kind of way she liked the excitement of being associated with it.

In the circumstances, being squired around a racecourse on a working afternoon by a man who looked like a movie star, she was prepared to concede that Len might not be as disgusting a specimen as she'd first thought. She just hoped he'd keep away from her office.

The first race was an easy victory for Salsa Sam who'd been drawn on the inside. He won easing down by ten lengths to the cheers of only a few. At 20–1, his victory was not anticipated.

Kathy tore up her ticket and turned to Steve. 'You told me he hadn't a prayer.'

'Not on his recent form. And he didn't look much in the ring – you said so yourself.'

So she had. Compared to her own fancy, the well-beaten favourite, Salsa Sam had looked a scraggy lightweight.

Steve had turned away from her, holding a mobile to his ear. He'd be checking in with Jerry to see how they had fared. Before the race he'd been buoyant. Punters had been plonking down their cash in a healthy fashion in all of his shops.

However, she could see that his fortunes had changed. Steve's face was as humourless as a brick wall.

'Bad news?'

For a second, Steve did not register her words. 'We took a big hit on that winner.'

Kathy was puzzled. She didn't think bookies lost money on 20-1 shots. It was when the hot favourites came home they were in trouble, wasn't it?

'What happened?'

'A lot of money was placed at the last minute.'

'Don't you cover that? Shorten the odds or something?'

'As a rule. But we didn't have time.'

'So Fairweather's must have caught a cold as well.'

She knew about the feud with the bully across the road. It was a remark intended to cheer him up.

'Let's hope so, eh?' A smile had returned to his face but she could read the worry in his eyes. Nevertheless, he took her arm and said, 'How about a drink?'

She wasn't thirsty but nodded her head all the same. Her boss looked like he could use one.

Tomas was late back from Beverley – very late. Ivana had planned to have an early night but that wasn't possible now. She wouldn't get to sleep with Milos's voice echoing in her head.

She called Tomas on his mobile but it was switched off, as it had been all evening. Then she rang Charlie – he might know if Tomas had been held up. But the call had been a mistake as it was answered by Louise; the background noise sounded as if she was in the car with him, driving back. Ivana asked after Tomas but got short shrift from Louise.

'I've no idea. I haven't seen him,' she said in her clipped English way.

51

Ivana knew Louise was suspicious. Her enquiry after Tomas was genuine but Louise would surely put a different interpretation on it. Damn.

Eventually she went to bed, listening out for the sound of Tomas's car. She must have dropped off because she was woken by the sound of banging at the front door. She lay frozen in bed, disorientated and frightened. Had Milos tracked her down already?

'Ivana! '

Relief surged through her – it was Tomas. She stumbled downstairs and found him shouting angrily through a crack in the front door; she'd fastened the security chain and he couldn't get in.

'Why the hell did you lock me out?' he exclaimed as she let him inside.

She didn't answer, just flung her arms round his neck and burst into tears. His irritation vanished when he realised how upset she was and he allowed her to cry herself out, standing in the hall, holding her to his chest.

'Tell me,' he said eventually, after he'd sat her down in the kitchen and made her some tea.

'It's Milos.'

'What about him?'

'He telephoned me here this afternoon. He wants to see me.'

'Tell him to get lost.'

'I did but he's not going to take any notice. I know him. He's sick.'

'Just ignore him.'

Did Tomas really think that would work? She remembered Milos and his game with lighted cigarettes. How he had beaten that horse till the blood flowed. Most of all she remembered Katerina.

The girl had called her at her mother's house after she'd left Uncle Kamil's yard; she'd said she used to go out with Milos and insisted they meet. When Ivana saw her she realised why the girl had been so keen. Katerina's face was a mess. The knife had split her cheek open from jaw to eyeball. It looked like the blade had first been put in her mouth and then used to saw through the flesh from the inside. Though the girl had been sewn back together, it was hardly an invisible mend.

'Milos did this to me,' she'd said. 'When I left him for another guy he said he'd fix me so I wouldn't look pretty.'

'What about the police?' she'd asked. 'He should be in jail.'

Katerina had given her a lopsided grin. 'He promised he'd kill me first. I believed him.'

And so had Ivana. That was the moment she'd realised she had to leave the country.

She made that decision again now. 'I've got to get away,' she said. 'I can't stay here where he knows he can find me.'

Tomas looked at her in bewilderment. 'Don't be silly, Ivana. Things are going well here.'

'For you maybe.'

'But you'll be safe here. You're with friends – everybody loves you.'

She laughed bitterly. 'No, they don't.'

He looked at her thoughtfully. 'Do you want me to come with you?'

She didn't. It was too much to ask him to pack in his future for her.

'Don't be silly. You've got Goldie to ride, a new agent, trainers interested in you. I don't want you giving that up for me.'

He looked relieved – and a little guilty. 'But I'm your brother.'

She gazed into his face, so earnest and warm and trusting.

'You're a good man, Tomas,' she said. Perhaps if she established herself somewhere else then he could follow her.

But where was she going to go? It had to be somewhere far away where Milos would never find her. The US maybe, or Australia – she could find jobs with horses there surely.

But how would she manage it? She didn't even have enough money for a plane ticket.

Chapter Four

Rose Wyatt – now Sidebottom, though she never thought of herself by that name – gave an extra polish to the walnut photo frame that contained her father's picture. It showed Geoff Wyatt in his prime, holding the reins of Have I The Right?, his King George VI winner, cigar in his other hand, a melon-sized smile on his lips. Rose was in the background, looking proudly on, her new dress daringly scoop-necked. She'd thought she looked so sophisticated. She could never get into anything like that now, the past fifteen years had done her figure no favours. That day at Ascot might have been the best of her life, except there had been plenty of other days like it, following her father into winner's enclosures and hospitality boxes and lavish receptions all around the racing world. It had been a life of laughter and excess, so vivid she could relive every day, close enough to touch though it was long in the past. It made her feel old. Only forty-four and she felt past it, her glory days long gone. It wasn't fair.

'Rosie?'

This morbid nostalgia wasn't fair either, at least not fair on those around her with whom she had a future.

'I knew I'd find you here.' Jason was in the doorway. She could see his reflection in the mirror over the fireplace. 'We ought to call this room the temple of Geoff.'

'Don't be mean,' she said but there was no anger in her voice. She knew he was right. Though they'd been married six months, she'd only just properly moved into his modest semi after the death of her father. Jason had been good about it, like he was about everything, but it was an unspoken fact of life that Dad came first in everything. She couldn't have left him to manage on his own, no matter how often he urged her to do so.

Jason had bent over backwards to make his house nice for her, insisting she annex the first-floor spare room for her remaining good things – the mementos of her former life. There was the piano – they'd only just squeezed it up the stairs – and her dad's old roll-top desk and the glass cabinet of trophies. And also the photos, some like the King George one in special fancy frames but most in the big leather-bound albums that were piled on the desk top. They were all that remained of a champagne lifestyle – the bailiffs had had the rest.

She put her hand on Jason's cheek: it was prickly with stubble and his jeans were flecked with paint – he'd been decorating the room upstairs, turning the spare room into a study for her, like he'd promised. She'd told him he didn't have to do it, she'd be happy working in this room, but he'd insisted. 'I know this isn't what you're used to,' he'd said, 'but you don't have to be cramped up in here with your dad's things. If you want a study you can have one.'

So she'd stopped protesting. Doing things for her made him happy, he said, and she believed him. Besides, it would be nice to have her own little place at the top of the house; there was a limit to how much privacy she could rely on at work. She needed somewhere for her own affairs and she could rely on Jason not to pry.

It was a pity she didn't love him in the way he loved her. A pity he looked more like a hobbit than an elfin prince, being short and wide with a face like a polished walnut. She sometimes called him Hobbit but he didn't mind. 'At least I don't have hairy feet, O Princess.' So he had a sense of humour, which counted for a lot, and a heart of oak. He was a former jump jockey. Her father always said that jockeys were the toughest and bravest of men and she'd grown up never doubting her father.

he knows how to get men to accommodate her.
retty good deal out of you.'
 Bella suggesting? Rob could feel his temper

aving this. Ivana has done a great job here and
cking her out, whatever you think.' He was
hadn't meant to.
ou expect me to think? She's done pretty well
ere and good luck to her. But now I think she
nd wiggle her hips somewhere else.'
a, you can be a real bitch sometimes.'
re a bloody fool when it comes to a
little tart like her.'
both shouting now, glaring into each other's
itching to smack that superior smirk off her
ooked as if she were about to drive her nails

' a voice wailed from the door.
ack. They hadn't heard her come in but they
wards her, as if caught red-handed – which

he quarrel had ended though it had not been
y had burst into tears and her mother had
er, steering her off to bed. Rob had slipped in
ater and apologised.
nything into it, Kathy, please. Your mum and
her very much. These things happen in
etimes.'
aud as he'd said it. After all, how would he
er been married before.
 had surprised him. 'I'm sorry I walked in
.'
t time, as far as he was aware, that he'd ever
ologise for anything.
red sleeping in the spare room but as he
throom considering whether that would
r worse, Bella had come in. She'd not said
rned the light off with one hand and put

His arm was round her waist, that thickening waist that would no longer allow her to slip into slinky Ascot dresses, and his whiskery cheek was pressing against her neck. Stupid though it was, the fact that she was three inches taller than him had been one of the hardest objections for her to swallow. But she was over that now.

'Have I mentioned you look smashing today, Princess?' His breath was hot on her cheek as he sought her mouth.

She kissed him briefly then disengaged. 'I've got to get to work,' she said.

'You're the boss, aren't you? Give yourself another half hour.'

'Don't be naughty.' She stepped away, but nicely, squeezing his big rough hand and smiling. 'Because I'm the boss, I've got to play by the rules.'

She could see he wasn't convinced, that she'd offended him again but she really did have to go. She ran the sales office for an expanding mail-order business and a lot of people depended on her.

'I'll see you tonight,' she said as she made for the door.

She knew some people thought she'd married Jason to please her father, but that wasn't the case at all. She'd married him because he loved her unconditionally. One day – soon, she hoped – she'd be able to return his devotion in the way he deserved.

Rob watched as Cape Fear stalked menacingly around his pen. He'd earned his living from horses, had grown up with them, knew these animals inside out – and this was the only one he'd ever been afraid of. Of course, he'd come across plenty you needed to treat with caution, horses you wouldn't turn your back on or walk behind for fear of a spiteful kick. But the big black stallion was an animal apart.

As a yearling Cape Fear had chased more than one groom from the paddocks. He'd bullied all the other animals and, in the end, had been turned out by himself. They'd contemplated gelding him but once he'd been broken in and sent off to be trained he seemed to settle down. 'Lucky

I didn't cut him,' Rob's father had said on many occasions after Cape Fear had won his first Group race but the fact was that Dad was getting frail by then and had nothing to do with the handling of the difficult colt.

In a career spanning three seasons, Cape Fear won two Group Two races and three at the next level down. He wasn't well enough bred and hadn't had quite enough class on the racecourse to seem an obvious candidate for a stud career but, with Goldeneye's arrival in his second crop of foals, the situation looked set to change. Sadly his temperament had only got worse.

The stallion had been back at Rushmore for less than a month when he had attacked Gwen, Rob's head groom. She had been mucking him out while he was chained to the wall, when Cape Fear threw his head back and snapped the links as if they were made of tin foil. Before Gwen had a chance to escape from the pen, the stallion had knocked her to the ground. He was kneeling on her chest, about to sink his teeth into her face, when Rob rushed in and hit him as hard as he could. Gwen scrambled to her feet and was almost clear when the horse lashed out from almost six feet. Fortunately for her the kick did not land squarely, though it threw her clear of the stable and left her sprawling on the cobbles of the yard, screaming in pain and fear. She'd never returned to the yard.

After that, Cape Fear became the mother of all bastards to deal with. Rob rehoused him in specially secure quarters and treated him with the utmost caution. The stallion's head collar was never removed and it was fitted with two large brass rings. When he covered mares, two handlers would stand either side of him equipped with long poles with hooks which they'd hitch up to the rings and lead the horse along like a bull. Leather muzzles and hobbles were used on him for treatment by the vet or the blacksmith and, on occasions, he'd be immobilised in heavy-duty stocks or tranquillised with a dart from a small handgun. After what had happened with Gwen, Rob wasn't taking any chances.

Rob rarely allowed things to get him down for long. He

the other on his chest inside his unbuttoned shirt. Her touch was electric, instantly reconnecting all the want and passion that he carried within him. He'd have taken her on the bathroom floor if it wasn't so close to Kathy's room.

'Carry me,' she'd murmured and he'd picked her up and borne her off to bed. What followed was selfish and cathartic and when they'd finished with each other there had been no energy left for talk. Their conflict had been put on hold.

Cape Fear had been standing still for once. He would do this in his presence on occasions, Rob had noticed, and he savoured these moments. It made him wonder if there wasn't, deep down in the horse's wild nature, a core of peace – if only he could get in touch with it.

Suddenly the horse jerked his head, his whole body twitching, and he stamped his feet in familiar fury. Someone was coming.

The door opened and Ivana entered the barn.

'Rob?' In the light of his disagreement with Bella, the Czech girl's soft, husky tones broke guiltily on his ear. 'Can I have a word with you, please?'

It was a surprisingly formal approach but, in the circumstances, Rob was grateful.

'Sure. What's up?'

She looked hesitant and when the stallion reared towards her, she jumped anxiously.

'Wait a moment,' he said and unfastened the gate which gave Cape Fear access to the paddock where he took his exercise. The enclosure, an area of about half an acre, was surrounded by a ten-foot-high security fence.

'He hates me,' Ivana said. 'I never met a horse so mean. He has a black heart.'

Rob shook his head. 'He's just anti-social.' Whatever the justification, he didn't like people running the stallion down.

'Huh.' She was unimpressed. 'Look, Rob, I've got something to tell you. I'm thinking of leaving.'

'What? Leaving the stud?'

'Yes. I'm sorry.'

He was amazed she was giving him notice. What were the odds of this happening so soon after his argument with Bella? As an employer, his impulse was to demand her reasons but all he could think was that this might be a solution to his current predicament.

'I don't want to lose you,' he said, feeling like a hypocrite. 'What's brought this on?'

She ignored the question. 'I'll need some money.'

'You want to borrow money?'

'No, Rob, I need cash quickly.'

He didn't know what to say. Was she asking him to give it to her?

'Look,' she said, 'I've worked hard for you. I've made a big contribution here, right?'

'Yes, and I've paid you for it.'

'I'm asking for help, Rob. As a friend.' Her hand was on his arm, squeezing.

'What's the matter? You're upset.'

She shook her head. 'It's nothing. I just need some money.'

'I suppose I might be able to scrape together a farewell present for you. A few hundred maybe.'

'That's not enough. I need more.' Her big green eyes implored.

'I'm sorry, Ivana, I don't have it.'

'But you've just won a lot of money on Goldeneye.'

'I haven't got it yet. Anyway, that money's needed for the business.' He wriggled uncomfortably under her accusing stare. 'Look, I'll do some sums, see what I can do, OK? Give me some time to think about it.'

He could see her calculating how hard to push the matter, her small pointed chin thrust aggressively at him, her cheekbones gleaming in her pale face. How come he had so many difficult women in his life?

She removed her hand and stepped back. 'Thanks, Rob,' she said as she walked away.

He watched her go, disappointed at this turn of events. She'd be a big loss and, if he could, he'd happily send her off with a cut of Goldie's prize money. But if he did, how could he keep it from Bella? If there was one thing guaranteed to convince his wife that he'd ever been romantically attached to Ivana, it was wishing her bon voyage with a large cheque.

Jason was happy with his handiwork. He'd never fitted a safe before but he could turn his hands to most things around the house. He'd thought it was a funny request, mind you, but anything Rosie wanted was all right with him.

He supposed it was coming from a background like hers, being brought up in a big house with valuable things all around. Geoff Wyatt would have had a safe in his study, bet your life. Probably hidden in the wall behind some fancy painting, where he'd keep a handy bundle of cash. He was always doling out money wherever he went. He remembered Geoff well from those days, when he'd been riding winners for him. Jason had been tipped a fair few quid too. Geoff Wyatt had been the most generous owner in the land, bar none, till the day he crashed.

Back then, Geoff's daughter Rose had seemed unattainable to Jason. A real English beauty, named just right. He'd fancied her in the way every red-blooded bloke fancied Lady Diana, she warmed the cockles, but he recognised that she was quite out of his reach. She was always on her dad's arm at race meetings, the pair of them like a married couple only they were father and daughter. He knew she worked in Geoff's firm – he was the Midlands' biggest brassware manufacturer – and the two of them were inseparable. Geoff's wife was some kind of permanent invalid and Rose, his only child, played her mother's part.

For all that, it had never seemed unhealthy. Geoff was always pushing Rose in the direction of eligible young men and it didn't take much to get him on the subject of the grandchildren he expected one day, to Rose's obvious embarrassment. Boyfriends came and went, smart business types with family money and rising young executives who were going places. Rumours would circulate about wedding plans – this time, it was said, Rose had found Mr Right. But there was always a hitch, none of these likely young bucks ever swept Rose up the aisle. There she would be, year after year, no longer a fresh-faced flower but now a mature beauty, forever on the arm of her father.

Only after Geoff sold his business was he seen about on his own. Jason got the story out of Rose later, at least the portion of it she was prepared to tell. Her mother's Alzheimer's had taken a turn for the worse shortly after the sale and Rose had switched allegiance to her other parent – she'd needed constant help and Rose wasn't prepared to hand her over to a team of nurses. Without his daughter's steady influence by his side, Geoff's gambling had soon got out of control. While Rose was tending her sick mother, the family's considerable fortune ran through her father's fingers. Rose had told Jason the figures – the old man had got through six million pounds in four years on horses, hotels and vintage champagne. The Inland Revenue had taken their slice too. Jason had always reckoned Geoff Wyatt was the most generous man he'd ever met and Rose confirmed that for her father charity did not begin at home. He'd funded innumerable benefits for racing causes and the monthly standing orders to the Injured Jockeys Fund were the last things she'd stopped as his creditors closed in.

Jason had situated the safe in the old built-in wardrobe. Placing it in there out of sight seemed the most obvious thing to do. He was coming round to the idea now, especially since it was fireproof. They could shove passports and insurance documents in there for safekeeping. Since Geoff's millions had gone down the Swanee it was unlikely ever to be used for actual money.

Some people were envious of the rich. Even now, people couldn't resist a little dig at Rose and her wealthy past. If they were in the pub with Phil and Liz, one of them would always say something like, 'Bit of a comedown, my lass,' or 'So it's come to this, has it?' when Rose asked for half a bitter shandy. It irritated Jason no end and he'd have had a word with Phil about it if Rose hadn't stopped him. She didn't care, she didn't even see the insult. 'But I've always liked shandy. You're so fierce, Jason.'

Actually, he wasn't fierce at all. He never spoke a cross word to anyone or took offence – except when it came to his new wife. He'd walk through fire for Rose. He'd defend her to the death and do anything she asked without question. She might not have got much when she'd married him but she'd got absolute commitment to her cause.

After Rose's mother had died and the creditors had closed in on Geoff, Jason had been able to help out, just a bit. It was really his uncle who'd got him involved with the Wyatts. Jim Sidebottom was a former farmer who'd tried his hand at training and he still worked in the racing business. Unlike some people, Jim had taken more of an interest in Geoff after his fortune had gone. Jim was a righteous man. He was more concerned with what he could give Geoff than what he could take from him.

One Sunday Jim had asked Jason to give Geoff a lift to church, where Jim was preaching. Jason had been surprised – surely Geoff could drive himself? – but he'd agreed. He discovered Geoff and Rose still living in the large detached family home, but everywhere he looked there were signs of decay. There was no longer a Bentley and a sporty runaround in the driveway, just a battered Renault which, it turned out, belonged to Rose. She greeted him like a long-lost friend and apologised for not driving her father herself but there was a problem with the starter on her car. All this was far from Jason's expectations but it was the sight of Geoff that really shocked him. The erstwhile life and soul of the party was a diminished figure, thin and hesitant, whose fingers limply returned his handshake and eyes stared dull and lifeless into his.

'Depression,' Jim told him later. 'They've got him on any amount of medication but that won't do him much good. The man needs to rediscover faith in himself.'

Jason knew what his uncle was getting at by his talk of faith and knew that Jim would do all he could to supply his own brand. As for himself, he tried to make a difference in a more practical fashion. That first Sunday, after he'd returned Geoff home – whether he'd benefited from the excursion was hard to tell – Jason stayed on to sort out Rose's starter motor. She was pathetically grateful. He dropped round later in the week to bring Geoff some racing videos and repaired a collapsing gate, a broken shower head and the lock on the kitchen door. It was the beginning of regular visits. He'd appointed himself the Wyatts' unofficial odd-job man. When he wasn't working – he put in a lot of mileage each week selling horse feed – he'd drop in to see what other household tasks he could perform.

When the Wyatts lost their home and moved into a rented terrace house, Jason was on hand to help. He could only imagine how much Rose was suffering as the props of her life were stripped from her one by one. As for Geoff, he appeared to be disappearing into himself, barely managing a word in response to a direct question. The result was that he and Rose started to talk to one another, really talk, about everything under the sun. Though he called her Princess for fun, he soon disabused himself of that Lady Diana nonsense. When it came down to it, Rose was an ordinary woman like any other, with insecurities and fears and a fragile confidence that needed bolstering. He bolstered with all his heart.

It was like an old-fashioned love affair really. He'd advance and she'd retreat but bit by bit he inched his way into her life. They'd married with Geoff's blessing – how could it have been otherwise? – though their living arrangements had maybe been a little unorthodox. Now here she was, at last making a proper home in his house, and it was ten days to their six-month anniversary.

When she got back from work, he'd show her her brand new office. And if there was anything she didn't like, he'd change it. She only had to ask.

Kathy left for work early. After walking in on her mother and Rob yelling at each other she didn't fancy hanging around at home. Talk about a shock. She'd thought Mum and Rob were made for one another. She was all in favour of their marriage. Though she knew plenty of girls her own age who had resented stepdads or -mums, she'd not had any problem adjusting. For one thing, Rob made Mum really happy. Other reasons were more selfish. Now Mum was on cloud nine with her new husband, she'd not half as much time to get on Kathy's case. Frankly, things had been a lot less stressed since Rob had come on the scene.

So last night was a real downer. Years back, she'd witnessed plenty of fights between Mum and Daddy and she'd thought that sort of thing was a distant memory. But she was older now; if this new marriage was going down the tubes she definitely didn't intend to stick around.

But surely it would be all right? They were allowed to lose their rags once in a while. She hoped that's all it had been. Mum would be unbearable if it all went wrong.

They'd been arguing about Ivana. She hadn't meant to eavesdrop but they'd been too worked up to notice her at first.

Surely Rob hadn't been having it off with the Czech woman? That would be a major turn-up. She knew lots of men fancied Ivana – Gary, for one. Even though he denied it, she could tell. And it was well known Steve had had a big fling with her in the past. But Rob didn't seem interested in her that way. Kathy had assumed that that was because he only had eyes for Mum. But maybe he was deliberately covering something up.

What a bitch Ivana was. Kathy used to think she was OK but she'd been distinctly unfriendly recently. Since Steve had taken an interest in her, in fact. No mystery there then.

In the circumstances, with all this domestic drama, going to work early seemed like a good idea.

She was surprised to find Steve in the office when she arrived. She'd discovered that he spent most mornings at home catching up on recordings of the previous day's races. It sounded like a bit of a chore to Kathy and she'd been wondering if she could help somehow. But now was not the moment to air her ideas. Steve looked as immaculate as ever but there was no enthusiasm in his greeting.

'What happened yesterday?' she said. The race at Hampton Waters must be what was on his mind.

'A lot of people seem to have got lucky at my expense.'

'You said there were lots of medium-sized bets.'

He nodded. 'Fifty to win on Salsa Sam. Each shop took around three or four bets like that, all within a couple of minutes of the off. All of them got twenty to one or better.'

Kathy began to calculate.

'I'll save you the bother. I'm down around twenty-five grand.'

No wonder Steve was not his usual buoyant self.

'Do you want to know something?' he said. 'As far as we can tell, most of these punters were women.'

That sounded curious. 'Did anyone ask them why they thought he would win?' Kathy asked.

'A few, but they weren't very helpful.'

'They must have said something.'

'They said they liked the name. Apparently salsa dancing is a bit of a craze. Can you flaming believe it?'

Rob had long learned that where horses were concerned appearances could be deceptive. Some of the scruffiest looking nags had carried him triumphantly round three miles of steeplechase fences; some of the most elegant had dumped him at the first ditch. The same principle applied to the men and women who owned horses. One of the richest he'd known wore spectacles held together by Sellotape; a woman who was guaranteed a winner at every Cheltenham festival appeared to dress courtesy of Oxfam.

So Rob wasn't put off by the visitor in the stained blazer and dirty trainers who emerged from the ten-year-old Escort with a crumpled front bumper. Mr Vladimir Petrov, as he'd introduced himself on the phone, could be a billionaire oligarch for all Rob knew. At any rate, he was happy to show round a prospective client and Petrov claimed to be interested in sending a mare to be covered next season.

His arm was round her waist, that thickening waist that would no longer allow her to slip into slinky Ascot dresses, and his whiskery cheek was pressing against her neck. Stupid though it was, the fact that she was three inches taller than him had been one of the hardest objections for her to swallow. But she was over that now.

'Have I mentioned you look smashing today, Princess?' His breath was hot on her cheek as he sought her mouth.

She kissed him briefly then disengaged. 'I've got to get to work,' she said.

'You're the boss, aren't you? Give yourself another half hour.'

'Don't be naughty.' She stepped away, but nicely, squeezing his big rough hand and smiling. 'Because I'm the boss, I've got to play by the rules.'

She could see he wasn't convinced, that she'd offended him again but she really did have to go. She ran the sales office for an expanding mail-order business and a lot of people depended on her.

'I'll see you tonight,' she said as she made for the door.

She knew some people thought she'd married Jason to please her father, but that wasn't the case at all. She'd married him because he loved her unconditionally. One day – soon, she hoped – she'd be able to return his devotion in the way he deserved.

Rob watched as Cape Fear stalked menacingly around his pen. He'd earned his living from horses, had grown up with them, knew these animals inside out – and this was the only one he'd ever been afraid of. Of course, he'd come across plenty you needed to treat with caution, horses you wouldn't turn your back on or walk behind for fear of a spiteful kick. But the big black stallion was an animal apart.

As a yearling Cape Fear had chased more than one groom from the paddocks. He'd bullied all the other animals and, in the end, had been turned out by himself. They'd contemplated gelding him but once he'd been broken in and sent off to be trained he seemed to settle down. 'Lucky

I didn't cut him,' Rob's father had said on many occasions after Cape Fear had won his first Group race but the fact was that Dad was getting frail by then and had nothing to do with the handling of the difficult colt.

In a career spanning three seasons, Cape Fear won two Group Two races and three at the next level down. He wasn't well enough bred and hadn't had quite enough class on the racecourse to seem an obvious candidate for a stud career but, with Goldeneye's arrival in his second crop of foals, the situation looked set to change. Sadly his temperament had only got worse.

The stallion had been back at Rushmore for less than a month when he had attacked Gwen, Rob's head groom. She had been mucking him out while he was chained to the wall, when Cape Fear threw his head back and snapped the links as if they were made of tin foil. Before Gwen had a chance to escape from the pen, the stallion had knocked her to the ground. He was kneeling on her chest, about to sink his teeth into her face, when Rob rushed in and hit him as hard as he could. Gwen scrambled to her feet and was almost clear when the horse lashed out from almost six feet. Fortunately for her the kick did not land squarely, though it threw her clear of the stable and left her sprawling on the cobbles of the yard, screaming in pain and fear. She'd never returned to the yard.

After that, Cape Fear became the mother of all bastards to deal with. Rob rehoused him in specially secure quarters and treated him with the utmost caution. The stallion's head collar was never removed and it was fitted with two large brass rings. When he covered mares, two handlers would stand either side of him equipped with long poles with hooks which they'd hitch up to the rings and lead the horse along like a bull. Leather muzzles and hobbles were used on him for treatment by the vet or the blacksmith and, on occasions, he'd be immobilised in heavy-duty stocks or tranquillised with a dart from a small handgun. After what had happened with Gwen, Rob wasn't taking any chances.

Rob rarely allowed things to get him down for long. He

was a man whose response to bad news was instant – usually explosive – then the dust would settle and the sun would reappear. But the sun wasn't shining at the moment as he stared moodily at the gleaming black shape of Cape Fear. Right now his company seemed appropriate.

The chief cause of Rob's ill-humour was Bella. He'd had disagreements with her before but not like last night's. He'd been foolish to walk out on her earlier in the day but he'd done it to avoid a row. He hadn't trusted himself not to lose his rag once she started on about Ivana and, on the spur of the moment, he'd fled. It had been a mistake.

She'd waited till they'd eaten supper and he'd settled himself in an armchair with a Scotch and the racing paper. His guard had been down – he realised that now.

'You know, Rob, running away never solves anything,' she'd begun. 'Nor does hiding behind a newspaper.'

He put it aside at once, knowing that he'd not be picking it up again in a hurry.

She didn't wait for him to reply. 'Have you thought any more about what I said this morning?'

'Sure.' He was determined to remain even-tempered. 'You're right, let's crack on with the foaling boxes and everything.'

'I meant about Ivana. I know she's been invaluable in the past and you don't like upsetting anyone but look at the facts. That cottage should be earning us more money.'

'Maybe but I'm not going to make Ivana move out.'

'Ask her to pay some rent then. It's a reasonable request, surely.'

'No, Bella, the cottage goes with the job.'

'If you're not brave enough, Rob, then leave it to me.'

She was standing over him, as lovely as ever but not in the way that was familiar to him. She seemed hard, armed with her beauty like a warrior.

He got to his feet. 'I thought you liked Ivana.'

'We get on fine.' Her voice was flat. 'I respect her as a resourceful woman who knows how to get what she wants.'

'What do you mean by that?'

'I mean she knows how to get men to accommodate her. She's got a pretty good deal out of you.'

What was Bella suggesting? Rob could feel his temper rising.

'I'm not having this. Ivana has done a great job here and I'm not chucking her out, whatever you think.' He was shouting, he hadn't meant to.

'What do you expect me to think? She's done pretty well for herself here and good luck to her. But now I think she ought to go and wiggle her hips somewhere else.'

'Jesus, Bella, you can be a real bitch sometimes.'

'And you're a bloody fool when it comes to a manipulative little tart like her.'

They were both shouting now, glaring into each other's eyes. He was itching to smack that superior smirk off her face and she looked as if she were about to drive her nails into his face.

'Please stop!' a voice wailed from the door.

Kathy was back. They hadn't heard her come in but they both turned towards her, as if caught red-handed – which they had been.

After that, the quarrel had ended though it had not been resolved. Kathy had burst into tears and her mother had taken care of her, steering her off to bed. Rob had slipped in to see the girl later and apologised.

'Don't read anything into it, Kathy, please. Your mum and I love each other very much. These things happen in marriages sometimes.'

He'd felt a fraud as he'd said it. After all, how would he know? He'd never been married before.

Her response had surprised him. 'I'm sorry I walked in on you like that.'

It was the first time, as far as he was aware, that he'd ever heard Kathy apologise for anything.

He'd considered sleeping in the spare room but as he stood in the bathroom considering whether that would make it better or worse, Bella had come in. She'd not said anything, just turned the light off with one hand and put the other on his chest inside his unbuttoned shirt. Her touch was electric, instantly reconnecting all the want and passion that he carried within him. He'd have taken her on the bathroom floor if it wasn't so close to Kathy's room.

'Carry me,' she'd murmured and he'd picked her up and borne her off to bed. What followed was selfish and cathartic and when they'd finished with each other there had been no energy left for talk. Their conflict had been put on hold.

Cape Fear had been standing still for once. He would do this in his presence on occasions, Rob had noticed, and he savoured these moments. It made him wonder if there wasn't, deep down in the horse's wild nature, a core of peace – if only he could get in touch with it.

Suddenly the horse jerked his head, his whole body twitching, and he stamped his feet in familiar fury. Someone was coming.

The door opened and Ivana entered the barn.

'Rob?' In the light of his disagreement with Bella, the Czech girl's soft, husky tones broke guiltily on his ear. 'Can I have a word with you, please?'

It was a surprisingly formal approach but, in the circumstances, Rob was grateful.

'Sure. What's up?'

She looked hesitant and when the stallion reared towards her, she jumped anxiously.

'Wait a moment,' he said and unfastened the gate which gave Cape Fear access to the paddock where he took his exercise. The enclosure, an area of about half an acre, was surrounded by a ten-foot-high security fence.

'He hates me,' Ivana said. 'I never met a horse so mean. He has a black heart.'

Rob shook his head. 'He's just anti-social.' Whatever the justification, he didn't like people running the stallion down.

'Huh.' She was unimpressed. 'Look, Rob, I've got something to tell you. I'm thinking of leaving.'

'What? Leaving the stud?'

'Yes. I'm sorry.'

61

He was amazed she was giving him notice. What were the odds of this happening so soon after his argument with Bella? As an employer, his impulse was to demand her reasons but all he could think was that this might be a solution to his current predicament.

'I don't want to lose you,' he said, feeling like a hypocrite. 'What's brought this on?'

She ignored the question. 'I'll need some money.'

'You want to borrow money?'

'No, Rob, I need cash quickly.'

He didn't know what to say. Was she asking him to give it to her?

'Look,' she said, 'I've worked hard for you. I've made a big contribution here, right?'

'Yes, and I've paid you for it.'

'I'm asking for help, Rob. As a friend.' Her hand was on his arm, squeezing.

'What's the matter? You're upset.'

She shook her head. 'It's nothing. I just need some money.'

'I suppose I might be able to scrape together a farewell present for you. A few hundred maybe.'

'That's not enough. I need more.' Her big green eyes implored.

'I'm sorry, Ivana, I don't have it.'

'But you've just won a lot of money on Goldeneye.'

'I haven't got it yet. Anyway, that money's needed for the business.' He wriggled uncomfortably under her accusing stare. 'Look, I'll do some sums, see what I can do, OK? Give me some time to think about it.'

He could see her calculating how hard to push the matter, her small pointed chin thrust aggressively at him, her cheekbones gleaming in her pale face. How come he had so many difficult women in his life?

She removed her hand and stepped back. 'Thanks, Rob,' she said as she walked away.

He watched her go, disappointed at this turn of events. She'd be a big loss and, if he could, he'd happily send her off with a cut of Goldie's prize money. But if he did, how could he keep it from Bella? If there was one thing guaranteed to convince his wife that he'd ever been romantically attached to Ivana, it was wishing her bon voyage with a large cheque.

Jason was happy with his handiwork. He'd never fitted a safe before but he could turn his hands to most things around the house. He'd thought it was a funny request, mind you, but anything Rosie wanted was all right with him.

He supposed it was coming from a background like hers, being brought up in a big house with valuable things all around. Geoff Wyatt would have had a safe in his study, bet your life. Probably hidden in the wall behind some fancy painting, where he'd keep a handy bundle of cash. He was always doling out money wherever he went. He remembered Geoff well from those days, when he'd been riding winners for him. Jason had been tipped a fair few quid too. Geoff Wyatt had been the most generous owner in the land, bar none, till the day he crashed.

Back then, Geoff's daughter Rose had seemed unattainable to Jason. A real English beauty, named just right. He'd fancied her in the way every red-blooded bloke fancied Lady Diana, she warmed the cockles, but he recognised that she was quite out of his reach. She was always on her dad's arm at race meetings, the pair of them like a married couple only they were father and daughter. He knew she worked in Geoff's firm – he was the Midlands' biggest brassware manufacturer – and the two of them were inseparable. Geoff's wife was some kind of permanent invalid and Rose, his only child, played her mother's part.

For all that, it had never seemed unhealthy. Geoff was always pushing Rose in the direction of eligible young men and it didn't take much to get him on the subject of the grandchildren he expected one day, to Rose's obvious embarrassment. Boyfriends came and went, smart business types with family money and rising young executives who were going places. Rumours would circulate about wedding plans – this time, it was said, Rose had found Mr Right. But there was always a hitch, none of these likely young bucks ever swept Rose up the aisle. There she would be, year after year, no longer a fresh-faced flower but now a mature beauty, forever on the arm of her father.

Only after Geoff sold his business was he seen about on his own. Jason got the story out of Rose later, at least the portion of it she was prepared to tell. Her mother's Alzheimer's had taken a turn for the worse shortly after the sale and Rose had switched allegiance to her other parent – she'd needed constant help and Rose wasn't prepared to hand her over to a team of nurses. Without his daughter's steady influence by his side, Geoff's gambling had soon got out of control. While Rose was tending her sick mother, the family's considerable fortune ran through her father's fingers. Rose had told Jason the figures – the old man had got through six million pounds in four years on horses, hotels and vintage champagne. The Inland Revenue had taken their slice too. Jason had always reckoned Geoff Wyatt was the most generous man he'd ever met and Rose confirmed that for her father charity did not begin at home. He'd funded innumerable benefits for racing causes and the monthly standing orders to the Injured Jockeys Fund were the last things she'd stopped as his creditors closed in.

Jason had situated the safe in the old built-in wardrobe. Placing it in there out of sight seemed the most obvious thing to do. He was coming round to the idea now, especially since it was fireproof. They could shove passports and insurance documents in there for safekeeping. Since Geoff's millions had gone down the Swanee it was unlikely ever to be used for actual money.

Some people were envious of the rich. Even now, people couldn't resist a little dig at Rose and her wealthy past. If they were in the pub with Phil and Liz, one of them would always say something like, 'Bit of a comedown, my lass,' or 'So it's come to this, has it?' when Rose asked for half a bitter shandy. It irritated Jason no end and he'd have had a word with Phil about it if Rose hadn't stopped him. She didn't care, she didn't even see the insult. 'But I've always liked shandy. You're so fierce, Jason.'

Actually, he wasn't fierce at all. He never spoke a cross word to anyone or took offence – except when it came to his new wife. He'd walk through fire for Rose. He'd defend her to the death and do anything she asked without question. She might not have got much when she'd married him but she'd got absolute commitment to her cause.

After Rose's mother had died and the creditors had closed in on Geoff, Jason had been able to help out, just a bit. It was really his uncle who'd got him involved with the Wyatts. Jim Sidebottom was a former farmer who'd tried his hand at training and he still worked in the racing business. Unlike some people, Jim had taken more of an interest in Geoff after his fortune had gone. Jim was a righteous man. He was more concerned with what he could give Geoff than what he could take from him.

One Sunday Jim had asked Jason to give Geoff a lift to church, where Jim was preaching. Jason had been surprised – surely Geoff could drive himself? – but he'd agreed. He discovered Geoff and Rose still living in the large detached family home, but everywhere he looked there were signs of decay. There was no longer a Bentley and a sporty runaround in the driveway, just a battered Renault which, it turned out, belonged to Rose. She greeted him like a long-lost friend and apologised for not driving her father herself but there was a problem with the starter on her car. All this was far from Jason's expectations but it was the sight of Geoff that really shocked him. The erstwhile life and soul of the party was a diminished figure, thin and hesitant, whose fingers limply returned his handshake and eyes stared dull and lifeless into his.

'Depression,' Jim told him later. 'They've got him on any amount of medication but that won't do him much good. The man needs to rediscover faith in himself.'

Jason knew what his uncle was getting at by his talk of faith and knew that Jim would do all he could to supply his own brand. As for himself, he tried to make a difference in a more practical fashion. That first Sunday, after he'd returned Geoff home – whether he'd benefited from the excursion was hard to tell – Jason stayed on to sort out Rose's starter motor. She was pathetically grateful. He dropped round later in the week to bring Geoff some racing videos and repaired a collapsing gate, a broken shower head and the lock on the kitchen door. It was the beginning of regular visits. He'd appointed himself the Wyatts' unofficial odd-job man. When he wasn't working – he put in a lot of mileage each week selling horse feed – he'd drop in to see what other household tasks he could perform.

When the Wyatts lost their home and moved into a rented terrace house, Jason was on hand to help. He could only imagine how much Rose was suffering as the props of her life were stripped from her one by one. As for Geoff, he appeared to be disappearing into himself, barely managing a word in response to a direct question. The result was that he and Rose started to talk to one another, really talk, about everything under the sun. Though he called her Princess for fun, he soon disabused himself of that Lady Diana nonsense. When it came down to it, Rose was an ordinary woman like any other, with insecurities and fears and a fragile confidence that needed bolstering. He bolstered with all his heart.

It was like an old-fashioned love affair really. He'd advance and she'd retreat but bit by bit he inched his way into her life. They'd married with Geoff's blessing – how could it have been otherwise? – though their living arrangements had maybe been a little unorthodox. Now here she was, at last making a proper home in his house, and it was ten days to their six-month anniversary.

When she got back from work, he'd show her her brand new office. And if there was anything she didn't like, he'd change it. She only had to ask.

Kathy left for work early. After walking in on her mother and Rob yelling at each other she didn't fancy hanging around at home. Talk about a shock. She'd thought Mum and Rob were made for one another. She was all in favour of their marriage. Though she knew plenty of girls her own age who had resented stepdads or -mums, she'd not had any problem adjusting. For one thing, Rob made Mum really happy. Other reasons were more selfish. Now Mum was on cloud nine with her new husband, she'd not half as much time to get on Kathy's case. Frankly, things had been a lot less stressed since Rob had come on the scene.

So last night was a real downer. Years back, she'd witnessed plenty of fights between Mum and Daddy and she'd thought that sort of thing was a distant memory. But she was older now; if this new marriage was going down the tubes she definitely didn't intend to stick around.

But surely it would be all right? They were allowed to lose their rags once in a while. She hoped that's all it had been. Mum would be unbearable if it all went wrong.

They'd been arguing about Ivana. She hadn't meant to eavesdrop but they'd been too worked up to notice her at first.

Surely Rob hadn't been having it off with the Czech woman? That would be a major turn-up. She knew lots of men fancied Ivana – Gary, for one. Even though he denied it, she could tell. And it was well known Steve had had a big fling with her in the past. But Rob didn't seem interested in her that way. Kathy had assumed that that was because he only had eyes for Mum. But maybe he was deliberately covering something up.

What a bitch Ivana was. Kathy used to think she was OK but she'd been distinctly unfriendly recently. Since Steve had taken an interest in her, in fact. No mystery there then.

In the circumstances, with all this domestic drama, going to work early seemed like a good idea.

She was surprised to find Steve in the office when she arrived. She'd discovered that he spent most mornings at home catching up on recordings of the previous day's races. It sounded like a bit of a chore to Kathy and she'd been wondering if she could help somehow. But now was not the moment to air her ideas. Steve looked as immaculate as ever but there was no enthusiasm in his greeting.

'What happened yesterday?' she said. The race at Hampton Waters must be what was on his mind.

'A lot of people seem to have got lucky at my expense.'

'You said there were lots of medium-sized bets.'

He nodded. 'Fifty to win on Salsa Sam. Each shop took around three or four bets like that, all within a couple of minutes of the off. All of them got twenty to one or better.'

Kathy began to calculate.

'I'll save you the bother. I'm down around twenty-five grand.'

No wonder Steve was not his usual buoyant self.

'Do you want to know something?' he said. 'As far as we can tell, most of these punters were women.'

That sounded curious. 'Did anyone ask them why they thought he would win?' Kathy asked.

'A few, but they weren't very helpful.'

'They must have said something.'

'They said they liked the name. Apparently salsa dancing is a bit of a craze. Can you flaming believe it?'

Rob had long learned that where horses were concerned appearances could be deceptive. Some of the scruffiest looking nags had carried him triumphantly round three miles of steeplechase fences; some of the most elegant had dumped him at the first ditch. The same principle applied to the men and women who owned horses. One of the richest he'd known wore spectacles held together by Sellotape; a woman who was guaranteed a winner at every Cheltenham festival appeared to dress courtesy of Oxfam.

So Rob wasn't put off by the visitor in the stained blazer and dirty trainers who emerged from the ten-year-old Escort with a crumpled front bumper. Mr Vladimir Petrov, as he'd introduced himself on the phone, could be a billionaire oligarch for all Rob knew. At any rate, he was happy to show round a prospective client and Petrov claimed to be interested in sending a mare to be covered next season.

His visitor had a beaky nose and hair tied back in a ponytail but he seemed an affable sort of fellow and certainly knew his way around a yard, asking a variety of questions in accented English.

'Where do you come from?' Rob asked.

Petrov made an expansive gesture. 'The East – all over.' Maybe he *was* an oligarch and owned half the Urals.

'Do you speak Czech? I have a worker here from the Czech Republic.'

'And you have Czech jockey too.' The man's hand gripped Rob's elbow. 'I saw on television that a Czech boy rides a horse bred here. That's why I think of sending my horses to you.'

Rob looked round for Ivana but there was no sign of her. It was possible she'd left in a huff after their earlier conversation, which was a pity. She could have given the visitor the tour, maybe in his own language – emphasising the East European connection wouldn't do any harm.

Petrov didn't seem all that impressed with Curtain Raiser, Rob's junior stallion, who was a small, neat horse. Rob wasn't surprised, his visitor was obviously not a man for subtlety, and so he quickly led him to Cape Fear's paddock. This was the point in his sales pitch at which things could go wrong, depending on the stallion's mood. Female owners in particular sometimes had second thoughts about placing their mares at his mercy.

The horse stood in the shade on the far side of the open space; he seemed not to have noticed them or, more likely in Rob's opinion, did not think them worthy of interest. Rob extolled the animal's virtues: his pedigree, his race record and the achievements of his offspring, finishing with a toot on his trumpet for Goldeneye's Two Thousand Guineas win.

His companion stared at Cape Fear through the mesh of the fence. 'Magnificent,' he pronounced.

Cape Fear turned his head in their direction and then stalked past them into his box.

'That is one fabulous horse,' said Petrov, 'but why this?' He rattled the fence. 'You afraid he's gonna run away?'

Rob explained. He believed it was best to be frank about the stallion's true nature, even if it meant losing some business. In this case, if he read the hawk-faced Petrov correctly, he didn't think it would make the slightest difference. They followed the horse into the barn and Rob pointed out the movable gate, which divided the horse's pen so a groom could clean without fear of attack.

His visitor was intrigued. 'I see. He's like a tiger in a zoo.'

Rob didn't disagree.

As they made their way back to the yard, he caught sight of Ivana approaching from the path that led to her cottage.

'There's the girl I was telling you about,' he said to his guest. 'She's from Czechoslovakia.'

Rob was about to call to Ivana when she caught sight of them. Without making any sign of acknowledgement, she turned into the foaling sheds.

Rob wanted to yell after her but she had disappeared. He had wanted to introduce her but what was the point? She'd soon be leaving anyway.

'Steve?' Kathy was feeling sorry for her boss. After only a fortnight's exposure to his business she could see that it was ailing. She'd spent a morning prioritising the unpaid bills and was fast developing a technique for fobbing people off on the phone. There was the unfair competition across the road and now the losses from the race at Hampton Waters. 'Do you think,' she continued, 'that this has got anything to do with Fairweather's?'

He raised a grim smile, the first of a long morning. 'Possibly. It could be the next step in their campaign to put me out of business. They're the only people I can think of who are big enough to organise a team to place twenty-five bets simultaneously.'

'But how did they know Salsa Sam was going to win?'

The smile faded. 'You've got me there, Kathy. I really don't know.'

'But the horse won like a train. Do you think he was on drugs?'

Steve shrugged. 'If he was, it'll show up. Anyway, I've already paid out.' He sighed. 'Maybe it's just my luck that half the salsa evening classes in town decided to have a flutter in my shops.'

Kathy couldn't believe she'd be feeling sorry for a bookmaker – it wasn't exactly in the script. On the other hand, Steve wasn't exactly her idea of a bookie. He was too good looking, for a start. The funny thing was, she fancied him even more now he seemed less than his usual cocky self.

'Steve . . .' she hesitated, wondering if this was quite the moment, then blundered on anyway. 'Do you like being a bookie?'

'Not right now, no.'

'I mean, have you ever thought of doing something else?'

For a moment she thought he was going to tell her to mind her own business. Then he said, 'When my dad was alive, I just wanted to be like him. Couldn't wait to get my hands on the business after he died. It was the only way I was going to get it. He'd have gone on till he was ninety if he'd been able to. I bet he's not happy about popping off at fifty-five, wherever he is.'

'When was that?'

'Four years ago. It's been a tough four years. So the answer to your question is, yes, I have thought about doing something else with my life.'

'What?'

He looked at her. His eyes, she thought, were like chips of blue sky.

'My dad had a lovely old mare and I kept her up at Rob's. He mated her with his stallion and look what we got – Goldeneye. A Two Thousand Guineas winner. The mare's dead now but I'd like more like her. I wouldn't mind breeding horses instead of doing this.'

That made sense to Kathy. She wouldn't mind breeding horses herself. But she stopped herself saying so – talk about being obvious. Now she had Steve's ear it was time to try something out.

'You know you keep a record of every race on video?'

For a second he was surprised by the change of subject. Then he said, 'Yes, you can't move in my house without falling over form guides and videos, if that's what you mean.'

'How would you like it available on computer? Any race you like just a mouse click away.'

'You mean play videos on the computer?'

'Forget videos. Record the races on DVD and store them on a portable drive, then you can use the drive on other machines. No piles of videos or discs, all in one place, easily get-at-able.'

'Sounds like hard work logging it all in.'

'Not if I do it for you. Get me the right equipment, hook up the racing coverage in here and I'll take care of it.'

He regarded her shrewdly, little crinkles at the corners of his eyes. Signs of age some might say; to Kathy it only made him look more attractive.

'You're sure you can fix this?'

'You bet. Although,' she added in a moment of inspiration, 'it would help if I could see your present set-up.'

'It's just a video machine and a mountain of tapes.'

'I mean, if I could see how you label them. You know, so I could devise a system to suit you.'

'Custom-made, eh?'

'Just for you.' She hoped she didn't appear too keen; Mum always said it was a mistake to chase the boys. But Steve was hardly a boy, though he might think she was just a child. She had to let him know she was available.

'You'd better come round then,' he said. 'Cut it short this afternoon and come on over to my place.'

It sounded good to her.

Ivana didn't know where she was going, she'd broken into a run once she was out of sight of the two men and now she blundered off the path into a small copse by the far paddock. What would an onlooker think? She didn't care, just so long as Milos wasn't coming after her.

What on earth was he doing with Rob? To see him standing there smirking at her had paralysed her with fear. Why was he here? Her imagination spun round in many directions but always with the same message: now he'd found her he was going to try and force himself back into her life. He was an obsessive – nothing would put him off.

But he hadn't come after her. The path back to the yard was empty. As she recovered her breath she heard the sound of a car engine and, after a minute, through the trees she made out the shape of an unfamiliar white vehicle winding down the lane leading to the main road.

Surely that was Milos – leaving, thank the saints.

What was he doing with Rob? Had he been talking about her? What kind of lies was he telling?

And when was he coming back?

Rob looked up from his desk as Ivana entered the office.

'I hope you haven't forgotten about tonight,' he said. 'I'm relying on you.'

Rob and Bella were attending a charity dinner at a hotel ten miles off and had booked a room so they could make a proper night of it. But they could only stay over if Ivana was on hand to take charge in case of an emergency.

Ivana nodded, it was a long-standing arrangement and she'd promised.

'Good.' Rob looked relieved. 'It's a pity you didn't meet the guy who came to look round earlier on,' he went on. 'His name's Vladimir Petrov and he comes from Eastern Europe, he didn't say where exactly.'

Ivana could have told him but was only interested in getting the information to flow in the other direction. 'What was he doing here?' she asked.

'He's just an owner who asked to look round. He's got a mare he might send to be covered next year.'

Oh really? Ivana felt that must be a lie but it was possible Milos could be representing someone. But why would he turn up at this stud now, so soon after their encounter at Newmarket? That would be too much of a coincidence. And why the assumed name?

There was only one reason he had shown his face at Rushmore. He was staking her out.

This was the third season Tomas had been picking up rides in England but it was the first time he'd ridden at Brighton. The course wound uphill and downhill in a left-handed curve, some four hundred feet above the sea. Though he'd ridden at Newmarket, another track which didn't form a circuit, he'd never seen anything quite like it. And he'd never seen anything like the broad-beamed female in a rose-patterned dress the size of a tent who was giving him instructions on the next race, addressing him as if he were a hundred yards off rather than standing in the shadow of her bulk: Betsy Beal, a south coast trainer who'd succumbed to Sammy Swan's sales pitch for his services. By her side was a sylph-like girl a quarter her size but with the same pink cheeks and strawberry-blonde hair: Julie, Betsy's daughter.

'And none of that Fancy Dan stuff,' the trainer was roaring. 'Get hold of him straight away or the other little sods will leave you for dead like last time.'

Tomas didn't understand half of what she was saying but he got the gist. He had ridden for her already this afternoon and had missed the break at the start of a six-furlong sprint. She was telling him not to make the same mistake again and he nodded his head confidently and said, 'Right you are,' a couple of times, a phrase he'd picked up from an Irish jockey which usually went down quite well. It plainly amused Julie no end.

The truth was he was far from confident, this course obviously favoured runners and riders who knew it well – which did not describe his situation or that of his mount, Cat's Whiskers. All the same, he was determined not to let Mrs Beal down, she'd taken a chance on him, as she'd said more than once, and he was determined to repay her faith. Besides, according to Sammy, she had some good horses back in her yard on the Downs, and was worth impressing.

Unlike the first race, the current encounter was spread over a mile and three furlongs, the entire length of the serpentining course. Tomas reckoned this gave him a better chance, provided he could stay close enough to the leaders to still be in contention when it came to the switchback run-in over the last few furlongs.

Cat's Whiskers proved to be a neat, nimble-footed type who coped well with the left-handed bend uphill at the start – a good sign. Tomas tucked him in at the head of the second group of runners, determined to keep the three leaders in his sights.

The horse was in a fair rhythm now and he had a feeling there was strength in reserve – 'Don't worry, he'll stay' had been the trainer's words. That was as well, because the final two furlongs were uphill and a killer for animals who'd shot their bolt by that stage.

Aware now of the course's sting in the tail, Tomas kept a tight hold on Cat's Whiskers as they began the downhill run on the turn for home. Even so, his mount was now up with the leading three, one of whom was beginning to roll with fatigue as the ground levelled out and then began to slope upward.

The tired horse just ahead lurched suddenly across his line and Tomas gave his mount a reminder with the whip, to keep him straight. Then, bang, the other horse barged into him and the whip was gone, knocked from his hand.

Tomas gripped tight with his legs, urging Cat's Whiskers on. The little horse dug in as promised and caught the animal in second within fifty yards of the winning post. As he dismounted he wondered what might have been if he hadn't lost his whip.

'Silly boy,' growled Mrs Beal, 'hold it tighter next time.' Then she grinned, her big ruddy face glowing like a red balloon. 'The owner's chuffed though, it's the first time his horse has finished in the frame all season.'

Chuffed? The English had some funny words in their language. What did it mean? All the same, he worked out from Julie's provocative smile as she congratulated him that he must have done all right.

* * *

Ivana felt like destroying the phone in her hand. She wanted to hurl the stupid plastic into the pile of horse muck at her feet and stamp on it. Except that the violence would be misplaced – it was the person on the other end of the line she really wanted to hurt. Instead she had to settle for a scream of Czech invective.

'You prick, Tomas. You can't do that to me!'

But it seemed he could. The little sod, today riding at Brighton, was staying with a local trainer so he could work a horse for her the next morning. He said he'd told Ivana about the arrangement a couple of days ago. She couldn't remember. All she could think of was that he wasn't intending to return that night.

'But Milos was here today,' she said urgently, repeating herself. Maybe Tomas hadn't realised how upset she was. 'He's tracked me down. You've got to come home! I need you.'

'Calm down. Even if he is still interested in you, he's not going to hurt you.'

'If he does, Tomas, my blood will be on your hands, you selfish bastard!'

She cut the call off. Jesus, he made her so mad sometimes. Didn't he realise that, when it came to it, the pair of them were on their own in this country? There were times when only his reassuring presence and the sound of their mother tongue on his lips would ease her fears. Times like now. But what did that matter to him? He was too busy sucking up to his new contacts to care that she was petrified.

Her phone rang. So maybe he'd thought better of his self-centred behaviour after all.

She answered the call. 'I hope you're going to tell me you've changed your mind.' The words tumbled out.

But her caller was not who she was expecting.

'Who is this speaking please?' said a voice in English. Clipped, cold and female. Ivana read the number on the LCD read-out.

'It's Ivana, isn't it?' The voice wasn't friendly.

'Yes?' That was a mistake but she wasn't thinking clearly. 'Who are you?'

'I think you know very well.'

Ivana finally worked it out. She recognised the phone read-out and placed those icy English tones. The number belonged to Charlie Moorehead and this was his wife, Louise.

'I want to know why you are listed on my husband's phone.'

'Because,' she thought quickly, 'sometimes I need to get hold of my brother.'

'But your brother has his own phone. The number is here too. And I can tell you that my husband talks to you more often than to him.'

Ivana could hear the rattle of paper in the background – was the woman going through Charlie's phone record? She could do without this kind of hassle right now.

'Sometimes he speaks to me when he can't get hold of Tomas. So what?'

There was a pause, as if Louise was taking a deep breath, then she started again. 'I'll tell you what, young lady. I don't know how single women behave where you come from but over here they don't go around throwing themselves at married men. Not unless they earn their living that way in which case we have a name for them. Now I'm not calling you a tart but if you don't stop pestering my husband I shall revise my opinion – and jolly well make sure that everyone in racing shares it.'

Ivana had had enough. 'Oh, go and screw yourself, you ugly bitch.' There was a gasp of outrage on the other end of the line and she realised she'd well and truly burned this bridge. In which case she might as well enjoy the blaze. 'You know why Charlie would rather make love to me?' she said. 'He works with horses all day, he doesn't want one in his bed at night.'

She savoured the stunned silence and broke the call as a screech of outrage cascaded down the line. That made the second caller she'd hung up on in ten minutes.

It didn't give her much satisfaction. She turned off the phone so the horrible woman couldn't call back.

* * *

As Tomas followed Mrs Beal's battered old estate along the narrow Sussex road, he replayed the conversation with Ivana in his head. How come she made him feel so guilty these days? Hadn't he done plenty for her in the past – and wasn't he always at hand when her life hit a rocky patch? Of course he was. She was his little sister and he'd always take care of her. But sometimes her dramas had to take a back seat. And now was one of these times.

He'd accepted an invitation from Mrs Beal – or Betsy as he'd now been instructed to call her – to stay the night at her farmhouse and ride out a couple of her promising two-year-olds the next morning. She'd been impressed with his handling of Cat's Whiskers. He'd be a fool to turn down the opportunity – he knew how Sammy would react if he did. 'I'll find you the openings, mate, but it's up to you to take them. And not just on the course. Get to know people. You're a bit more interesting than most lads, coming from Czechoslovakia and all. Make the most of it.'

So how could he suddenly cancel on Ivana's hysterical say-so? The fact that the trainer's pretty daughter would be there too had nothing to do with it.

It was weird that creep Milos suddenly showing up at Rushmore but there was probably an explanation. Coincidences did happen in life. And even if Milos had come looking for Ivana, it was probably just to see if he still had a chance with her. Some people never gave up.

He was suddenly aware that the road ahead was empty. Jesus, where had the bloody woman gone? He put his foot down on the accelerator and gritted his teeth as the car lurched into a bend. A hundred yards ahead he spotted the navy blue tail end of the trainer's vehicle as it disappeared round another twist in the road. It was all very well for her but he didn't know these lanes.

He put his sister from his mind as he concentrated on keeping his new benefactor in his sights.

* * *

Ivana was just finishing her hair when she heard a knock at the front door. She peered carefully down into the yard. A dirty white car was parked there – why hadn't she heard it? She'd had the hairdryer going, that's why. Not that it mattered.

The knock sounded again. Without showing herself at the window she couldn't see who it was but she knew. She recognised the car as the one she had watched drive out of the yard at Rushmore. It was Milos, who else? Just as she had feared.

What was she going to do?

If she kept quiet and still, in the end surely he would go away.

But maybe he'd heard the hairdryer or the remnants of the bath water draining away and knew someone was at home. He wouldn't go then, would he?

More knocking, loud and insistent this time.

'Ivana!'

It was him, all right. She was standing stock still, not daring to move, hardly daring to breathe. She couldn't believe this was happening. Just as she had predicted. Prepare for the worst and pray it never happens, that's what her mother used to say to her. There had to be something better she could do than pray.

She heard a clicking noise, the bastard was looking through the letter box. What would he see that might betray her presence?

Her handbag on the hall table. And her mobile phone sitting next to it.

'Ivana, hello! It's me, Milos.'

If she had a gun she could defend herself. She could stick the barrel in his beaky face and tell him to shove off.

But there were no guns. She should have made Tomas get one. Too late for that now.

He was rattling the front door and her heart leapt into her mouth. Suppose the lock gave? Suppose he broke in and came up the stairs? She'd be done for, there was nothing to defend herself with up here. At least downstairs there were knives in the kitchen. And her phone – she could call for help. But if he was looking through the letter box he'd see her.

The rattling stopped. The door was solid, thank God.

There was silence, then footsteps on the gravel. Oh please, please, please say he's going to drive off!

She craned her neck to look carefully out of the window. The car was still there, empty. She leaned closer to the glass, holding her breath. No sign of Milos. No shaggy black clump of hair and hulking shoulders in that stupid striped jacket. Where had he got to?

Then she heard a sound from the back of the house. He was at the kitchen door!

She moved without thinking, not even making a conscious effort to be quiet, though her bare feet were muffled by the carpet. In the hall she dug her feet into a pair of slip-on shoes. They belonged to Tomas – too bad. Behind her, from the back of the house, she heard the rattling of the kitchen door as Milos banged loudly. It wasn't as solid as the front door. He could be inside in seconds.

This was her only chance.

As noiselessly as she could, she eased open the front door and shut it behind her. It was fifty feet across the yard and the lane beyond. A quick scramble over the fence and she was running behind the hedgerow, doubled over out of sight from the lane, heading for the woods at the top of the field.

She'd done it. She'd escaped!

This time.

Chapter Five

Ivana blundered through the undergrowth, uncaring of the branches that whipped into her face or the brambles that flayed her legs. She ran until she reached the summit of the wooded hill and scrambled over the stile that skirted the long meadow on the top. From there she could look back down on the metalled lane that led to the cottage and, over the hedgerow at the bottom, see most of the yard in front. The white car was visible but there was no sign of Milos. Had he broken into the cottage only to find her gone? Or was he charging up the hill after her, concealed by the trees?

She listened hard, willing her breath to calm and her heartbeat to slow. There were no sounds above the birdsong and breeze in the branches. She didn't think he was coming after her but she wasn't going to hang around to find out. And she certainly wasn't going back to the cottage.

She crossed the meadow and took the path downhill on the far side. She had no plan beyond getting away but she knew, deep down, which way her feet were taking her. They were following a route she had denied herself for the past eighteen months, since the failure of the only relationship that had stirred her since her days of innocence with the bastard now hunting her below.

Only one person apart from her brother knew about Milos. And even though Steve had failed her in the past, he'd understand her present predicament. He'd help her surely. She didn't intend to leave him any choice.

* * *

Kathy felt rather like a naughty schoolgirl on the brink of being found out, though she didn't really know why. It was perfectly reasonable her being here at Steve's place. He *was* her boss, after all, and they'd only been in his study, going through his library of videotapes, like she'd suggested.

But there was more to it than that, she was sure of it. A certain something in the air. A crackle of electricity as their fingers met while they shuffled tapes around. The pressure of his hard, lean thigh against hers as they squashed together on the little sofa to watch horses dancing across the turf on the TV screen in front of them. Body heat, that's what they called it.

She wished she looked better. What she'd give to be in her new skirt which her mum said was obscene but which did real justice to her best feature. Was Steve a leg man? she wondered. Whatever, she knew she looked good in jeans too. Gary said that with a figure like hers she'd look good in a potato sack but he'd been nuzzling her neck at the time and pawing her with trembling fingers.

Steve hadn't touched her yet, or said anything which indicated he might, but she'd seen him looking at her. And the lazy way he smiled tied her thoughts in knots even as she rattled on about how she would sort out his racing archive and set up a new system in the office which would free up his time to do all the important executive things that he had to do. Shut up, Kathy! she told herself and she made herself sit next to him in silence, savouring that body heat, gauging the slightest move he made. Like the way his arm moved casually to lie across the back of the sofa. All she had to do was lean back an inch or two, like this, and if he just moved his hand inwards then she'd be in his arms and he could turn his head and plant that lazy smile right there on her lips—

'Do you fancy a drink?' he said suddenly.

She could think of something she'd like better but, all the same, it was a step in the right direction.

So things were going swimmingly as they went downstairs and he was about to usher her into his gorgeous front room, where she'd never been before, when the doorbell rang. Not good timing but, with luck, just a minor hiccup.

'I'll only be a moment,' he said and turned to answer the summons.

Kathy watched from the doorway of the sitting room, mildly irritated but not perturbed.

He opened the door and said, 'Oh,' in an unreadable tone.

'Hello, Steve,' said a familiar voice.

Kathy edged herself further into the hall so she could see round her host but she knew the unwanted visitor was Ivana. Knew too that her assumptions about the rest of the evening had just gone up in smoke.

'Are you all right?' Steve said.

Kathy could see Ivana clearly now. She did not look her usual composed and elegant self. Her face was flushed and her breath was short, as if she had just come off some arduous workout at a gym. Her shirt tails hung in a ragged fringe over a stained denim skirt and her bare legs were streaked with dirt and scratches. On her feet were a pair of dusty men's shoes.

She fell into Steve's arms – threw herself, it seemed to Kathy – and clung fast to him. 'You've got to help me,' she said and began to sob.

Kathy ducked out of sight, into the sitting room. What on earth was Ivana doing here now?

What was she doing here at all? It was all over between her and Steve ages ago, wasn't it? That's what everyone thought.

'Kathy?'

Steve was standing next to her but there was no sign of Ivana. Had she gone? But she knew by the expression on Steve's face that that was not the case.

'Sorry,' he was saying, 'I didn't realise how late it was. You must be wanting to get on home.'

'No, I'm fine,' she said brightly. Go on, chuck me out in favour of her, she thought. Why should I make it easy?

But the grinning, roguish Steve had been replaced by the

hard-eyed businessman. 'We'll talk about new equipment tomorrow and I'll bring the tapes in. It's a good idea, Kathy. Well done.'

Somehow he'd steered her into the hall. There was no sign of Ivana – where had he hidden the Czech bitch?

'There's no need to rush into the office tomorrow,' he said as he opened the front door. 'Have a lie-in.'

'Yeah, OK,' she heard herself say. 'Thanks, Steve.'

The door closed behind her.

Thanks for nothing.

Steve opened the bottle of white wine and poured. It was a Viognier, a new discovery of his and one that went down well with the girls. He'd been intending to try it out on Kathy but that possibility had disappeared out of the door in something of a sulky huff. Which was probably just as well. Ivana's arrival, bad timing though it seemed, had probably done him a favour.

He handed the glass to his visitor who drained half of it in one gulp. She was breathing easier now and she'd washed her face in the bathroom while he was making his excuses to Kathy. All the same, standing in his pristine woodblock and gleaming chrome kitchen, she looked a mess – a beautiful mess.

She finished her wine and thrust her empty glass at him. He refilled it and waited for her to speak. It was a long time since she had stood in his house drinking wine with him. On that occasion she had told him never to come near her again – and he'd kept his word.

'I once told you about a man back in Czech who beat me,' she said at last. 'Do you remember?'

He remembered all right. It was the second or third time they'd gone to bed, after the first frenzy, when he'd taken time to discover her secrets. And he'd found the marks high up on her arm, on the inside where the flesh is most tender: a pattern of small overlapping circles, pinker than the pale skin surrounding them. Little haloes of hate where some man had marked her with the glowing end of a cigarette.

He'd kissed the scars and vowed to himself never to hurt her. A pointless promise as it turned out, though the pains he'd inflicted had not been physical.

He sighed. 'Milos.'

'You remember his name?'

It wasn't the sort of thing you'd forget. The burns had been made to form the letter M, like marking your belongings – M for Milos. The brute had made them over the course of a few weeks, she'd told him, waiting till each scar had healed before inflicting the next. And she'd put up with it – that was almost the most extraordinary thing of all.

But it didn't explain what she was doing here now. Unless . . .

'He's found me,' she said. 'He's living here now – he saw me at Newmarket and he's come after me.'

Bella looked up as Kathy entered the yard. 'So there you are,' she said. She was examining the off fore of Chopsticks, a retired event horse. 'I was beginning to wonder where you were.'

Kathy's impulse was to tell her mother to mind her own business. The anger inside her was itching to boil over, it had scarcely cooled in the half-mile drive back from Steve's place. But she made an effort to resist the urge. If she got into a scene with Mum, she might end up telling her all about Steve and her frustration at being shunted out of his house like some irritating kid. That would be a big mistake. She mustn't give her mother any ammunition to put an end to her new working arrangement.

'I've been at the office,' she said, not without a trace of pride. It sounded good.

Bella looked puzzled. 'Why would you want to hang about there? I thought you told me it was a complete dump.'

'Not any more. I've been straightening it out. Clearing junk, redecorating, reorganising.' Kathy could see disbelief on her mother's face. 'Honestly, Mum, I can do stuff like that, you know.'

Bella blinked, plainly having trouble picturing her

daughter with her sleeves rolled up. It was insulting really, Kathy thought. It wasn't as if there was any point in taking charge at home when it wasn't her responsibility. Besides, she was being paid at Steve's.

'Anyway, Mum, you can talk. I thought you were meant to be going out tonight.'

'It's not far. It won't take me long to get ready.'

This was true. One of the irritating things about her mother was that she could throw on her clothes in a flash and always look great.

Kathy turned for the house but Bella hadn't finished. 'You might keep your phone switched on. I've been trying to ring you.'

Oh? Kathy was about to deny receiving any calls when she realised she didn't have her phone with her. Now she thought about it, it was sitting on the desk in Steve's study; she'd been so thrown by the speed with which he'd ejected her that she'd walked off empty-handed.

'You should call Gary Moorehead, he's been trying to get hold of you.'

Oh Christ, hadn't Gary got the message? Gary didn't interest her much at the moment.

'OK,' she said, intending to do no such thing – not at the moment anyway.

She started to walk back to the house, pondering the best way to reclaim her phone from Steve, when Bella called after her. What now?

'I don't suppose you feel like taking Milkshake out, do you?'

Milkshake was Kathy's horse and she'd been neglecting him recently. She resented being made to feel guilty, even if it was justified. Then she had a bright idea.

'All right, Mum. I'll take him later.'

She strode purposefully back, suddenly pleased with herself. If she rode past Steve's place she could drop by to pick up her phone. He couldn't complain about that, could he?

* * *

Ivana watched Steve closely as he talked on the phone and made the arrangements for her to stay with his sister in London. He was going to drive her down himself after work the next day and that would be the end of her time at Rushmore. She hadn't told Rob her departure was so close but that was a detail; today's events had changed her timetable, that was all.

Steve glanced at her frequently as he talked, casting her looks of reassurance. He was having to do some persuading but everything was OK. His look said, you're in my hands now, you're safe. And his mouth turned up at the corners as he smiled and cajoled and she knew that Yvonne's objections had been overcome and he'd sweet-talked her into agreement. He was very good at that.

It had taken her five seconds flat to fall in love with him – a delayed five seconds maybe, because they'd first met when she was newly arrived from Czechoslovakia, struggling with her English and the strangeness of everything and the damage Milos had done her. But after a couple of months, when she'd fitted into life at Rushmore and her future in England seemed assured, she'd registered that Rob's friend always had a word for her. Then suddenly it was Christmas and she was in the pub, on the fringe of a conversation that was passing too fast. Steve appeared in front of her, shutting her off from the group and said, 'Tell me about Christmas in Czechoslovakia.' That was the crucial five seconds – the time it took for her to register that he wanted to talk about her and that, up close, he was by far and away the most handsome Englishman she'd met.

They'd had an unforgettable holiday time – though in fact she'd worked solidly throughout because Rob had gone off to Spain with some weighing-room pals for the New Year and left her in charge of Rushmore. Steve took it upon himself to help out and the pair of them had set up home in the main house, as if they were a newlywed couple. After a start like that, no wonder she'd got too many ideas about the future.

She didn't love him any more. It had taken a long time for his magic to fade but it was OK now. She'd accepted finally that he wasn't the marrying type, that he couldn't commit to one woman, that the grass would always be greener somewhere else. That's what she'd told herself and she'd given him a wide berth. At least her expectations were not at risk in the arms of Charlie Moorehead. Not now anyway.

Yet, having found herself in a hole, here she was back in Steve's house, expecting him to dig her out. But that was OK, because they had significant history. All things considered, he owed her.

He put the phone down. 'Yvonne says yes. She's just concerned how long you want to stay.'

'Until I can get a flight to the States. Or Australia. Like we said.'

He'd promised to help her. He'd said he didn't have contacts in overseas yards but he knew plenty of people who did. He was going to take care of her.

Just one thing remained.

'I can't go back to the cottage tonight, Steve. Not with Tomas away.'

He put his hand over hers. 'It's all right, darling, you can stay here with me.'

Darling. It was almost the way things used to be.

But she mustn't get sentimental or she'd never have the courage to do what she had to do.

She'd never planned to betray her benefactors who had given her a new life in England. Even when she'd put the disk in her special hiding place she'd had no intention of using it.

Now she had no choice.

Kathy trotted Milkshake, her little grey horse – he was nearly white, hence his name – along the bridle path that ran round the perimeter of Rushmore farm. She'd set off on a circuitous route, intending to skirt the farm and follow the bridle for a couple of miles before returning on the path that would take her past Steve's place. Just in case she got distracted at Steve's. This way Milkshake would definitely get his exercise.

It was a glorious early-summer evening, with a gentle breeze propelling cottonwool clouds across a picture-postcard blue sky. Kathy looked without seeing, her mind on more earthbound matters.

Like the conversation she'd just had with Gary. He'd called again, just as she was about to leave the house, and asked her out that night. A group of kids he knew were holding a barbecue party at a house with a pool and Gary was proposing to drive over and pick her up. No thanks, she'd said.

Then Gary had begun to insist, like she was his girlfriend and she was supposed to go to the party with him. I mean, *please*. Where was he coming from? Just because she'd sat on his lap at Nick's place the other week didn't mean she was *married* to him all of a sudden. Not that you could tell from the way he'd reacted.

'Are you saying it's all over between us?' he said.

'It can't be over because it never started,' she pointed out, to which he replied, 'That's what you say now,' and other things which implied that she'd been leading him on. It made Kathy mad. She couldn't stand it when boys started reading all sorts of things into innocent remarks.

Steve Armstrong – now he would be a different proposition. She wouldn't need to beat around the bush with him. Anyway, she'd play a game he liked – if she got the chance.

Would that ever be? she wondered. Surely she hadn't misread the signals he'd given her earlier, when they were scrunched up side by side in his study?

'Let's go and find out, shall we, Milky?' she said, slowing the horse and turning him in a shallow curve across the corner of a field. Then she headed back down the path in the direction of Steve's house.

Steve had never expected to find himself back in bed with Ivana. Life was full of unexpected pleasures if you had the guts to grab them – and they were all the sweeter for it. He knew that, had he so wished, he could have spent every night of the week with the Czech beauty. But in that case the pleasure would have been entirely expected and much diminished.

The moment she asked to stay he knew where the evening would end up. He'd just accelerated the process and she hadn't appeared to object. There would be a price to be paid though, there always was with women.

'Stephen?' She rarely called him Stephen, only in bed.

He found the sensitive point on the back of her neck, then pressed down hard the way she liked it.

'Ooh,' she murmured.

'Is that nice?'

'You know it is.'

He did it again and kissed her full lips. She was languid and loose in his arms, not like she'd been half an hour ago. He'd eased the tension from her limbs, banished the fear and anxiety from her mind. He'd always been able to take her to a better place – for a while anyway.

She pulled her mouth away. 'Stephen, we've got to talk.'

Here comes the price.

Then the doorbell rang. Reprieved. Good timing.

She rolled away from him, her face unreadable as he pulled on a thin blue bathrobe.

He did not expect to find Kathy on his doorstep. She held a riding hat in one hand and the reins of a horse in the other. The animal blinked at him, docile and friendly. Kathy smiled, those cherry-red lips parted in now familiar fashion, her eyes huge and hungry.

'I think I left my phone here.'

'Oh.' It took a second for him to take in what she was saying.

'I'm sorry to disturb you. Looks like I caught you at the wrong time.'

She was staring at his robe. He was aware of his bare chest and legs.

'Yes.' He tightened the cotton belt round his waist, thinking quickly. 'I was about to have a shower. Where's the phone? I'll have a look.'

'I must have left it in the study. You know, when we were going through those tapes . . .'

Her voice tailed off. Her eyes were no longer on his but

trained over his shoulder. The smile had gone. The cherry lips were turned down in a pantomime of dismay. This was a girl whose feelings were sketched on her features. Were all eighteen-year-olds so transparent?

'Hello, Kathy.' Ivana's voice came from behind him, soft, low and accented. He watched it land like a club on the girl's open face.

'Oh,' Kathy said. 'Hi.'

Ivana was halfway down the stairs. She wore a towel.

Silence stretched awkwardly.

'I'll just have a look for that phone,' he said. 'It's in the study?'

'Just give it to me at work. I shouldn't have come – I mean, it's not important, I can manage.' She was putting the hat back on her head, fastening the chin strap. It looked as if she couldn't get away fast enough.

'Here's your phone.' Ivana was in the doorway by his side, holding it out,

Kathy snatched it with a muttered thanks and scrambled onto her horse's back. How on earth did she manage it in jodhpurs that tight? Then she was off down the drive, urging her little grey horse into a trot.

Steve closed the door and met Ivana's gaze. His reprieve was over.

Rob stood in the bedroom, fumbling with the cufflink at his wrist. He reckoned he was pretty nifty with his hands but some things were a skill that had to be learned – and he'd not been brought up to wear cufflinks more than once a year.

'I don't know how people manage these things,' he said.

'They have servants,' Bella said, turning from the mirror to look him steadily in the eye. They were almost the same height. 'I'll be your servant tonight,' she added and took the little silver fastener from his fingers and slipped it through the matching holes in his cuffs.

Rob recognised the gesture for what it was – a peace offering after their argument of the night before. Now Ivana had handed in her notice, their difficulty had been resolved.

Just in time too; their evening at the charity dinner wouldn't have been much fun if they weren't on speaking terms.

Downstairs the front door slammed. It was followed by the clump clump clump of furious footsteps on the stairs and then – anticipated by both Rob and Bella as they locked glances – the crash of Kathy's bedroom door. Such a dramatic arrival was not unknown, but Rob could not remember it being enacted with such violence.

Bella was already on her way out of the room. There was a case, Rob felt, for letting the young woman quieten down. Give her the space to bawl into her pillow and come to terms with whatever was currently bothering her. But her mother was for direct intervention and he knew better than to get involved. 'Good luck,' he murmured to Bella's departing figure.

It wasn't that he was unsympathetic to Kathy's adolescent moods. He remembered his own vividly enough: shouting red-faced at his father after underage drinking sprees in the Star and Garter, refusing to do his early morning shifts on the farm when there was snow on the ground, leaving the old man to fetch and carry for his mother when she was lying upstairs surrendering to the suffocating embrace of pulmonary lung disease.

For years after his mother's death he'd been fierce on himself for behaving as he'd done. He'd been selfish and stubborn, resentful of the desperate drama being enacted around him. But when he'd finally had a heart-to-heart with his father about it, the old man had said, 'Lighten up, son. Most people don't ever learn anything except the hard way.'

So whatever Kathy's problem, in the end she'd have to sort it out herself. He doubted her mother could do it for her and, if she did, how would Kathy ever gain knowledge? She was a smart young lady at heart and he had every confidence in her.

The phone rang, a short interruption as it turned out and he was still considering it when Bella returned, exasperation and anguish in her expression. 'Kathy wouldn't tell me what's up.'

Rob nodded; he wasn't surprised. But he could see that Bella wasn't going to let the matter rest.

'Gary Moorehead rang her just before she went out, it might be something to do with him. Maybe they've split up.'

'I didn't realise they'd ever got together.'

Bella rolled her eyes. 'I'm not happy with Kathy working for Steve,' she said. Predictably, to Rob's mind. 'It was going all right with Gary till Steve started taking an interest in her.'

'Steve's not going to start mucking around with Kathy.'

'You want to bet?'

'He wouldn't want to upset you. Or me, for that matter.'

'I've met plenty of men like Steve. They don't give tuppence who they upset when they've got their trousers round their ankles.'

Rob laughed, he couldn't help it. The expression conjured up a comical image of his friend. Bella grinned too.

'Who was that on the phone?' she asked.

'Ivana. She's decided to leave tomorrow.'

'What?' He'd already told her that Ivana had handed in her resignation. 'That's a bit sudden. Why?'

'She didn't say but I'll find out. She wants to have a serious talk with me.'

'She *is* coming to work tomorrow, isn't she?'

Rob nodded. Ivana had confirmed the arrangement.

He expected Bella to complain that Ivana should have given them a decent notice period but she didn't. It was a relief to think that soon the Czech girl would no longer be a bone of contention between them.

'Your turn.' Bella had stepped out of her robe into her dress and was now asking him to zip her up. He did as she asked and she turned to face him. 'What do you think?'

Peacock-blue really suited her golden colouring.

'Wow,' he said with feeling.

He thought he was in for a good night.

* * *

Gary Moorehead searched in the fridge for a cold one. It was one thing about living at home, he could make free with his father's booze and there was always plenty about.

He downed half the beer in one and flipped the top off the next bottle. He could still go over to Nick's barbecue but he couldn't be arsed. They'd want to know where Kathy was and he'd have to make up some story or tell them that she'd chucked him. They'd enjoy that, the way he'd been dropping little hints about her for the past few weeks. They'd take the mickey out of him and then they'd all get tanked up together – the usual crew of losers. He'd rather stay here and watch TV. Or do nothing at all.

He wandered into the hall and kicked his shoes into the corner. Then he heard a noise from upstairs. Mum and Dad were out tonight, at the charity dinner, and he'd been banking on slobbing out with the place to himself.

He froze. Then heard the sound of a cupboard slamming. Without thinking he ran upstairs in his stockinged feet, empty bottle in hand. If some bugger had broken in he'd soon find out he'd picked the wrong place to turn over.

He walked slap into his mother coming out of the bathroom in her dressing gown. Objects leapt from her hand and scattered onto the floor.

'Oh, it's you,' she said dully.

'Mum, what are you doing? It's the charity night, isn't it?'

'As you can see, I'm not going.'

There was something very odd about his mother. She was not her usual bright-eyed and bossy self. She wouldn't meet his glance, instead she knelt down to pick up what she'd dropped.

He stooped to help her. 'You're not ill, are you?'

'Go away, Gary. Mind your own business.'

'Where's Dad?'

'At the fucking dinner, so he says.'

Gary blinked in shock. His mother never swore. She'd rather cut her own tongue out, or so he thought.

'Or just fucking,' she added and the smell of neat gin hit him full in the face.

Around them on the floor were scattered cartons of pills, Anadin and Neurofen and other pain relievers.

He put his hands on her shoulders, his own concerns driven from his mind. 'Mum, what's going on?'

She looked at him properly this time, her lip trembling and the tears welling in her eyes. 'Oh Gary, am I really so ugly?'

He held her tightly while she wept, waiting for an explanation, in dread of what it might be.

The waiters were already serving the hors d'oeuvres by the time Rob and Bella took their seats for dinner. Rob didn't know how he always managed to cut things so fine. He was relieved to see an empty chair at the table – at least they weren't quite the last. The familiar figure of Goldeneye's trainer sat on the other side of the empty space and he realised who was missing.

'Where's Louise?' he asked Charlie who had greeted him with a slowly raised hand.

'She's not feeling too bright.'

Charlie didn't look too bright himself. His mouth was set in a thin, tight line and drops of sweat beaded his hairline.

'Don't worry,' Charlie added, 'it's nothing serious.' He flashed an unhappy smile. 'Unfortunately.'

Rob didn't accept the opening. Charlie and Louise were both strong-minded parties and their occasional fights were legendary. Rob had no intention of getting caught in the middle.

'Why didn't you bring young Gary along? He'd have enjoyed it.' The evening was in aid of Racing Welfare – a dinner followed by an auction for the cause.

Charlie shrugged. 'I left Gary waiting for the vet. He's taking another look at that horse of yours.'

Goldeneye's fitness had been the cause of much recent concern. He'd been suffering from sore shins since his victory in the Guineas, caused by the hard going at Newmarket. Though he was entered for the Irish Two Thousand Guineas in a week's time it was touch and go whether he'd make it to the Curragh.

'What are his chances, Charlie?'

It wasn't the first time Rob had posed the question. So far Charlie had sat on the fence, mixing optimistic noises with notes of caution. Now he regarded Rob balefully.

'I wouldn't bother calling Aer Lingus, if I were you. I don't think he's got a prayer.'

'Oh.' That was a bit of a slap in the face. Rob had been clinging to the hope that Goldie would make it. He rather fancied a weekend away with Bella in the Emerald Isle although, given the imminent staff change at Rushmore, maybe that wouldn't be so easy to organise.

'I know how you feel,' said Charlie. 'Bit of a bastard, eh?' He sloshed some wine into Rob's glass and filled his own, not for the first time, Rob guessed. 'This plonk tastes like vinegar. Better than nothing though.'

Rob ignored the remark. Charlie was a wine buff whereas he would rather have a beer, if he drank anything at all.

'Perhaps it's just as well about the Irish Guineas,' he said. 'One of us would have had to stay behind now Ivana's leaving.'

Charlie's big head swivelled round to face him. The whites of his eyes were grey and watery, the sockets dark. He really didn't look well.

'What did you say about Ivana?'

'She's handed in her notice and says she wants to leave tomorrow.'

'Why?'

Rob shrugged. 'I honestly don't know though I intend to get it out of her before she goes. She's been a bit odd recently, not her usual self.' He took a sip of wine. 'You're right, this does taste like vinegar.'

Charlie wouldn't let it drop. 'So you really don't know what's behind this?'

'No. Some screwed-up relationship, I expect. There's always man trouble with Ivana, isn't there?'

'Jesus Christ.' Charlie emptied his glass down his throat and stood up abruptly. 'I'm off to get a decent drink.' He squeezed Rob's shoulder. 'If you want me, I'll be in the bar.'

Rob watched him go with some concern. The trainer was an energetic, indestructible sort but tonight he looked ponderous as he moved to the far door.

'What's the matter with Charlie?' asked Bella, who had been talking to the couple across the table.

'I think he's off to the bar to get drunk.'

'What were you talking about?'

'How he doesn't like the wine. And about Ivana suddenly buggering off.'

'Ah.'

Rob read the concern in her face. 'Is that what's caused it, do you think?' A penny suddenly dropped. 'Do you think he's worried Tomas might decide to go too?'

She shook her head. 'No, Rob. Anyway, why would Tomas want to leave? Surely he's doing too well.'

That was true, there would be no sense in Tomas leaving. What a relief. Although there would be plenty of good jockeys keen to take his place, Tomas had proved himself on Goldeneye and Rob would hate to see their partnership broken up. Charlie must feel the same way. He'd catch up with him later and put his mind at rest.

Kathy had cried herself out – for the moment at any rate. Later, though, she knew the tears would fall again, when she replayed the pictures in her head of her visit to Steve's. The distant look on his face as he saw her standing there, as if he was trying to remember her name. Ivana, the Czech bitch, sashaying down the stairs in that obscene little towel. The pair of them standing side by side, half naked, the heat rising off them like steam. She must have disturbed them doing it – shagging. It was disgusting. Like when her friend Val had shown her downloaded porn on her brother's computer.

She couldn't believe it of Steve. He'd been so kind and considerate to her. Confiding in her, listening to her ideas, treating her like a proper grown-up. And looking at her with that penetrating strip-you-bare gaze as if he wanted to fold her into his arms and . . . screw her like that wiggly, slinky Ivana.

He didn't think of her like that, did he?

Obviously he didn't. That's why he'd pushed her out of his house. So he could get Ivana into bed. The lewd revolting slut.

Were all men so basic?

Was Gary?

She used to look up to Gary, being a few years younger than him, impressed by what he'd been doing with his life. He'd seemed so much more mature than her. Then she'd realised what a kid he was really, compared to someone like Steve.

But maybe Gary was best for her. She'd thought she could handle Steve but she wasn't sure about that now – not as a lover anyway. Not if it meant she'd have to compete with tramps like Ivana in her little towel.

She picked up her phone, dismissed the thought of the half-naked Czech bitch handing it to her with a smirk, and dialled Gary's number. It rang for a long time and she wondered if he was at the barbecue having a good time without her.

'Hello.' He sounded strange. Snappy.

'Hi, Gary.'

'Who's this?'

Surely he recognised her voice? 'It's me, Kathy.'

There was silence.

She plunged on. 'Did you go to the barbecue?'

'Look, Kathy. I don't know what you're up to but I'm not interested in your little games. I don't want to talk to you now and I don't know when I will.'

It wasn't the kind of reception she'd been expecting. Maybe she had been a bit off with him but all the same . . .

'Come off it, Gary, there's no need to be mean.'

Then she realised she was talking to herself. He'd hung up.

Chapter Six

Ivana could hardly believe this was her last morning at Rushmore. Things had moved so fast. It wasn't the way she wanted to go, she'd spent years here and now there was scarcely time to say goodbye. She felt bad about Jacko, her loyal co-worker, but she'd write to him and explain. Charlie was more of a problem. She'd not wanted to call him from Steve's and her mobile was still in the cottage where she'd left it in her flight last night. She'd have to ring from London and explain. Maybe they could meet up properly to say goodbye before she left the country. After all, it wasn't him she was running away from.

She had not gone back home before starting work – she kept spare clothes in the tack room. After yesterday the thought of being in the cottage on her own gave her the creeps. Tomas would be back in the afternoon so she could return to pack up her things. Her brother thought she was mad – he'd said so when she reached him last night – but he'd offered to come back at once. It had been a bit late by then. He wasn't happy with this turn of events but he'd promised to help her pack up. God, she hoped she was doing the right thing.

Thinking like this, it was tempting to put it all off. There were so many reasons to wait and plan her departure properly. But if she waited, Milos would come back, she was sure of it. And this time he might catch her. She thought of Katerina and her disfigured face. Maybe she was a coward but she didn't want to end up looking like that.

Even if she went to the police, what could they do? There were no grounds to have Milos arrested. And as long as he was free she knew she would always be in danger.

Later, she'd make a round of the mares and the yearlings to say goodbye. For the moment though, she was dealing with her least favourite animal. She wondered why she was bothering to muck out Cape Fear – except it was a chore that had to be done. She'd never shirked a job at the stud and she didn't want to start now. So she'd decided to put in a proper morning's work and leave with no hard feelings. She didn't want any petty resentments to cloud her final conversation with Rob.

The big black stallion eyed her morosely as she walked along the side of his fenced-off exercise area, only the flicking of his tail revealing the antipathy he felt whenever she was in his presence. He was a magnificent beast to look at, she could appreciate that. His photograph on the Rushmore website went a long way towards selling his wares. The lustrous coat, the elegant carriage, the noble head – these princely features all gave the impression of a racehorse oozing class. But when you got to know him, you came face to face with the black-hearted devil within. In Ivana's experience, he was the only horse who had never relaxed his enmity towards her. Or any other female for that matter.

From outside, she opened the sliding gate that separated the stallion's stable from his exercise area. Some mornings he'd charge out to let off steam, on others he'd have to be lured with food or prodded with a pole through the bars to get him out. Today he looked at her with disdain and stood his ground for a few seconds, before ambling into the larger space. She rolled the gate shut behind him with a firm push. Now she could enter his night quarters. She slid open the outside gate and stepped inside, safely separated from the stallion.

Maybe it was a good thing she was doing this. She would miss many things about working at Rushmore, not least the other horses, the mares and their foals, but she'd be very happy never to set eyes on the magnificent Cape Fear ever again.

He was watching her through the bars, his eye glistening like a wet coin, as midnight black as his coat.

She smiled at him as she positioned the wheelbarrow in the doorway and began to shovel the horse's soiled bedding. 'This is the last time I'm clearing up your shit, mister.'

The horse raised his head and made one of his irritated nickering sounds. She laughed. Sometimes it was amusing to get under his skin. Suddenly he swung round away from her, his ears flat against his head, a squeal of real anger echoing round the confined space. It wasn't caused by her, she knew. Someone else was approaching.

Kathy considered her face in the mirror. It was not a pretty sight: swollen eyes, hedgehog hair and smeared make-up that she'd not removed last night. You'd think the buckets of tears she'd cried would have washed it all away.

She'd not slept much, half her usual eight hours, but the sleep had been profound and now it was as if she were being winched to the surface from a subterranean well. And she had to face the working day. Oh God.

In the small hours, as she was crying into her pillow and reliving every moment of her humiliation on Steve's doorstep, she would have sworn that she'd never have the nerve to return to the Armstrong office again. The job, as her mother had predicted, had turned out to be a complete failure.

But that was last night and as she contemplated her pathetic state this morning she was aware of how stupid she must seem. Of how doubly stupid she would seem if she ran from the job now. How her mother would savour the I-told-you-so, even if she had the grace not to utter it.

Kathy stood under the hottest shower she could bear and finished off with a full minute blast of cold. The freezing drops jetting into her scalp did the trick. In the bedroom she pulled her baggiest sweater and most shapeless work trousers from a drawer, towelled and brushed her hair viciously and applied the merest touch of eye make-up. She wasn't tarting herself up for Steve bloody Armstrong any more.

It took a moment for Ivana to recognise the figure making its way down the barn. Though Gary Moorehead was hardly a stranger to the stud, it was unusual to see him here at a time of day when his father's yard would be at its busiest. He walked briskly towards her, his mouth set in a grim horizontal that suggested that this wasn't a friendly visit.

'Hi, Gary.'

'I want a word,' he said. It came out as a high-pitched bark but there was no denying the intensity in his voice.

'Go ahead,' she said, putting down her pitchfork.

'Is it true you're committing adultery with my father?'

For a moment she was struck dumb. Then the laughter burst out of her, she couldn't help it – he sounded so formal. She could see it only enraged him further and his cheeks blazed scarlet.

'What's funny?'

She made an effort to control herself. 'It's the way you put it, Gary. So stuffy. And anyway, I can't commit adultery because I'm not married.'

'Don't get clever with me. Are you or are you not screwing my father?'

All amusement had gone now. He looked big and threatening standing there with his fists clenched. Fortunately, the wheelbarrow stood between them in the open doorway, a handy barrier should he decide to close the gap between them. And there had been times in the not too distant past when he had wanted to get close to her. Was that what was fuelling his anger?

'You're jealous, aren't you, Gary?' she said. 'You don't like to think that your father has succeeded where you failed.'

'I don't know what you mean.'

'You like to watch me, don't you? I know what goes on in your head, it's written on your face. You'd like to do more than watch, wouldn't you? But all these years we've known each other, you've never had the nerve to ask me out.'

'That's crap. I wouldn't touch a slag like you with a bargepole. I don't know what I'd catch.'

She sighed. 'Don't be childish. In answer to your question, yes, I have slept with your father. He's a real man. One day maybe you'll be like him.'

'And how do you think my mother feels?'

Ivana shrugged and said nothing. Louise Morehead was not her concern.

'Do you know how upset she is? What a misery you're making of her life?'

Ivana could hardly believe that, but so what? The woman was like a glacier, she could afford to melt a little round the edges.

'I'm warning you,' Gary hissed, his face twisted. 'Stay away from my father and stay out of our lives. Or I'll make sure your precious brother never rides for our yard again.'

Then he bent down and tipped the wheelbarrow into the stall.

She jumped backwards, alarmed by his sudden violence. But Gary was not about to come after her. Instead he seized the stable gate and slid it across the opening, shutting Ivana into the enclosed space.

'Hey, what are you doing?' she cried as she saw him bend down. But she knew what he was up to, he was fastening the peg on the runner which locked the door in place, imprisoning her in the stall.

He glared at her through the bars, a smirk of triumph on his face. Then he was off.

Clive's reception team on the desk at the Crown Gable Hotel had enjoyed a busy morning so far. There had been the usual stream of businessmen checking out early, plus the horseracing over-nighters from the big dinner – horsey people were keen on their early starts. But Clive was concerned that one face had been missing at the breakfast table and in the lobby – the gentleman in number 42. Clive wasn't much of a racing follower but he liked to keep up with his guests. Number 42 was a top horse trainer who, according to his sources, had trained the winner of the Two Thousand Guineas. He had specifically asked for an alarm call at 6.45.

The call had been made but not answered. It had been repeated at regular intervals since and it was now getting on for nine and still there had been no sign of number 42.

There could be several reasons for this lack of response. The trainer could have left in the small hours while the night porter was dozing. It wasn't unknown for guests to suddenly disappear in this fashions – though, in this case, Clive had no doubt that such a well-thought-of gentleman as Mr Moorehead would soon be on the phone to settle his account.

It was more likely that the trainer had overslept after a good night and abandoned his plans for an early start. In which case, why hadn't he responded, even if angrily, to the repeated calls to his room? It must have been a good night indeed for him to sleep through a telephone blaring from the bedside table at regular intervals.

Alternatively – and this was the theory that seemed the most likely to Clive – the guest hadn't spent the night in room 42 at all. Clive had observed that the room had been booked in the name of Mr and Mrs Moorehead, yet the gentleman had arrived without a female companion. Possibly he had unexpectedly found himself footloose and fancy free for the night and made the most of the opportunity. There were many possibilities once hanky-panky entered the equation. In these circumstances, experience had taught Clive to tread softly.

But two hours had gone by without response and he was worried. There was always the worst-case scenario. Fishing the pass keys from his pocket, he made his way to room 42 and rapped smartly on the door.

There was no response from within. Enough was enough – he'd risk getting his head bitten off by the winning trainer of the Two Thousand Guineas.

A minute later Clive was dialling the ambulance service. The worst-case scenario had come true.

* * *

Ivana cursed in her mother tongue.

The door was solid up to four feet from the floor. There was no way she could reach through the bars and pull out the peg. She was trapped.

Rob and Bella couldn't be much longer, surely.

Then she heard the sound of the barn door opening and of footsteps making their way towards her. She couldn't yet see who it was but she didn't care.

'Hello!' she called.

Someone was coming to let her out.

As Kathy dumped her cereal bowl in the sink – who said she never did a hand's turn in the kitchen? – she looked through the window and caught sight of Gary Moorehead striding into the courtyard in front of the house. What was he doing here? He must be coming to see her.

She hastily reassessed last night's telephone conversation. He'd been pretty rude to her but he probably had cause. She hadn't intended to lead him on but, thinking about it in the light of her own humiliation at the hands of Steve and Ivana, maybe she had been a bit naughty. Gary could be very sweet sometimes and, a big plus, she knew where she stood with him. He was probably on the way to apologise for hanging up on her. All things considered, she was prepared to be magnanimous.

She stopped in front of the hall mirror – thank God she'd used that eyeliner, it stopped her looking like a complete frump – and waited for the knock on the door. She'd be kind to him this morning. It was in her gift to make someone's day and she wouldn't harden her heart. Not like some people would.

But the knock didn't come. She idly flicked through yesterday's newspaper left on a chair in the hall. She wasn't going to look for Gary – let him come and find her. She might be softening towards him but she wasn't intending to throw herself at his feet. Time ticked by. Where was he? Then came the sound of a car engine firing and, after thirty seconds or so, retreating. Kathy couldn't contain herself any longer and she opened the front door.

Gary's Mini was just visible as it made the turn into the lane and accelerated away through the fringe of trees.

So he hadn't come to see her. Unaccountably, she felt miffed.

Maybe he'd come over on yard business, something to do with Goldeneye possibly, and he'd been talking to Rob. But she didn't think Rob was back yet.

When she'd seen Gary out of the window he'd been striding down the path from the big barn, where that brute Cape Fear was kept. Perhaps Rob had gone straight up there – it was quite possible. She headed in that direction herself. She was curious.

She knew something was wrong even before she entered the barn. The squealing and roaring of an angry horse split the air, a sound familiar to those who lived around Cape Fear. But this was worse than usual, sounding a new pitch of excitement and hysteria. It freaked Kathy out.

All the same, she broke into a run and dashed through the barn door and up to the fence that bordered the exercise area. The sounds were louder in the enclosed space but the animal was not immediately visible. Then she saw his black bulk blocking the internal doorway into the stable, kneeling on a white shape on the floor, working at it with his great jaws.

Jesus, the shape was a person in a work coat.

Why on earth was the security gate open?

Kathy began to scream as she ran towards the stall.

Rob had put his foot down on the drive back. It was only a twenty-mile journey but it had been a good idea to stay over. He could tell from Bella's air of sleepy contentment over breakfast that she'd enjoyed it too. They'd have to see if they could organise getaways like this more often.

All feelings of contentment vanished the moment he stepped out of the car. The yard looked just the same but the air was filled with sounds of danger and distress. Yells were coming from the barn – a woman's voice and other cries all too identifiable as those of Cape Fear. He ran as hard as he could, his one thought, 'Oh no, not again.'

But last time, with Gwen, he'd got there before the stallion could do more than give the stable groom a monumental fright. This time he wasn't so lucky. And neither was the groom.

Kathy fought the horse with a broom. She didn't know where she'd got it or how she found the courage but there wasn't time to think only to *do*. She'd flung open the door to the stall and jabbed the bristles into the animal's face, aware that she was still screaming, that a wheelbarrow lay on its side between her and the shape on the floor and that there was blood. Lots and lots of blood, crimsoning the white coat beneath the enraged horse, thickening the straw underfoot and leaking into her trainers.

Rob seemed to come from nowhere, appearing at her shoulder with a pole he drove into the breast of the stallion. She could stop yelling now help had arrived but she didn't. She dashed the broom again and again into the horse's face. Then suddenly the beast was gone, rearing back into the open space beyond, and Rob was rolling the gate across to prevent a return.

'Are you OK?' he said, as he knelt on the floor by the bloody shape lying broken and crooked.

'Yes,' she managed, squatting beside him, watching as he felt for a pulse and listened for a breath. Searching for any sign of life.

Kathy had never seen a corpse before but she knew he was wasting his time.

She'd spent half the night wishing that Ivana were dead.

Be careful what you wish for, she thought, it might come true.

Part Two
Summer

Chapter Seven

Kathy held her mobile to her ear as she sat in the front seat of the old Fiesta, which she liked to think of as her car though technically it belonged to her mother. She was only pretending to make a call while she kept a watch on Steve's Seymour Street shop twenty yards away on the other side of the road. It was probably a pointless subterfuge – who would be taking any notice of her? – but it amused her all the same.

She was on a special assignment for Steve. The targeting of his business that had taken place back in May at Hampton Waters had continued throughout the following two months: an unexpected flurry of medium-sized cash bets being laid at the last minute, always successfully. It had been Kathy's idea to follow one of these punters after she – it was always a she – had collected her winnings. Steve was inside the shop. In a moment he would call her with her instructions on which one to tail.

Though she was apprehensive, she was also excited. This was better than fielding phone calls and transferring endless horserace videos onto DVD in that poky office – the hub of Flagship Armstrong, as Steve sometimes referred to it.

But these were not the days for jokes. Ivana's death was a marker on a timeline, an indicator of Before and After. In Kathy's mind, Before lay her childhood. Then she'd found the Czech woman's broken body and knelt by Rob's side as he searched frantically for signs of life, her clothes

111

drenched in the dead girl's lifeblood. After was life now as an adult, grimmer, less joyful and full of uncertainty.

She could have run away. She could have gone to her father in America or to her mother's parents who trained showjumpers in Devon. Certainly she could have turned her back on Steve and his office job and pitched in at the stud where events had thrown life into chaos. She did her bit there anyway, mucking out first thing in the morning and helping with the yearlings when she got home at the end of the afternoon. But, to the surprise of others – and herself – she went into the office every day and dealt with Steve's paperwork and other secretarial tasks. It just seemed the adult thing to do. And it gave her time on her own to get used to what had happened and to try to make sense of it.

Ivana, her love rival, was dead. 'Love rival' was a trashy term though that's how Kathy had thought of Ivana that night after she fled Steve's house, her heart broken by the thought of the man she wanted bedding down with his old flame. Of course, her heart wasn't broken, not in any real sense. She'd been hysterical, self-indulgent, childish. Ivana lying in bloody shreds under the stallion's hoofs, now *that* was real. She was dead and Kathy had wished it on her. She couldn't get around that fact.

Was that why she had not said a word to the police about Gary? He'd been up there with Ivana and Cape Fear. She'd seen him walking away from the barn a few minutes before she went up there herself. How long exactly? Five maybe, she wasn't sure.

If he'd been with Ivana, maybe he could shed light on what had happened. He could say if the security gate had been open and what had been on Ivana's mind. Had the Czech woman been careless, as they'd suggested at the inquest? Distracted by the thought of her departure that day and all the things she had to do before Steve drove her to his sister in London. Or were there other things on her mind?

Gary had looked serious as he strode into the yard. Kathy had thought at the time that he was on his way to talk to her.

She'd assumed he was preoccupied with putting his case to her in the best light. Obviously that wasn't how it was at all. Maybe he'd been thinking about Ivana.

She'd not spoken to Gary about it. In fact, they'd not spoken a word since the accident, barely even nodding to each other at the funeral. He was still angry with her, it seemed. It was as if their little romance had never taken place. He'd not called her, nor she him though she felt bad because his father had had a heart attack and Rob had told her Gary was trying to fill his father's shoes in the yard. But the last time she had rung him he had accused her of playing games. She wasn't going to get caught out like that again.

In the end, she had sent Charlie a card, saying she was sorry to hear he was ill and hoping he would soon be better. She liked Charlie. There was no reason why a quarrel with his son should stand in the way of that. She wrote the card without calculation – there was no reason to think Gary would see it anyway.

All the same, she thought about Gary in quiet moments in the office – and there was no shortage of those. This would all blow over eventually and then she'd ask him what he'd been doing in the yard that morning. He must have been the last person to have seen Ivana alive. She could understand he might not want to discuss it right now.

Kathy ruminated on other aspects as well. She'd wished she'd known Ivana was intending to leave the yard. The night with Steve must have been a farewell fling. 'Ivana and I used to be very close,' he'd said to her on the first day she'd returned to the office. He'd made it sound very formal, as if he were giving her a prepared statement. She supposed he wanted to clear the air. 'When Ivana turned up that evening, she told me she'd decided to get away and asked if I would help her. It was our last night. I should have said no but, to be honest, I don't regret a damn thing now.'

He'd looked shell-shocked, beyond tears. She understood what he must be feeling; well, she had an inkling at least. It put her own emotions into perspective. She'd never slept with a man, nurtured a relationship over time, tried to put another person first in any aspect of her life. She was callow and ignorant. She'd only read about love, listened to the songs and imagined how it must be. All she'd felt so far had just been a product of her own self-obsession. Ivana's death told her that she knew nothing about real passion between men and women. And so she dismissed the pang of jealousy that gripped her as Steve talked about his last night with Ivana. Her feelings did not count for much when weighed against his grief.

They'd not discussed it since. Ivana's death had hit hard – she could respect that.

The phone in her hand suddenly vibrated, alerting her to her current task.

'Yes?'

'Leaving now.' It was Steve's voice. 'Girl in a pink top. Plumpish – you can't miss her.'

Too right she couldn't miss her. A woman in her mid-twenties shouldered her way out of the bookie's onto the busy high street, stuffing her purse into a white shoulder bag. The pink top was more a fuchsia red, with white lettering on the front which Kathy couldn't read at this distance. The woman must have weighed getting on for eighteen stone and, as she crossed the road towards the Fiesta, the letters formed the slogan 'Fight Anorexia' above a boxed cartoon of a grimacing warrior holding a spear.

How very PC of Steve – 'plumpish' was understating the matter.

Kathy was sure of one thing: she wouldn't like to get on the wrong side of this daunting female. Considering her orders were to follow her, that was always a possibility.

Right now she was in a quandary. The woman was being carried along in the sea of pedestrians heading down the street. She should get out of her car and track her on foot but she only had twenty minutes left on her parking permit. Was there time to get another ticket? No, the red top, beacon though it was, was disappearing fast. Kathy quickly locked the car and headed after her through the crowd. She'd have to risk a parking penalty even though she'd get it in the neck from her mother. She'd have to get Steve to cough up, which wouldn't be easy – despite first impressions, he wasn't awash with money. Why hadn't she thought ahead and bought a longer permit?

Damn. Distracted by these thoughts she'd lost her quarry. Some espionage agent she was turning out to be. Where the hell had the woman gone?

Then a stroke of luck. She looked across the road into the short-stay car park and spotted a flash of red. Yes! The woman was unlocking a dusty-looking dark blue van.

Kathy turned and bolted back up the road. If she was quick she could be in position to pick up the van as it turned out of the car park.

She grinned as she forced her way into the traffic stream, bringing an indignant hoot from the driver behind. Ahead she could see the van approaching the exit barrier. Perfect. This was more fun than balancing the petty cash. More fun than shovelling horse dung. Perhaps she'd found her true calling.

Tomas sat in a pool of silence in the jockeys' changing room at Leicester. He'd always been a popular figure with his fellow riders, even at the beginning when his conversational skills were strained by the quickfire to and fro of their banter in a foreign tongue. But he had a warm smile and was gracious whatever his fortunes on the course. After a while he became known as Bouncer.

'You know why, don't you?' said Ed Christie, a young Irishman with a middle-aged face.

'I think it's because when things go bad, I bounce up again,' he'd said. He'd pondered the mystery and rather liked this notion.

Ed had laughed. 'No, mate. It's because you're a Czech. You know, bouncing Czech.'

And they'd had to explain it. Privately Tomas preferred his own version but he smiled just the same.

He wasn't smiling much these days and the other lads left

him to inhabit his own circle of gloom. It wasn't that they did not sympathise, rather the opposite. Ivana's horrible end had reverberated throughout the weighing room. And now they gave him as much space as he required in the changing room. He appreciated it. One day the Bouncer would bounce back, but not just yet.

He'd taken a fortnight off after Ivana's death. 'Take as much time as you need,' Sammy had advised, adding, 'but your sister wouldn't have wanted your career to fizzle out, would she?'

Anyhow, riding was good for him. The intensity of the races themselves provided escape from the nightmare, they were better even than sleep because Ivana was nightly in his dreams. But the contest was always over too soon. And then the glow of success or the ache of disappointment was diminished, useless as a buffer against his feelings. Those feelings could be summed up in one word: guilt. It was proving a heavy burden.

The verdict of the inquest – accidental death – had been of some help. As the only member of Ivana's family, the coroner had sent him a copy of the post mortem result in advance of the hearing, so the verdict wasn't a surprise. Rob had enlisted the help of a doctor friend who had interpreted the medical phraseology.

'She suffered a nasty selection of injuries,' the doctor told them. 'Broken ribs and multiple bite wounds.'

'What actually killed her?' Rob had asked. Tomas was grateful – it was what he needed to know but he wasn't sure he could get the words out.

'Skull fracture. The back of her head was shattered, pushing fragments of bone into the brain. I'm sorry.'

But Tomas had been grateful for the blunt explanation. It was a fact and he had to know the facts.

'How?' he said.

'These kind of reports are not usually cut and dried. But it says her wounds were consistent with the horse banging her head on the concrete floor.'

So there it was. The enraged stallion had gripped her in

his great jaws and slammed her repeatedly against the hard floor of stable where the soiled straw covering had been swept away and not replaced. Tomas could picture it in sickening detail. That horse had been mad. Rob had had it put down the next day but that was of little comfort.

Tomas had downed two large brandies after the doctor left and then vomited them up. But the explanation had made him feel better, just a bit. If the horse had killed her for sure then Ivana's death had been nothing to do with Milos. In that case, whether or not he had returned home in response to Ivana's phone call, it would have made no difference. If her death was not at the hands of the ex-lover whom Tomas had discounted, then there was no reason for him to feel guilty. But he still did.

The post mortem didn't answer the main mystery – why was the security door open? He found it hard to credit that Ivana would have put herself at such risk. At the inquest, the coroner had implied that she must have become careless. That she was so used to the horse and distracted because this was her last day that she had overlooked basic safety precautions. That hadn't sounded right to Tomas. Unless her distraction was not so much her imminent departure as the reason for her wanting to go: Milos. The bastard had completely freaked her out. Maybe he didn't actually have to be present to do his damage. He'd nearly destroyed her once before and, from the way Tomas looked at it, this time he had succeeded.

So he wasn't guiltless after all. If it was down to Milos, it was down to him too. His sister had appealed to him to protect her. He had failed her and now he was going to have to live with it. He got to his feet to weigh out with a heavy heart.

Kathy had never been fool enough to think that tailing another vehicle would be as easy as it looked in the movies – and it wasn't. She managed pretty well on the crowded urban shopping streets, where the cars stop-started down one-way systems through innumerable traffic lights. Even if some obstacle cut her off from the blue van, she could count on a corresponding hold-up to slow her quarry down and keep her in sight.

Then they were speeding away from the town centre and red T-shirt woman found a bit of space on the dual carriageway. She was not a respecter of the speed limit. Kathy bit her lip as she noted the camera signs by the side of the road. She'd only been driving for six months – passed her test at the first go, to her mother's surprise but no one else's – and she didn't want to get done for speeding.

They were now out on the three-lane ring road and the blue van was hammering along in the outside lane. Kathy had no choice but to follow. There was fifty feet between them as the junction light ahead turned amber.

'Stop, you idiot!' she yelled at the vehicle ahead.

The van accelerated and shot over the intersection just as the light changed to red.

Kathy followed, her knuckles white as she gripped the wheel, the blare of horns loud in her ears as she charged the red light.

Her heart was hammering. She was doing sixty in a forty zone. She was enjoying it.

Suddenly the van was gone. Where? Then she saw it in the inside lane. How had it got there?

Red top lady didn't appear to believe in indicators. Kathy watched in frustration as the van took the left turn-off, leaving her no chance of cutting across the crowded lanes of traffic inside her in time to follow. All she could do as she swept by was to note the road sign: Otley Manor Business Park. She supposed that was something. It was all she had.

As he took his place in the starting stalls for the mile handicap, Tomas narrowed his focus to the task in hand. It was a relief to know he did not have to think about anything but the race ahead. His mount, Jack of Hearts, shifted his feet nervously as they waited for the other eighteen runners to load. Tomas calmed him with a pat on the shoulder. Ivana would have liked this neat, gentle animal. Together they were going to win this race for her.

Being honest, Tomas doubted whether the docile Jack of Hearts had it in him. Gary had delivered his father's instructions – Charlie was still not well – in the parade ring: 'Keep him covered up. If he sees daylight he'll run too free. If you're in the mix at the top of the slope then go for it.' Both Tomas and Gary knew these words were simply for the owner's benefit. Jack of Hearts had had three previous outings and had never been 'in the mix' in any of them.

The gates flew open the second the last runner was loaded and Tomas was almost left at the start. They set off down the straight mile in pursuit of the rest of the field. No wonder Jack of Hearts had failed to register in the sprints over five and six furlongs at Salisbury and Brighton. He just wasn't a speed merchant compared to some of his bigger, long-striding contemporaries. The only ray of light in his performances to date had come at Sandown over seven furlongs. When the quick starters around him had flagged, Jack of Hearts had plugged on, finishing just outside the frame in fourth. The theory was that the extra furlong in this race was what he needed.

Tomas wasn't convinced. But you had to have a plan with a horse, if only to keep the owner happy.

The runners were making the most of the downhill slope of the course and Jack of Hearts was still last as they hit the uphill gradient in the middle section. However, as some of the more headstrong around them slowed, the horse started to get himself into the race, steadily picking off the back markers.

'There he goes.' Gary injected enthusiasm into his voice for the benefit of the steely-eyed matron by his side. 'All is not lost, Mrs Pryce.'

Jack of Hearts' owner replied with a back-of-the-throat grunt that said, more eloquently than words, that she was not convinced. Having watched her horse flop on three consecutive occasions, this experienced horsewoman was going to take some persuading of his merits.

Gary said nothing further. In his place, his father would be full of encouragement and, if necessary, sympathy – always tempered with the observation that this run had been no failure because lessons had been learned and that next time they could do X instead of Y. His father was ever conscious that an owner's expectations had to be managed as diligently as his horse's capabilities.

Once, Gary would have played his father's part to the letter, but right now he didn't give a stuff. Frankly the horse was a waste of space and he didn't have the energy to pretend otherwise. There was enough pretending going on in the rest of his life.

He didn't know how he had held himself together in the days following Ivana's death – though at first his argument with her hadn't seemed significant. By the time he was halfway home he'd regretted locking her in the stable but reasoned that someone would soon let her out. When he arrived back he'd found his mother in shock because she'd received a call from the hotel to say his father had been taken away in an ambulance with a suspected heart attack. In the subsequent hours at the hospital, he'd not given another thought to Ivana.

It wasn't till the next day, when his father was pronounced out of immediate danger, that he heard the news of Ivana's death.

He had sleepwalked through his duties at the yard. Had he played a part in the accident at Rushmore? The thought nagged at him.

The double blow had thrown a pall over everyone. Even his mother, the one person in the world with good reason to rejoice at the death of her rival, had been affected by the accident to Ivana.

Louise had hugged him. 'That poor girl. What a terrible end.'

He'd held her as she wept. It was all wrong.

'For God's sake, Mum, she was no friend of yours.'

'Oh, I'm not crying for her.' She stepped back and wiped her eyes. 'I'm crying for Tomas.'

Gary had not considered Tomas. Gary's own sister, Claire, was three years older and was living with her boyfriend in Leeds. He never saw her for months on end but to imagine her dying, not being there to nag and laugh at him – it was unthinkable. Tomas would be devastated, it was true.

'And,' his mother added softly, 'there's your father to think of. He doesn't know yet. I'll tell him when he's strong enough.'

Gary said nothing. He didn't have much sympathy. His father ought to suffer over Ivana. He'd been selfish and uncaring, putting his wife through hell. Gary loved his father but he'd done wrong and he deserved pain. Why didn't Mum realise that?

When Gary had charged off to have it out with Ivana it was an attempt to get her to back off. If she realised the damage she was doing surely she'd stop playing with a man old enough to be her father – a married man whose wife was self-destructing bit by bit.

But it had blown up in his face. Ivana had treated him with contempt, made fun of him, put her finger on his weakness. He hadn't been motivated by personal jealousy or in competition with his father. Not consciously.

And now his father's mistress was dead and things were worse even than they were before.

Gary couldn't understand why the police hadn't come for him. He'd considered seeking them out and confessing, except that it would have made it worse for Mum and Dad. It would probably have finished his father off completely if he'd been arrested.

So now he had to live with the knowledge of what he'd done.

'Oh, I say!' Mrs Pryce's exclamation brought him back to the present and he blinked at the field of runners storming towards the finish. There was a hint of girlish glee in her tone as she squealed, 'I can't believe it.'

Neither could Gary.

*   *   *

Things had looked up for Tomas and Jack of Hearts around the six furlong marker. They were in the thick of the action with bigger horses on all sides and Tomas expected the horse to be intimidated. He gave him a tap with the whip, just as a reminder, and in response the horse lengthened his stride. That was interesting.

The game plan was to run Jack of Hearts over a longer distance and see if he could make up in stamina what he lacked in speed. There was only one way to find out if they'd been thinking on the right lines.

A barrier of horses blocked his way, five of them spread across the course, chasing the favourite two lengths further ahead. The riders were gearing themselves for a final push to the line. Tomas could see a small opening between the two horses to his right – but he had little faith that Jack of Hearts had the courage to go through it. He decided to make the horse's mind up for him and hit him hard behind the saddle. To Tomas's surprise Jack of Hearts stuck his nose out and edged forward into the space.

He knew that once he got his mount's shoulders level with the quarters of the horses in front he would be safe. But if the horse lost his nerve and allowed the other two animals to come together there was every chance their legs would tangle and Tomas would crash to the turf at the fastest point of the race.

But Tomas didn't care if he got hurt. Regardless of his own safety, he drove Jack of Hearts forward.

For a few strides, the three horses seemed glued together. They were in the final furlong now, unknown territory for Jack of Hearts. The horse picked up the pace, finding strength that was failing his opponents. He liked this new territory – it was his. At the death, Jack of Hearts burst past his two rivals to claim second place, half a length behind the leader. And if they'd not held him up, who knows? He might have won. Certainly Mrs Pryce thought as much.

'I'll be keeping an eye on you,' she told him. 'That's the bravest piece of riding I've seen this year.'

Tomas was gratified but it irked that he'd not managed to get home in front. He'd badly wanted to win for Ivana – he owed it to her.

'Where exactly is this place?' Steve had been stirring the cup of coffee Kathy had made him for the last thirty seconds. His mind was evidently elsewhere, on the information she had just given him about the woman in the red T-shirt.

'Otley Manor Business Park.'

'Never heard of it.'

'It's off the ring road, just before you get to the hospital.' That's where Kathy had turned off once she realised the van had given her the slip. Then she'd doubled back and found her way onto the business estate. 'I went back and had a look round.'

He nodded. She couldn't tell if he was impressed or annoyed that she'd lost the woman in the first place. She couldn't read much from him these days.

'It's quite big. There's warehouses and offices and odd little businesses like a fish smokery and a place where they make greenhouses.'

'Did you see the van?'

No, she hadn't, and that had been a big let-down because there were vehicles parked all over the place.

'I had a good look. There's underground parking at some of the offices so she could have gone there but they all had security guys, so I didn't fancy going in to look.'

'Quite right.' He shot her a quick grin. So he wasn't annoyed with her – that was a relief.

'There's one thing,' she said. 'Though it's quite a big area, it's self-contained. There's just one road in and one out. She must have gone into one of those places, she couldn't just have driven through on the way to somewhere else.'

'Thanks, Kathy. I appreciate you doing something like this.' The grin turned into a proper smile – it was nice to see him smile again.

'That's OK.' She wouldn't mind doing it again. Despite the

hairy moments, it had been a bit of a thrill. 'How much did she win?'

'Six hundred quid. A hundred on Culloden at six to one. The favourite went off at five to two and there was another runner at five to one. But I could have told you before the off that this Culloden was going to win.'

'Because she wasn't the only one?'

'We got a string of bets like hers across all the shops. A hundred to two hundred quid a time, all on Culloden to win. We laid off as much as we could but I'll still end up paying out ten grand.'

'Is it always the first race at Hampton Waters?'

Steve nodded but she knew the answer to that anyway from previous discussions. She also knew it didn't happen at every meeting but frequently enough to bleed significant money from his business. Hampton Waters held weekly meetings throughout the summer; even if only a proportion of them were loaded against him the loss was potentially huge. Now Steve was wise to what was happening, she knew he could offset some of the loss by identifying the likely winner and hedging money elsewhere. But the bets were always placed at the last minute. Since that first occasion back in May, he estimated he'd lost over a hundred thousand pounds to this scam.

'Can't you identify who's placing the bets and ban them?'

'I've been trying but it's not easy when there's lots of different people putting the money down. Bookies don't stay in business long if they ban too many punters. Anyway, this lot keep changing the personnel – I don't know how they manage it.'

'Haven't you talked to any of the people who place these bets?'

'Sure. They just say they fancied the horse – someone gave them a tip at work, or they liked the name. There's a million reasons you can give for having a bet. None of them have to be the truth.'

'You could try putting the thumbscrews on them.'

He shot her a baleful look. 'Don't think I haven't thought about it. But I can't run my business from prison.'

'I wasn't serious, Steve.' She could understand why he wasn't amused but she didn't want to let the matter drop. 'So the woman I followed today is typical?'

'Only because she's female. They can be all sorts of women, provided they're old enough to bet. Shop girl types, grannies, middle-class housewives.'

'Do you get lots of women in betting shops?'

'Hardly. If a woman wants a bet there's a good chance she'll get a man to put it on for her. Most women don't even know how to fill out a betting slip.'

'But these ones do?'

'Oh yes. And they know what's going to win in the first race at Hampton Waters. How the bloody hell do they know that?'

He slammed his coffee mug onto the desk, slopping a wave of cold coffee over the rim. The question hung unanswered in the air.

Despite Jack of Hearts' good showing at Leicester, there was no air of satisfaction in Tomas's car on the drive home from Leicester. All the same, Gary – whose Mini wasn't reckoned reliable enough to make the trip – looked at Tomas with some admiration.

'That was a bloody stupid bit of riding,' he said. 'Are all Czech jocks as mad as you?' He'd been saying similar things since the beginning of the journey.

'There was a space. I went through it, that's all.'

'You threaded him through the eye of a needle, mate, that's what you did. Old Mrs Pryce nearly swallowed her false teeth.'

'She looked happy enough to me afterwards.'

'She wouldn't have been so happy if you'd broken her horse's neck.'

Tomas shrugged and pulled out to overtake a Golf, despite the fact that they were cresting the brow of a hill. Gary flinched as they cut back inside to avoid a head-on smash with a lorry. The Golf's horn sounded a protest. Tomas put his foot down.

'Steady on,' Gary said. 'You're not on a horse now.'

Tomas grinned and slowed the car a fraction. 'I'm sorry.'

'Are you on a death wish today, or something?'

Tomas did not respond and Gary wondered if he'd upset him. It was awkward enough driving with Ivana's brother. He'd always liked Tomas and they got on well but these circumstances were a strain. He could only imagine how the loss of Ivana was hurting Tomas but he didn't dare talk about it lest he let something slip. He didn't want to be any more of a hypocrite than he was already, sitting here by Tomas's side, the responsibility for Ivana's death weighing him down.

Tomas's voice broke the silence.

'My sister did not die by accident, you know.'

Gary froze in his seat. Was he a bloody mind-reader?

'There were things going on in her life,' Tomas continued. 'Things that were not discussed at the inquest.'

'What do you mean?'

'My sister did not choose her men friends well. They screwed up her mind. That's the only reason she would have got careless with the stallion.'

'You mean she deliberately opened the gate to Cape Fear's pen?'

'No, not deliberately. But there was a man who had been frightening her. He wanted her and could not have her and that completely freaked her out.'

Jesus! What was he getting at? Gary said nothing.

'I think this man had so upset her she did not know what she was doing.'

'Did you tell the police?'

Tomas shook his head. 'I don't trust police. In my country you have to pay them, then they do what you want.'

'It's not like that here.'

'Huh,' Tomas did not sound convinced. 'Would they listen if I said my sister was so upset by a man she did not protect herself against a mad horse? It doesn't make much sense, does it?'

Put like that, it didn't.

'But I know it to be true.'

So did Gary.

'That's not all, my friend.' Tomas spoke with fierce intensity, his eyes on the road ahead. 'I know who this man is.'

Gary swallowed hard.

'I know who he is,' Tomas repeated. 'And one day soon I'm going to kill him. Then they can lock me up for the rest of my life. I don't care.'

Panic gripped Gary. If Tomas carried out his threat then he would be responsible for another death.

Another thought occurred to him. Perhaps Tomas knew about his row with Ivana. Knew that it was Gary who had imprisoned her in Cape Fear's stall so that her only way out was to open the safety gate and make for the door on the far side of the pen.

Maybe Tomas's death threat was not aimed at some unknown man. It was aimed at him.

The car roared on into the evening, dangerously over the speed limit. This time Gary did not protest. A head-on crash would solve everything.

Chapter Eight

Rob stood in Cape Fear's old exercise yard, hands in pockets, dark thoughts running through his head. The steel gates, the ten-foot high fence, the specially constructed exercise area stood empty and useless. A great deal of thought had gone into building a secure home for the dangerous beast in the light of what had happened to Gwen. What had *nearly* happened to Gwen – the girl had got away without a scratch though she'd had the fright of her life. Rob had considered getting rid of Cape Fear at the time but he'd blamed the poor state of the stallion's quarters – the horse hadn't been properly restrained. Also, he'd had a hunch the stallion had a future at stud and he'd been right about that, at least – Goldeneye was the proof. And, as he'd said at the time, it was Cape Fear's first offence. Everyone deserves a second chance.

Now he bitterly regretted his decision. He should have sold the evil beast, even at a knock-down price, and spent the money on another stallion. Now he had a woman's death on his conscience. And he had no stallion either.

Bella had not wanted Cape Fear put down but Rob had barely listened to her, just instructed the vet to do it quickly. He'd learned a lot about Bella recently. How could she even think of sparing the horse that had killed one of their team? Was it because the victim was Ivana, whom she'd taken against? Or was she simply concerned with the financial loss?

She'd laid into him for getting rid of Cape Fear. 'You're too impulsive. Somebody would have taken him off our hands. Now we've lost our best stallion and I don't know how we're going to replace him.'

Is this really the woman I married? he'd asked himself. Surely not everything could be measured in pounds, shillings and pence.

Now he stood morosely in the empty barn. In his mind it still echoed with the roars of the enraged horse and Kathy's shouts as she fought Cape Fear with a broom. She was a game girl. Her mother would have done the same thing, he knew. The pair of them had the same core of steel.

He resolved not to let this terrible event poison his marriage. Bella was a realist at heart. Perhaps he was too sentimental. Time to toughen up.

He could start by recognising that Ivana's accident was not his fault. The inquest had cleared the stud of any deficiencies in safety precautions and the coroner had gone out of his way to commend the security arrangements in the workplace. And, though he had couched his opinion in gentler terms for Tomas's benefit, it was plain that he considered the girl's death was due to her own carelessness.

Rob had been relieved, there was no getting round it. To have been publicly implicated in her death would have been a blow.

So why couldn't he absolve himself? In his position, Bella would. In the car driving home from the coroner's court she'd said, 'So it was Ivana's fault. I hope you'll stop blaming yourself now.'

But Bella hadn't been up here with Cape Fear and Ivana on a regular basis. It was the Czech girl's job to muck him out on the mornings Jacko wasn't available and Rob knew how much she hated it. It was the reason he helped her when he could. If only he'd been here that Friday . . .

He remembered now the way Ivana had reacted the day before when she'd come to say she was leaving the stud. The stallion had snarled at her then and she'd been a bag of nerves. What had she said? 'He hates me – he's got a black heart.' Something like that. It was hard to believe she'd take any risks with him the very next day.

He walked to the stable end of the enclosure, where the metal gate could be rolled back on a runner to separate the horse from its sleeping quarters. He tested the gate and the catch which held it in place – the hundredth time, maybe, he'd examined it since the accident. And he'd not been the only one. It worked as designed every time.

'Is there any way,' the coroner had asked the local authority Health and Safety Inspector, 'that this safety gate could have been opened by accident?'

'No.'

'It couldn't have been insecurely fastened so that movement by the horse would have shifted it?'

'The gate is held in place by a spring latch which has to be gripped and pulled. It is designed so that only a person could release it.'

'And in your opinion was this gate functioning correctly on the day of the accident?'

'I have no doubt about it, sir.'

Which left only one possibility: that Ivana had unlatched it herself. But why?

One theory, the only one that seemed to make any sense, was that it was quicker and less awkward to take the wheelbarrow of muck through Cape Fear's exercise yard, rather than manoeuvre it round the perimeter. It was certainly a shorter journey. If Ivana was looking to cut corners, might she not have taken this route? The coroner had seized on the possibility.

Rob found it hard to believe. Nobody ever did that. He stood in the doorway that separated the stable from the yard and measured the distance to the far gate. It was a shorter trip all right but Ivana would have been completely exposed to the horse's ill temper. She'd not have got far before he'd be after her.

Actually, she'd gone no distance at all. Cape Fear had killed her right here in the doorway, where he now stood. But why hadn't she tried to escape? At least she might have attempted to climb up the bars. She wouldn't have been able to climb out of the pen – there was a roof of netting – but maybe she could have scrambled clear of the stallion's reach and gained some valuable time.

Her death was still a mystery to Rob.

The place was clean now, with scarcely a scrap of straw to be seen or scent of horse to trouble the nostrils. But Rob could see the pool blackening the floor beneath Ivana's body, her hair spread out like weed in the puddle of gore, the smell of blood and manure filling the air. He remembered holding her, her flesh warm and wet, her limbs heavy and awkward, searching for a pulse in her wrist or a flicker of breath in her throat – and being so damned clumsy he'd not been able to tell. It turned out his efforts had been futile.

The animal she'd been most scared of had killed her and that animal had belonged to him. No wonder he could not absolve himself of blame.

He closed the stable door behind him and began to walk along the corridor between the barn wall and the fence – the perimeter walk that Ivana had decided not to take with the wheelbarrow. Possibly.

His eye alighted on the canvas duffel bag hanging on its hook outside the stable door. This was Cape Fear's bag, containing his individual grooming kit: dandy brush, body brush, curry comb, hoof pick and other implements – not that it was used very often in Cape Fear's case. Rob supposed he ought to tidy it up; the bag must have been overlooked in the cleaning-up operation.

He took it down. There was no point in leaving it here now Cape Fear was gone. He opened the drawstring that held the bag together and examined the contents. Most of the implements were in pristine condition. Even the stable rubber – a white cotton cloth the size of a tea towel used for wiping down a horse – was folded neatly, as clean as if it had just come from the laundry.

Rob lifted the cloth out and examined it. Something bothered him, plucking at the sleeve of his thoughts. Why was this insignificant scrap of cloth, an everyday item of equipment at the yard, important? But he had a feeling it was.

Uniformed police had arrived as Ivana was being taken away in the ambulance. They'd told Rob not to touch the place of the accident but later that afternoon, after other officers had examined and recorded the scene, he was told he could clear up. He'd done it on his own, hosing, sweeping and washing down the whole area. He'd performed the task stoically, saving his shock and grief for when the job was done.

Having to dispose of the blood-sodden work coat she'd been wearing had been the hardest part. In the pocket of the coat he'd found a bloody stable rubber just like the one he held in his hand. He'd not been surprised at the time. It made sense for a horse's groom to have the animal's cloth in her pocket. Later he'd burned it along with the overall and the bloody straw from the floor. He'd not thought about it since.

But now, running the cloth through his fingers, a thought surfaced: if this was Cape Fear's stable rubber, and it must be because he'd just found it in the stallion's bag, where had the other one come from? And what was it doing in Ivana's pocket?

Not that it mattered. The girl was dead and, however he looked at it, he was still responsible.

As always, Len appeared in the doorway of Kathy's office without warning. Steve had fitted a lock downstairs as requested but it made no difference.

'Miss de Lisle,' he said, his tone neutral, the sarcasm implicit rather than stated. Since their first meeting he had been unnecessarily polite and she imagined that Steve had spoken to him. All the same, she sensed the antipathy. She'd concluded it wasn't personal – this was a man who disliked his fellow human beings on principle. Or maybe he was simply antagonistic to women.

As a rule, Len came by looking for Steve and a couple of times she'd seen him hand over envelopes which, she assumed, contained money. Another defaulter must have been persuaded to pay up.

Once, she'd noticed grazed knuckles on the hand with the envelope. On another occasion, there were ugly furrows down the broad plane of one cheek – scratches made by a woman's nails, she concluded. She didn't want to imagine the circumstances.

'So where's this Otley Manor business place?' he asked.

For a moment she was lost for words. Why did he want to know?

He repeated the question slowly. It was plain he thought she was dim.

She described the location and, when prompted, the blue van she had followed.

'What's the reg. number?'

'I don't know.' It hadn't occurred to her to make a note.

'You mean you followed the van for half an hour and you don't know the number?'

She felt like an idiot but she couldn't remember it at all.

His small flinty eyes glared at her in disbelief. She could tell he was dying to tell her what he thought of this obvious incompetence but restrained himself.

'Keep your eyes peeled next time,' he said finally. 'If there is one.'

Then he was gone, leaving her musing uncomfortably on the conversation.

What had her car chase the other night got to do with this thug?

Even someone as dim as Len thought she was could work that out. Steve had now called in his heavy guns to sort out the mystery of the Hampton Waters losses.

On reflection, Kathy wasn't unhappy she had failed to note the van number. She didn't want Len turning up at anyone's door because of her.

Gary was alarmed to see his father in the yard when he came down off the gallops. He'd thought the doctor had made it clear Charlie was supposed to stay away from the yard while he recovered. On the other hand, Gary wasn't surprised. It was already high summer and the days of the

134

Flat season were slipping away, with key meetings coming up fast. No self-respecting trainer would want to be left on the sidelines when his horses were so busy.

His father was sitting on a bench with a white cricket hat shielding his eyes from the sun. His walking stick was resting on the seat beside him. He looked pasty-face and his hand shook as he moved the stick so Gary could take a seat beside him.

'What on earth are you doing here, Dad?'

'Oh, don't you start.' The voice sounded reassuringly firm and familiar. If Gary didn't look directly at Charlie, it was much like being with the dad he'd known all his life.

'Your mother brought me over,' his father continued, 'after I'd spent half an hour telling her a spot of sunshine would do me good. I had to get Phillips on the blower to convince her.' Phillips was Charlie's specialist. Having an unscheduled phone conversation with him was unheard of. Gary reckoned it was probably easier to talk to the Queen.

'Why didn't you just go out into the back garden? Why come all the way over here?' Not that it was far, but a hundred yards in his father's state took a bit of doing.

'Why do you think?'

Gary couldn't avoid his father's gaze now. He tried not to look at the loose lip and slack cheeks with the stray clumps of hair that the razor had missed – his father insisted on shaving himself. Instead he focused on the older man's cloudy grey eyes, anxiously checking that the real Charlie was present. It had been the worst part of his father's 'turn', looking into his eyes as he lay on the hospital bed, tubes snaking everywhere, and finding only swirling incomprehension. His father had been absent. It had been a terrifying moment.

But that was over now, thank God.

'Well?' Charlie was insistent. 'Why do you think I've braved your mother and flogged all the way over here?'

It was obvious, now Gary thought about it.

'You want to see Goldie, don't you?'

135

This morning had been Goldeneye's last piece of work before his next race, the Prix Jacques Le Marois at Deauville in Normandy. It had taken the horse an age to recover from the sore shins he'd acquired at Newmarket and key races like the Irish Guineas and the St James's Palace Stakes had come and gone in his absence. This French race, a tempting prize for Europe's top milers, was a chance to get back on the racecourse and re-establish himself. And his trainer, Charlie, was forbidden from making the trip. No wonder he'd risen from his sickbed specially to look the horse over.

'He'll be along in a moment, Dad. Tomas is just bringing him down.'

'How did it go this morning?'

'Fantastic. He gets better every day.'

'Don't get carried away, this is the toughest thing he's taken on. He's got to handle the journey for a start.'

Goldeneye was being driven down to Portsmouth the next day to catch the ferry to Le Havre. He'd never made a sea crossing before.

'I've been talking things over with Pete,' Charlie continued. Pete was the travelling head lad who'd be in charge of the horse on the journey. Gary could well imagine that he would have been over to share his father's bench, some of the other lads too. 'Pete says you're not doing badly,' his father added. 'I knew that already.'

Gary put his hand over his father's. In the recent emotional turmoil, it was necessary to get the things that mattered right.

'Great to see you in the yard, Dad.'

'I'm not going to rush back, son. And when I do, I'll be relying on you.'

That was good to know. Maybe now was the time to ask another important question. 'What about Mum?'

There was a long pause. Gary hadn't been there when his mother had broken the news of Ivana's death but he knew his father had taken it badly. It had clearly set back his recovery, no matter how he tried to disguise it, and Gary knew how much Mum resented it.

His father had to realise what he was getting at, didn't he?

Eventually Charlie said, 'I don't know why she still puts up with me. Without her, I reckon I'd be dead.'

'Does she know that?'

'I tell her every ruddy day. She'll get so big-headed she'll never get her Ascot hat on again.'

That was all right then.

The sound of hoofs echoed in the distance. That should be Goldeneye. His father was fumbling in his jacket pocket. He produced an envelope and pushed it towards Gary. 'Kathy sent me a card.'

Gary looked at it – a Stubbs painting – and read the message on the back in round schoolgirlish writing.

'Your mother says you're not talking to each other. God knows, I'm no expert in the romance stakes, but I think you're a bloody fool.'

The sound of the approaching horse grew louder.

Gary handed the card back. 'Like you say, Dad, you're no expert.'

Then Goldie entered the yard with Tomas on his back and there was no other topic of conversation.

Rob found Jacko with Curtain Raiser, now the stud's only stallion, who'd been suffering from colic for the past few days. Come to think of it – and he often did – Rushmore wasn't much of a stud farm these days. If they lost CR they'd be completely emasculated.

Jacko was brushing the stallion's caramel-brown quarters. His coat looked dull to Rob, without its usual lustre.

'How do you think he's doing?' he asked the big man.

'OK.' Jacko pulled a face which, typically, said more than his words. The horse must still be suffering. You had to read Jacko's expressions to get the best out of him.

'Everything set for this weekend?'

Jacko spent most of his time on his father's farm and it was understood that that was his priority. But he was an obliging fellow and would help Rob whenever he could. It was particularly important that he lent a hand when Rob and Kathy were away in France for Goldeneye's race. Bella was due to hold the fort but Rob was concerned that assistance would be on hand should she need it.

'Yup,' Jacko grunted, still brushing and not looking in Rob's direction. But that was all right. Jacko's grunt was good enough for him.

There was another question that had to be asked and Rob was apprehensive about raising it. Jacko had adored Ivana and taken her death hard, not that many would have noticed. But Rob was used to Jacko and knew that he wouldn't want to talk about what had happened. All the same, there was an issue Rob wanted to clear up.

'I was sorting out Cape Fear's bag,' he began.

Jacko stiffened but carried on with his work; he was listening closely though.

'I don't think anyone has been near it since the accident.'

'Well, I haven't.' Jacko turned to face Rob, waiting for him to continue.

'Do you know if there were two stable rubbers in the bag?'

Jacko was a young man, in his early twenties, but there was something middle-aged about the deliberate way he did things. He ran a big hand over his square jaw. 'No,' he said at last. 'Was there two there?'

'No, just one. But –' this was awkward – 'Ivana had another one on her. I found it in the pocket of the coat she was wearing.'

Jacko blinked, his pale yellow eyes unnaturally wide. Something was going on in his great head.

'We was missing a stable rubber in this boy's bag.' He laid a big meaty hand on Curtain Raiser's shoulder. The horse took it as his cue to walk off. Jacko didn't appear to notice, he was thinking hard. 'I had to get a spare from the tack room.'

'When was this?'

'Just after it happened. The next time I came in, I couldn't find CR's rubber.' He shook his head. 'Jesus.' There was a weight of emotion in the word.

Rob knew Jacko was thinking the same as him. Ivana would have mucked out Curtain Raiser first that morning. Was it possible she had taken the stable rubber that had belonged to him and carried it with her up to Cape Fear's pen?

Some stallions were notoriously jealous of their peers; one thing absolutely guaranteed to enrage Cape Fear was the scent of his rival, Curtain Raiser. The two stallions had been housed at opposite ends of the yard and kept well apart.

The cloth which had been used to rub down Curtain Raiser, heavily impregnated with his individual scent, would have been quite enough to send Cape Fear into a jealous frenzy.

'It was in the pocket of her coat?' Jacko was understandably puzzled. Separate coats were kept for each stallion: what was true of the stable rubber was also true of the coats the grooms wore to tend to each animal. Ivana would have taken off the coat she used to muck out Curtain Raiser and left it hanging outside his stall. Then she would have donned a fresh coat to deal with the other stallion – as she had done. The garments were clearly marked to avoid confusion and Rob had noted Cape Fear's name, stitched in red, on the collar of the coat he had burned.

So how had Curtain Raiser's stable rubber found its way into the pocket of Cape Fear's coat? That was the question bothering both men.

'She must have got it muddled up with her clothes,' Rob said. 'Maybe she forgot about it when she was putting the bag away and shoved it in her jeans. Something like that.' He was thinking out loud. 'She had a lot on her mind.'

Jacko shrugged. 'That bastard horse didn't need no excuse to go for her anyway.'

That was true enough. But if she'd been carrying the scent of another horse on her, it would have made it a stone-cold certainty.

Steve waited while Len drank lustily. The big man placed the empty glass on the table top and wiped the orange moustache from his lip with the back of a beefy hand. If

Steve hadn't been so tense he'd have had trouble keeping a smile off his face. It wasn't every day you saw a bruiser like Len down a pint of carrot juice.

Above their heads a wide TV screen regurgitated an early-season football match. The over-excited commentary provided useful cover for their conversation. As did the yelping of two energetic toddlers nagging their mothers for change for the jelly-bean machine. Steve couldn't understand why Len didn't belong to a proper gym, an old-fashioned sweat and liniment place above a boozer with pictures of boxing heroes on the wall. Except those places probably didn't exist any more.

Despite the unlikely ambience, Len looked as if he'd made the most of the facilities on offer. His broad chest was barely contained by a white singlet and his usually pale complexion was tinged with the pink of recent aerobic effort. He smelt vividly of deodorant and aftershave.

'You'll be pleased to hear,' he said, 'that our Mr Doogan won't be staying.'

Doogan was the new manager of Fairweather's in Seymour Street; the third since the branch had opened.

That was good news. The first two managers had been locals, unable to cope, but Doogan was a hard man, brought down from head office in Manchester.

'The family have had trouble settling in apparently,' Len said.

'Why's that?' Steve had to ask.

'The local yobbos have been making a nuisance of themselves. Chucking bottles, bit of graffiti – that kind of thing. And Mrs Doogan don't like rats.'

'Rats?' That was a new one.

'They've been turning up at their house. They had the pest control round three times last week. I think it was the dead one in the kids' sandpit that really freaked her out.'

Steve could understand that. The Doogans had a child of two and a baby just starting to crawl. He knew mothers were completely paranoid about kids at that age – if his sisters were anything to go by.

The spring of tension inside him unwound a notch. So they'd seen off another of Fairweather's army. Who said the little guy couldn't fight back?

Steve put the envelope on the table and Len's hand covered it as if it didn't exist. Three grand in cash seemed a lot to pay for a couple of dead rats. But if it helped stem the steady leak of money from his shops it was worth it.

Finally a smile tugged at his lips. A rat in a sandpit – the things you had to do to survive in business these days.

Tomas ran the video for the fifth time. Or was it the twenty-fifth? He'd lost count. It was two in the morning and he ought to go to bed. But he knew he wouldn't sleep so what was the point? Watching race videos of his rivals in the upcoming Prix le Marois at least seemed like a useful way of passing the sleepless hours.

The trouble was, by this stage he was scarcely looking at the screen. His mind kept turning to other matters: like Ivana and the circumstances of her death and the man who had, surely, been the cause of it.

Tomas had been trying to track him down. Milos had told Ivana he was living in England now. Given that he must have a job, it was likely he could be found at a yard somewhere. There were plenty of East European workers to be found at British stables and Tomas had been asking around. After all, it was reasonable for him to seek out fellow countrymen and he'd met plenty as a result. Good fellows all – and none of them with a ponytail and a beak of a nose.

It would, of course, be much easier if he involved the police. Maybe they were different here in England. But the traffic cops who stopped him were the same sarcastic bullies he recognised from back home. People who stared at you as if you were dirt and who disbelieved every word that came out of your mouth – even if they did call you 'sir'.

Back home, the police had not done much to help his mother, had they? Even when his father put her in hospital with three broken ribs they'd not charged the bastard.

He didn't think the cold-eyed bullies here would be any different. Like he'd told Gary, he didn't trust the police. They'd laugh at him. The inquest had delivered a verdict and they wouldn't want to go against that. He doubted if they'd even start to look for Milos.

So it was up to him.

He'd even gone so far as to ring Julie Beale, the trainer's daughter from Sussex. He'd not wanted to do that. The thought of her filled him with guilt and self-loathing. She was blameless, of course, but he couldn't bear to think of that pretty pink face and provocative smile.

If it hadn't been for her, would he have answered Ivana's plea and gone home that night after the Brighton races? It wasn't just having to renege on his promise to ride work the next morning but the thought of Julie's company that had held him back. English girls liked him and he liked them. But he wasn't in the mood for them any more. So calling Julie to ask about Czech stable workers had been painful. And, it turned out, a waste of time.

She'd sounded pleased to hear from him but could shed no light on Milos.

'A ponytail and a big nose? Doesn't sound like my type.'

And what exactly is your type? he could have replied, which would have been unnecessary as he knew very well. He was her type, as she'd made clear that evening when he should have been driving home to protect his sister.

'I'll ask around for you, shall I? I can give you a call if I hear anything.'

He'd agreed with reluctance. It was not her fault but he never wanted to hear from her again.

On the TV screen, the crowd was cheering and a horse and jockey were being feted. He couldn't even remember which horse it was. The race had passed without him taking in one detail.

He rewound the tape. No matter. He had all night.

Chapter Nine

There was no denying Bella would have enjoyed a weekend in France. And when Rob had tried to insist that she, not him, should travel to the race meeting at Deauville, it would have been easy to agree. But it wouldn't have been the right decision. Much as she would love to see Goldeneye square up to the challenge of the Prix Jacques Le Marois, he was not her horse. Rob owned half of him and it was only right that he should be there to participate in Goldie's triumph or failure. To her mind, all other things were incidental: the chance to savour some fine French food, to stroll the boardwalk and survey the chic sunbathers, to slip into the brand-name couturiers and stunning boutiques of the town they called Paris-on-sea – too bad, she couldn't afford it anyway. Given that one of them had to stay and mind the business, it was plainly her job.

The one thing that might have changed her mind was the knowledge that both Kathy and Steve would be among the Goldeneye party. She'd tried to get Kathy to stay home and help her on the stud but Kathy had been resistant.

'Don't think I'm giving you the money,' Bella had said.

'There's no need.'

'Steve's not paying, is he?'

Kathy had laughed. 'You're joking. He's got no money. I'm paying for myself, thanks very much.'

There wasn't much Bella could say to that, though one or two things puzzled her. Admittedly Kathy was earning some sort of wage so she probably could fund her own trip, though Bella hoped she wasn't piling up a debt somewhere. Steve having no money didn't sound convincing, however. He always seemed to be chucking it around – at least, that was the impression she'd gathered in the past.

Not that she cared about Steve's finances. All she cared about was whether he was intent on seducing her daughter, in which case, a hotel in Normandy would be as good a location as any.

'You'll keep an eye on Kathy, won't you?' she instructed Rob. 'Make sure she gets off to bed on time. On her own.'

Rob knew how seriously she took the matter so he hadn't made a joke out of it, though she could see he'd been tempted.

Instead, he said, 'I don't think you should worry about Kathy and Steve. If they want to have a fling, they can do it here. Anyway, I don't think she fancies him any more.'

Now Bella thought about it, she realised Rob's assessment was probably correct. Since that night when she'd come home in tears – which Bella was convinced was down to Steve – Kathy had shown no signs of her early crush. However, that was the night before Ivana was killed and that had had an effect on everyone.

Reassured to a degree, Bella had seen them off early on Saturday morning. When Jacko had turned up she'd left Rushmore to him so she could concentrate on the job she had set herself for the weekend.

Ivana's cottage had always been an issue for Bella and now, at last, she had vacant possession. Admittedly the circumstances of the vacancy were troubling but that was hardly her fault. After Ivana's death she had wondered how long she could wait before getting Rob to evict Tomas – or else to lease it to him at a realistic rent. Rob, she knew, would happily let him stay on for nothing and she was gearing herself for an argument, when Tomas had told them he was moving in with his friend, Ed Christie, who had just bought a house near Stratford.

'Without Ivana, the cottage is not a happy place,' he said. 'Anyway, I don't like to live on my own.'

So Bella's self-imposed task for the weekend was to clean out the cottage.

Bella wasn't a hypocrite. She had never been a fan of Ivana's and the woman's death had not changed her opinion. Rob had told her about the stable rubber from the other stallion in her pocket. How stupid could you be? Though, frankly, it was a bit of a surprise. Calculating, predatory, immoral – these were the charges Bella would have laid against the Czech woman were she called to justify her dislike. But stupidity would not be amongst them. All she could think of was that Ivana had been so keen to shake the dust of Rushmore from her heels that she'd got careless and cut too many corners. Somehow she had managed to muck out Cape Fear with Curtain Raiser's stable rubber in her pocket. If that wasn't suicidal behaviour, what was?

More interesting to Bella, and she mused on the subject as she hoovered and washed walls and banged rugs, was why Ivana had been in such haste to quit. It had to be a guy. Bella wouldn't mind betting it was a middle-aged man with money, married of course, probably a trainer or an owner. Maybe it had been Charlie – she was sure from the trainer's reaction to the news of Ivana's departure at the charity dinner that the rumour of their affair had been accurate. Or perhaps Ivana was chucking everything in for a new lover. Maybe that's why Charlie had keeled over with a heart attack, because he'd lost Ivana to another man.

Bella dismissed the thought as a flight of fancy. It probably had nothing to do with reality at all.

She couldn't believe the state the cottage had been left in. The living-room carpet had been pulled up and the side of the bath had been removed. She was on the kitchen now, which was less fun than spring-cleaning the bedrooms. Kitchens always attracted cringe-making grot, decaying foodstuffs and burned-on messes which only serious elbow grease could dislodge. She made a quick decision not to bother with the cooker – it would have to be replaced anyway. Similarly, they'd need new cupboards and appliances and cooking surfaces. You couldn't skimp on a kitchen if you hoped to let at a decent rate.

The Welsh dresser, however, was an asset, as was the solid old kitchen table. They'd scrub up pretty well, she reckoned.

She started by emptying the drawers. Soon she had a pile of place mats, cutlery, old champagne corks, chewed-down pencils, playing cards and bashed-in ping-pong balls, among other things. She decided to remove the drawers to give them a proper clean. That's when she made her discovery. Turning the right-hand dresser drawer over to tip the dust out, she found a white paper rectangle taped to the underside.

She recognised the little packet at once: a CD-ROM. She unstuck it and examined the small silver disk. There was no label.

Her mind began to race. This was better than phantom lovers and illicit liaisons. The disk had been hidden, so it must contain something of significance. Hidden, what's more, by Ivana, otherwise Tomas would have taken it with him.

When she got back home she'd pour herself a large drink and slip the disk into her computer. It was something to look forward to at least while her husband and daughter were living it up in France.

Kathy was taken aback by the opulence of the hotel. Her room was small but luxurious with a view down the long golden beach from the balcony outside. Her bed had a brocaded canopy and on the bedside table was a small silver box with matching ribbon containing a tiny bottle of Hermès perfume. Fantastic!

Rob and Steve were sharing the room next door – a gesture of frugality, she supposed. If so, she thought as she took her seat beside them in the beachfront bar, it was the only one. A bottle of something cold and fizzy was nestling in an ice bucket next to the table and a dark-eyed waiter with a curling lip poured her a glass without being asked.

She gulped enthusiastically then put the glass down.

Mustn't get hammered straightaway, she told herself. She wanted to make the most of this. Portraits of familiar faces peered down on the tables. She recognised some of them: Robin Williams and Harrison Ford. Who were the others?

Steve saw the direction of her gaze. 'They have a film festival here in September. For American films. And this month half of Paris is here – it's a hot little town.'

Kathy could feel the buzz in the air. She polished off her drink, what the hell.

The waiter stepped forward to refill her glass and she shook her head. 'Can I have a Coke instead, please?'

Was there a flicker of contempt in his eye as he nodded and glided away? Should she have tried to ask in French?

'Er, *merci beaucoup*,' she mumbled as he reappeared with her request. She could swear his lip curled further.

Rob grinned at her and raised his glass. 'Here's to Goldie.'

They toasted the horse and Steve added, 'If he doesn't win tomorrow, we'll be sleeping on the beach.'

Rob winked at her. 'He's only joking.'

Maybe, thought Kathy, but she'd seen the number of invoices flooding into Steve's office, often the same ones over and over, insistently demanding settlement. Not to mention the phone calls and, occasionally, the irate personal callers. Somehow she was always on her own in the office when these individuals turned up. Despite appearances, Steve's finances were stretched wafer thin.

At least he paid her on time, not that her wages would go far in a place like this. She'd not been entirely truthful with her mother on the financing of this trip. She'd forked out for her own Eurostar fare but Rob had promised to pick up the hotel bill, which pretty much amounted to her mum paying for her after all.

'I won't tell,' he'd said. 'And if she sees it on my credit card bill I'll say you paid me back. Don't worry about it.'

But Kathy did. She was too much like her damn mother.

The waiter was hovering again, finishing off the wine with his latest round of top-ups. He gestured to her glass.

'*Oui, merci*,' she said.

The waiter smiled at her.

'We ought to look in at the casino after dinner,' said Steve. 'What do you think, Kathy?'

She nodded enthusiastically.

To hell with her mum.

Bella's imagination worked overtime as she booted up the computer. Upstairs she could hear the water trickling into the bath – the plumbing was so pathetic in this old house it would take another ten minutes to fill. She took a long pull of the gin and tonic in her hand and waited impatiently as the screen flickered through its start-up procedure.

What would Ivana have preserved on disk and then hidden in such a manner?

If it had been her, Bella thought, it would be online access security details: bank and building society passwords, other website log-on stuff – things she'd want to keep secret if her computer was stolen. And business accounts. In fact, she backed up encrypted accounts for Rushmore on the office computer.

But Ivana didn't have a business to run and was unlikely to have more than a couple of accounts to keep track of.

Suppose it was more personal than that? Love letters, for example. But would you write love letters on computer and keep a file copy? It didn't seem very romantic. And, anyway, wouldn't such letters be in Czech?

That depended who they were addressed to. Letters to Charlie, for example, would be written in English.

Oh Lord, please don't let this have anything to do with Charlie. It would be so embarrassing. She resolved that if this disk contained letters to Charlie she would chuck it away without reading the contents.

She pushed the disk into the CD-ROM player and listened to it whirr into action. A Windows box asked her what she wanted it to do. Above it was a small icon labelled 'Pictures'.

Of course – photographs.

She hesitated for a moment. What kind of photographs would Ivana keep secret? Bella had a pretty good idea. Dirty ones, probably. Photographs of Ivana taken by some lover. Possibly professional ones. With her looks, Ivana could easily have tried out as a model. These could be samples of some obscene alternative career.

She'd come this far so she had to continue, even if the prospect of seeing the dead girl exhibit herself seemed a bit sick.

Bella clicked 'open folder to view files' and watched as a series of small rectangles filled the screen. Even in miniature she could see at once that her assumptions had been incorrect. There were no immodest displays here, just what appeared to be a succession of views and scenes of Rushmore.

She right-clicked on one of them and opened in the Windows Picture Viewer. A shot of the Rushmore foaling sheds filled the screen. A horse she instantly recognised, Good Timing, poked her big grey head out of her box. The next shot was similar, only this time Rob was in the shot, his hand on the horse's neck, grinning happily into the camera. Bella recognised the dreadful old sweater he was wearing, with its frayed hem. She'd made him throw it out. These pictures must date from years ago, certainly before her marriage to Rob.

She scrolled quickly down the row, her excitement now diminished. Most were of horses and she recognised a spindly-legged foal with a patch over one eye – Goldie. She looked for people. There were plenty of Tomas and several of Steve looking hungrily at the picture-taker, Ivana presumably. Maybe these dated from the Czech girl's early days at Rushmore. Then there were shots of Ivana herself and a series of her snuggling into Steve's chest, dressed in a scarlet minidress with snow-white trim. Bella had seen other photos of that ridiculously skimpy outfit – the Czech girl had worn it to a Christmas party and caused a bit of a stir. That was the dress, so she'd heard, that had hooked Steve, though not for long. It had all ended in tears later.

Bella shut down the machine. She couldn't think of one good reason why Ivana should have kept these photos hidden away. Was it because they captured the heady days when she'd fallen in love? She could understand that that would be reason enough to treasure the disk but why conceal it? The photos couldn't be of interest to anyone else.

Oh God, she'd forgotten her bath!

She raced up the stairs, the mystery of Ivana's pictures quite forgotten.

The English racing set were out in force in the casino so Steve was relieved that no one had observed his little difficulty with the cashier. Where the credit on his bastard Mastercard could have disappeared he couldn't quite explain – he must have been running closer to the wire than he'd calculated. As it turned out, it hadn't much mattered as his Visa was still good for some cash. But he'd have to be careful or he'd end up at the races tomorrow unable to have a bet. It was laughable really, a bookie too skint to have a flutter, but it hadn't yet come to that.

He had a choice of roulette or baccarat or blackjack. Normally it would be no contest, as the first two were simple games of chance – with an edge in favour of the house, naturally – while blackjack required at least some measure of skill. On the other hand, blackjack also required a bit of privacy and concentration. With the room full of Brits and little Kathy, looking scrumptious tonight in a pale, turquoise cocktail dress, heading across the room towards him, it was best to play a more sociable game.

'Has Rob deserted you?' he asked.

'He's playing the slot machines. I got a bit bored.' Her eyes were wide at the activity around the room. 'This looks a lot more fun.'

'Oh, it is. Are you familiar with roulette?'

She wasn't. He steered her towards the tables and they watched for a moment.

'Would you like to play?'

'If you tell me what to do.'

'It's not difficult but I'll get you started.' He found her a seat at a table and bought her some chips.

'What's this lot worth?' she asked.

'Five hundred euros.'

'Steve!' There was a warning note to her voice.

'Try not to lose it, sweetheart. It's all I've got.'

It was the simple truth. The funny thing was he trusted her more than he did himself.

She placed a chip on black and the ball spun. Black 17. He grinned. It was a good omen.

'Hello, Stephen.' The dark brown voice oozed directly into his ear and a hand gripped him by the elbow. He turned to look into the chiselled countenance of Hal Cheviot. The Old Etonian was just the kind of endangered species Steve had expected to find in this milieu. Had rather hoped to find, if the truth were told.

'Good to see you, Hal.' He accepted the soft handshake. 'Are you here for the horses, the gambling or the sales?' The Deauville yearling sales took place during the August meeting.

'What do you think?'

As the bloodstock adviser to an Arab oil sheik, Hal Cheviot never missed a significant sale of horseflesh. Not that he missed much in the way of top-flight Flat racing either.

'Deauville in August is de rigueur, as the Frogs say. Too many bloody people, if you ask me. Personally, I'd rather be sitting by a babbling Hampshire stream, watching the trout go by.'

'This must be hellish for you then.'

'You're too right, Stephen.' There wasn't a hint of irony in the man's tone, though Steve was well aware that casinos and racecourses were Hal Cheviot's dedicated environment.

Sitting in front of them, Kathy ventured half a dozen chips on black and a single on two vertical rows of numbers. Both bets came up. She flashed a smile of triumph at Steve, then turned back to her task.

Hal raised his eyebrows. 'I can see you've found some compensation. Or did you bring her?'

'She's a bit of an honorary niece.'

The other man snorted. 'Nice work, uncle.'

'She's also my current PA.'

'So this is just a business trip, is it?'

'Absolutely. Goldeneye's in the Prix Jacques Le Marois tomorrow.'

'I'm aware of that.'

He would be. For all his languid manner, Hal knew the form and breeding of every quality runner in Europe.

Kathy pushed back her chair and stood up. She was clutching a mound of chips, somewhat more than Steve had paid for in the first place. He helped her cash out.

There was a smile of triumph on her face. 'Quit while you're ahead, that's what my dad says.'

Steve grinned. 'I thought Johnny kept losing his shirt.'

'That's what he says, not what he does.'

Hal was regarding Kathy with interest. 'Johnny who?'

She shot Steve an inquisitive look, so he quickly made the introductions.

'Oh, Johnny de Lisle,' said Hal. 'How's he finding life in exile?'

Steve wasn't surprised Hal knew Kathy's father – it was his job to know everyone. He watched with some amusement as the other man dredged up an amusing reminiscence of when they'd played polo together. Within a minute or two he was proposing to escort Kathy to the bar to introduce her to the delights of the local *digestif*.

'Go ahead,' Steve said, calculating that it might be a good move to let the Sheikh Al-Mazin's bloodstock adviser show off to Kathy: her fresh-faced beauty was guaranteed to make an impression. He could trust her not to say anything indiscreet about his business.

It hadn't been Gary's idea to visit the casino, but Pete, his companion for the last couple of days as they'd accompanied Goldeneye on the ferry to France, had insisted. 'You don't have to gamble, mate, but you've got to see it. Looks like a wedding cake and it's all marble and chandeliers on the inside, really ritzy. Not to mention that it's packed to the gills with high-class totty.'

'Are you out on the pull then, Pete?' The thought of this balding Brummy copping off with some sophisticated mademoiselle was amusing.

Pete, to his credit, could see the funny side. 'Unfortunately for the footloose females of Deauville I am a happily married man, so I shall devote myself to the tables. You, on the other hand, mate, might get lucky. So, come on.'

Though eaten up with nerves for the day ahead – the biggest race in the career of the yard's best horse for years and he was in charge – Gary had shrugged himself into a suit and tie and now stood admiring the activity around him in the gaming salon.

As Pete had promised, there were indeed many attractive women in attendance, all of them, whatever their years, polished and well-presented, in dresses and gowns that showed them off to best advantage. But Gary was immune to all this. Ever since he'd entered the room and caught sight of a familiar face at a roulette table, he'd lost interest in the heady display all around.

He'd been expecting to encounter Kathy at the racecourse tomorrow. And he'd decided to blank her, possibly to favour her with a distant nod if politeness demanded it. But tomorrow he'd be working and there would be plenty of important distractions on hand. Seeing Kathy here, looking so dazzling and confident in this sophisticated company, was unexpected and it knocked him for six. All his resolutions to avoid her melted. Instantly he knew he must reclaim the friendship he'd decided to put behind him. He wanted to dash over and tell her that she was the loveliest woman in the room by far and that, next to her, all the pampered and perfumed Parisiennes in their couture gowns were just a collection of leathery old bags.

But just as he was waiting for his moment, not wanting to disturb what looked like a decent run of luck at the table, she suddenly stood up and turned to two men behind her.

Gary had not noticed Steve standing behind her chair and he didn't know the other man, a dapper figure in a dinner jacket. Even from out of earshot, Gary could imagine the casual upper-class drawl with which he spoke and he noted with dismay the glitter of interest in Kathy's eyes as she listened.

Next, even worse, the man had placed a proprietory hand on Kathy's elbow and was steering her from the room, while Steve watched them go.

A lance of jealousy pierced Gary. He cursed himself for his reticence. Would she have been going off with some smooth character if he had made his move a bit quicker?

Who cared anyway? Kathy was no good for him. He'd been right to cut her out of his life.

Steve was approaching with a grin on his face, eager no doubt to find out how Goldie had handled the crossing.

Gary forced himself to return the smile and resolved not to ask who that man was, the one who had just stolen Kathy away. He really didn't care.

Almighty and most merciful Father, we have erred and strayed from thy ways like lost sheep. We have followed too much the devices and desires of our own hearts. We have offended against thy holy laws.

Rose was not a regular churchgoer. She'd attend a carol service at Christmas maybe and weddings and christenings. And funerals. All the usual social gatherings that obliged a C of E agnostic to stumble through the occasional hymn and mumble a prayer. Dad had never been one for the church, not even at the end when he'd had nothing left to live for except the love she had to give him and any that the church might offer. Neither, it turned out, had been enough to stop him stretching his own neck.

She closed her eyes, willing herself to find meaning in the words. The trouble was, she had no belief in God's holy laws, only in the laws of man. And if she was judged by those she'd be looking at a couple of years in prison.

Kneeling by her side was the iron bulk of Jim Sidebottom. Unlike her, Jason's uncle had absolute faith in God's law but she doubted somehow that he prayed for forgiveness in the way she did. He'd probably get an even longer sentence than she would. His faith would sustain him in jail, however. If the day came when they locked her up, she could do with a portion of Jim's religious dedication. She could ask him for instruction but she had no intention of doing so. She absorbed just enough of Jim's fervour for her purposes; more would be tedious.

Besides, it was important that Jim believed her devotion to be without flaw. The point of her being here today and on every Sunday morning was to show a unity of purpose. After all, they did share a common belief, even if hers was more circumscribed than her companion's. Revenge was quite enough to sustain Rose's piety, there was no reason to let Jim know that was as far as it went.

We have left undone those things which we ought to have done, and we have done those things which we ought not to have done, and there is no health in us.

She didn't believe that either. It seemed to her perfectly healthy to get your own back on the man who had driven your father to bankruptcy and, more significantly, robbed him of his standing and self-esteem so that he felt he had no option but to end his life.

Unlike the pious man by her side, the righteous instrument of her vengeance, she did not believe she was morally justified in stealing. Even though the money that she took was not for her benefit, she couldn't use altruism as an excuse. When all was said and done, what drove her to pursue her vendetta was that it made her feel a damn sight better. And she would continue with her unholy mission until she was fully healed.

Amen.

Jason spent Sunday mornings catching up on local work calls, ones he'd let slip during the week. Since horse yards of all descriptions were hardly a five-day week proposition, there was always someone around to sign for a delivery. It was funny how often his route would take him past St Martin's, where Uncle Jim and Rose were at their devotions. It gave him a good feeling just to see Rose's little red Fiat parked up in the lane by the church. He wasn't checking up on her or anything, but he did like to know where she was.

Working on a Sunday morning had not been what he had in mind when he'd got married. The notion of a Sunday lie-in was part of what married life was all about, in his opinion. At least, it had been back in the early days of his first marriage – the very early days before Jennifer had turned into a mercenary shrew and he'd stopped coming home on Saturday nights.

That was nearly twenty years in the past but he remembered some good times. The kind of times he wouldn't mind coming round again. Just because a man and a woman were in their forties didn't mean they couldn't have some fun together. And to end up marrying the woman of his dreams and be denied that enjoyment was galling. Not that he was complaining, certainly not to Rose, but he could admit it to himself. He might not be the world's greatest lover boy but, in his own way, he was a man of passion.

He'd reluctantly concluded that the same could not be said of his wife. Rather than lie abed on a Sunday morning with him, she preferred going to church with his Uncle Jim, a poker-up-his-arse type who mentioned the good Lord every other sentence.

For all that, Jim was a handsome man. He didn't look unlike poor old Geoff Wyatt.

Jason wasn't the kind of fellow who put much store by psychology but you'd be a fool if you ignored some things in life that were as plain as the nose on your face – that Rose, for example, was not a woman who gloried in carnal pleasures. It wasn't just that she wouldn't cuddle up to him on a Sunday morning but she had no history of enjoying herself with a man. She hadn't been a virgin on their wedding night but she'd obviously had little experience of 'that sort of thing', as she put it. Jason remembered all those boyfriends who'd tried and failed to prise Rose away from her dad. And then he thought of Jim – safe, older and her regular consort on a Sunday morning. A father figure.

That was OK, he supposed. He wasn't exactly jealous – he didn't want to be Rose's dad himself. But he wouldn't mind being more of a husband than he was at present.

Since this was how things were, he would just have to live with it. But it was a crying shame.

Rose impatiently willed the two grey-haired ladies in front of her to shuffle along a little faster. The church organ sounded particularly sombre today and she was eager to get into the fresh air. It had been raining before the service but now, beyond the figure of the vicar framed in the church doorway, she caught a glimpse of blue sky. She wanted to get home.

At her side Jim muttered, 'Not a bad sermon.' The emphasis was on the word 'bad' and the implication was clear: it would have been better if it had been his turn in the pulpit.

'It was OK, I suppose.' She hadn't listened to a word of it but it was best to agree with his judgement. Hypocrite that she was.

They reached the vicar and Jim exchanged a few words, avoiding mention of the sermon, Rose noted. The sun was indeed shining. That was something to give genuine thanks for.

He walked her to her car. Here was her opportunity to make her wishes clear. Jim didn't carry a mobile – in any case, she wouldn't want his number showing up on her phone records should things go wrong. Hence her sudden attention to her devotions on Sunday mornings.

'Doctor Wu,' she said. She'd spent some time studying the runners in the first race at Hampton Waters for the following evening.

Jim nodded.

'He's drawn in two,' she added, just so there would be no misunderstanding.

It was always a horse drawn in the first three. It wasn't possible to fix it so that a horse in an outside lane could get the advantage.

'I hear you.' His storm grey eyes were unfathomable but she knew he would not fail her.

He opened the car door for her as he always did and watched as she carefully inched out of her parking space. A silver-haired gentleman bidding his middle-aged niece farewell after morning service. They hardly looked like two perpetrators of a criminal gambling conspiracy.

Out on the main road Rose put her foot down. Jason appreciated a proper Sunday lunch.

Chapter Ten

Kathy was having the time of her life. The luxury hotel and chic surroundings were a far cry from the uninspiring Midlands office where she spent her working week and she loved being somewhere glamorous and exotic which was not, well, too foreign. She'd spent enough holidays in France to feel comfortable.

So far she'd thrown herself into the experience with a determination to make the most of things. After her night at the casino, she'd responded to Rob's suggestion of an early-morning walk along the beach to admire the horses stretching their aristocratic limbs across the sand. They'd bumped into a string of people doing exactly the same thing, including the amusing fellow who'd plied her with apple brandy the night before. Rob had scrutinised Hal suspiciously but when Kathy explained that he knew her 'other' father, that had broken the ice.

Then she'd sunbathed back at the hotel until a sudden cloudburst had driven her from the pool. Fortunately, it was time for aperitifs and lunch. Suddenly fiercely hungry, she had gobbled down asparagus, steak and a mountainous gooey meringue that tasted like honeyed air. Steve and Rob had restricted themselves to a sandwich which made her feel guilty as they were probably thinking of the bill. Then she realised that they were just plain nervous about Goldie's race, which didn't stop them ordering a succession of beers to calm the jitters, so they couldn't have been considering the bill at all.

Happily the sun reappeared so she opted for her rose-red summer dress with the bootlace shoulder straps and the three of them headed for the racecourse. At the end of their abbreviated taxi ride she noticed Steve handing over a hundred euro note.

He caught her glance and raised his eyebrows. 'It's only ten when there's no racing on. They don't call it Doughville for nothing.'

There was no denying that this was a place where you needed money in your pocket. Luckily, she had some – her winnings from roulette the night before. And after her punt on the first race she had even more, despite not quite understanding the funny French betting.

Really, things were going so well that she should have expected something to spoil it. All the same, it had been a surprise when she'd dashed up to Rob, her winnings in her hand, and found Gary standing next to him.

'Hi, Gary,' she'd said, in her excitement quite prepared to overlook their recent estrangement.

He'd stared at her as if she were some kind of alien life form then turned to Rob. 'I'd better get back,' he announced and strode off through the crowd.

He'd cut her dead completely. How dare he?

Her face flushed scarlet, as if she'd been slapped. And she had been.

Tomas liked to think he didn't suffer from nerves. Why should he? Even though he was only just now making it into the big time, he'd been around a bit. He'd ridden in all sorts of places before he'd pitched up in England, he'd even had a couple of races here at Deauville. That was when he'd been a very green apprentice at a yard in Germany. He'd travelled to the meeting from Cologne in the horsebox and shared a shoebox-sized room in a *pension* ten miles along the coast. Today, courtesy of his landlord Eddie, he'd hopped a ride on a chartered jet from Farnborough and was booked into one of the ritzy hotels on the Deauville seafront. And he had three rides at the classiest meeting of the French summer season, the pick of them being on Goldeneye, the lightning-fast three-year-old with whom his fortunes were teamed.

But Ivana was not here. Life might have changed but not necessarily for the better.

He pictured his sister for a moment. She was not dead, she was with him always, she would help him today.

Then he consciously put her image aside and began to pull on his riding boots.

'It's a bit like Ascot, isn't it?' Rob said. He was trying to stay cool and detached – the seasoned horseman surveying the scene before the big race. The biggest race of his life as an owner. He'd ridden in Grand Nationals and Gold Cups but had never felt like this. Not long now, just a few minutes to go. He bounced on the balls of his feet. 'I think I'm going to be sick,' he added.

'Too many beers,' said Kathy.

'Not enough, sweetheart.'

She wormed her hand into his and squeezed. What a great kid she was. How come she and Bella didn't get on?

'It's nothing like bloody Ascot,' said Steve, looking up from a racecard covered with so many scribbles it was almost unreadable. 'The toffs don't pitch up to Ascot in shorts.'

This was true. Rob had been amazed to see the French racing aristocracy parading in polo shirts and shorts with ironed-on creases and prominent designer labels.

'I meant the course,' said Rob. 'It's a right-handed oval with a spur for the straight sprints. Mind you, the oval's not an oval at Ascot and there's a load of ups and downs but the layout's similar.'

'Give it a rest, mate.' Steve sounded grumpy, nerves must be getting to him too. 'I don't like the look of the Irish horse. Or that French one, Elba.'

By which Rob assumed Steve liked the look of these horses rather too much.

He couldn't be bothered to respond. They'd been having

this conversation since they'd boarded the Eurostar at Waterloo: which of Goldeneye's opponents was likely to cause the biggest threat. Goldie had beaten half of the eight-strong field in the Guineas so it had been narrowed down to Leading Me On, the Irish horse, and two French-trained runners.

Steve was still talking. 'The rain makes a difference. Tabouleh goes in the wet and Goldie only just got to him at Newmarket. The same could be said for—'

'They're in,' said Kathy urgently, cutting him off.

On the big screen opposite, the last horse had been loaded into the starting gate.

They were off. Thank God for that. Rob angled his binoculars across the track at the eight coloured blobs beginning their charge towards the stands.

Tomas had picked up Goldeneye's uncertainty the moment they left the parade ring and began the long canter to the start. The recent rain had made the surface sticky and it was evident that Goldie was not his usual sure-footed self.

Unfortunately the change in conditions did not appear to have had the same effect on his competitors. When the gates shot open, the other runners launched themselves forward and Tomas found himself instantly some lengths in the rear.

There was no call for panic but, all the same, Tomas was at a loss. His prearranged tactics – keep the horse handy, push the button a furlong out and rely on his finishing speeds – were of no use in this position. They were now five lengths in the rear and Goldie was tripping suspiciously over the tacky surface.

Tomas resisted the temptation to use the whip: he knew that would be a disaster. First he had to help the animal find his feet, and if the race was over by the time he'd managed it, then that would be too bad.

Sitting quietly but gripping tightly with his knees, he urged the horse to the right, away from the stands rail where most of the runners ahead were bunched. It seemed an age but eventually Goldeneye appeared to drop into a rhythm.

Maybe he'd discovered marginally better ground or had simply come to terms with the surface. Either way, Tomas didn't much care. They were a good half-dozen lengths off the penultimate runner but at least they were racing, even if they weren't yet in the race.

Though he'd ridden at the course before, Tomas was disoriented. He'd got used to the big white furlong markers on British tracks; here the poles were small and their orange discs unreadable. All he remembered from his previous experience was that, from the point where the circular main track was joined by the straight used for sprints, two and a half furlongs remained to the winning post. And they were almost at that junction now.

Tomas worked harder, squeezing the horse's back with the his thighs – *pick it up, get amongst them* – and the horse obeyed, the ground no longer an issue, the urge to run with the herd gripping him with familiar fever.

They were in the thick of it now, all their beaten rivals from Newmarket behind them bar Tabouleh but Tomas could see that he was rolling and Goldie cruised past with ease. They must be in the last furlong. The crowds were on their left and the stand was looming up. Inside him and still ahead were Elba and Leading Me On, the joint favourites. Tomas applied the whip.

Fantastic – it was like having another gear. Goldie lengthened his stride and drove with all his power.

As they passed the winning post, Tomas caught a glimpse on the big screen to his right of a brown streak with a white-blazed face thrusting his head across the line ahead of his rivals.

A jockey could only dream of being on a horse like this – but it wasn't a dream.

In Kathy's opinion the celebration dinner was the best she'd ever had. They ate lobster and drank champagne but it wasn't just the food that made the occasion memorable. They toasted absent friends: Charlie and Bella – both of whom were conjured up on the phone and forced to listen to the drunken sentiments expressed in their honour. Then Rob asked them to raise their glasses to Ivana, the one truly absent friend, and even Hal, who had never met her, looked suitably sombre for a moment.

Hal was by Kathy's side once again. It was flattering, he seemed to have been there the entire weekend, but she laughed off his suggestion of a stroll on the boardwalk, to be followed doubtless by the suggestion of a last drink in his room. Steve had asked her to be nice to him, not that she needed much persuading, but she had no intention of being that nice.

The excitement of the race and Goldie's triumph had almost wiped Gary's behaviour from Kathy's mind. It was funny how one little thing could irritate so much, even on such an occasion.

In the parade ring before the race, Rob, Steve and Kathy gathered round Gary, as they would have gathered round Charlie had he been in charge. Hal had attached himself to their group and Kathy noted the ungracious way Gary received the introduction; he could learn lessons from his father in more ways than one. Then Tomas had arrived, looking splendid in his red and black silks. He'd clasped hands with them all, accepting their good wishes with a nod of the head which could have been interpreted as arrogance. Kathy knew that wasn't so, he was just concentrating on the task ahead. She stared into his eyes as she wished him good luck but she could see he was barely present.

She couldn't make any excuses for Gary, however. She'd planned to hug him and let him know that she was living every moment of this big test with him. But, as he chatted awkwardly with the others, his eyes passed over her as if she didn't exist. And afterwards in the euphoria of victory, when Gary had allowed himself to be back-slapped by both Rob and Steve, had been pummelled and mauled by a phalanx of people he couldn't possibly know, he'd still managed to snub her.

'Well done, Gary, fantastic!' she cried, planting a kiss on his cheek, but he'd contrived not to look at her, just to accept her congratulations as if he'd never seen her before in his life.

And now, at the dinner, he'd placed himself at the far end of the table, where he was out of any kind of contact.

She wasn't going to stand for it any longer. At the risk of ruining the evening, she was going to sort this matter out. Gary was staying at her hotel so it shouldn't be that difficult to get him on his own.

Her one problem, she'd imagined, would be giving Hal the brush-off but he was far too urbane to put himself in that position. He'd taken the hint and was already arranging to take to the Calvados with Steve.

Pleading tiredness, she left the party and headed back to the hotel. She'd thought of sitting in the lobby and waiting for Gary to appear. But Gary was liable to show up with Pete, which would be awkward, especially since Pete could be guaranteed to draw the wrong conclusion. Also, she felt conspicuous sitting by herself. After ten minutes she'd been subjected to two unsolicited approaches and many inquisitive stares.

She went upstairs and rang the desk for Gary's number. If she waited directly outside his door, there was no way he could avoid her. She took up her station at eleven thirty.

By twelve she was slumped on the floor, wedged up against the door, her head pillowed on her knees. She ignored the occasional passers-by, returning to their rooms. Some laughed at the sight of her, others were openly disapproving, all of them she tuned out. She'd not been lying when she'd said she was tired; her day had started early.

A hand woke her, shaking her shoulder.

'*Mademoiselle,*' the voice was gentle, '*qu'est-ce que vous faites ici?*'

Kathy forced her eyes open. A woman in a navy tunic was bending over her, concern in her big brown eyes. There was a clipboard in her other hand – a hotel functionary of some kind.

'Er . . . *pardon, madame.*' Kathy groped for an

explanation. *'J'attends mon ami. J'ai perdu mon clef.'* I lost my key, not bad for someone who had nearly failed GCSE French.

'Oh la.' The woman made a clicking sound in the back of her throat, selected a key from the bunch hanging from her waist and the next moment the door behind Kathy was swinging open.

This wasn't exactly what she had envisaged but Kathy was not going to look this gift horse in the mouth. With a flurry of *merci beaucoups* she scrambled to her feet and into the room. It was laid out in almost exactly the same way as hers but she didn't bother to reconnoitre. She turned on the standard lamp in the far corner of the room, kicked off her shoes and threw herself onto the bed.

She was asleep in seconds.

Gary had turned down Pete's proposal to go back to the casino.

'But it's our night, man. We're winners! Anything we chuffing touch is gonna win, guaranteed.'

'You go, Pete. I'm fine.'

'Oh no. I promised your old man I'd keep an eye on you and I'm gonna. Forget the casino, you're right. What we need is beers.'

So they'd ended up in a racing bar where the visiting British were out in force, winners and losers alike, rehashing the day's events. It was a strange sensation for Gary. He'd never been the centre of this kind of attention before. He'd basked in the glow of his father's achievements from time to time but tonight the spotlight was on him, the winning trainer of the Prix Jacques Le Marois.

'My dad should be here really.' he repeated regularly. 'I'm just an understudy.'

'Bollocks,' Pete would chip in – he seemed to have appointed himself Gary's guardian – 'you've looked after this horse for the past six weeks. You're the guv'nor, son, it's in the blood.' Unlike Gary, Pete did not appear to have turned down a drink since Goldeneye had crossed the line.

Finally, people started to drift off and Gary realised he was dog-tired. It had been a heck of a day. He thought he'd made a clean getaway until he felt a hand on his arm in the hotel lobby.

'You trying to run away?'

Oh God, it was Tomas. Gary didn't think he had the strength left to deal with a man on a mission to avenge his sister.

Tomas, he knew, was stone-cold sober. Gary had watched him all evening – he always kept an eye on Tomas – and admired the air of quiet calm that surrounded him. No wonder he was such a good jockey, part of him was always ice-cool, controlling his emotions.

Gary lived in fear of Tomas. Since that conversation in the car driving back from Leicester, he'd been waiting for him to make his move. But horses like Goldeneye did not come round very often so for the time being Tomas was probably just playing with him.

'I'm off to bed,' Gary said.

Tomas nodded. 'Sensible. I just wanted to say . . .' He paused.

Gary's blood froze. What was he going to say? *I know about you and Ivana?*

'Today is a special day. We must not forget it.'

'No, we mustn't.'

'Everything went right. I was lucky and you were lucky.'

Was that it?

The grip tightened on his arm. 'But we must not forget that tomorrow it might all go bad.'

Was that a threat?

'Goodnight, my friend.' And with a final squeeze of his arm, Tomas was off.

Gary stepped gratefully into the empty lift and pressed the button for his floor.

Maybe he'd got Tomas completely wrong. How could the jockey know anything about his row with Ivana? It was just guilt that lent an edge of menace to the other man's gloomy remarks.

It was up to him, Gary, to get over what had happened. He must toughen up and live with his involvement in the woman's death. What good would it do to tell anyone? It wouldn't bring her back and it would ensure a lot of grief for many people.

Including you, said an internal voice. You coward.

He was so preoccupied as he entered his room he didn't notice the soft light shining from under the bedroom door. He stood in the small lobby, shrugged off his jacket and kicked off his shoes. He stepped into the bathroom and splashed water on his face. Lowering the towel, he found himself staring at a woman in a pale blue cocktail dress standing in the bedroom doorway.

For a second he thought he'd somehow got into the wrong room.

Then he realised who it was.

Kathy.

'How did you get in here?'

'The housekeeper let me in. I want to talk to you.'

'No.' This was wrong. He'd been doing his best to shut her out of his life, couldn't she see that?

'It won't take long, Gary.'

'It won't take any time at all.' He took two steps to the door and pulled it open. She had some bloody cheek. 'I want you to go right now.'

She stood just where she was. 'It's OK. I don't want to know why you won't talk to me. I'm not looking for an apology for the rude way you've treated me all day. I just want to know what you were doing in our yard the morning Ivana was killed.'

He hadn't expected that. He'd been looking in one direction and the punch had come from another. Thump, straight into his guts.

'I saw you from the kitchen window. You were coming down from Cape Fear's barn. I thought you were on your way to see me but you weren't. You got in your car and drove away, didn't you?'

Gary said nothing, his eyes riveted to her face. Her hair

was a tangle and she looked as tired as he felt. She was beautiful and his enemy.

And she knew.

He closed the door quietly behind him.

Steve considered the number his companion had just written on a napkin and pushed across the table, where it nestled next to his brandy balloon. He checked and rechecked the row of figures. There really were a lot of noughts.

Opposite, Hal Cheviot was returning his Mont Blanc pen to the inside pocket of his jacket. He wore his customary look of arrogant detachment and appeared to be stone-cold sober. Steve didn't know how he managed it.

It was late and most of the hotel revellers had stumbled off to bed, only a hard core of drinkers remained. Away from prying eyes, it was safe to talk business.

This was the third figure Hal had written down. Steve had laughed at the others but he wasn't laughing at this and he guessed Hal would not be improving it. The money on the table was the most he was going to get. If it had been up to him he would have jumped at it. But there was a complication.

'You're quite sure Jimmy won't settle for just my share?'

Jimmy was Hal's employer, a sheikh with a passion for horseracing almost as deep as his pockets. The sheikh had suffered a couple of blank years without a top-class horse and was looking for a prospect to change his luck. According to Hal, Goldeneye's victory in the Prix Jacques Le Marois had put him at the top of Jimmy's shopping list.

Hal considered Steve's question. It was an issue that had come up before in the course of their discussion and he looked slightly peeved as he disposed of it again.

'Jimmy's not interested in owning half a horse. He can't be arguing over trainers and jockey and races. If the sheikh buys him, he'll make all the decisions.'

'In practice, that means you, doesn't it?'

Hal's mouth twisted into a sardonic grin. 'Much as I'd

169

love to pretend I pull the strings, honesty forbids. I'm just the face of Team Jimmy. I can make recommendations, that's all.'

'So, you could recommend Goldie remains at Moorehead's yard and the Czech boy keeps the ride?'

Hal shrugged. 'I could but I wouldn't. Charlie's a good trainer but he's just had a heart attack. Who's to say he'll ever work again?'

'Young Gary knows the horse inside out. Look at today's performance.'

Hal sighed and sipped his nightcap ruminatively. 'He did a good job for this race but I wouldn't rely on a kid like that. I'd want an established trainer, not some up-and-comer.'

'He's got the benefit of his father's knowledge to fall back on. Believe me, he won't let you down.'

Hal sniffed. 'It's still too much of a risk. And the jockey's a bit of a Flash Harry in my opinion. Anyway, what's it to you once you've banked your cheque?'

'It's not that simple.' It was a question of convincing Rob to sell and Steve had a feeling that more than money would be needed to persuade him. If he could say that the purchaser had promised to keep Goldie's existing training and riding arrangements in place, it would be a help. He picked up the napkin and tucked it into his pocket. 'Let me see what I can do.'

Gary shut the door and stepped towards her, his face a mask of – what? Kathy couldn't read his expression. He didn't look like the Gary she knew. But his jaw jutted obstinately, like it had that morning in the yard when he was stalking towards his car.

He spoke softly, the words difficult to pick out at first. Then he repeated them louder. 'It's my fault Ivana's dead,' he said. 'I killed her.'

Kathy felt a stab of fear. She was on her own with an unfamiliar Gary who stood between her and her only means of escape.

But what he said didn't make sense and she saw now

that the jutting chin was trembling. He was fighting back tears.

'Gary, come here.'

She took his hand and led him into the bedroom. He fell onto the bed, the sobs bursting from deep within, the sound of his gulping breaths loud in the small space. Once or twice he tried to speak but it was impossible. She sat on the bed beside him at a loss. All she could do was hold him, rub his back, murmur, 'It's OK,' like her mother had done to her when she was a child.

Eventually his tears slowed. She went to the bathroom and, avoiding her messed-up reflection in the mirror, soaked a hand towel in cold water and wrung it out.

'Here.'

He took it from her gratefully, burying his swollen tear-stained face in its damp folds.

'Look,' she said. 'Before you say anything I want you to know Ivana was a bitch to me. Not that I wanted her dead or anything. But I didn't like her much.'

He managed a wan smile. 'Did you know she was having an affair with my father?'

'Really?' It would never have occurred to her.

He looked stricken. 'She was. I didn't know until the night before. I found my mother in a terrible state and got it out of her. I don't know if you remember but that's when you rang me.'

So that's why he'd been so odd.

'Sorry. Bad timing.'

He ignored the intervention. The words were tumbling out. 'I knew Ivana would be up at your place because your mum and Rob were out at that charity do – and so was Dad. So I went up to have it out with her. It was really stupid. As if what I said would make any difference. And it turned out she was leaving anyway. The whole thing was a fiasco.'

'What happened?'

'She was in Cape Fear's stall, mucking out. The horse was in the exercise pen.'

'What about the security gate?'

'It was shut. There was no way the horse could get at her, not when I was there, I swear.'

'But you said you killed her.'

'I must have done.'

He caught the incomprehension on her face. 'I mean, we had a row, of sorts. I told her to lay off my father and did she realise that she was making life hell for my mother and she just laughed. So I chucked the wheelbarrow of muck into the stall and locked her in.'

'Locked her in?'

'I shut the door and put the peg in the runner. You can't open it from the inside, can you?'

Kathy thought about it. Thought hard. 'No.'

'I was so angry with her I left her to stew. I knew someone would come along eventually and free her. I never thought she'd try and get out by moving the security gate back.'

Kathy was still chewing on her thought. 'And that's why you said you killed her?'

He nodded. 'I'm the one who trapped her in. She wouldn't have gone into the stallion's yard if it wasn't for me. I was sure I'd be found out. I spent days waiting for the police to come and question me and they never did. Then I realised that I hadn't been seen. At least, I thought I hadn't been, not till now.'

'I watched you come down from the barn. I waited for you to come to the house but you didn't. You just drove off.'

'I was angry. She'd made such a fool of me.'

There was silence. They were sitting facing each other on the bed. He leaned forwards and grabbed her wrist. 'Have you told anyone you saw me?'

This was the moment she could lie. If she didn't trust him, it would be the right thing to do.

'No, Gary. I never mentioned it.'

'You didn't tell Tomas?'

She blinked in surprise. 'No. Why would you think that?'

'Because he thinks someone killed Ivana. I thought he suspected me.'

'But you didn't kill her.'

He took his hand from hers. 'I'm responsible, Kathy. I blocked off the only safe way out because I was angry. In my heart I wanted her dead and suddenly she was. I can't get around it.'

'Yes, well . . .' She got off the bed and opened the minibar. There was Coke – just what she wanted. She'd had enough of the fancy French booze. She knocked the cap off the end and drank from the bottle. That was better. Time to put him out of his misery.

'Look, Gary, I'm telling you that you did not kill Ivana. I found her, you know that, don't you?'

He should. It had been widely reported and she'd been a witness at the inquest – though, come to think of it, he'd not been present. In the circumstances, she wasn't surprised he'd ducked it.

She took another swig and continued. 'I went up there after you'd gone. I was curious because you'd come from the direction of the barn. I thought Rob might have come back and gone straight up there. But he hadn't and I was the one who found her.'

'I'm sorry,' he said.

She ignored the remark. 'The point is, I ran round to the stable door, grabbed a broom and tried to push the horse off her. Luckily Rob came along. It was foul and bloody and I was in a panic but I remember everything. It all happened in slow motion and I can replay it in my head. And that door wasn't locked.'

He stared at her, almost as if he wanted to contradict her.

'Gary, there was no peg in the runner. I'd remember if I'd had to bend down and undo it, believe me.'

'You mean, Ivana could have walked out of the stable door?'

'Yes.'

'But the horse got her first.'

'He must have done.'

'Jesus.' He looked at her strangely. 'You're not just being nice to me, are you? You know, saving me from myself because what's done is done and you don't want to see me suffer?'

173

She suppressed the laugh that rose within her. If she started she wasn't sure she could stop this side of hysteria.

'Get real, Gary. Have some Coke.'

He took the bottle from her and emptied it down his throat. Then he grinned. 'There was really no peg?'

'No.'

'But I put it in. She tried to open the door and couldn't. She must have found a way of dislodging it.'

Kathy nodded, marvelling at the jaunty way he now yanked open the fridge to extract another bottle. It wasn't often you got a chance to lift a burden of guilt from someone's shoulders. She was glad she'd had her thought.

Then she had another.

'I suppose,' she said, 'that someone else could have come along after you and opened the gate.'

His arm froze halfway to his lips. 'And then what happened?'

But she had no answer to that.

Rob didn't feel like going to bed. Anyway, what was the point in turning in when Steve would come blundering into the room in the early hours? He'd seen his roommate ensconced in the bar with that oily Cheviot bloke and had chosen not to join them. He'd also noticed Hal chatting up Kathy and didn't want to encourage him. Doubtless it was pure class prejudice on his part but he couldn't warm to the bloke. You didn't come across many of his type when you were up to your knees in horse muck in the Black Country.

He strolled outside and walked the boardwalk in the balmy night air. There were still lots of people about, couples mostly, holidaying Parisians and visiting race-goers, or so he assumed. He wished Bella was by his side. It was the first time they'd been apart since their marriage. He had the urge to call her but it was one in the morning and she'd be asleep, in preparation for her customary early morning start. Besides, they'd already talked since the race.

174

The last time just a couple of hours ago. It wouldn't be fair to wake her up, even if it was to tell her how much he missed her.

She might give him a hard time about money and harbour some unexpected prejudices – like those against Ivana – but who said marriage was easy? They loved each other, that was what mattered.

He'd reached the end of the boardwalk and turned round to stroll back past the rows of beach cabins named after film stars. Away to his left the sea swished companionably on the sand and a soft breeze snatched at the furled beach umbrellas. He stood aside to let a group of exuberant youngsters pass by on the way to some nightclub. They didn't give him a glance, which was fine by Rob. He felt content in his anonymity.

Ahead he saw a familiar figure approaching: Steve. He was on his own, Rob was pleased to see.

Steve was beaming, Rob guessed there was no reason to ask why. They were the owners of the horse who'd won the day's biggest race at the classiest meeting of the French summer season. And they were due to share a prize of around £200,000. Rob felt his own face split into a grin as he greeted his old friend.

Steve pointed down the beach. 'Fancy a look at the sea?'

They stepped off the covered walkway and crunched their way across the sand, out of the fringe of the light cast by the boardwalk lamps.

They didn't speak, there was little left to say. There were stars in the night sky and softly hissing waves broke in squiggles of white surf just a few feet in front of them.

A perfect night to follow a perfect day.

So why did Rob feel a flutter of anxiety as Steve cleared his throat? Maybe he hadn't brought him down here for a moment of companionable celebration.

'Hal Cheviot's just made me an offer for Goldeneye.'

So there it was. The ulterior motive exposed – he knew his friend well.

'How much?' He had to ask, it was what you did because,

apart from anything else, it gave you time to control that lurch of panic in your guts.

'Two million.'

Jesus H. Christ! He didn't have to work out what that would mean because the sum was so large it needed no calculating. His share would wipe out the mortgage, fund all the stud refurbishment they had planned and then some.

'Hal says the sheikh's in love with Goldie. He's never had a Breeders Cup winner like his brother. He's desperate.'

Rob was silent. He could have said a lot of things. Such as: if Goldie could win a Breeders Cup race in the States for the sheikh he could win for them too, and if they sold him he'd just vanish from their lives, whisked off to some state-of-the-art training operation. And though Rushmore would suddenly be solvent and set fair for the future, he'd never have the chance to bring his home-bred Classic winner back to stand at stud as he'd been dreaming of.

Doubtless all these things would soon be said. And Steve would counter. Anything could go wrong with a horse. He could break a leg tomorrow and never even make it to America, let alone win a Breeders Cup. The time to cash in was now. A bird in the hand and all that.

There were other opinions to consider. Bella would consult her calculator, look at the proposition in the way he should but couldn't. This was business. Bella, he was sure, would not think twice about selling Goldie for the right price.

But he knew his father wouldn't have sold and he wasn't going to give up without a fight.

Steve had fallen silent, waiting for his response.

'Can I think about it?' said Rob.

'Sure you can, mate.'

The waves were still murmuring on the sand and the night air was like a lover's kiss on his cheek. But Rob didn't notice any of that now.

Kathy was sitting on a chair, Gary on the bed opposite her. She supposed she ought to go back to her own room but she hadn't achieved what she'd set out to do when she'd come in search of him. Not directly anyway. Somewhere along the way her anger had disappeared and her mission with it.

All the same. 'So are we OK now?'

He looked puzzled. 'What do you mean?'

'You're not going to avoid me? Ignore me in conversation? Look through me like I'm not there?'

His shoulders slumped a fraction. 'I'm sorry, Kathy. You mucked me about and I decided the best way to handle it was . . .' He shrugged. 'I don't think I'm much good with girls.'

For goodness' sake. 'Don't be wet. Anyway I'm not "girls". We're connected.'

He thought about it. 'My dad showed me the card you sent him. He was chuffed.'

'How's he doing?'

'It's slow. He says when he comes back he's going to lean on me.'

'So he should. You did a great job today.'

'Come off it. It's Pete and the lads back home more than me.'

'Whatever.' She yawned. She didn't really want to go back to her own room. 'Budge over,' she said, getting to her feet.

'What?'

'I'm tired. Can I lie down next to you?'

'I'll sleep in the chair.'

'Don't be stupid, there's plenty of room.'

He fetched her a glass of water, arranged the cover over her and lay down by her side. She closed her eyes.

Sometimes it was better to be with someone. Not just anyone: a friend.

Part Three
Autumn

Chapter Eleven

Jason was disappointed to see that Rose had taken the day's *Racing Beacon* from his jacket which was hanging in the hall. He kicked himself, he should have left the paper in the car but he'd wanted to go through the runners before tonight's meeting.

Rose was reading the page he'd marked up so maybe she hadn't seen the spread on Deauville and everything would be all right.

She looked up as he approached and he could see that things weren't right at all. She had that tightness around her mouth and her full lips were stretched thin, making her look tense and angry. So she had seen the pictures of the victorious runners at the chic French meeting.

He really should have left the paper in the car.

'Three hundred thousand euros,' she said with bitterness in her voice, 'that's what you get these days for winning the Prix Jacques Le Marois. I don't think Dad got even a tenth of that when he won.'

He wouldn't have done, it was probably back in the eighties. But Jason leapt on this remark – a meander down Memory Lane might cheer her up.

'I didn't know Geoff had a winner at Deauville.'

'Why shouldn't he? He had winners all over the world. Whippersnapper won the Prix Le Marois just after my twenty-first birthday and Dad gave me ten thousand francs to play roulette. I lost it all. He thought that was very funny. It was the first time I'd ever been in a casino.'

Her mouth was softening, returning to its usual pretty shape. He had the urge to kiss it but he daren't. Still, his strategy was working.

'Whippersnapper was a nervy little horse. He had a white splash on his face too, a bit like this Goldeneye. We all expected big things of him but he never won another race.'

'Maybe Goldeneye has shot his bolt too.'

Rose shook her head. 'I don't think so. He's the best miler around.'

Jason knew better than to contradict her. When it came to Flat racing, he trusted her judgement implicitly. He thought it no accident that old Geoff's gambling knack had deserted him once his daughter wasn't by his side at the races. The thought gave him an idea.

'Why don't you come with me tonight, Rosie?'

'No thanks.'

'But I don't understand, you never go to Hampton Waters and it's right on the doorstep.'

'You know I don't enjoy all-weather racing.'

She always used the artificial surface as an excuse but Jason wasn't entirely convinced. They'd had trips to Wolverhampton when she'd got just as carried away as any day out to Epsom or Newbury. Horseracing was one thing Rose was passionate about.

'Come on, love, we can say hello to Uncle Jim.' Jim was the groundsman, he'd been there for donkey's years.

She shook her head. 'I saw Jim yesterday. That's quite enough.'

The little flame of jealousy flickered inside him for a moment. Was she boxing clever? Pretending that her only interest in Jim was as a fellow worshipper on a Sunday morning?

If so, she was very convincing. In all honesty, father figure or not, Jason didn't believe Rose was interested in his strait-laced uncle in that way. There was something funny about the way she went to church with him though. Rose wasn't religious, he knew that for a fact. And if she knew Jim wasn't going to be at the service she wouldn't go.

'All right then.' He gave in gracefully. He could see that he wasn't going to persuade her and it was time he was off. He hadn't yet missed an evening meeting at the new Hampton Waters course.

If she wasn't coming with him there was one thing she could do. He pointed to the paper. 'What do you fancy then?'

Her eyes dropped to the page and the race listing.

'Doctor Wu in the first is a possibility,' she said.

He took a pen and placed a large cross beside the name. She had a bloody good record at Hampton Waters. He'd have a fiver on it.

Kathy was excited. She was hovering at the counter just inside the door of Steve's betting shop in Seymour Street. The result of the first race at Hampton Waters, Doctor Wu, had just been announced and a queue was forming in front of the pay-out window.

She'd been hoping to see the woman from the previous week amongst them but the statuesque figure was not present. Nor was her blue van in the car park – Kathy had looked. It was a pity. Kathy had been looking forward to resuming their duel and this time she was determined not to let the van out of her sight.

Some people – her mother for one – would have thought her mad to be so keen to work on her first night back from France. But Kathy had unfinished business. Not that she'd told Steve what she was up to. He wasn't in evidence. On the train back he'd said he was off home to catch up on his kip – he'd certainly looked like he needed to. Kathy was short of sleep too, but so what? If she didn't get after van woman tonight she'd have to wait another week.

There were other females in the queue, collecting money. Forget about the large woman, one of these would do. She'd already had a word with Jerry who was overseeing events behind the counter. He hadn't been surprised when she'd asked him to help her, he knew all about the beating they were getting at Hampton Waters.

A small middle-aged woman in a suit was accepting a

healthy bundle of notes from the counter clerk, quickly folding them so they fitted into her purse. She seemed flustered, as if she couldn't wait to get out of this unfamiliar environment.

Kathy looked through the glass screen at Jerry. He nodded. The lady in the suit had just picked up her winnings on Doctor Wu.

She wasn't blue-van woman but she would do. Kathy followed her out of the shop, relieved to see her advance upon a Honda Accord parked three doors down. Kathy walked quickly to her own car across the road, her heart thumping, all tiredness gone. This was it.

The woman took her time. She made one phone call, then another. Go on! Kathy urged, eager to get going.

At last the woman started the car and moved off, nervously entering the line of traffic. As a driver, she was a different proposition to the blue-van woman. This lady drove hesitantly. No chance here of being left in the starter's blocks.

The Honda driver gave Kathy a different set of problems. Apart from driving slowly, the woman was plainly unfamiliar with the route she was following. She crawled through the town traffic, dithering at junctions and only signalling at the last minute. Kathy, trying to lag behind and ape the woman's movements, found herself unpopular with her fellow road-users. Maybe it was a natural hazard of tailing someone, you ended up getting hooted at.

The woman eventually found her way onto suburban roads where there was less traffic. Now she stopped to consult a piece of paper, forcing Kathy to pull over abruptly thirty yards back. After a minute the woman started off again and Kathy had no choice except to follow. She hoped she hadn't been spotted but reckoned it unlikely. This driver was barely attuned to the manoeuvres of other vehicles.

Now they were moving down a narrow road of stone-clad houses bristling with satellite dishes. The woman ahead was driving slower than ever and Kathy had a feeling the end of their journey was at hand as Honda woman crawled along, maybe looking for a house number. At last she stopped and began an elaborate parking manoeuvre. Kathy reversed into a handy space and waited for developments.

After a lot of back and forth the woman emerged and carefully locked her car. Then she crossed the road and rang the bell of a smarter than average semi with a neatly trimmed hedge and a clematis with purple flowers on a trellis. The front door opened, welcoming the visitor inside without offering a glimpse of the interior or the occupant.

Kathy settled back to wait. To be honest, she was starting to doubt the wisdom of this expedition. She should have gone over to Gary's, like she'd told Mum. Though she was intending to do that later.

The hotel in France seemed a world away now. She'd stayed in Gary's room all night. They'd not touched once, just lay side by side, dozing and talking. Breathing the same air. She didn't feel about Gary the way she'd felt that night at Steve's. She'd been desperate for Steve to kiss her, to squeeze her in his arms. She'd have gone to bed with him if he'd asked and it wouldn't have been just to talk.

But she'd not felt like that about Steve since. The Ivana business had changed everything. She was so relieved she'd not let him make love to her. As it was, there was something about Ivana turning up and the way he'd turned his attention to her that made Kathy feel a bit soiled. Even the horror of the next day hadn't completely wiped that away.

Thank God she'd mended it with Gary. Being close to him, sharing their secrets and fears through the night, had felt good. She didn't know whether she fancied him, or he her, after what had happened. She just felt close to him, properly close for the first time, and that was good enough.

Twenty minutes had gone by and the woman was still inside. Maybe she was visiting for supper. Kathy might as well go to Gary's now. His dad was looking forward to seeing her too, and her mum, so he'd said on the phone. Time to go now, then home to bed and some proper sleep.

Only one thing stopped her. What on earth was a woman like that doing in a bookie's? A middle-aged ditherer who double-checked her car locks and took five minutes to park. Was Steve's business being ripped off by an army of maiden aunts? It didn't make sense.

Just when Kathy was about to quit, the door reopened and the woman emerged. This time Kathy got a look at the householder, another woman. It was hard to tell her age. It could be the same as her visitor but comparing the two was like measuring chalk against cheese. Even in a loose shirt worn over jeans this other woman was upright and elegant. Her hair was thick, a rich chestnut tangle that fell to her shoulders, and her face handsome.

The pair said goodbye with an elaborate politeness that did not suggest intimacy. So they probably weren't related, or even friends. Kathy wondered about Honda lady's careworn suit. Maybe it was some kind of business meeting. She'd been inside for twenty-five minutes, time enough to drink a cup of coffee and discuss – what? Life insurance? The next school governors meeting? The local fete? On the face of it, it didn't seem likely to be a betting scam.

The woman was back in her car and revving the engine unnecessarily. Kathy supposed she'd have to follow her and hope that this time she went straight home. Then she'd have an address she could give to Steve and leave him to follow it up.

She had her hand on the car key, about to start the engine, when she caught sight of a familiar shape in her wing mirror. A blue van coming down the road, indicating that it was about to park. She did not turn the key.

The blue van slipped into the space vacated by the Honda and the woman she'd followed before, unmistakable in her bulk, strode across the road and rang the bell of number 19.

Kathy took her phone from her bag. She'd better let Gary know she might be some while.

Gary put his phone away. If Kathy wasn't coming over just yet, he had no excuse not to talk to Tomas who, at this moment, was downstairs with his father. And the talk might be difficult.

Be honest, it might be an effing disaster. And it wasn't a talk anyway, it was a confession.

But it was the right thing to do. Last night, when Kathy had lifted the burden of guilt from his shoulders, a load of fear had gone with it. He wasn't proud of the part he'd played in Ivana's death and he'd been particularly ashamed of the lies of omission he'd told to Tomas.

He could put that right now.

Downstairs he heard the click of a door and his mother's voice. She was showing Tomas out.

He took the stairs two at a time.

'I didn't know you were back,' his mother's voice accused. 'We've just been raising a glass to Tomas's marvellous ride yesterday. You could have joined us.'

'Sorry, Mum.' He hoped she hadn't been raising too many glasses, though to be fair she was looking like her old self these days. There was something to be said for his dad being laid up; his mum was now firmly back in the box seat and thriving on it.

'I thought I'd take Tom out for a quick drink now,' he added.

Tomas shook his head. 'Can we do it another day?'

'I'll walk you to your car. I just need a quick word.'

If Tomas was surprised to be escorted ten yards to his vehicle he didn't show it. He said a polite goodnight to Louise and the pair of them stepped outside.

'What do you want?' the jockey asked as the door closed behind them. His face looked drawn in the lingering dusk. 'Everything's OK with Goldeneye, isn't it?'

It occurred to Gary that Tomas was regarding him simply as the trainer of his best ride.

'He's fine.'

The jockey looked relieved. 'You don't mind if we don't go for a drink?'

'No, but I need to talk to you.'

'Can't it wait?'

'If I wait, Tom, I'm scared I'll never have the nerve to tell you at all.'

Gary led him round the side of the house to a garden bench that faced a bed of roses. The scent enveloped them as they sat down. Gary opened his mouth.

Where to begin?

Rose was still trying to call Dee, her last punter, when she heard Jason's key in the lock. The silly girl must have turned her mobile off. Knowing her, it had probably run out of juice.

Apart from Dee's failure to show up on time, tonight's operation had gone well. All her other ladies had turned up and the cash was stowed out of sight upstairs. The safe had been a brainwave and Jason had installed it without a murmur, even accepting that it was exclusively for her use. Weren't husbands meant to be more suspicious? She had a gem in Jason, in so many ways.

However, she could have done without him appearing at this juncture, before Dee had shown up. She would have liked to have stashed all the money before Jason came home.

She met him at the door.

'How was it?' she asked. She hoped he'd had some luck. For a former jockey you'd think he'd be a better judge of what might win.

He pulled a goofy grin, one of his standard expressions. 'All downhill after the first, I'm afraid. I did my lot.'

She rolled her eyes. 'How much did you lose?'

He calculated. 'About sixty quid, I reckon. Half of that was what I won on the first so let's say thirty. Sorry, darling.'

She wanted to laugh, except it might be misinterpreted. He'd lost thirty pounds and he was sorry. Her father had lost millions.

'Never mind,' she said with a straight face.

At that moment the snarl of a motorbike engine sounded in the street and a bike squealed to a halt in front of their gate. The rider jumped off and headed towards them with a swish of leather. It was Dee. Jason gazed in amazement as she swept off her helmet and a mass of red ringlets tumbled out.

'Sorry I'm late,' she began. 'But I was watching the baby and I couldn't get off till my auntie came round and then she kept me yakking. She can be a right old gasbag sometimes. Howdja do.' This was to Jason, who was giving her one of his mad grins – with justification, in all fairness.

Rose was forced to make the introduction.

'Lovely to meetya,' Dee continued, scrabbling inside her jacket with her free hand. 'Anyhow, here it is,' she was pulling out banknotes. 'Six hundred, all right? I think it's all there. He bloody well bolted up, didn't he? I watched it in the shop.'

Rose took the crumpled bundle, folded the notes into a discreet wad and slipped them into her back pocket. All the same, she could sense Jason's eyes on her every movement.

Dee was stuffing the helmet back onto her head and issuing further excuses for being late and now, sorry, don't want to be rude, but she had to shove off smartish because she was meeting some bloke in a pub and it was bloody miles off. She vanished in a roar and the street fell silent.

'One of my sales girls,' said Rose quickly. 'She's quite a character.' She steered Jason inside, indiscreetly spilling information about Dee's complicated personal life and working out what she was going to say about the money when he asked – and he was bound to ask. Just as soon as she let him get a word in.

Kathy had witnessed the whole scene from across the street. She'd thought she'd done pretty well even before the motorcycle girl arrived, but this was even better.

The woman at number 19 had had a succession of visitors throughout the evening. After Honda woman and the driver of the blue van, a string of other females had pitched up at the door. They had disappeared inside for only a minute or two though some stayed longer. Only one had transacted her business on the doorstep and that was the girl on the motorcycle. Most revealing it was too, confirming all Kathy's expectations.

What's more, while the blue-van lady had been inside,

Kathy had got out of the car and strolled past the van. There wasn't much to be seen in the front, apart from mess – a balled-up sweater, crisp wrappers, takeaway coffee cups. But in the back, she managed to glimpse boxes through the rear windows.

Kathy didn't dare linger. She returned to her car. The boxes contained what looked like clothes catalogues and, from the number of them, maybe this woman was some kind of sales rep.

She wondered, as she finally slipped the car into gear and drove off, if all these visitors were sales reps too, selling designer-imitation dresses and suits. It might explain why they were all women.

But not why they were taking Steve to the cleaners.

Jason allowed Rose to babble, which was significant in itself. She never ran off at the mouth like some women. He appreciated that. She'd fetched him a whisky which, again, was out of character. He'd once come home a bit squiffy from the races when he'd run into an old mate and ever since she'd suspected him of boozing on his nights out. Tonight, though, she'd poured him a hefty few fingers of Famous Grouse of her own accord. He might be excused for thinking she wanted him pissed – and forgetful.

'Is she punting for you then?' he asked as she handed him the glass. No point in beating about the bush.

She knew what he meant but pretended not to. So he spelled it out.

'Is that girl putting bets on for you?' he asked. It was all he could think of. Maybe Rose had got herself barred at some bookies and used someone at her work to place her bets. 'Only what's the point of that? If you want money on, I'll do it for you. I'm not a man who minds his wife having a flutter. Bloody hell, given what you and I have been up to in our lives, what would be the point of that?'

Rose looked him in the eye. 'Dee is not betting on my behalf, Jason. She follows the horses so I gave her a tip, that's all. Like I did with you.'

That was true enough but it didn't explain everything.

'What about the money? She gave you six hundred quid. So she said anyway.'

'That's quite separate. That's money for orders she's taken over the past month.'

Rose was still looking at him in that bold way, as if she was daring him to disbelieve her. His instinct was to pursue the matter. The way the girl had spoken, it certainly sounded like the money came from a bet. She hadn't said, here's the money for last month and thanks very much for that horse you tipped me. The way it had come out, it had all been one thing. And, anyway, if the money was from catalogue sales, shouldn't there be paperwork with it? An invoice record to show who had paid for what?

Unless there was something hooky going on. Though he couldn't believe that of his wife. She was as straight as they come.

All the same, he had to ask. 'This is above board, isn't it, Rosie?'

Her gaze was unblinking. 'Of course. I know it looks a bit odd but Dee's just disorganised, that's all. I wouldn't keep her on if she wasn't such a good seller.' She laid a hand on his arm. 'Promise me you won't worry about it.'

He covered her hand with his. 'I promise.'

What else could he say?

When Gary had finished, the pair of them sat in silence. He wasn't sure how he had expected Tomas to react. He might have attacked him physically or shouted abuse or even walked off into the night, never to speak to him again. Instead he said nothing. The narcotic perfume of Louise's old-fashioned tea roses, Blue Moon and Silver Wedding, hung heavy in the air around them.

'I'm sorry,' Gary said. He'd said it several times.

'Why didn't you tell me this before?'

'Because I thought I was to blame. I thought that by locking Ivana in I'd forced her to go out through the exercise pen and the stallion had attacked her.'

'And you were scared of owning up.'

'Yes.' He couldn't hide from that basic fact.

'But now you're not scared.'

'I'm bloody petrified, if you must know. You could go and shop me to the police. Tell whoever you like. Bash my head in with a brick or something.'

'I won't talk to the police, I told you that. The brick is not a bad idea though.'

Tomas's voice was calm and he was joking. That was something.

'I am so sorry,' Gary said again.

'You English apologise too much. I can understand you hated my sister at that moment. I'm ashamed she was playing around with your father. I should have done something about it.'

Relief flooded through Gary. He'd been expecting a hard time.

'What could you have done?'

Tomas exhaled heavily. 'I should have tried but my sister's love life has always been bad news.'

Gary seized his chance.

'So, it's not going to spoil our friendship?'

Tomas shook his head. 'I'm grateful you told me. Your information is very interesting.'

There was silence. From somewhere inside the house came the rumble of Charlie's voice.

'I'm glad your father is getting better,' said Tomas. 'But we've done all right without him, I think. You and me make a good team.'

In the dimness the jockey held out his hand and, with relief, Gary took it.

Rose hated lying to Jason but it was for his own good. She waited till he was watching TV before she slipped upstairs and put the money in the safe with the rest of the cash.

She knew how things would look if she got caught. The police would put her through the wringer and Jim too. That was only to be expected. Girls like Dee and all the others who wagered for her would also be questioned but they weren't on her conscience. It wasn't a crime to put a bet on for someone and that's all she asked them to do. And none of the women did it that often anyway, as she made a point of rotating the request. With an area sales force of 150, she had plenty to choose from. And even if some of them ended up enduring an unpleasant hour or two, they'd been paid and, of course, they could bet their own money on her tip. Most of them took advantage of that. So far, nobody had turned down a request to place a bet on her behalf.

But if things turned sour, then Jason would also be in the firing line. This troubled her a great deal. As a former jockey, he'd probably be seen as the instigator of the fraud. She hated to think of him being blamed along with herself and Jim. Even if he escaped jail, he might well be warned off racing like her father had been. What a terrible irony that would be.

The only way she could think of protecting him was to keep him absolutely in the dark. If the worst came to the worst, he could genuinely plead innocence and she and Jim would make it as clear as they could that Jason had played no part. Jim was in whole-hearted agreement that the exoneration of his nephew was an absolute priority.

There was one other way to protect him, of course. That was to stop the scam.

But not yet.

In Tomas's situation, many people would have been angry with Gary. To have withheld the story of what had happened between him and Ivana just a few minutes before her death – some might have found that unforgivable. But Tomas was aware that in his circumstances he didn't have the luxury of falling out with the present trainer of Goldeneye.

There was more to it than that. Though he resented not having been told all the facts – and during those car rides together to and from the racecourse when he had confided in Gary, surely his confidences could have been reciprocated? – at least he knew them now. And he had been

193

honest when he'd told Gary he understood his quarrel with Ivana. The guy had been watching his parents' marriage fall apart around him. His sister had a lot to answer for. She'd been selfish with her pleasures and done damage.

But she didn't deserve to die for it.

At least now, thanks to Gary, he had a better idea of what had happened to Ivana. Someone had been responsible for her death and it wasn't Gary, no matter how stupidly he had behaved. Someone else had been there that morning. He'd always suspected it but now he knew. Someone had unlocked the stable door and gone into the box with Ivana.

And then what?

He didn't know but at last the picture was becoming clearer.

Chapter Twelve

Envy filled Rob's heart as he drove through the white gates of Lonsdale Manor Stud and up the never-ending drive flanked by shimmering green parkland. Here were some five hundred acres laid out for a state-of-the-art operation that he and Bella could only dream of. Lonsdale contained one hundred and fifty boxes with seven isolation yards and employed a permanent staff of twenty, augmented to almost thirty during the covering season. The five standing stallions produced a stream of high-achieving offspring who, in turn, fed the demand for Lonsdale stud services and upped the covering fees. Just one of those stallions would revolutionise his own business.

At least he had the prospect of Goldeneye standing at Rushmore – provided Steve didn't get his way. He banished the thought for the moment.

The purpose of his visit was to check out the double foaling boxes that had recently been installed at Lonsdale Manor; a friend had put him in touch with Tania, the stud manager. It was also on Rob's mind to look over Lambrusco, Lonsdale's newest stallion and a classy performer in his racing career. It might be worth sending a mare to be covered by him next season.

Tania was a cheerful Scots girl who found a stud hand to show him the stallion. The animal was a perky show-off, only too keen to parade for Rob, and afterwards Tania played him a video of the stallion's racecourse victories.

As they left the office, Rob caught sight of a figure

crossing the opposite corner of the yard. For a moment he struggled to place him and then remembered with sudden clarity: Vladimir Petrov, the fellow who'd visited Rushmore the day before Ivana's accident. He'd not heard from him since but if he was interested in these Lonsdale stallions it was not much of a surprise.

'Hey, Vladimir,' he called out but the man did not break stride, instead he speeded up.

'Excuse me,' Rob said to Tania as he ran after the fellow.

Petrov had disappeared round the corner but was still in sight as Rob followed. His hand was on the door of what might be a tack room.

'Vladimir – Mr Petrov.' The man turned.

Rob wasn't mistaken, it was him all right. The hawk face was unforgettable.

'Rob Harding,' he said as he caught up to his quarry. 'You looked round my stud farm back in May.'

The man's face showed no recognition. 'You mistake,' he said in a heavy accent. 'I no know you.'

Rob was flabbergasted. Surely this was the man who'd visited his yard, laughing and joking? But that man had spoken fluent English, with an accent certainly, but not thick like this.

'You came to visit my stallions. You said you might send a mare to me next season. I've been waiting for you to get in touch.'

The man shrugged, his ponytail jogging on his neck. 'I no understand.'

Rob stepped back, no longer certain of himself. 'I'm sorry. I was sure it was you.'

'No problem.' He knew that much English anyway.

With a nod of his head, the man stepped into the tack room and closed the door in Rob's face.

Rob retraced his steps to Tania who looked at him with curiosity. He apologised for running off.

'I thought I knew that fellow.'

'Micky?'

'I thought he was called Vladimir.'

'His real name's Milos.' She pronounced it Meelosh. 'He got us all to say it one night in the pub but he answers to Micky.'

'He doesn't have an identical twin, does he?'

She laughed. 'Not that I know of.'

'How long has he worked here?'

'Since February. He's on a short-term contract but I think he might stay longer. He's an entertaining fellow.'

Entertaining? That didn't fit the profile of the man who'd barely stumbled through a conversation just now. Though it did fit the man who'd shown up at Rushmore.

'His English isn't up to much.' Rob was irked, he felt he'd been shown up as a fool, running after a complete stranger. 'Where does he come from?'

'The Czech Republic. Actually, his English is pretty good these days. You should come down to the Duck sometime and meet him properly.'

Rob shook his head, he had to get back. There was no point making an issue out of this.

But as he walked back to his car he noticed another vehicle parked nearby that reversed his best intentions: a dirty white Escort with a crumpled front bumper – the same car that 'Vladimir Petrov' had emerged from that day at Rushmore.

He felt like marching back up to the yard and demanding an explanation from the man who'd just lied to him. But what good would that do?

Get over it, he urged himself. But he thought of nothing else as he drove home.

When Steve had inherited his father's bookmaking chain, he thought he'd acquired a licence to print money. After all, the old man had done well out of it. When his father had died and he'd laid claim to the family home and the business, naturally his two sisters had to be kept happy. Steve had mortgaged to the hilt and beyond to pay them off. Again he thought how foolish he'd been to have refused the offer from Fairweather's.

So the last thing he needed this morning was to discover that he'd been turned over at Hampton Waters again last night. He shouldn't have gone home to catch up on his sleep. He'd taken his eye off the ball and lost another twelve grand. Jesus. That was a chunk of his prize money from the win at Deauville down the drain already.

Thank God for Goldeneye, was all he could think. He had money owing in every direction and those bastards over the road were deliberately trying to sink his only asset. But he owned half of a horse who was coveted by a man with a bottomless fortune. Steve needed the sheikh's money in his hand today, if not yesterday. Needed it like a drowning man needs a lifeboat.

Rob's agreement was crucial. He hadn't actually come out and said he wasn't prepared to sell but Steve knew the signs. Why not apply a bit of pressure?

He picked up the phone. 'Hi, Bella. Is Rob at home?'

He knew damn well he wasn't because Rob had told him about some trip to a stud near Newmarket. But it was time to broaden the discussion about the offer on Goldeneye and he sensed that, on this topic anyway, he and Bella might see eye to eye.

He wasn't altogether surprised to learn that she knew nothing about it. He lost no time in bringing her up to date.

Rob found Bella waiting for him when he got back and she didn't look much like the contented wife who'd seen him off. Their reunion after the Deauville trip had been almost as good as the trip itself.

'I should go away more often,' he'd said as they lay in bed, feeding each other the cheese and pâté he'd brought back from France.

'Not without me,' she'd said. 'The presents are lovely but I'd rather be with you.'

He had brought her back an outfit from one of the smartest boutiques in the rue Eugene Colas. Luckily Kathy had been on hand to give advice but it would have been better if Bella had been there. All the same, his gift – funded in the carefree knowledge that Prix Le Marois winnings would offset the credit card bill – had been well received.

It had been a fine homecoming but now, from the look on Bella's face, it was hangover time.

'Steve rang,' she said.

Rob could guess what was coming next.

'He wanted to know if you'd made your mind up about the offer on Goldeneye.'

There was accusation in every syllable. He'd not told her about the offer. For one thing, he'd not wanted to spoil the mood – it would have hijacked their reunion completely. For another, he wasn't sure how to tell Bella that he'd cut his right arm off rather than sell the horse. Perhaps he should say just that.

Instead he apologised. 'I didn't want to spoil things last night.' Her face softened. 'Did Steve tell you the size of the offer?'

'Yes.'

'So I suppose you want me to accept.'

'No, Rob.' She looked exasperated. 'I want us to sit down and discuss it properly. Let's do some figures and work out what's best for you.'

'Us.'

She grinned – that was better. 'The business.'

It was as he'd imagined. She wanted to get the calculator out.

'Let's get on with it then,' he said with a heavy heart. In his experience calculators never delivered good news.

But to Rob's surprise, Bella's methodical way of assessing the deal did not necessarily favour selling Goldeneye. It was possible to predicate an even more lucrative – and fun-filled – future by keeping him. If he stayed healthy. If he could land at least one more big race as a three-year-old. If he was able to perform at stud.

If Goldie could do these things they'd be mad to sell him.

In assessing the profit and loss on a horse's future they needed a crystal ball not a calculator.

'So what's your gut feeling?' said Bella.

'Do you have to ask? I want to keep him. What's yours?'

She considered, her full pink lips turning down at the corners as she thought. 'You think I'm a mercenary cow, don't you?'

'I think you're better with figures than me. More level-headed.'

'I know, sensible.'

'If you like.'

They were facing each other across the table in the kitchen. She placed a hand over his.

'I couldn't bear it if I turned on the TV and saw Goldie winning a race somewhere and he was no longer ours. I'd be heartbroken.'

Quite. That was exactly how he felt.

He leaned across the table and kissed her fiercely.

Kathy sat before her computer screen, rerunning the first race at Hampton Waters again. She'd already watched Doctor Wu's comfortable victory three times. The horse had slipped effortlessly into the lead from the start and he'd stayed there without appearing to break sweat. He'd won by six lengths but she had the feeling it could easily have been more. On previous form he'd looked to have little chance against the two horses behind him but who knew?

The lady at 19 Black Vale Avenue.

Kathy was in a quandary. Her impulse was to tell Steve all about her exploits last night, how she had tracked down the source of his losses from Hampton Waters.

But if she did that, she knew what his response would be – he'd send in the heavy brigade. The thought of being responsible for Len showing up at Black Vale Avenue turned her stomach.

On the other hand, the woman was cheating Steve's business out of serious money. Just because she looked like a harmless suburban housewife didn't mean she wasn't a thief. She could even be in league with Fairweather's, in charge of a team of punters dedicated to putting Steve out of business – and her out of a job.

Even put like that, she didn't want Len involved any more than he was already. Someone could get hurt – the woman with the chestnut hair, or the little man with a face like a garden gnome who seemed to live there with her.

Also, if she told Steve and he handed it over to Len, that would put an end to her own involvement. She'd enjoyed her sleuthing around so far and was reluctant to bow out now.

Her theory was that the women placing bets distributed the catalogues she had seen in the back of the blue van, probably for a company based in Otley Manor Business Park. A sales force would provide a ready-made pool of people able to place bets, wouldn't it? Obviously the woman and the man organised them.

She had their address, and she wondered what else she could find out about them.

The door opened and Steve stepped into the office. The face of a carefree racehorse owner, fresh from a Group One triumph in France, had been replaced by the look of a businessman staring down the barrel of misfortune. Last night's loss must have been substantial. For a moment, she considered telling him what she had found out but just at that moment the phone rang.

She answered it. 'Stephen Armstrong. How can I help you?'

It was Rob. Her professional phone-answering technique was rather wasted on him.

She handed him over to Steve.

'Hi, mate,' he said.

By the time he put the phone down, the moment had passed – she'd keep her discoveries to herself.

Jason was prepared to let the matter of Dee and the money drop. He'd thought about it all morning as he made his deliveries. Much as he hated to admit it to himself, he was sure Rose had been lying. He replayed Dee's comments as she handed the notes over and he had no doubt she'd been placing a bet for Rose. In which case, he felt a number of

201

things. One of them was that it was none of his business. He'd been brought up to respect a man's betting habits. If a mate was playing the horses and wanted to keep the details to himself, that was his affair. And, when it came down to it, though this mate was his wife and, by definition, a woman, what difference did it make? If Rose wanted a bet on the side she was entitled, provided she didn't land them in bankruptcy like her old man.

That led to another thought. People's character flaws ran in the blood, it was well known. Though she'd always seemed the reliable one, Rose was her father's daughter. He hoped she wasn't going to go off the rails like Geoff.

So he'd have to keep an eye on her – surreptitiously, because he didn't want her to think he no longer trusted her. And he did trust her in everything else. Even in the matter of her funny church-going with Jim.

He felt happy enough when he came to this conclusion. So what if she had a few hundred on the odd runner? Actually, given her record, she was probably well ahead of the game. He was embarrassed to think she had given him the tip of the night and he'd won thirty quid, which he'd promptly lost, while she'd finished six hundred to the good. Still, next time it could be different.

When he dropped home at lunchtime to grab a sandwich, he ran into Mrs Forsyth from opposite, encouraging her constipated sausage dog to crap in the gutter.

'There were a lot of people at your house last night,' she said. 'Do you have a regular social engagement on Mondays?'

He didn't know what she was talking about.

'I just happened to notice when I was taking Darcy for his walk. Lots of strange cars in the street. People coming and going from your door. Then I realised it was Monday. Not that I mind, though I did have to turn the wireless up a bit.'

He finally managed to untangle what she was saying and apologised for disturbing her. The gathering, he explained, must have something to do with Rose's work.

Indoors, he puzzled over the information as he worked on

his cheese-and-ham sandwich, which he ate without tasting despite the extra mustard.

So Dee had not been Rose's only visitor last night. There'd been a string of them popping in and out. And this was a typical occurrence on a Monday evening according to Mrs Forsyth.

His first instinct was to dismiss this as rubbish, Mrs F was not the most reliable of witnesses. He couldn't recall any evenings when people had called round one after the other. But he was often out on Mondays – at the races.

There was no reason to think that these other mystery visitors were punting for Rose as well. As he'd said to the neighbour, it must be to do with Rose's work. She was always on the phone to 'her girls' of an evening. They were women with other part-time work, children to care for, full lives to lead. According to Rose, one of the advantages of being a catalogue sales agent was that you could fit it round the rest of your life. These days, both employer and employee had to be flexible.

Did flexible mean taking part in a regular Monday night betting coup?

Surely not. At most he'd seen one woman hand over cash for one race and he'd built this whole mountain of supposition on it.

All the same, as he thought about it, he wished he knew what was in that safe he'd installed upstairs.

Rob hadn't seen Charlie Moorehead in a week or so and the difference in him was marked. He'd lost his ghostly pallor and seemed to rely less heavily on his stick, though he kept it by his side all the time.

'So,' Charlie said, 'which race are we going for next? The Queen Elizabeth?'

The Queen Elizabeth II Stakes was the last big contest of the season for three-year-old milers. Charlie had been arguing that it was the logical next step for Goldeneye and would provide an opportunity to end the season with a bang.

'It makes sense,' Rob said.

'You don't sound sure.'

The hesitation in Rob's voice did not stem from any misgivings about the race. But it was only fair to mark Charlie's card about the offer for Goldeneye.

The conversation with Steve had not gone well.

'I've decided I don't want to sell,' Rob had said.

There had been a sigh of disappointment on the other end of the line. 'It's a heck of a lot of money.'

'Yes, I know.'

'Have you talked it over with Bella?'

'She doesn't think I should sell either.'

'Really?' Steve had sounded surprised. He'd probably been banking on Bella being seduced by all those noughts. Well, he'd got it wrong.

'She thinks like I do. It's not every day you get to own a Classic horse. We don't want Goldie running under anyone else's colours. When it comes down to it, it's not about the money.'

'Jesus, mate, I wish I could afford to think like you.'

'But Steve, if he keeps improving he's going to make you even more in the end.'

There had been a long pause at that point. 'I can't afford to wait.'

So that's where they ended the conversation, in stalemate. But with a lot of other questions unanswered.

Rob gave Charlie a quick précis of what was going on. To be honest, he needed an experienced man to talk to. Even though Charlie wasn't physically fit, his brain was all there. And if Charlie looked at him and said, 'You'd be foolish not to take the money,' then his stance might change. But Charlie didn't say that.

'Can't Steve just sell his half of the horse?'

'Not to Sheikh Al-Mazin. He'll want complete control.'

Charlie pulled a face. 'That puts me out of a job then.'

'And Gary and Tomas and Pete and everyone else. We'd all be reduced simply to watching him on the TV. I'm not having that.'

'You can't blame Steve for wanting to cash in though. Can't you buy him out?'

Rob laughed. 'I wish.' He'd spent half the afternoon doing figures with Bella but they simply couldn't stretch that far. If he'd not been so cavalier in destroying Cape Fear they might have had a chance. But he'd been right to put the stallion down.

'What about you?' he said to Charlie. 'We could be partners.'

The trainer shook his head. 'I'd love to but I can't risk it. Not if Steve's looking for a million. It wouldn't be fair on Louise and Gary if anything went wrong.'

They sat in silence for a moment.

'Steve could force a sale,' Charlie said, 'if he's really determined to sell.'

Rob was aware of it. Goldeneye could be entered in the September horses-in-training sales at Tattersalls and, if Rob wanted to keep the horse, he'd have to bid for it, in effect raising the money for Steve's half anyway. And he'd probably be bidding against Hal Cheviot. He might even have to pay more than he was being offered at the moment.

The truth was, he probably couldn't afford to keep the best horse he'd ever had. It was sickening.

Kathy didn't want to get involved in the dispute over Goldeneye. It was an awkward situation, with her boss wanting to sell and Rob looking to squash the deal.

'Sometimes,' Steve had muttered with scorn, 'your stepfather is a complete prat.' As if it were *her* fault! And then he'd stormed out of the office.

Kathy could understand why he was so uptight. She saw the bills going across his desk, not to mention Fairweather's and the Hampton Waters losses. But she could also understand Rob's point of view and, personally, she'd be really upset if he cashed Goldie in now. Then there was Gary – he'd be heartbroken.

So her loyalty was being pulled in two directions. Especially when Hal Cheviot came on the phone.

'Kathy, sweetheart, I do hope you've recovered from that tedious weekend in Frogland.'

She'd laughed, she couldn't help it. She'd never met anyone as affected as Hal before.

'I should imagine Stephen's told you I'm trying to take the divine Goldeneye off his hands for an extortionate sum of money.'

Kathy couldn't imagine any sum of money would be too great where Goldie was concerned and she said so.

'What a loyal little treasure you are. And wasted in that provincial backwater. If you could persuade your boss to extract the digit and give me a favourable answer I'm sure I could find you a far superior position.'

Kathy allowed the double entendre to pass without comment but she noted it all the same. Did she want to get involved with this character?

'I'll tell Steve you're waiting for his call.'

'Don't bother, darling. I've left messages on his mobile. I only rang this number for the delight of talking to you. We must get together soon.'

'Love to, Hal.' In your dreams, she thought.

After she'd finished her daily chore of logging the previous day's races onto DVD, she was left with her customary boredom. Naturally, she returned to the issue of the woman in Black Vale Avenue.

She had her address, therefore she must be able to find out her name. If she were a real detective she'd bet it would be easy. Note down the numbers of the cars outside and check them on the Police National Computer – that's what private eyes did in the books she read, since they were all ex-cops or had contacts in the police. But she didn't know any policemen.

There were direct ways, like knocking on the door and pretending to be doing market research or petitioning for something. A couple of times, at school, she'd gone down streets trying to get sponsorship for a charity swimathon. Lots of people got all snotty and refused to cough up because they didn't know her. But some were really generous, and she'd come away with their names and addresses.

But maybe, despite their benign appearance, the people in the house were genuinely shady. If she thrust herself so blatantly into the firing line, she might be putting herself in danger. There must be other ways. Like the electoral roll. Only didn't you have to start with a name, not the other way round?

She typed 'electoral roll' into Google on her computer and clicked on the UK electoral roll site. Within seconds she had the answer to her query: no, she did not require a name, she could do a reverse search based on the address for the princely sum of £6.50.

'Brilliant,' she said out loud as she typed in her credit card details.

It didn't take long for her answer to appear: Jason Francis Sidebottom was the voter registered to 19 Black Vale Avenue. There was no mention of a Mrs Sidebottom or another adult. Still, one out of two wasn't bad, providing it was the same man.

She typed 'Jason Sidebottom' into Google and got over fifteen thousand hits – academics and members of school teams, some called Jason and some Sidebottom. She linked the two words and the list dramatically shortened. And she had him.

He was a former jump jockey who had retired some ten years ago – which was one reason she hadn't recognised the name. Another would be that he was hardly a legend of the turf. In his best season he'd managed just over forty winners, most of the time he averaged considerably less.

This page of biography supplied a photo of Sidebottom in his prime, a small moon-faced figure barely recognisable as the bulky character at the door of number 19. But the print was vintage. There was no mention of a woman in his life but, this being an archive of jockeys past and present, that was hardly surprising.

No matter. Kathy felt a sense of triumph. After all, who needed friends on the force and access to the PNC? She gave herself a pat on the back, which was more than she'd be getting from anyone else. She'd keep this information to herself.

Rob had just got off the phone to the vet when Tomas appeared in the stud office. Rob had a list of other calls to make, not to mention more practical tasks. His long weekend was catching up with him, together with the realisation that they would have to replace Ivana soon – unless he could persuade Kathy to give up her office job and sign on full-time at the stud.

'Bella says she found some of my things at the cottage,' Tomas said. 'But if you're busy I'll come back some other time.'

Rob shook his head. He was pleased to see the Czech jockey.

'Come up to the house. She left a bag for you somewhere. I'll see if I can find it.'

'Look,' he said as they walked across the yard, 'you ought to know that Goldie might have to go to the sales.'

That stopped the jockey in his tracks and Rob could understand why. If the horse changed hands, there was no guarantee Tomas would keep the ride. In fact, if Goldie ended up in the hands of the sheikh, it was certain he would lose it.

'I'm trying to avoid it,' he continued, 'but we've had an offer and Steve wants to accept it.'

Tomas said nothing.

'If I were you, I wouldn't worry about it. I just didn't want you to hear it from anyone else.'

The jockey nodded. 'If you want my opinion you would be mad to sell that horse. We haven't seen the best of him yet.'

Rob agreed with him all the way but it didn't make him feel any better.

At the house, he found the carrier bag Bella had put aside. He handed it over. Tomas looked inside and lifted out a navy blue cable-knit sweater.

'I thought I'd lost this. Very good for the winter.'

He held up a pair of pink espadrilles. 'These are Ivana's. Perhaps they would fit Bella or Kathy.'

Rob took them, suddenly aware of how sensitive this matter was.

'Or just throw them away,' Tomas added.

'I'm sure they would love something of Ivana's.' He wasn't at all certain that was true, but the white lie seemed permissible in the circumstances.

There was an awkward silence as Tomas replaced the sweater in the bag. Rob cast around for something to say.

'I met a fellow countryman of yours yesterday, at a stud in Newmarket.'

'A real Czech? For sure?'

'To be honest, no. Nothing's for sure about this fellow. I've met him before and he spun me a line.'

Tomas's smooth brow creased in puzzlement. 'What do you mean?'

'He came up to the stud and I showed him round because I thought he was an owner. He spoke good English but when I ran into him yesterday he pretended he couldn't understand me.'

'Was he definitely the same man?'

'Apart from the fact he looked identical, he drove the same car. I've got no doubt about it.'

'What's his name?'

'When he was pretending to be an owner he was Vladimir Petrov. Yesterday he was called Milos.'

'Milos.' Tomas echoed the word, his voice expressionless.

'That's right. One of the girls there said they called him Micky and he spoke good English. Not to me he didn't.'

Tomas made a brittle sound, like a laugh that had died in the back of his throat. 'You want me to go with you and talk to him?'

'There's no need to get involved.'

'I could speak to him in Czech and find out what's really going on with him. Maybe there's an explanation and you can still do business.'

209

Rob considered the offer. Frankly he didn't think there was a hope in hell of doing business with the man – he was an obvious time-waster. But he'd love to see the look on his face if he turned up with an interpreter. That would put his big nose out of joint.

'Are you serious?'

'Deadly serious, my friend.'

Chapter Thirteen

Gary was taken aback by the favour Tomas asked of him. It meant laying his hands on an item that wasn't, technically, his and handing it over to the Czech jockey, but it was only for one night.

'You will have it back tomorrow, I swear,' Tomas said as Gary slid into the front seat of his car so he could pass him the package unseen. It was important there were no witnesses, just in case something went wrong.

But what could go wrong? Tomas had assured him he wasn't going to do anything illegal with the gun. He trusted Tomas and he owed him.

It was his late grandfather's pistol, a semi-automatic Colt which, reputedly, Grandad had been given by a GI during the Second World War; his dad kept it in the gun cabinet with the shotgun. Gary used to play with it on the quiet when he was a kid, until Dad caught him one day and scared him witless about stealing stuff out of the cabinet. Charlie was a big man with a loud voice and the kind of stare that went through the back of your head. He didn't need to lay a finger on a boy to reduce him to a snivelling heap of remorse.

All that was a good ten years in the past but it still played on Gary's mind. Even with his dad only able to hobble from room to room at a snail's pace, Gary was a bag of nerves retrieving the key to the cabinet from its old hiding place and sneaking into the back room. He felt like a little boy again as he lifted the old pistol into the light. He'd not touched it since his youthful crime. Funny how familiar it felt in his grip.

He wrapped it in a yellow duster and slipped it into his gym bag.

So he was feeling edgy as he sat in Tomas's car. Silly, really. He wasn't afraid of his father's temper any more. Charlie was no longer such a big man, in more ways than one. All the same, he didn't like lending out the old gun. He wouldn't have let anyone else have it but Tomas was the kind of guy who could keep secrets – at least, Gary hoped he was.

'Why do you want it?' he asked, still holding on to the package.

Tomas shook his head. 'Don't ask me.'

'Is it something to do with Ivana?'

'I can't say.'

'You promised you wouldn't do anything illegal. So why can't you tell me?'

Tomas sighed heavily.

'If you don't say, I'm taking it back.'

'OK. There's a Czech guy who used to be Ivana's boyfriend. He saw her at the Guineas – unfortunately.'

'What's his name?'

'Milos. Why do you want to know?'

'A big guy with a ponytail?'

'That sounds like him.'

Jesus. He'd met the guy at Newmarket too and he'd given him Ivana's address. He'd thought he might get into her good books.

He listened with mounting horror to Tomas's story.

And then he handed over the weapon without a murmur.

The Duck, the pub closest to Lonsdale Manor Stud, was not somewhere Rob would have chosen to spend any time. It was dark and stale-beer smelly, with piped music and noisy fruit machines. But it was within walking distance of the stud and he guessed the staff didn't have much choice.

Tania broke away from a group by the pool table when

she spotted him. She'd sounded surprised when he'd rung her up and distinctly less friendly. Then he'd twigged that she thought he was asking for a date and had hastily told her he wanted to bring a Czech friend of his along to meet Milos.

Now, as she caught sight of Tomas, he could see that he would have no trouble gaining her cooperation. She recognised the jockey at once.

'Why didn't you tell me you were bringing a celebrity?' she said to Rob.

The answer was that he didn't know he was. He'd been vaguely aware that Tomas had been picking up mentions in the racing press for his recent performances. As he listened to Tania he realised that mainstream papers had also begun to single him out. Given the jockey's overseas origins and tragic recent history, it wasn't so surprising. The fact that he was such a handsome lad couldn't harm either. Tania seemed to appreciate it.

Tomas didn't appear to notice the stir he had caused. 'Where's Milos?' he said.

Rob couldn't see him in the pool table crowd and they were the only other occupants of the bar.

Tania looked puzzled. 'He always comes in after work.'

'Did you mention that we'd be here?'

'I did, as a matter of fact.'

Damn. He should have asked her to keep quiet about their visit.

'Don't worry,' she said. 'He'll probably be along in a minute.'

Rob had a funny feeling he wouldn't be.

Tomas had been listening closely. 'So he's not coming?'

'He still might.'

'We should go to his address.' Tomas turned to Tania. 'Can you tell us where he lives?'

Rob could see that the request took her off guard. The welcoming grin had vanished from her face.

'Why don't you wait a bit longer?' she said. 'Have a drink.'

Rob was prepared to go along with the suggestions – he

213

didn't want to antagonise her. But Tomas, to his surprise, was keen to press the point.

'Look,' he said, stepping closer to Tania, 'I don't know Milos personally but I believe he knew my sister.'

Rob saw the change in the girl's face. She knew about the accident at Rushmore. Everybody in the business did.

'So,' the jockey continued, 'it is very important for me to meet him. Do you understand?'

Tania was already writing on a piece of paper she'd pulled from her bag.

'He lives in a village about five miles away. He's got a flat in the house opposite the post office.'

'Good.' Tomas almost ripped the paper from her grasp. 'We must go.'

Rob lagged behind as the jockey marched to the door, embarrassed by Tomas's abrupt manner.

'I'm sorry about this. He's not normally so—'

'Rude? That's OK.' The smile was back on her face. 'Just get your friend to give me a call and he can make his own apologies.'

Tomas was unlocking his car as Rob stepped out of the pub. They had arrived in separate vehicles at the jockey's insistence.

'Wait up, Tom. I'll come in yours and you can drop me back here after.'

Tomas shook his head. 'You should go home now. I'll go see Milos and talk to you later.'

What?

'Don't be ridiculous. I want to hear what he has to say about wasting my time.'

'We will be talking in Czech. It will be boring for you.'

Rob considered the jockey's stern face. He seemed like another man altogether from the polite and friendly fellow he thought he knew.

'What's going on? Why did you spin that line about Milos knowing Ivana?'

'Because she did.'

The jockey's gaze was unwavering. Rob realised he must

be telling the truth – there was no point in lying to him, after all. He waited for Tomas to continue.

'She met him years ago back in Czechoslovakia when she was working at our uncle's stables. He was her first boyfriend but he turned out to be crazy.'

'Crazy how?'

'He wanted to lock her up and keep her for himself. And he was also cruel to the horses. She wouldn't stand for that. That's why she came to England, to get away from him. But he ran into her at Newmarket, the day of the Two Thousand Guineas.'

'So what was he doing at my yard?' But Rob knew that was an unnecessary question even as he uttered it. Milos may have posed as a customer but it sounded like his real purpose was to see Ivana.

And he had seen her. Rob remembered the moment when Ivana had appeared on the other side of the yard and he'd called out to her. She'd run away.

'Is that why Ivana wanted to leave so quickly?' he said.

'Yes. She was petrified of him. I told her she should stay where she was and tell him to get lost. She said he'd come after her anyway – and she was right.'

'What do you mean?'

'That day, after he'd been up to the yard, he went down to the cottage and tried to get in. She managed to get away to Steve's. She rang me later and told me about it.'

'So . . .' Rob was trying to make sense of this information, 'what is your purpose in finding Milos now?'

Tomas considered the question. 'I want to look the bastard in the eye and ask him if he murdered my sister.'

Rob gaped at him. He'd always thought Tomas was a well-grounded guy but maybe he'd been mistaken.

'You're joking, right?'

'Believe me, I wouldn't joke about this.'

'Look, mate, nobody murdered Ivana. It was a terrible accident, the inquest said so.' Rob didn't mean to be insensitive but Tomas was coming over as a bit flakey. Losing your sister might do that to you.

Tomas stared at him hard. Rob had not noticed the delicate brown of his irises before, shading to black at the rims. The look was a challenge.

'You think Ivana would have been careless?' The emphasis lay heavily on the last word. 'You really think she would have been so stupid as to go in with that horse?'

Rob had never thought that. It had always worried him but Tomas didn't give him a chance to say so.

'The coroner was a nice man. Very kind to me. But he did not know Ivana or that bastard horse. She was terrified of him.'

'So what did happen, Tomas?'

'I don't know for sure. But someone else was at the yard.'

What?

'How do you know that?'

'I can't tell you.'

'Of course you can bloody tell me.' Rob was getting angry.

'Please, my friend. Don't ask me to betray a confidence. The security gate was pulled back and Ivana would never have opened it.'

And Curtain Raiser's stable rubber was in Ivana's pocket, guaranteed to rouse Cape Fear's fury to fever pitch. But Rob hadn't told Tomas about that and he didn't intend to mention it now. He was more concerned about what Tomas was going to do next.

'You can't go on your own,' Rob insisted.

'It would be best if you don't get involved.'

'Bugger that, I *am* involved!' Not as deeply as Tomas maybe but it was true enough. It was his yard, his stallion and the whole terrible business was on his plate. He couldn't avoid some of the responsibility. Unless Ivana really had been murdered.

Tonight was Jason's turn to be alone in the house. Rose was having one of her regular suppers with Mrs Summersby, an old friend of her father's. As a rule he accompanied her, even though an evening with Pat Summersby could be a chore. Old Pat had enjoyed a middle-aged fling with Geoff in years gone by and his death had granted her the status of honorary widow – at least in her eyes. Personally, Jason reckoned it was one of Geoff's better decisions in his later years to have staved off a trip down the aisle with Pat. And, given the parlous state of Geoff's finances at the end, a lucky escape all round.

Secretly he knew that Rose agreed with him, she would have hated to see her father remarry. However, she was loyal to Auntie Pat and enjoyed their chance to get together and chew over more glamorous days. Tonight Jason had cried off – there was a limit to the amount of reminiscence about old Geoff that a man could take.

In any case, it gave him an opportunity to get to grips with the mystery of Rose and the money.

He realised that, to many men, his willingness to install a safe for his wife's exclusive use might seem incredible. He knew that one or two of his old mates made jokes about exactly who wore the trousers in the Sidebottom house. Not to his face they didn't though and, when he looked at the blowsy drudges they were hitched to, he knew who had got the better bargain.

Rose had asked him if he minded her keeping the combination to the safe secret. She explained that she intended to use it to store sensitive documents in connection with her work. 'It's not that I don't trust you,' she'd said, 'but if any of this stuff leaked into the hands of our competitors there might be legal repercussions. If you don't know the combination, then no one can suspect you.'

So the secrecy was to protect him. He hadn't really believed her and now he reckoned it was a load of baloney for certain. Rose was up to some dodgy punting scam and she was stashing the proceeds in the safe. And – this thought was even more disturbing – if she had one secret from him, how many more might there be? Like the mystery of Jim.

He reckoned he could handle almost any discovery about Rose except the fact that she might have another man in her life – though surely not his strait-laced bible-bashing Uncle Jim. But suppose there was someone else? When you set out to pry into a loved one's secrets, you had to be prepared to discover the worst. And the worst was the idea of another man lying in bed with his Rose, enjoying the kind of easy intimacy that he longed for and which she found so hard to give. If she was involved with another man then he didn't know how he might act.

At any rate, he had been happy to go along with Rose's scheme to put in her personal safe and the kind he'd chosen – approximately fifty centimetres square with a door pocket, a shelf and seven live-locking bolts 'for extra security' – was opened by means of an electronic digital lock. He could have chosen a model operated by keys, or both key and code combined but, as he'd explained to Rose, a digital keypad was much simpler. All she had to do was programme in a five-digit code and she had no dilemma about where to hide the key.

Jason did not know the code she had chosen. But he did know his wife. Though their married life together could be measured in months rather than years, he was familiar with her habits. He knew the PIN numbers she used for her cash card, her mobile phone and for security access to their joint account. What's more, he knew the passwords she used for her internet accounts – for the online bookstore she used and the racing forum she occasionally signed on to. And he had every confidence he could guess almost any password or code she might devise for security purposes in the future because Rose always used the same one, give or take a number or two, depending on requirements. She wasn't naïve enough to choose her own birthdate as a template, she chose her father's instead.

Geoff Wyatt had been born on 31 March 1931. His lucky numbers, he always said, were 3 and 1 or any combination of the two. He never shied away from 13.

So, though Jason could say with absolute truthfulness he did not know the code for Rose's safe, he was pretty damn sure it would be 31331.

He tapped in the numbers and held his breath. If the first sequence didn't work he knew a number of variations.

Beep. A green eye winked on the keypad and the door lever yielded to his grip. He was in first time, just as he'd expected.

Finding Milos's address took a while. Privately Rob thought they should have spent more time getting precise directions from Tania. Eventually they found the right street. A terraced row of houses faced the post office and a dirty white Escort with a crumpled bumper was parked outside. At least the object of their quest was at home.

'Maybe you should wait in the car,' said Tomas.

Rob rejected the suggestion irritably.

'For your own good,' the jockey added. 'I don't want to land you in trouble.'

'There'll be trouble if I don't go. He could beat you to a pulp.'

'That will not happen.'

God knows where Tomas got his confidence from.

They got out of the car and Tomas took a jacket from the boot and put it on. As if this were some kind of formal occasion. Rob reminded himself that the jockey was from a different culture. Obviously different rules applied.

'OK,' said Tomas. 'We go together but it's best if you keep quiet. Whatever I do, you stay out of it.'

'Why? What are you planning to do?'

The jockey put his hand on Rob's sleeve. 'Just trust me. I promise I'm not going to hurt him.'

Hurt Milos? The thought was preposterous, Tomas was half the other man's size.

There was no time to debate the matter as they were standing in front of the end door of the terrace, which opened directly onto the pavement: 27 Oak High Street. Tomas pressed the bell marked 27B, the address on Tania's scrap of paper.

Rob waited nervously, unsure of what reception he might get. A punch in the face maybe. He tried to put the thought of violence out of his head. It was Tomas's fault.

It wouldn't have surprised him if Milos had refused to answer but at last he heard footsteps in the hall and the door swung inwards.

The man stared at Rob. He didn't seem that surprised. 'How did you get this address?'

'From the yard. Sorry to turn up out of the blue.'

Milos's face screwed up in irritation. 'I told you. I no speak you.' Not that again.

Then the big man's face changed. Tomas, who had been standing to the side of the door, now stepped into view.

The two men exchanged remarks in Czech which sounded polite enough to Rob. He noticed that the jockey had inserted his body into the doorway and, after a moment, Milos stepped back and held the door open. They were being invited inside, albeit with bad grace.

As they entered a scuffed lino-covered hallway and followed Milos through an internal door and down a narrow staircase, Tomas turned to Rob and flashed a quick thumbs-up. Rob wasn't exactly sure what that meant.

The basement flat stank of cigarettes and fried food. The living room had a partially curtained-off kitchen area where dirty plates were piled high in the sink. Rob took a seat on the sagging sofa next to Tomas while Milos faced them from a creaking wicker chair. Rob noticed a decent looking music player and an untidy rack of CDs; a guitar was propped in the corner. They were not offered refreshment.

Tomas and Milos spoke fast, in Czech. The pair of them, it seemed to Rob, expressionless in their delivery. He couldn't read anything from their faces.

Suddenly Milos turned to him. 'I'm sorry. I came to look round your place for fun, that's all. It's interesting for me to see how things are done in this country.'

His English sounded pretty good now.

'You've found your tongue, I notice.'

Milos smiled sheepishly. He understood. 'Forgive me. I was ashamed to have tricked you. Sometimes, as a foreign person, it is the easy way.'

Rob could see that. 'I understand. Apology accepted.' It was that simple – from his point of view.

Milos smiled in proper Petrov style. 'So no hard feelings? Good. One day maybe I will have my own mare to send you.'

'Now that's settled,' said Tomas, 'we can talk about my sister.'

The Petrov grin vanished. 'I am very sorry for the terrible thing that happened to her.' He said something in Czech to Tomas, who nodded stiffly in response. A formal commiseration maybe.

Milos turned to Rob. 'I knew Ivana from Czechoslovakia.'

'Why didn't you say so when you were up at the yard?'

The big man shrugged. 'It wasn't your business. And things were complicated between us.'

'Is that why she ran away when she saw you?'

'I suppose.'

'Isn't that why you came in the first place?' Tomas cut in. 'You weren't interested in looking round, you just wanted to see my sister.'

Milos began to reply in Czech but Tomas interrupted him. 'Speak English.'

The other man looked suspiciously at Rob then said, 'I saw Ivana at Newmarket but she was not very friendly. So I thought I'd try again.'

'When she ran away from you, was that not clear enough?' Tomas's voice was cold.

'Sometimes a woman does not know what she really wants.'

'Ivana didn't want you, that was for sure. You went after her later, too, didn't you? You went to the cottage.'

Milos looked surprised.

Tomas carried on. 'She told me she was hiding inside while you were banging on the door, shouting through the letter box. She was petrified.'

'I only wanted to talk. We used to be close, like man and wife.' Milos seemed genuinely aggrieved.

'And then what happened?'

'What do you mean? I got no answer so I gave up and

came home. I was going to write to her but the next day I heard about the accident.' He shrugged helplessly. 'I wanted to go to the funeral but I was embarrassed about everything. I should have gone.'

'That's it?'

Milos nodded.

Tomas got to his feet. Rob was surprised that he seemed so easily placated but maybe honour had been satisfied. Then he saw the blood drain from Milos's face.

Rob turned. Tomas was holding a gun.

'What the hell are you doing?' he shouted.

'Shut up, Rob. I need to get the truth.'

'For Christ's sake, put the gun away.'

Tomas was standing by the fireplace, far enough away to be out of reach. He was holding the gun steadily and now it was pointing at Rob.

'Stay out of this or I'll shoot you too.'

The metal mouth gleamed in the dim light. Rob felt his insides shrink. No one had ever aimed a gun at him before.

No wonder the jockey had not wanted him to come along. What had he said outside? *I promise I'm not going to hurt him.*

Jesus Christ, he'd better not.

A string of words that Rob did not understand cascaded from Milos's mouth but his voice was urgent, pleading.

'Now,' Tomas sounded remarkably calm, 'just answer my questions. If you tell the truth I promise I will not shoot you. Do you understand?'

'Yes.' The big man's eyes implored Rob to help.

Rob sat immobile. *Trust me.* That's what Tomas had said. What else could he do?

'Where were you the next morning, after you went to the cottage?'

'I was here.' Milos's voice was soft but firm.

'Where exactly and what time?'

'I was here all night. I went to work at six thirty like I always do.'

'You are telling me you didn't drive back to Rushmore Farm?'

'Yes.'

'You're lying.'

'I'm not. I never went back. I can prove it.'

'That's what you say but I find it hard to believe a man who beat my sister.' Tomas looked at Rob. 'He used to kick her in the ribs where the bruises wouldn't show. And he branded her with cigarettes on her arms. Didn't you, you bastard?'

'Yes – yes, I did but—'

'But what? You can't justify that to me, you dog. Perhaps I'll put a bullet in you anyway. One in the stomach so you can suffer like she did.'

'Tomas!' Rob couldn't just sit here and let it happen.

The jockey shot him a withering look. *Shut up.*

'So, tell me, Milos my friend, did you not get back into your car and return to Rushmore where my sister was mucking out the big black stallion? You'd looked him over just the day before, hadn't you? You'd seen the layout of the exercise pen and the special security gate. Isn't that right, Rob?'

'Yes, it is.' It was true. Milos had taken a great interest in Cape Fear's arrangements.

'I wasn't there. I was at work, I swear to you.'

'It just seems too much of a coincidence to me that the day after you show up and look around, Ivana allows the horse she hated to attack her. Especially since I know someone was in the pen with her.'

'It wasn't me!' Milos's voice rose in pitch.

'I don't believe you.'

'Ask them at work, I can prove it, I wasn't there!'

'Say your prayers, Milos.'

Tomas's finger was whitening on the trigger.

'No!' shouted Milos. 'For the love of God!'

The finger tightened. Rob shut his eyes. There was a click. Silence.

The man on the wicker chair sat as if frozen.

223

Tomas stepped closer and thrust the gun into the other's face. *Click, click, click.* He pulled the trigger several times but there was no explosion of blood and bone.

He turned to Rob. 'Just as well I'm inclined to believe the gutless bastard.'

'Jesus, Tom!' Rob got to his feet, his knees felt unfirm. He put his hand on Milos's shoulder. 'It's OK, mate,' he said. 'You're not dead yet.'

Tomas was tucking the pistol back into his jacket pocket. So that's why he had worn it. 'Come on, let's go.'

Rob considered the seated man. 'I'll see you in the car.'

Tomas nodded. He looked at Milos. 'I'm going to check out your alibi. It had better be the truth.'

As the sound of his footsteps faded on the wooden stairway, Rob stepped into the kitchen area. He rinsed out a cup and found an open bottle of wine.

Milos took the cup from him. 'The little prick,' he said. 'I could have pulled his head off.'

'So why didn't you?'

Milos drank the wine in one gulp and stood up. 'Come. I want you to see something.'

Rob hesitated. 'You'd better make it quick.'

'Follow me.'

Milos went ahead of him down the corridor to the next door along. He threw it open and motioned Rob forward.

Was this a trick? Rob wondered. Was Milos about to get his own back for the humiliation he'd suffered?

He looked through the open door. There was a bed, table and wardrobe, dirty clothes piled on a chair, an electric guitar and a coil of cables but Rob barely took these things in.

The wall opposite dominated his sight. It was covered with photographs of a girl with pale creamy skin and dark ringlets: Ivana. Some had been enlarged, others were just ordinary sized prints fastened with pins. He stepped closer and saw pictures that had to be recent – of Ivana in the candy-striped blouse she had worn to Newmarket. In others she was younger: wielding a pitchfork in an unfamiliar landscape, posing in jeans and T-shirt in front of some rackety horseboxes, standing waist deep in a blue lake, coyly glancing over her bare shoulder.

A central image of Ivana on a white horse dominated the display. She wasn't wearing a riding hat and her blue-black hair streamed behind her in the wind; she was laughing.

Beneath this breathtaking picture gallery was a small table draped in a maroon cloth with gold trim; on it stood a crucifix and a small burning candle.

Rob stared at this shrine to the object of a man's obsession. He did not know what to say.

'I loved her,' said Milos. 'I did bad things to her maybe but I always loved her. You don't believe me?'

He'd caught the look of cynicism on Rob's face.

'I believe you.' But did that make it more or less likely that he killed her? 'Each man kills the thing he loves' – Oscar Wilde, wasn't it? But Rob wasn't about to give Milos a lecture on Victorian poetry.

'I went to prison because of her,' Milos continued. 'I had much time to think and I changed big time. I just wanted the chance to show her.'

Rob glanced again at the crucifix. Maybe Milos had discovered religion. He wouldn't be the first to find salvation after he'd hit rock bottom.

'I used to be a bit mad but not now. I would never have hurt Ivana any more, I swear. Or her brother – he has a right to be angry. You go tell him.'

Rob rejoined Tomas in the car. He had no intention of saying anything about the Ivana shrine or his conversation with Milos. Besides, he had a bone to pick.

'You complete idiot. What the hell did you think you were doing?'

'What I said.'

'He could be on the phone to the police right now.'

Tomas shrugged and started the engine. 'He wouldn't dare. Anyway, we just say he's making it up.'

Rob was still boiling. 'Where did you get the bloody thing anyway?'

'I can't tell you.'

'You pointed it at me!'

'Calm down, Rob. It was all for show, I would never have shot you.'

Rob stared at the road ahead, seething quietly. Eventually he said, 'This is England. You don't go around shoving guns in people's faces.'

Tomas laughed. 'I bet in my country I could have got some bullets. In my opinion Milos got off lightly.'

Rob thought of the look on the jockey's face as he'd levelled the gun. He did not disagree.

Jason made sure that there was no evidence of his violation of the safe. By the time Rose returned – by minicab, Pat being a famously heavy-handed dispenser of the gin and tonic – Jason had tidied everything away and was settled in front of the television, pretending to watch the news.

Rose wobbled slightly as she kicked off her shoes in the hall and allowed herself to be steadied by an arm about the waist. She even granted him a moist kiss on the cheek as he held her.

'I'm worn out,' she said. 'It's been a long day.'

And a longer evening, Jason had no doubt. He sat her down and fetched her cocoa. He couldn't abide the stuff himself but Rose was partial to bedtime milky drinks. He also filled a basin with hot water and brought towels and a flannel from the bathroom.

'What are you doing?' she asked as he knelt in front of her.

He didn't answer, just lifted her bare left foot and lowered it into the water.

'Oh,' she said in surprise. And pleasure.

He took the flannel and began to wash.

'Oh, that's heavenly,' she said, smiling at him over the rim of her mug.

She had long bony feet, strong and solid, without corns or calluses. In Jason's opinion she had beautiful feet. But then, everything about his wife was beautiful to his way of thinking. Especially tonight.

There was no evidence of marital infidelity in the safe, or any evidence of romance past or present. So those suspicions had been quite unfounded, not that they had ever been founded on anything more than his own fear.

That didn't mean the safe was empty, however. He'd found money, £8,750 in notes, and bank books. The account was in the name of R.J. Wyatt and the balance stood at £146,890.55. The accompanying documents showed a detailed record of horseracing bets: dates, money wagered and money won. Jason imagined that this was not only the product of a tidy mind but an insurance against any formal investigation. These days you couldn't pay large sums of cash into a bank account without someone asking where you had got it. These papers did just that. They also showed just as effectively how one chain of bookmakers was being systematically bled dry: Stephen Armstrong.

Jason knew how badly his wife hated Armstrong and he knew why. Revenge is a dish best eaten cold, they say. He wouldn't like to get on the wrong side of Rose.

'Ooh, that's lovely,' she sighed as he turned his attentions to her other foot, massaging the flesh of her sole as he washed. 'You have the most fantastic touch.'

He smiled silently and kept on working with his fingers and thumbs. There were so many questions spinning round his head but he couldn't ask any of them, not without revealing that he'd been snooping. How come she had a ninety per cent success rate in finding the winner of the first race at Hampton Waters whenever her team placed bets? That wasn't luck, nor even judgement. It was fixed, it had to be.

There had been no mention of Jim in the papers in the safe but Jim, the groundsman at the racecourse, had to be in on the fix.

He couldn't credit it. His God-bothering Uncle Jim who lived in a cottage with bare floors and no central heating, no mod cons of any kind, who took no strong drink or fancy foreign holidays, and who never placed a bet. Or so he said, much to the amusement of other racing folk whose prayers tended to be directed rather more to William Hill than Jesus Christ. That Jim should be fixing races was inconceivable. But it had to be.

Jason was towelling her feet dry now. The flesh was pink against the whiteness of the towel, soft and pliant under his gentle rubbing.

She'd put her cocoa aside and was resting her head against the back of the chair, her eyes closed, her mouth half open, a flush on her cheek.

If this was the most pleasure he could give her, then so be it. How he worshipped his beautiful, mysterious, devious wife.

Chapter Fourteen

Though it wasn't yet ten, by the time Rob reached home the house was in darkness. Bella must have gone upstairs and there was no sign of Kathy. But she was an independent young woman these days.

He poured himself a brandy, stuff he rarely touched, and let the strong spirit spread a warming glow through his veins. Brandy was good for shock, and shocked was how he felt after the events of the evening. Whatever you called it, a good stiffener was what he needed.

He heard the soft tread of footsteps and turned to see Bella in the doorway wearing a long white T-shirt, her bedtime attire.

'How did it go?' She knew he'd been to find Milos with Tomas.

'He's just a harmless joker.' That was true enough. He didn't intend to give her a blow by blow account. 'Bit of a waste of time. How are you?'

She put her arms round him. 'Exhausted.'

He wasn't surprised, she'd been holding the fort here almost single-handed while he'd been distracted elsewhere. They'd finally agreed to find a proper head groom to fill the void left by Ivana but so far he'd made no progress.

'I'll find someone soon,' he said. 'I'll hit the phone tomorrow and see who I can drum up.'

'I've had an idea. Why don't you get Gwen back?'

Gwen. Ivana's predecessor. The girl Cape Fear had failed to kill – just.

'I thought she'd gone to live in Ireland.'

'She's back. Louise told me she'd seen her in town waitressing at some pizza restaurant. Apparently she's only doing it until she can find some decent work.'

Rob thought about it. 'I don't know if that would work. She left in hysterics, swore she'd never set foot in the yard again.'

'But it was Cape Fear who terrified her, wasn't it? And he's not here any more.'

That was true. There were obvious advantages to re-employing someone who knew the yard and the job. Rob wondered if he could persuade her.

Bella yawned and leaned her head wearily on his shoulder. 'Louise told me the name of the place she's working at. It's on the pad in the study.'

'OK,' he said, steering her towards the door.

Pizza for lunch tomorrow then. At the present moment the thought of food made him feel sick.

'I don't know why we're watching this junk.' Kathy threw a kernel of popcorn at Gary, who was lolling in the armchair with his long legs hanging over one arm as he gawped at the television.

They were sitting in the back parlour of the Mooreheads' old farmhouse; Gary's parents had gone up to bed an hour ago.

Kathy wouldn't have minded a trip to the movies or even a ride over to one of Gary's pals, whom he complained he was losing touch with now he was working so hard. But Gary had seemed morose and said that he couldn't be bothered. He added in a half-joking fashion that, as they weren't going out together and he didn't have to impress her, did she mind if they just hung around at home? She had the feeling that he'd pulled a fast one somehow but she agreed all the same and they'd ended up mooching the evening away in front of the box.

'As a matter of fact,' she chucked more popcorn because he hadn't even looked her way, 'I know why you're watching it. You fancy the dark one, don't you?'

On screen, a bikini-clad girl with black curly hair was sitting in the *Big Brother* jacuzzi, squealing. She made sure her glistening cleavage – which she had confided to the watching world she intended to surgically enhance as soon as possible – was visible above the foam.

'No,' said Gary guiltily, looking Kathy's way for the first time in five minutes.

'Course you do. It's all right, Gary, I'm not offended. I'm not your girlfriend, after all.'

'Good point.' He turned his head back to the screen.

'She reminds me of Ivana,' she said. She waited for a response from Gary but didn't get one. So she followed up. 'You used to fancy her too, didn't you?'

She knew she'd got to him even before he turned his head. His leg, which had been irritatingly swaying back and forth, froze its motion.

'Don't bother to deny it, Gary. You weren't the only one. I'd just be interested to know if you had any luck.'

He flicked the remote and the TV shut down. Finally, she'd got his full attention.

'I never went out with her, Kathy. Honestly.'

'You'd have liked to, though, wouldn't you?

She was aware she should tread carefully. Their 'friendly' understanding was new and, maybe, delicate. She didn't want to upset him. On the other hand, real friends spoke to each other about real things.

He didn't responded to her question, just shrugged it away evasively.

'Does it feel strange to think your dad's had an affair with a girl you fancied?'

'Jesus, Kathy!'

'Tell me to shut up if you want to. I'm just curious. I can imagine how I'd feel if some boy I liked starting sleeping with my mum.'

'You really think you can imagine that?'

'Yes.' He still hadn't answered her question, had he? Maybe this was his way.

He sat up straight now and turned to face her properly.

'So how would you feel if this boy had it away with your mum?'

'I might freak out. I'd want to teach him a lesson. I might . . .' she paused. Dare she say it?

'Go on.' His eyes glittered in the dim light.

'I might lock him in a stable with a vicious stallion.'

His eyes went flat and cold, like his face. 'I guess I asked for that.'

'Gary, I'm serious. I'd do something just like you did. I want you to know it makes perfect sense to me.'

His expression softened, but before he could reply a sound from outside the room destroyed the moment. It came again. Someone was tapping on the open casement window.

It must have taken Gary by surprise as much as it did her, but he reacted quickly. All she could think of, as Gary moved across the room, was: had they been overheard? It was a hot night and the windows were open to let in the cool night air. Had their voices carried?

'Hey, Gary.' She knew that voice – Tomas. 'I've brought this back.'

'Oh, hi, Tom.' Gary leaned forward, blocking the space, but she saw something in his hand that had been passed over the sill. Then he whispered some words she couldn't catch, though she could have sworn one of them was her own name.

'Good evening, Kathy.' Tomas was leaning through the window. She got up to say hello.

'Aren't you coming in?' she asked.

He shook his head. 'No, I was just passing by.' Then he was gone.

It was odd – passing by at midnight? And what had he given Gary?

Whatever the jockey had handed over seemed to have been squirrelled away.

'What was that all about? What did he give you?'

Gary shrugged, looked shifty. 'Just some DVDs I lent him.'

So why hadn't Tomas said, here are your DVDs back? Why be so elusive?

'Go on, let's have a look then. What kind does he like?'

'Er, just action stuff. You know, *Kill Bill* and things. I've put them away.'

Already?

She decided not to quiz him any more, she'd been nosy enough as it was. But there was something about this she didn't like.

It wasn't drugs, was it? Hash or coke or something. She didn't know much about drugs and she didn't want to, they gave her the creeps. Was that why Gary had been so reluctant to go out? Because he was waiting for Tomas to show up with some dope?

'It's time for me to go.' she said.

'OK.' Did he look relieved? Whatever, she was profoundly disappointed, she'd made a real effort with him. Maybe she'd just been wasting her time.

It was almost three o'clock by the time Rob arrived at Patsy's Perfect Pizza. The end of the lunchtime service, he calculated, should be good timing for his purpose but the small stuffy room on the high street was full of people taking refuge from the summer storm outside. The squeals of tired toddlers filled the air and the staff looked harassed. Rather than find a table he asked for Gwen.

'You a friend?' said a red-cheeked girl in a tight pinafore.

'Yes.' Well, he was.

'Stay here and I'll tell her you're waiting. She's serving upstairs at the moment.'

Rob was stuck in a small corner between the till and the door. He busied himself holding the door open for mothers with buggies and laden-down shoppers with wet umbrellas. He was just beginning to wonder whether his message had got through when he heard a familiar voice.

'Rob?'

He hadn't seen her for over three years and she'd changed. Her face seemed a different shape, though it was probably just the new haircut – short, with blonde streaks –

and the make-up. He preferred her less sophisticated look of former times but he didn't say so.

'Gwen, you look great. Will they let you out of this hellhole so I can buy you a drink?'

'Not now. I've got customers waiting.'

'When then?'

'Can we do it another day? I'd love to chat but right now is a bit difficult.'

'Gwen!' a voice sounded above the general chatter, proving her point. 'Table five are asking for their bill.'

'There's a pub over the road,' he said. 'I'll wait for you there.'

'What's so urgent?'

'I want to offer you your old job back.'

'Oh.' Under the make-up her face blanched.

'Gwen!' came the voice again, insistent.

'I might be a while,' she said.

At least she hadn't turned him down flat.

The pub was a haven of civilisation after the restaurant. What's more, it had a television tuned to the racing at Warwick where Tomas was riding. Rob bought a pint and a ploughman's and settled down to watch.

Tomas had rung that morning, full of apologies for the night before. Rob had been as cold as he could manage. Tomas had used him and, despite the lad's expressions of remorse, would play the same hand exactly the same way again. But Rob found it hard to sustain a sense of injury.

Once the apologies were out of the way, Tomas had not wanted to discuss last night and Rob had decided the less he knew the better.

'I just spoke to Tania,' Tomas said. 'She said she thinks Milos was at her yard on the morning Ivana died.'

Rob wasn't surprised to hear it. If the man had been lying last night, he was a fine actor. Rob was also a bit put out. He'd just made a similar call to the stud but the stud manager had been too busy to take it.

'You spoke to Tania?'

'Why not? She put her number on the paper she gave me last night.'

On reflection, that wasn't surprising.

On the TV screen, the three thirty at Warwick had just finished; Tomas's horse had finished third.

'I see Tom is getting somewhere at last,' said a voice at his shoulder. Gwen had finally managed to get away. 'He probably won't want to know me now he's such a star.'

Gwen and Tomas had worked side by side at Rushmore when he'd first arrived. She'd been in charge of him, as Rob remembered.

'Of course he will.'

'Really? He always thought he was too good to be mucking out with me.'

Rob was surprised to hear her sound so jaundiced about Tomas, he thought they'd got on well, perhaps rather too well. He ordered the coffee she requested. 'Come up and see us and I'll get him over.'

She blew on the hot liquid. 'No offence, Rob, but I don't want to go back to Rushmore ever again. Too many bad memories.'

Rob's heart sank.

'And,' she continued, 'it turned out I was the lucky one. When I heard about what happened to Tom's sister I thought, that could have been me. It damn nearly was.'

'I had Cape Fear put down.'

'So I heard. Good for you.'

'So you won't have to deal with him if you came back to work for us.'

'To be frank, Rob, you've got a nerve asking me.'

'Come off it, I'm doing you a favour. Surely you don't want to carry on skivvying in that dump across the street? Any horse has got to be better than a bunch of squalling kids puking up pizza.'

She laughed. 'Shame on you. And you're a stepdad now and all.'

So he was. He'd missed out on Kathy's kiddy tantrums. On reflection, he wouldn't have minded them.

He grinned apologetically. 'I'm just trying to persuade you, Gwen. I never wanted you to go in the first place. I felt terrible about what happened. And since Cape Fear isn't around any more, I wondered if you might consider it.'

She sipped her coffee. Then spoke again.

'Rob, I've got to be honest. After what happened with Cape Fear I decided I wasn't cut out to be working on a stud.'

'Rubbish. You shouldn't let one incident play on your mind.'

'Cape Fear was a horrible horse, the nastiest animal I've ever dealt with, but when he went for me he was only following his instincts, wasn't he?'

'All horses have instincts, Gwen. I've never come across one as vicious as Cape Fear.'

'What I mean is, he couldn't help himself. I've never told anyone this before but it was partly my fault.'

'What are you saying?'

'I'd been mucking out that other stallion of yours, Curtain Raiser. And I'd somehow managed to take his stable rubber with me. That's what set Cape Fear off.'

Rob froze. He'd never understood that phrase about the hairs standing up on the back of your neck when fear strikes. But he did now. He felt as if he could count them one by one.

Kathy was glad the weather had turned. The fat raindrops rolling down the office window suited her mood.

Damn Gary. Damn men in general. So many of them acted like little boys. Even the so-called sophisticated ones like Hal. He'd been on the phone again, probing about Steve and the offer on Goldie, dangling carrots in front of her – dinners, jobs, weekends away – and all because he wanted to get into her knickers. At least, it amounted to that though he had a la-di-da way of putting it.

There was something wrong with her situation. She was only eighteen, for heaven's sake. She just wanted some fun with boys – and no hidden agendas.

She'd thought she might have a straightforward relationship with Gary once they'd cleared the air. And they were doing well, no heavy-breathing pressure, just good conversations, building foundations of trust for the future – when Tomas had appeared at the window last night.

Was she making too much of that? The jockey had passed something to Gary which he'd clearly not wanted her to know about. And Gary had lied about it, she was sure. She'd bet if she asked Tomas whether he'd enjoyed *Kill Bill* he wouldn't know what she was talking about.

Now she thought about it, it could have been porn: dirty-movie DVDs which Gary might have been embarrassed to tell her about, though that would have been silly. She had no objection to blue movies unless they were sick. On second thoughts, maybe she did have objections.

Anyway, Gary's furtive manner had bothered her. He didn't have to lie to her, especially when they'd been making a point of being honest with each other.

They'd talked a lot about his part in Ivana's death. That was a big thing for him to come clean about, so why would he conceal something trivial? Unless it wasn't trivial. Like drugs.

The only thing she'd kept back from him – though it was hurting her to do so – was what she'd been up to at work. She'd been dying to tell Gary about following the women from Steve's shops to Black Vale Avenue and tracking down the ex-jockey, Jason Sidebottom, on the net. But she reasoned that if she hadn't yet told her employer then she shouldn't tell Gary. It wouldn't be fair.

Last night, before Tomas had turned up, they'd discussed 'the mystery man' in the yard on the morning of the accident. There had to be a mystery man, or else how had the peg come out of the runner? It was a conversation they'd had a few times now and since there was nothing new to add, it tended to slip into silliness.

'Suppose Jacko killed her,' she'd suggested. 'He comes in secretly and sees you lock Ivana in. He opens the security gate from outside the pen and, when the stallion jumps on her, he unpegs the gate so it all looks normal.'

'Motive?' he'd asked.

'He's been carrying an unrequited passion for Ivana for so long he can't bear to see her leave. He'd rather she died so no one else can have her.'

Gary hadn't been impressed. 'Pretty feeble, Sherlock. Jacko was at the market with his dad that morning, he told me. What about your mum?'

That had taken her by surprise.

'It doesn't have to be a man, does it?' he said. 'She gets back with Rob, nips up to the stable before him and does the business with the gates.'

'But why?'

'Jealousy. She thinks Rob has had a fling with Ivana and wants her gone. You told me they'd been rowing over her.'

'Yes, but Mum knew Ivana had just handed in her notice. There's not much point in killing her under those circumstances, is there? Anyway, you lay off my mum. What about yours? She's the one with the real motive.'

His face fell. 'Very funny.' He'd picked up the TV remote. 'Anyway, it's all bollocks. It was an accident.' And he'd clicked the TV on.

Come to think of it, he'd been pretty moody even before that sneaky business with Tomas.

Damn Gary.

Rob asked Gwen to explain again. He couldn't understand how an experienced hand could mix up the stable rubbers. More to the point, he couldn't fathom how two experienced hands, Gwen and Ivana, could do the same thing.

Gwen told him she'd simply stuffed it into her pocket after grooming Curtain Raiser and forgotten it.

She stirred her second cup of coffee thoughtfully.

'I wasn't thinking.' She was repeating herself. 'My mind was elsewhere.'

Rob waited for her to carry on. After a moment she spoke again.

'I'd just had a row with someone. A man. I told him I was

going to have his baby and he . . .' Her milky blue eyes were big and wet. 'He asked if it was his.'

He nodded. On the surface, it didn't seem an outlandish question.

'I told him of course it was. And it was, I was in love with him. And I thought he loved me too but it turned out he didn't.'

'And that's what he told you that morning?'

'Yes. Just before I started work, so it was all going round my head. He was horrible to me. I realised he'd just been stringing me along because I was a handy shag and now he didn't want to know. And what's more, I was pregnant and what the hell was I going to do about it? So maybe me carrying the wrong stable rubber was some kind of death wish. What do you think?'

Rob ignored that question and asked one of his own. 'What happened about the baby?'

'Cape Fear solved that problem for me, didn't he? I had a miscarriage that night and the bastard father said, every cloud has a silver lining. I think he thought I'd go back to warming his bed twice a week.'

Rob covered her hand with his. 'I'm sorry, Gwen.'

She managed a smile. The milky blue eyes were dry now. 'I appreciate your offer, Rob. But I can't possibly come back if there's any chance of running into him again.'

'Why? Who was it?'

She shook her head. 'I'd rather not say.'

It didn't matter. Rob had a pretty good idea from the remarks she'd made earlier and from his recent observations. Girls liked Tomas no matter how he treated them – look at Tania the other night – and there was no denying that the Czech jockey could be a ruthless operator.

'Good to see you, Rob, but I'd better get back to work.'

He was sorry to see her go. She was wasted in a pizza parlour but he could understand how she might prefer it.

Kathy had never been in a car accident before. She didn't know whether to laugh or cry.

Strictly speaking it wasn't much of an accident. 'A minor shunt' was how the policeman referred to it when summoned by the driver of the other vehicle. Mrs Greening was an elderly party barely large enough to see over the steering wheel. In Kathy's opinion compulsory re-testing of senior citizens couldn't come quickly enough.

'You don't look old enough to have a licence' had been Mrs Greening's opening gambit after her ancient Volvo tank had lumbered into Kathy's path as she tried to shoot up the inside lane. 'You're just a child. I've been driving for forty-seven years.'

You'd think in that time the old bat would have learned to look in her wing mirror.

The galling thing was that the other woman's car bore hardly a scratch. Kathy's front bumper and driver's headlight had not been so fortunate. She hoped that would be the extent of the damage.

'Sorry, love, it'll be off the road for a bit,' said the man in the garage. 'I'll give you a call in a day or two.'

Kathy cursed the slippery road, doddery old drivers and the fragility of cars in general as she trudged back to the office in the rain. But most of all she cursed herself. She'd been going too fast. And the reason for that was the glimpse she'd had of a blue van in the distance. It was like a reflex at the moment, whenever she saw a vehicle that resembled one of those she'd followed from the bookie's, she was after it in a flash. Too much of a flash.

Finally she had a stroke of luck – Steve was actually in the office. He could give her a lift home.

'Are you all right?' he asked as she threw her coat on the floor and slumped into a chair. She must have looked frazzled for he made her a cup of tea and listened to her woes.

'My car's off the road. Mum's going to be furious.'

'I'm sure she'll just be thankful you're not hurt. Are you sure you're OK? You can get a delayed reaction to these kind of things.'

He was being nice to her. She supposed now would be a good time to tell him she knew the identity of one of the people who was ripping him off. But the thought of Len kept her mouth shut.

'I've got an idea,' he said. 'How do you fancy dinner on Monday night?'

The proposal took her by surprise. He hadn't made this kind of overture to her since her first week.

Monday seemed a funny night to pick.

'You've not been to the big restaurant at Hampton Waters racecourse, have you? Fantastic views of the track.'

Of course – there was another evening meeting.

'Is this business or pleasure, Steve?'

'I hope it's going to be both.'

'I just want to know if I can refuse.'

He shook his head. 'I'd take a dim view of that. It wouldn't do your career prospects any good in this organisation.'

She laughed, as he no doubt intended. 'OK, I'll come.' She wondered if Jason Sidebottom would be there. It could be interesting.

'Excellent. Hal would never have forgiven me if I'd not brought you along.'

'You never said he was going to be there,' she protested.

'We're privileged. His Highness's representative on earth rarely deigns to bless us with his presence. He must have really got it bad for you.'

'In that case I'm not coming.'

He chuckled. 'Don't be daft, Kathy. He's got his eye on a horse. And you're coming all right. You can have the afternoon off to make yourself look particularly smashing.'

The exchange still rankled as he drove her back to Rushmore. She wasn't sure she wanted to be railroaded into an evening in Hal Cheviot's company. Then she thought of something that cheered her up. Gary would be really pissed off.

She couldn't wait to tell him.

Bella was not pleased to hear of the damage to her old Fiesta. But most of all, when her daughter appeared at the door, looking bedraggled and white-faced, with the word 'accident' on her lips, she'd felt an instinctive lurch of alarm. She flung her arms around her and hugged her tight, as if the intensity of her grip could wipe out the bad memory. Not that you could do that for your children.

She got Kathy indoors and sat her down in the kitchen while she made tea, listening to the story of the whole drama – which didn't turn out to be all that dramatic. Naturally she invited Steve in too. It had been kind of him to look after Kathy and bring her home. To be fair, all her misgivings about his interest in her appeared to be unfounded.

'Do you mind if I go and have a bath?' Kathy said as she finished her tea. 'I feel such a mess.'

It made sense.

'I'll be off,' said Steve.

Bella was surprised. 'Don't you want to twist my arm about selling Goldie? Now's your chance. Rob's not here.'

'I would if I thought it would make any difference.'

Maybe it was her opportunity to have a go at him. 'Steve, you do realise you're giving up something very special, don't you? He's a once-in-a-lifetime horse.'

He shrugged. 'You might be right but I need money now. You won't change my mind, Bella. I've got to cash in my share.'

'The hard-hearted businessman.'

'Don't get me wrong, I love the horse. I've now bred a Classic winner. I'll probably never do that again.'

A thought occurred to Bella. 'Do you want to see some pictures of Goldie as a foal? There's some really good ones.'

He followed her into the living room and then she realised exactly what she was asking him to look at. What an insensitive cow she was.

'Look, Steve, I've just remembered that Ivana took these photos. I found them on a disk when I cleared out the cottage.'

He took in the implications of her remarks. 'Are there pictures of me?'

'One or two. Maybe you shouldn't look.'

She wondered how she would feel in his shoes, to see photos taken by a dead lover of the time in their lives when they'd first fallen for each other. It would be upsetting but she wouldn't turn down the chance. Neither did Steve.

'It's fine, Bella. I'm curious.'

She pushed the disk into the CD tray and the pictures began to load.

'Where did you find these?' His tone was sharp.

'In a bit of an odd spot. The disk was taped to a kitchen drawer.'

'How do you mean?'

'When I was cleaning the dresser I took the drawers out. I found it taped to the underside. That's how spies hide things, isn't it?'

'I wouldn't know.' The picture programme was opening.

'Mum!' Kathy's voice echoed from up the stairs. Bella immediately recognised the sound of a child expecting a parent to fetch and carry. Maybe her grown-up young daughter wasn't so grown up in some areas.

'I expect Kathy's forgotten her towel. I'll leave you to look at these on your own.'

He nodded, his eyes fixed on the screen ahead. Perhaps it was best she left him to it anyway.

Twenty minutes later she was still attending to her daughter, Kathy having asked if she would do her hair like she used to. Bella acknowledged to herself that sometimes it was nice to be wanted by your child, especially when she'd just had an unpleasant experience. It was good to know that when the chips were down, mums still mattered.

By the time she went back downstairs, Steve had gone. He'd probably called out goodbye but his words would have been drowned by the sound of the hairdryer. She hoped he hadn't thought her rude.

Kathy thought Gary didn't sound too bright when she got him on the phone. However, he perked up when he realised it was her. Good.

She gave him an expurgated version of the accident; she was aware Mrs Greening's abilities deteriorated with every retelling but too bad. He sounded suitably shocked and concerned, so she played up the drama a teensy bit.

Oh crap, why was she game-playing with Gary? Just when she thought she'd found a man she could be totally honest with.

Tell me, Gary, are you smoking dope?

People didn't want that kind of honesty. She wasn't sure that she did.

Suppose he said yes?

He didn't sound stoned though. He was offering to come over and pick her up, since she didn't have transport. She ducked it, tonight she was too tired and she decided to be too busy over the weekend. Before she could say so, he declared his own unavailability; he'd be tied up at the two-day meeting at Goodwood.

'I can't do Monday,' she said. 'I'll be at Hampton Waters Races.'

'So will I. We've got a couple of runners.'

'I'll try to get along to see you,' she said, 'but I might be having too good a time in the restaurant. Someone's taking me to dinner.'

'Who?'

At last a chink in his armour. The question had come just a bit too fast.

'What did you say, Gary?' Might as well make the most of the opening.

'Who's taking you to dinner?'

He was absolutely wide open now.

'Hal Cheviot, actually. Remember him from Deauville?'

There was silence. Then, 'I'm sure you'll have a very good time.'

What a feeble response. Downed by a sucker punch, no doubt about it.

After she'd put the phone down she rather regretted that he hadn't put up more of a fight.

Chapter Fifteen

Rob recognised Tania's voice on the phone before she announced herself. Her gentle Scots lilt – was she from the Western Isles? – was unmistakable.

'You were asking if Milos was at work here on the morning of May the thirteenth. I've now checked back in the diary and I can confirm that Milos was indeed at work in the yard that day. He started at six thirty.'

'Tomas said you'd already told him.'

'Ah, yes, but that was off the top of my head, based on what I could remember. This is official. So even if Milos had come round to your place the day before, he couldn't have been involved in the death of Tom's poor sister.'

Rob nearly dropped the phone. 'Where on earth did you get that idea?'

'From Tom. We had a wee get-together the other night and he told me all about it. It's terrible, isn't it?'

Rob heard the coy note in her voice when she spoke the jockey's name. The mist was beginning to clear.

'What's terrible, Tania?'

'That someone killed that poor girl and it's just been passed off as an accident.'

'Is that what Tomas told you?'

'Oh yes. He's not sure exactly how it was done but he thinks somebody must have knocked her unconscious and put her in with the stallion. Disgusting. Anyway, I'm glad it couldn't have been Milos. I'd have felt a bit funny seeing him in the yard every day.'

'You haven't told anyone there about this, have you?'

'Certainly not. Tom swore me to secrecy. But you're different because you know about it.'

Did he? Not this latest version of events. It was incredible the lengths a man would go to impress a girl.

'Anyway,' Tania continued, 'I was wondering whether Tom had mentioned anything about his plans for the weekend.'

'No, but I don't see him every day. I know he's riding at Goodwood.'

'But he'll be back Sunday night, won't he? And the lads here are planning a barbecue. I just wondered if . . .'

'Call him, Tania. Do you need his mobile number?'

'I've got it but I don't like to pester him. Would you ask him for me?'

Oh, for God's sake.

But he agreed to do it. He'd been intending to ring Tomas in any event.

'What on earth have you been telling that girl Tania?' he began. 'You can't go around saying people have been murdered.'

'You are very keen to tell me what I can't do,' the jockey replied.

'But you've no evidence that it wasn't an accident, just like the inquest said. At least, not now we know it wasn't anything to do with Milos.'

'Someone was there, Rob. I know that for sure.'

'But you won't tell me how you know that.'

'I can't. It would betray a confidence.'

God save us. Rob was standing on the path leading up the hill above the yard where the reception was best. He booted a stone into the hedge in frustration.

'Tania says you told her someone knocked Ivana unconscious and opened the gate for the stallion.'

'That is what I think.'

'You never said that the other night.'

'I have only just worked it out. It's possible.'

'Knocked her unconscious how? Nothing showed up in the postmortem, did it?'

'The postmortem report said that the back of her skull had been fractured by the horse banging her head into the concrete floor. Suppose someone hit her first on the back of the head, then slammed her head into the floor until she was dead. After that he opened the gate to let the horse in.'

'They'd be able to tell if she was hit on the head.'

'Really? If her skull was all smashed up? And if it looked like an accident in the first place?'

Rob didn't like the sound of this. He didn't want to believe it.

'The point of the post mortem is to discover the truth. It would have been spotted.'

'You are very trusting, my friend. You think the English authorities always get it right.'

'They do.' He sounded more confident than he felt. Was it possible a postmortem could miss something like that?

He could go to the police. Tomas might be sceptical of their powers but he had a different perspective. On the other hand, he'd have to be on very sure ground. And – the thought came suddenly – might he not be putting himself under suspicion? He couldn't prove exactly where he was at the time. Some might think that he himself attacked Ivana and then hid till Kathy discovered the body.

This was a can of worms he wasn't going to open without complete conviction.

'I must go,' said the jockey.

That was fine by Rob. He needed time to think this through.

There was one thing though. 'Ring Tania, will you? She wants you to go to a barbecue on Sunday night.'

Tomas laughed softly. 'I'll think about it.'

Jim's face was a picture when he saw Jason walking down the nave alongside Rose. If he hadn't been in church, Jason would have had a chuckle to himself but, irreligious though he was, he knew how to respect other people's holy places. He nodded gravely to his uncle as he ushered his wife ahead of him into Jim's pew.

Rose had been surprised, too, when Jason had announced his intention of accompanying her that morning.

'I thought you hated all formal religious occasions,' she said. He suspected she was quoting back to him words he had used to avoid such services in the past.

'They don't seem to be doing you much harm, sweetheart,' he'd said. 'Besides, I like a good old hymn sometimes.'

So here he was, growling his way through 'Dear Lord and Father of Mankind' which, in his opinion, was being feebly rendered all around. In his, admittedly limited, experience, that was usually the way. Unless you took a bunch of Welsh folk along with you the congregational singing in churches these days was bloody awful.

By his side, Rose was barely singing at all and her face was strained. He knew that look, she was struggling not to laugh. But if Jim's expression was anything to go by, his thoughts were most un-Christian. Jason turned down the volume. After all, he wasn't here to make a spectacle of himself. His purpose was quite the opposite.

Having concluded that Rose and Jim were operating a gambling scam together, it wasn't difficult to work out that it must have some connection to their regular Sunday morning church attendance. Why else would she be going? He found it difficult to believe she had seen the light. If she had, she wasn't the kind of woman who'd keep it secret from him. At least, he didn't think she was.

So here he was at her elbow, surreptitiously keeping an eye on the pair of them as they sang hymns, knelt side by side to pray and listened to the sermon. So far, they'd hardly communicated. A surly greeting from Jim, a smile and a few whispered words from Rose when they'd taken their seats, that was the extent of it so far. Maybe they got together after the service for a little chat. In which case, his presence would throw a spanner in the works, which wasn't his intention. He wanted to see what happened between them. It was a pity he couldn't be a fly on the wall.

As they filed out of the church at the end of the service,

Jason lagged behind, his eyes fixed on his two companions. Would they start whispering to each other? Or go into a quick huddle as they got outside? Some planning had to be involved surely.

Maybe they talked on the phone. But phone calls leave records and he'd checked through theirs, including Rose's mobile phone account. She'd made no calls to Jim on that and the two references to Jim's number on the house landline had been his. In any case, if they planned by phone, why these Sunday morning meetings?

'I don't believe I've had the pleasure, Mr . . . er?'

'Sidebottom.' Damn, he'd been caught by the parson who was hovering by the door. Naturally he'd be keen to talk to the unfamiliar face in his insubstantial congregation. Still, Jason reckoned he knew what to say to parsons.

'Superb sermon, vicar. Most inspirational.'

'Really?' The little man blushed. 'You found ten minutes on the evils of false prophets inspirational?'

'Absolutely. Touched a nerve.' Jason was looking over the clergyman's shoulder. Jim had been waylaid by two small ladies of some antiquity and Rose had walked ahead down the path.

'It's a pleasure to meet someone who actually listens,' the parson continued, his voice alight with pleasure.

Why wasn't Jim giving the old dears the brush-off? Surely this was their chance to exchange information – if that was what they did.

'Sorry, vicar, I didn't catch that.'

'I was saying – oh, never mind. I hope we'll be seeing you again.'

Jim was saying his goodbyes and stepping towards Rose, waiting by the lychgate.

'I doubt it. I just came along to keep my wife company.'

'Oh.'

Jim had caught up with her and she was leaning close, speaking into his ear.

'Bingo,' Jason murmured to himself. He didn't think he'd said it out loud.

'As a matter of fact, gambling in all its forms is the subject of next week's little sermon, Mr Sidebottom.'

But Jason had had enough. With a matey pat on the clergyman's surpliced arm, he was off down the path.

'I should have warned you not to get caught by the vicar,' said Rose as he caught up.

'Hopeless speaker,' said Jim. 'Every hackneyed phrase in the book.'

Jason nodded though he thought the sentiment a bit rich, having suffered a couple of Jim's efforts in his time.

'I'll see you tomorrow night then,' he said as he parted from his uncle.

It was all he could do to stop himself challenging Rose outright as they drove back. But it wasn't time for that yet. He'd see for himself at Hampton Waters tomorrow night. And before he went he'd get a tip from Rose for the first race. This time he'd risk more than a fiver.

'Are you listening to me?'

In truth, Rob wasn't paying much attention to Bella as he trawled the internet. As he'd suspected, he found that post mortem error was not unknown. Though they made for fascinating reading, these cases were increasing his anxiety about Ivana's accident.

It was the stable rubber in her pocket that really worried him. It was the element that guaranteed that the stallion would attack her.

Suppose Tomas's scenario was correct. Someone had hit Ivana, positioned her close to the movable gate and battered her head on the floor. Then put the stable rubber smelling of Curtain Raiser in her pocket before opening the gate. Cape Fear might have ignored a motionless body on the floor. He would not have ignored the scent of the other stallion.

So why hadn't he told Tomas about the stable rubber? Was his reluctance based on anything more than caution, the feeling that such a revelation would simply have increased Tomas's conviction that Ivana had been killed?

It seemed to Rob that the jockey had bought into the idea that Milos had murdered his sister and, when the facts proved otherwise, he wouldn't let it drop. Instead he'd simply cast around for another suspect. Call it paranoia, call it grief, whatever it was it seemed to be a theory that existed without proof. After all, Tomas wouldn't tell him how he knew there was someone else in the yard at the time of Ivana's death. The whole hypothesis was based on that.

'Rob, pay attention, for God's sake.'

He turned to face Bella. 'Sorry. What's up?'

'Did you give Tomas the bag with those things I found in the cottage?'

'Yes.'

'I wish you'd told me. I've been looking for it because there's something I forgot to add.' She peered over his shoulder at the desktop. 'Have you seen a disk in a white sleeve?'

Rob pointed to a square paper envelope propped against a mug which held pens and pencils. 'That it?'

She picked it up. It was empty. 'I know. It'll be in the CD player. I was showing it to Steve after he brought Kathy home.'

Rob opened the CD player. The tray was empty.

Bella looked perplexed. 'It was here. I left him looking at it. He wouldn't have taken it, would he?'

Who could say? If he had a clue what she was talking about he might be able to help.

'It's a disk of photos Ivana took that first New Year after she'd arrived. They were of the yard and the horses. And of Steve – I thought he'd be interested.'

'And was he?'

'It looks like it. He must have borrowed it.'

'Fair enough.' Rob had had enough of this protracted interruption. 'I'll ask him to give the disk direct to Tomas when he's finished with it. OK?' Then he turned back to the screen.

Surfing the internet, in Rob's opinion, was a fine occupation for those with abundant leisure time to dispose of. He did not think he fell into that category. Each time he set out to discover something apparently simple with the aid of the computer, he ended up on a long journey, with many unexpected twists and turns, which was not guaranteed to take him where he wanted to go. It was diverting, entertaining and, often, frustrating.

So here he was, trawling through endless sites devoted to gruesome death. There were plenty of cases where the wrong reading of a post mortem had secured a murder conviction. He read about an elderly woman who fell dead of natural causes whose injuries sustained in the fall were attributed to an assault which had brought on a heart attack. The poor fellow who found the body served twenty-three years before being declared innocent. Then there were the cot death cases – mothers whose lives were already ruined by the loss of their babies being wrongly imprisoned for their murders; and wrong readings in drug death examinations resulting in prosecutions.

If it was possible to make mistakes which wrongfully implied murder, Rob thought, surely the opposite was just as likely? Might the pathologist – like the one who had failed to spot a suspicious result in a Manchester post mortem in 1994 – have bungled the examination? It was particularly unfortunate in the Manchester case because it involved one of the victims of serial killer Harold Shipman, who went on to claim a further hundred victims.

Rob closed down the browser, he was getting sucked into places he didn't want to go. Computers were brilliant but they could waste your life.

His eye fell on the empty white envelope which had held Ivana's missing disk.

What had he been thinking a moment ago? That computers were brilliant.

Let's see.

He opened the photo-imaging programme that he'd installed when they'd bought a digital camera. Kathy was good at working it and she'd given him a few tips. Bella, on the other hand, just operated on a need-to-know basis.

He clicked on 'Select a folder' and a dropdown list appeared. He scanned it and came upon 'Rushpix'. He didn't recognise the name.

A message read: 'Select the folder you wish to import.' He imported Rushpix and there they were, postage stamp-sized photos, loading up across the screen. Even at this size, Rob could see that these images were unfamiliar to him, though they had been taken right here at Rushmore Farm.

Bella, without realising it, had copied Ivana's disk onto the computer's hard drive.

He began to enlarge the photos and prepared to wallow in nostalgia. It would be a damn sight more entertaining than reading about Harold Shipman.

By the time Rob had viewed all of Ivana's photos the warm glow of nostalgia had been replaced by something close to nausea. Panic gripped him. The kind that follows an unexpected revelation that has just turned your life upside down.

He found Bella in the kitchen.

'Come and look at this.'

'Give me a moment, Rob. I've got the potatoes to do.'

'They can wait.'

She followed him back into the front room and took the seat in front of the computer as instructed.

'Oh,' she exclaimed with pleasure, 'you found the disk.'

An image of Ivana cuddling an obviously newborn foal was displayed full screen.

'I didn't find it. You copied the contents.'

'Did I? Clever old me.'

Rob didn't disagree though in some ways he wished she hadn't been quite so smart. There are some pieces of information you wish you had never discovered. This was one of them.

'It's a lovely photo, isn't it?' said Bella. 'I recognise Goldie from the marking on his face.'

That was Goldeneye all right. Rob wished to hell it wasn't but there was no mistaking the little animal with the caramel coat and the white patch around one eye.

'See that building in the background?' he asked, pointing to the left of the screen, behind Ivana's shoulder. 'We knocked it down when we built new quarters for Cape Fear.' The stallion had become a complete liability in the old boxes. Rob had raided the Rushmore piggy bank to invest in high security for the animal.

Bella looked puzzled. 'So?'

'The condition of the planning consent was that once the new stables were built, the old barn was to be pulled down. Like most things, we never got round to it and some nosy neighbour reported us. We got a visit from the planning officer who gave us until the end of the year or we'd get fined. It was actually demolished on New Year's Eve, according to Ivana. I was in Spain at the time.'

'What's your point?'

'My point is that if the barn was still standing after Goldie was born, then he was born before the end of the year, not after.'

'Oh.' She looked at him with an expression that he recognised. It masked those same feelings he had felt himself ten minutes earlier. Disbelief and dismay were the emotions she was feeling right now. Everyone in the world of horseracing and breeding would know just what she was going through.

All horses in the northern hemisphere have the same official birthdate of 1 January, irrespective of the day they were foaled. If Goldeneye had been born at the end of December, then in the eyes of the racing world he would have become one year old at the turn of the year.

For Rob and Bella the repercussions were enormous. They spelt disaster.

Rob kicked his heels irritably while he waited for Steve to show up at Rushmore. His co-owner had made excuses at first and then, when Rob had said he wanted to talk to him urgently about Goldeneye, he'd agreed to cut short his evening. In the background Rob heard laughter and raised voices, male and female, and remembered the bars he used to visit with his friend in his bachelor days. On reflection, he didn't miss them much.

It was late by the time Steve strode in. He wasn't drunk but there was a well-oiled spring in his step and a grin on his face. It seemed he'd jumped to a conclusion.

'So you've finally seen sense,' he said. 'We're going to cash the horse in and bank some serious money. About bloody time.'

'It's not that.'

'Well, I hope it's good, mate. We could have done this tomorrow.'

Bella brought him coffee. He'd be needing it, in Rob's opinion.

There was no point in beating about the bush.

'When was Goldeneye born, Steve?'

The bookie spooned some sugar into his cup. 'How do you mean?'

'Do you remember when he was actually born? I was away but you were here keeping Ivana company. Your mare was in foal. You must have known all about it.'

Steve stirred slowly. 'Sure, but I can't say exactly when it was. It all seems one big blur from this distance.'

Rob passed him a colour print he'd generated off the computer. It wasn't the best quality but it was clear enough. The shape of the barn was unmistakable. Rob pointed to it.

'This was knocked down on New Year's Eve. Goldie must have been born in December.'

Steve looked suddenly sober but he did not look shocked.

'You knew about this, didn't you? That's why you took the disk of photos the other day.'

Steve said nothing, just sipped his coffee.

Bella spoke for the first time. 'You could have asked, Steve, I wouldn't have said no.'

He shrugged. 'I was doing you a favour. The fewer who know about it the better.'

'You weren't doing me a favour when you let me go ahead and register the horse on the wrong date.' Rob wasn't happy. Technically, he was the one who had perpetrated the fraud.

He felt like a fool. 'We're going to have to make a public apology. Say it was an honest mistake.'

'Why should we say anything at all?'

'Because it's wrong, that's why. We've been racing him as a three-year-old and he's not, he's four.'

'Don't go all po-faced on me, Rob. I bet it happens all the time. The only difference is, nobody else is stupid enough to admit it.'

There was an awkward silence, broken by Steve. 'You realise what will happen if we come out with this?'

'Of course. They change the race records and we'll have to pay back the prize money he's won. He will lose all his two-year-old successes and the Guineas. He won't even keep Le Marois.' Though the Deauville race had been for three-year-olds and upwards, as a four-year-old Goldie should have carried extra weight.

'Just think what that will do to his prospects at stud,' Steve said. 'And his sale value,' he added, putting the final nail in the coffin of their hopes, 'will be halved at a stroke.' He leaned forward, palms outstretched, imploring. 'Please don't do this, Rob.'

Rob was silent. It would be easy to agree to keep quiet. He could rationalise such a course without much difficulty – it was a technicality, others must have done the same thing, it was too late to rectify a genuine mistake. And, if he came clean, he'd be kissing goodbye to a heck of a lot of money.

But he now knew the truth. He wished to God he could somehow unknow it but that wasn't possible. How could he enjoy any future success that might come Goldie's way knowing it was based on a lie?

There was another reason. No matter how deep the truth was buried, it usually found its way into the daylight.

'Did you know about these photos, Steve?'

'Not until the other day.'

Rob took another of the prints. It showed Ivana kneeling by the newborn foal squinting up into the pale winter sunlight.

'You didn't take this one then?'

Steve stared at it closely. 'No.'

'Who did then?'

The question hung there. Someone had taken the shot of the smiling groom and the premature foal. The shadow of the photograph-taker stretched across the bottom of the print.

Steve stared long and hard, a muscle working in his cheek. 'So what?'

'Someone else knows.'

Steve shrugged. 'They've kept their mouths shut so far.'

Rob looked at Bella. Only she could persuade him. His financial health was not his alone to consider.

'You don't have any choice,' she said. 'You've got to own up now you know. If it comes out later there'll be a bigger price to pay.'

'Jesus!' It was Steve's turn to bang the table. 'What a pair of sanctimonious idiots you two are. You're not at some sodding Boy Scouts jamboree. You're blowing off a fortune! For fuck's sake, what difference does a couple of days make?'

Rob was well aware of it but he didn't think he had any choice.

'OK.' Steve got to his feet, sending his chair toppling backwards. 'Can we just have two days to sort ourselves out? We'll have to prepare a statement. And I've got a few financial arrangements to make – it's going to be bloody difficult. Can we just keep quiet about it until then?'

Rob nodded. He hadn't thought through the logistics of the thing. 'Seems reasonable.'

'I'm glad something does.' Steve's parting remark was bitter.

He slammed the door on the way out. Hard.

'Poor Steve.'

Bella stared at Rob in astonishment. 'What do you mean? He's the lying sod who's landed us in this mess.'

Rob nodded. 'I know, but he's obviously up to his ears in debt. Now he won't be able to sell Goldie. I can see his point of view, that's all.'

Bella was tempted to put the boot in harder. She'd always mistrusted Rob's old friend but it was pointless to say 'I told you so' right now. It wouldn't help.

She put her hand on Rob's shoulder. Nor was it the time to fall out.

The Lexus touched a hundred on the road to Birmingham. Steve didn't care.

Those photographs. He thought he'd looked everywhere in that bloody cottage. At least they'd given him an idea of how to get out of this mess.

He couldn't believe Rob's attitude. All he had to do was keep his mouth shut. What did it matter if someone else knew? Now he thought about it, it was probably Tomas who had taken that photo. Ivana's brother, who else? In which case it was a stone-cold certainty that Goldeneye's jockey would keep his mouth shut. It wouldn't be in his interests to see his best victories chalked off his CV.

The fact of the matter was that no one was going to ask any awkward questions about Goldeneye. There was not the slightest suspicion about his age.

There would be plenty of awkward questions now if Rob opened his mouth.

He blamed Bella. If she'd not been involved he could have squared it with Rob, he was sure. Now the pair of them knew about it, he was stuffed.

But not yet. While the phoney registration remained a secret he still had a chance. He'd got two days' grace out of the pair of them. That might just be enough to make them see sense. Right now it depended on getting to a club in Brum before a certain party disappeared into the night. In clubland, it was still early, so there was a chance he'd make it in time.

He'd never resorted to this kind of thing before. But he'd never been this desperate.

Chapter Sixteen

Contemplating the card for the first race of the evening at Hampton Waters, Jason realised it was the first time in his life he had felt truly confident of the result. His observations of Rose's behaviour, the contents of the safe in the upstairs room and his wife's Sunday morning meeting with Jim all pointed to Magna Carta, the horse due off in stall number three, as a dead cert. More to the point, Rose had tipped him.

Given these unique circumstances, and the fact that he intended to make sure they didn't arise again, he bet the hundred pounds in his pocket at 11-2. He could justify it on many grounds, but most of all in the knowledge that he'd kick himself if he didn't.

He observed Magna Carta closely in the parade ring. To Jason's mind he was a bit small and he wore bandages on both front legs, which would have discouraged him in other circumstances. Purely on his own judgement, he'd choose either the favourite in stall six, or the runner from Charlie Moorehead's yard, Landslip, who was due off in two. Landslip was the better price and he had that young Czech jockey on board who'd been catching a few eyes recently. For a moment Jason regretted not having a spare tenner to back his hunch. Then he laughed out loud, causing the gent on the rail next to him to give him a disapproving stare. He grinned at the chap and moved off, there was no way he could explain. And there was no point in backing his fancy because it was certain to get beaten.

* * *

Landslip was an athletic sort with a reasonable turn of speed, a bit of a specialist on an artificial surface. That's what Gary had told him and Tomas had every confidence he was on a genuine contender in this race. He'd had a bit of luck in his previous rides at Hampton Waters and he had hopes for this outing, an optimism apparently shared in the ring.

'He's joint favourite now,' Gary said as he lifted Tomas into the saddle, 'but I think that's down to the draw.'

Tomas didn't care about the betting. He just wanted to win. He'd enjoyed a decent weekend at Goodwood, two wins and a place from half a dozen starts. No one could complain about that. His agent Sammy Swan was content. One of the victories was on a horse from a West Country trainer with a big yard full of decent animals. Sammy was optimistic he'd be able to pick up more spares from that quarter in the future.

So his career was looking up. He was 'going forward' with his life, as people said. He even seemed to have acquired a woman friend who was worth bothering with. Tania was smart and interesting. He'd told her more than he should have done about Milos and Ivana, but she was a good listener and all this stuff was inside him, just churning around, waiting to burst out.

What had happened to his sister was wrong. She was no saint but she did not deserve her fate. Someone was responsible but he didn't know who.

What a pity it hadn't turned out to be Milos.

Kathy had deliberately not told her mum or Rob that she was going to the races. What with all the agonising over Goldie, she didn't want to admit she was off wining and dining with Steve and Hal Cheviot, the representative of the man who wanted to buy the horse. When push came to shove, she was on Mum and Rob's side – selling Goldie would be horrible – but Steve paid her wages. For the moment she just wanted to stay out of the quarrel.

At any rate, things worked out OK. No one was in the house when she got ready, and she didn't make a big palaver out of it (it was just a business dinner after all). Steve had told her to take a cab and it rolled up on time and, as far as she knew, unobserved. She left a note saying she'd be back late and that was that.

All the same, as Steve ushered her to the table in the restaurant where Hal was waiting, she felt a bit guilty because of Mum and Rob, and because of Gary, too, though this was part of her strategy.

'Kathy, you look ravishing,' said Hal and bent to kiss her hand. He wore a suit that looked as if it had been hand-stitched and the gold in his starched cuffs gleamed. Smooth he might be, but a bit of matinee-idol smoothness made a change from everyday West Midlands rough and tumble. And no one had ever called her ravishing before.

'Champagne?' he asked, not bothering to wait for her response as he poured the bubbling yellow liquid into her glass.

Not so long ago, she would have preferred Coke. Not now.

'Thank you, Hal.'

'Here's to a special evening.'

Steve, who had been looking worn and tense, cracked a smile. 'Amen to that.'

Kathy said nothing, just sipped her drink. She hadn't been looking forward to this occasion but, honestly, what was there to be worried about?

Landslip lived up to his billing, as far as Tomas was concerned. As the twelve runners went down the home straight for the first time his horse clicked straight into the pace of the race. He took a pull on him as they entered the first left-hand bend of the oval-shaped track, he didn't want Landslip shooting his bolt.

On his inside against the rail, the front-running Magna Carta was two lengths in the lead and going very easily. Tomas wasn't bothered, he expected the real competition to come from the favourite, Haussmann. On form, Magna

Carta's challenge was not likely to endure beyond a mile and this race lasted for another furlong.

Turning for home, he asked Landslip for a bit more effort and the horse obliged. But they made no impression on Magna Carta. The other animal still appeared to be cruising. Haussmann was in the picture now, having cut inside to race alongside Tomas. The rest were behind him somewhere and he trusted they'd stay that way.

Halfway down the home straight he really went to work and Landslip found another gear. Haussmann fought back and the pair battled it out in front of stands, going head to head to the line, Landslip finally winning a contest that could only be settled by close study of the photograph.

It would have been the best finish of the evening, except that Magna Carta had already won the race, easing down, by a clear five lengths.

Kathy could see that her good fortune on the opening races had made an impression on Hal. He pushed his programme across the tablecloth towards her.

'Would you care to mark the rest of the card for me? I can tell you have local insight.'

'Just luck,' she said and smiled innocently – or so she hoped.

The second race had indeed been luck though she'd seen her hunch run here before, when Steve had brought her, and liked the look of him. But the first race benefited from some inside knowledge. It hadn't been that difficult to work out. The winner was certain as it would be the only front-runner in the race – that had been the pattern for the last few months. The runner in lane one was a hold-up horse. That left Landslip in two and Magna Carta in three. Ordinarily she'd have gone for the Moorehead-trained horse but if the race was bent she couldn't stomach the thought that Gary and Tomas would be in any way involved. So that left Magna Carta by the simple process of elimination, and he was a front-runner. She was pleased with herself.

One look at Steve dampened her self-satisfaction. He looked as though he'd taken another hit.

'Will you excuse me?' he said, getting to his feet. 'I've got to make a few calls.'

'No problem.' Hal was recharging glasses. 'It'll give me a chance to pick Kathy's brains on the next.'

Steve shot her a penetrating look over the other man's head. She knew what that meant – keep him sweet. Steve was terrified Hal would go cold on the Goldeneye deal before the horse went to Tattersalls. He had some nerve using her as a sweetener. It was lucky for him that, on this occasion, she didn't mind.

'I think we need a drop more bubbly.' Her companion was looking for the waiter.

'Not yet, Hal. Let's go and look at the runners first.'

'OK.' He turned his attention back to her. 'Good suggestion. This evening, I'm entirely in your hands.'

'Come on then.'

First off, she'd see if she could track down Gary. He was going to hate her for this.

As a rule Jason steered clear of his uncle when he visited Hampton Waters racecourse. Jim could rain on any parade. Tonight was different, however.

He caught sight of the ramrod-straight figure passing the entrance to the stand.

'I can't speak to you now,' was Jim's opening remark. 'I've got work to do.'

'We've got to talk, Jim.'

'When did you stop calling me Uncle? And what were you doing making a spectacle of yourself on Sunday?' Jim sniffed. 'No respect, these days, that's the problem.'

'How about after the last? I'll buy you an orange juice.'

'I'm busy then, too. You pick your time, don't you? This is a working night for me, lad.'

'Don't fob me off, Jim. I know.'

The older man glowered at him and his lips drew tight.

They were five yards from a party of cheerful punters, an

office group on a night out, Jason guessed. Maybe, like him, they had pockets lined with tenners courtesy of his uncle's endeavours.

Jason leaned his head closer, though there was no chance they'd be overheard. 'I know about you and Rose. Why she goes to church with you on Sundays.' Maybe some lip-reading security man had binoculars trained on them. Call it paranoia, but he didn't dare say more.

Jim's eyes glinted and his jaw slackened. He'd heard and he'd understood.

'Go on back to the cottage after,' he said. 'I'll be as quick here as I can.'

Jason nodded, grinned for the benefit of the security man in his mind and said, 'Thanks, Uncle. I'll see you later.'

He watched Jim walk away. He didn't seem as ramrod straight as before.

Tomas had never ridden in the United States but, from what he had gathered, a track like Hampton Waters was not a million miles removed from the US experience: a tight flat left-handed oval; and the artificial surface underfoot was probably more like American 'dirt' than standard British grass.

He planned to ride in the US someday and experiences like his victory in the third race of the evening, a six-furlong sprint around three sides of the oval, would surely help him achieve that ambition. The leading runners had been bunched so close it seemed as if they were all drawing the same chariot. Every inch counted and Tomas liked that. He enjoyed the precision of the short distance, the tight finish, and being on an intelligent, nimble horse like Tactful. He must have won by a nose hair but he didn't care, it only added to the thrill.

He received fulsome congratulations on his victory from the owners, a local butcher and his wife, but Gary didn't seem that impressed. His 'Well done' as he helped Tomas dismount was distinctly offhand. That was OK. Tomas knew what he'd done and didn't need a boost to his ego. But he was surprised by Gary's manner; nobody had expected Tactful to win.

Then he spotted Kathy de Lisle and the man by her side and understood in a flash the cause of Gary's mood. Poor guy. He'd make a point of telling Gary later that the girl wasn't worth the heartache. Only, in this instance, he suspected that she was. Kathy wore a blue satin sleeveless summer dress with a matching cardigan thrown over her shoulders. The clothes were simple but she looked great. He could tell that her new companion thought so too.

'You remember Hal, don't you, Tomas?' she said.

'Of course.' They'd met in Deauville and he knew plenty about Sheikh Al-Mazin's bloodstock adviser. He was the swine who was going to steal Goldeneye from Gary's yard – and possibly Kathy too. Tomas didn't like him on principle. But he shook hands and smiled all the same. This was business.

Kathy seemed less interested in the victory on Tactful than his ride in the first.

'How do you account for Magna Carta?' she asked. 'You didn't get within a mile of him.'

Tomas shrugged. He'd been mulling over the same question and he couldn't account for it.

'He was too good. It's like he went round on roller skates and the rest of us had army boots.'

'That's racing, son,' Hal Cheviot butted in. 'Come on, Kathy, methinks it's time for more champers.'

Tomas caught Gary's eye as Cheviot, his hand on her shoulder, steered Kathy away. He made a gesture that he'd picked up in the yard – the universal sign for 'wanker'.

Gary, poor fellow, couldn't even raise a smile.

Kathy felt bad about Gary. He'd looked so crestfallen when she'd shown up with Hal – as if it was some surprise, when he'd known that Hal would be there. Honestly, if the boot had been on the other foot, she'd have positively oozed grace and condescension, no matter what she might be feeling within. Especially if she was standing in the winner's enclosure. As it was, he'd simply handed victory to Hal on a plate and then allowed himself to be patronised.

She disengaged herself from Hal who seemed eager to get back to the restaurant. What was the point in coming racing if you weren't going to look at the horses? The runners for the next were prancing round the ring. To her mind it was almost the best bit.

'I'll go back and order the bubbly then,' said Hal. She had the impression he wasn't that interested in the racing on offer. But then, he must see so much, the evening was probably a bit of a busman's holiday.

'Do you mind awfully, Hal, if I just have a Coke?'

Was that contempt in his eyes? No, she was just being self-conscious. She was sure that look in his eyes was desire – for her. Why then didn't she feel flattered?

'I'll see you in a moment,' she said.

In the ring she picked out a small black horse who looked alert and interested in everything around him. He was a mean price, she noted, but she could afford a decent wager. Then she changed her mind. She'd keep hold of her winnings and treat Gary to a meal in the big trackside restaurant. They'd have a good laugh about this evening.

As she turned to make her way back to the grandstand, she saw a figure she recognised. A short round man with a balding head and bowed legs: Jason Sidebottom. He was talking to a lean, silver-haired gentleman in green overalls. The pair of them were standing in front of a group of rowdy punters, their heads close together, speaking urgently.

Kathy's pulse raced and she forgot all about Hal and Steve and the table upstairs. Could Sidebottom be fixing races right in front of her? Should she follow him and see who else he spoke to?

At that moment the group of punters turned for the stand and swirled around the two men. At the same time, the crowd by the parade ring began to break up, rushing to get on last-minute bets as the horses went down to the start.

And Jason Sidebottom was gone, lost in the melee.

Damn, she'd missed her chance.

So what did it prove, the ex-jockey being here at the races? Absolutely nothing.

By the time she'd got back to the table, she'd missed the race. The small black horse had won, naturally, but she didn't care.

'Terrible queue in the ladies,' she said as she took her seat.

Steve seemed to have recovered some semblance of good humour, thank God. So maybe he hadn't taken a beating in the first race. He and Hal were debating the deficiencies of the handicap system. Boring.

Their table was right by the window. She wondered if Hal had had to pay a premium to get it. It looked out over the track, now being prepared for the next race. She watched idly as a tractor chugged round the circuit trailing a contraption to smooth out the surface.

She watched, no longer idly, as the machine progressed down the straight right below her.

She had a magnificent view of the driver – a silver-haired man in green overalls.

She drank from her glass, the fizzy brown liquid cold in her throat, but she didn't taste a thing. She was thinking too hard.

'Cheer up, man. You should be celebrating.'

Gary turned his head sharply at the sound of Tomas's voice. The jockey seemed to have appeared from nowhere. He'd changed out of his riding clothes into jeans and a casual shirt of a startling tropical blue that Gary would never have had the nerve to wear.

'Where are you off to, done up like that?'

'To meet a friend.'

'The new friend who works in Newmarket with the nutter?'

'Nutter?'

Tomas's English was good but occasionally he could be caught out.

'Milos. The guy who stalked your sister.'

'Ah.' Tomas tilted his head back in a familiar gesture. He understood and he didn't deny it. He'd only just met this new girl and he must be keen if he was off to Newmarket at this hour. Gary felt a stab of envy.

'What are you up to now?' Tomas asked.

Gary shrugged. He wasn't going to say what his plans were. Why advertise your stupidity?

'I thought you travelled with the horses,' Tomas said, 'but I've just seen the box leaving. How are you going to get back?'

'I don't know.'

'Come on, man, I'll give you a lift.'

'No, thanks. Anyway, you're off to Newmarket.'

'I'll go later. Let me take you home.'

'No.' What was it with Tomas? He was acting like his father. 'Look, Tom, I want to be left alone. You buzz off and see your new girlfriend. I'll be fine.'

The jockey studied him for a moment. 'OK,' he said finally and headed off towards the car park.

Thank God for that. It was bad enough loitering here trying to catch sight of Kathy coming out of the restaurant with another man, but to be caught at it by a fully paid-up Romeo like Tomas would be humiliating. As if he didn't feel humiliated enough already.

The last race had come and gone and the three of them were still sitting at the table. To Kathy, the evening seemed to have taken on an unreal glow. Outside on the floodlit oval beneath them, groundstaff were busy on the track. Driving their tractors, smoothing the ground with ploughlike contraptions. Steve said they were called levellers. That was a good name. Making things level. As in 'a level playing field'. Making it fair for all the runners.

But that tractor driver there. The one with silver hair who shouted at the other men a lot and waved his arms, he wasn't playing fair, was he? She'd seen him with that big butterball of an ex-jockey, Jason Sidebottom. The pair of them were fixing races somehow. Right here. Always the first race. Always one of the inside lanes. She was almost there. It just needed a bit more thought.

'Kathy.'

The voice came from a distance but Steve was sitting right next to her. She swivelled her head slowly and looked into his eyes. In the daytime they were such a piercing blue but here in the artificial light of night-time they were black and bottomless. He looked mean and thrilling like some louche hero in a film with subtitles. He was talking, she must make an effort to listen.

'Hal's invited us back to his hotel for a nightcap.'

Ah-ha. That wasn't a question. He hadn't asked if it was all right with her to go back to Hal's hotel room. Interesting.

She turned her head – it seemed to take forever – and considered Hal. He had such a fascinating mouth. Full and wide and exquisitely shaped. As if it was chiselled out of marble. A woman would be proud of lips like those. On a man whose face was all hard planes and sharp bones, it was – what was the word?

Steve was standing, Hal was getting up too, there was a hand on her arm. 'Come on, Kathy. I'll give you a lift home after.'

Corrupt. That was the word she was searching for. If she kissed a mouth like that she would be exquisitely corrupted.

They were leading her along the level towards a door. You could go directly from the restaurant to the hotel next door, they said. That was handy.

They were on either side of her, like two guardsmen, each with a hand on the bare flesh of her arm – which was just as well because her legs weren't functioning as normal. When she looked down, her feet seemed to sink into the carpet so she held her head high and let the laughter inside her rush out of her throat like the bubbles from champagne.

All that champagne. She must have drunk too much. Well, so what? She had her two handsome guards to protect her.

Gary had got fed up waiting outside. A steady stream of people had been leaving the restaurant but there'd been no sign of Kathy.

But there were other ways out, weren't there? Damn, why hadn't he thought of that?

He rushed up the stairs, against the flow of traffic, and came out at the top of the enormous room.

The rows of tables were set in a steeply raked bank facing the great windows which overlooked the track. From here he could look down and survey the remaining diners.

Where was she?

'Excuse me, sir, can I help you?' A waitress was at his elbow. She carried a tray of dirty glasses and her face bore the unmistakable expression of someone who can't wait for the slog of the evening to be over.

'No, I'm just looking for some people.'

'Do you know where they are sitting, sir?'

There was Kathy, getting up from a table on the bottom level. Steve was helping her.

'It's OK, I've just spotted them.'

He set off down the steps, unsure how to play it. He couldn't exactly pretend he was just passing. But he could say he was stranded and ask for a lift home. It was the truth, after all.

A group were blocking the aisle in front of him. One was an old lady with a stick, moving very gingerly while a younger woman guided her. Their male companions, one senior, one junior, were poring over a pile of discarded betting slips that littered the table.

'For pity's sake, Dad,' the young woman said, 'it's not there. You must have dropped it.'

'I'm not goin' till I've been through this lot. You can all get on without me.'

The lost betting slip drama – in other circumstances Gary might have been sympathetic but not right now.

'Excuse me, I'm sorry, can I just . . .'

He got past them at last, in time to see the trio he was following reach the door at the far end of the room, the men almost obscuring Kathy's body from his sight. Just as well he'd come up here after them, he'd have missed them otherwise.

He speeded up, drawing level to the table they'd occupied. He stopped abruptly, halted by a flash of blue on the seat where Kathy had been sitting. Her cardigan. He snatched it up.

By the time he'd reached the door, they were out of sight and he rushed down the corridor ahead. Somehow the cardigan lent legitimacy to his intended intrusion. She'd be pleased to get it back.

He found himself standing in the reception of the hotel next door. It was a busy area, full of people keen to keep the evening fun going.

He squeezed into the crowded bar and looked around.

There was no sign of Kathy.

Steve wasn't out of the woods – indeed he was heading deeper into the forest – but at least he was doing something as he eased the stumbling Kathy into Hal Cheviot's hotel room. The evening had been an agony, making dumb racing chit-chat while he timed his move. Fortunately, Kathy had been away from the table when the waitress had arrived with the last round of drinks and it had been easy to get Hal to check out a horse on the far side of the course with his binoculars so he could put the powder in the Coke.

It had taken him half the night to track down Cyril in Brum. It seemed the man did the rounds of practically all the clubs in the city, but he had customers to deal with, after all. 'Gotta keep people happy,' he'd explained. 'I'm in the happy business.' Steve had wondered how long the business would remain solvent as Cyril plainly test-drove the merchandise himself. But that hadn't been his concern.

'So you want Roofies?' Cyril had giggled. 'I never thought Prince Charming would stoop so low. A man like you could snap your fingers and the pussy come runnin'.'

It had been a tedious business buying the Rohypnol from Cyril. He thought he was so funny.

He'd assured Steve that the tablet was tasteless and odourless and would not turn blue when mixed with a liquid. 'Some stuff does,' he'd conceded. 'But not my shit,

271

believe me. You want my advice? Grind it into a powder and it'll vanish just like that. Fairy dust, man.'

Cyril had been a pain in the butt but Steve had had no option.

In the event he'd been relieved when Kathy had ordered Coke – it wouldn't turn that blue. And it obviously didn't taste funny because she'd drained the glass.

The next twenty minutes were the worst. If the bloody stuff didn't work, he'd have to fall back on Plan B and he wasn't sure that Hal would go for that. Ravishing a comatose maiden was one thing, holding her down kicking and screaming was a different proposition altogether.

But then the girl started going slack around the mouth, gazing at them both with eyes like two-pound coins and Steve had felt a thump in the gut as the adrenaline kicked in. They were on. He had everything to do but he knew he could do it.

He'd get out of these shitty woods yet.

Gary racked his brains to think what Kathy had said when she'd told him Hal was deigning to pay a visit to Hampton Waters. Had she said he was staying in a hotel? He must be. If so, there was a good chance it was this one – it couldn't be more convenient for the race meeting.

Convenient also if you wanted to seduce your dinner guest. From table to bed in ten minutes or less.

He couldn't believe that that was what was going on. Kathy wouldn't fall for that, surely?

But Kathy was drunk. He'd seen it in the way Steve had had to help her to her feet. In the way the two men had almost carried her out of the restaurant – and she'd left her cardigan behind. She didn't know what she was doing!

Steve was with her though. He wouldn't just abandon her to some upper-class lech.

He might, whispered a little voice in Gary's head, especially if he thought it would help to sell his share in Goldeneye.

Suppose the sheikh had gone cold on the horse sale now

that the owners couldn't agree? What better way to keep the sheikh's man sweet than to serve him up Kathy for the night?

Gary took a deep breath. He'd drive himself mad if he thought like this. First things first. Where was Cheviot's room?

He asked a smartly turned out receptionist.

'Certainly, sir.' She picked up a phone. 'I'll just tell him you're here.'

'No.' That was no good. Hal would come down, collect the cardigan and that would be the end of it. Or else Steve would appear and offer him a lift back, which was no good either. He had to get Kathy out of that room.

'No, don't bother,' he continued. 'Just tell me the room number and I'll pop up.'

'I'm sorry, sir, I can't do that. You have to be announced.'

Gary's mouth flapped open but he could think of nothing convincing to say. *I think a girl I know is about to be seduced by one of your guests. She's probably had a bit too much to drink.*

That probably happened every night in this place. It was the point of hotels, wasn't it? Or one of them.

'OK, I'll leave it then.' He turned away from the desk and blundered outside into the car park.

'So, Gary, how's it going?'

A familiar figure in a startling blue shirt had appeared by his side. Tomas.

'What the hell are you doing here? Your new girlfriend's not going to be very impressed.'

Tomas made a dismissive gesture with his hand. 'I rang and said I was delayed.'

'Not on my account, I hope.'

'Of course, on your account. You think I'd drive off and leave you so you can get in a fight or do something stupid over Kathy? So, what's happening? Tell me.'

Gary contemplated telling him to get lost. Some people just couldn't mind their own damn business. A fight sounded good; perhaps he'd start by thumping Tomas.

He took a deep breath. Tomas wasn't his enemy. In fact, right now, he was his only friend.

So he told him.

Oh, that's so nice!

Kathy wasn't marching any more. She'd been held up by her two strong guardsmen and frog-marched along corridors and through doors and into a lift and then along more carpet, miles of it. Until at last she could lie back on this bed. So *nice*.

She said it out loud, only no sounds came out. Who cared? The pillow under her head was soft. She knew her dress had rucked up over her thighs but she didn't care about that either.

'Kathy?'

The voice seemed to come from far away but the man's face was near. His mouth – that mouth – was whispering in her ear. Was she feeling all right?

'Bliss,' she managed. She'd meant to say blissful, 'This bed is blissful,' but only half a word came out. It would have to do.

There was a shifting on the bed. A weight pressed down next to her. Hal. Handsome Hal with the cruel mouth. She couldn't believe she was lying on a bed with him. So what? It was a hoot.

'Get her out of her clothes.'

That wasn't Hal. That was another voice, further away. Steve. Her boss.

So that was all right. Steve would look after her.

Hal had his arms round her, rolling her towards him. She giggled. It was funny.

Zziiiip!

She heard the soft metallic purr, followed by a whisper of cool air all down her back. They were taking her dress off.

That was kind. They must be taking her things off to put her to bed properly. So she'd be able to sleep.

There were fingers all over her, unfastening and tugging and removing. Lots of fingers – well, there would be. There were two of them, so that made four hands, which meant twenty fingers.

Or was it sixteen, with thumbs extra?

Who cared anyway?

Ooh, that was bright – a sudden flash of light that stopped her giggles. Why was there flashing light in here?

And again. More lights. She knew what they were now. Someone was taking photos. It was a pretty odd thing to be doing, wasn't it?

'Kathy?' It was Hal again. Why did he have to talk to her? Why didn't he just put her under the covers, into the blissful bed?

'Kathy, you are absolutely, utterly, amazingly gorgeous.'

Was she?

Oh heavens, he was kissing her. With that mouth.

Why not?

'OK.' Gary was pleased with himself as he rejoined Tomas in the car park. 'The room number is twenty-four.'

They'd talked through how to discover the number and the trick had worked like a dream. Gary had returned to the reception desk and asked a different receptionist if he could leave Mr Cheviot a note. Then he had watched closely as the girl placed it in a pigeonhole behind the counter. Pigeon-hole number twenty-four.

'So what are you going to do now?' Tomas asked.

'I'll go up there and give her back her cardigan.'

'Suppose he won't let you in the room?'

'He'll let me in all right.'

Tomas smiled, his teeth flashing white. 'Sure, but don't be a hothead. Steve's there, too, isn't he? It could all be legit.'

'You're probably right. I just have to see for myself what's going on.'

'Women have strange taste in men sometimes. If Kathy's having fun, promise me you'll just walk away.'

'Yeah. OK.'

It was easy to promise.

'And I'll bring my car round to the front here and take you home afterwards.'

'Thanks, mate.'

It was good to know he had some back-up.

It was just getting interesting when the knock sounded on the door.

Steve froze.

Hal took no notice, just carried on nuzzling the girl's small alabaster-white breasts.

The knock came again, louder this time.

'Mr Cheviot!'

Hal raised his head. 'Who's that?'

In other circumstances Steve would have admired the casual elegance of the girl's nude body. But there was no time for that.

'Hotel security, Mr Cheviot. Sorry to disturb you.'

The voice didn't sound sorry. It also didn't sound as if its owner would go away.

'Answer the door,' Steve hissed, slipping the digital camera into his pocket. 'Get rid of him.'

Hal got to his feet, tucking his shirt into his trousers. Just as well he still had them on, Steve thought.

'What is it?' Hal called out, managing to inject irritation into his voice.

'It's about your car, sir.'

'My car?'

Steve relaxed a fraction, a car problem was not his problem. All the same, as Hal reached the door, Steve snapped off the overhead light and backed into the small bathroom.

He heard Hal opening the door. 'What's the matter with my car, I hope nobody's—' Then Hal's voice changed. 'What the hell are you doing here?'

And Steve realised it was his problem after all.

Gary had dreamed up the line about the car as he stood outside the door of room 24. It was the one thing guaranteed to get a prick like Hal Cheviot rushing to open up. God forbid anything should happen to his precious Porsche or Mercedes or whatever it was he drove – it was bound to be expensive.

When the door opened, Cheviot was dishevelled but clothed – that was something.

When he recognised his visitor and started to protest, Gary thrust his body into the doorway.

'Where's Kathy?'

The room in front of him was dark but enough light spilled from the corridor behind him to reflect off the pale shape on the bed. A naked woman.

Cheviot's hands were on his arm, hauling him back.

'Get out of here, you little turd. Mind your own business.'

For a moment Gary hesitated. If Kathy had gone to bed with him of her own free will, he had probably just lost her friendship forever. On the other hand . . .

'Kathy! Are you all right?'

'Of course she's all right, you fool.'

But Kathy said nothing. She didn't move a muscle.

Oh Christ.

He rammed his shoulder into the other man, loosening his grip. Then hit him with all the pent-up fury and frustration that boiled within his body. Hal squealed in pain and slumped against the wall.

Gary leaned over the body on the bed.

Her eyes were closed and her lips were half open.

'Kathy!' He put his hand on her shoulder. It was warm to the touch.

He shook her gently, then more urgently.

No response.

He heard a rustling of movement behind him and a whimpering sound. He must have hurt Hal. Good.

'Kathy, wake up!'

He found a pulse in her neck. It was strong and steady. Thank God for that.

He took the opposite corner of the counterpane and pulled the cover over her body.

Then he stood up and took his phone from his pocket.

As he dialled Tomas, he noticed that a door opposite was ajar, spilling more light into the room. It hadn't been open before, had it?

'You bastard.' Hal Cheviot's voice was thick, as if he had a mouth full of liquid. 'I'll have you done for this.'

Gary ignored him. He'd thump him again but he was no threat.

'Tom, can you get up here? I need your help.'

Steve didn't pass Tomas on the way out. He took the stairs and moved fast. He didn't think Gary had seen him but, frankly, that was academic.

In some ways, this was the best end to the evening. He had the shots he wanted in the camera and Gary would take care of Kathy.

It was a pity Hal had got hurt but he didn't think it would make any difference. The sheikh still coveted the horse.

And hadn't Kathy looked sumptuous laid out on the bed? He was looking forward to seeing the photographs.

Chapter Seventeen

Jason lay awake half the night. He'd intended to confront Rose with what he'd learned from Jim but it had been late when he'd got in and he hadn't the heart. She'd been groggy with sleep by the time he got upstairs and managed just a polite enquiry about his evening.

'Any luck?' she'd murmured.

'I had the winner in the first,' he said, watching her intently.

But her eyes were closed, her face serene on the pillow. 'Well done,' she managed.

I got the winner in the first, he wanted to say, because you ruddy well fixed the race!

But he didn't, he just let her slide off into dreamland, looking as innocent as a baby. He, by contrast, the truly innocent party in all this, had no chance of sleep, his mind was a whirlwind.

Jim had kept him waiting a fair while in his car before he'd finally driven down the narrow track to his cottage. He'd barely grunted a greeting as he unlocked the battered front door with a key from a vast bunch attached to his belt.

'I suppose you'll be wanting a drink,' he said, tramping ahead of Jason down the squeaky-floored hallway into the kitchen. 'You'll get no liquor in this house but there's tea or coffee.'

'Coffee will be fine.' Jason resented the way his uncle still tried to claim some kind of moral high ground. What an old hypocrite he was.

Jason waited till Jim had brewed a kettle and dumped granulated Nescafe in two suspiciously brown mugs. They sat at the kitchen table, as stained and cracked as everything else.

Ideally Jason would have liked to ask questions and be given direct answers. How are you fixing the races? How did Rose get involved? How long's this been going on? And, most important, what on earth do you think you're playing at? You could go to prison – and take Rose with you, you stupid old fool! But things were never straightforward with Jim, his straight-citizen uncle.

'Does she know you're here?' Jim said, getting in first. Meaning does she know you know?

'No.'

Jim nodded his silver head and sighed. 'Her father was a great man in his way.'

Oh dear, Jason did not want to travel down the winding road of nostalgia.

'Look, *Uncle,* I've found cash, bank records and a betting log. I've seen how you tell her which horse is going to win. Just fill in the blanks for me, please.'

Jim fixed him with a steady stare. 'As I said, Geoff Wyatt was a great man. He loved the world of horseracing and he was a benefactor to everyone in it. If a racing man was down on his luck, all he had to do was confide in Geoff and Geoff would find a way to ease his burden.'

Jason couldn't believe he was hearing such a mellow appraisal of his deceased father-in-law. 'As far as I'm aware he blew millions on gambling and the high life. And he was utterly reckless with his own family fortunes. I'm surprised you'd stick up for him.'

Jim drank with a slurp and carried on as if he hadn't heard. 'Geoff's trouble was he couldn't say no to anyone. He loved the horses, true enough, but he spent more money on other people than himself. He gave it left, right and centre. When I tried my hand at training years ago, when I was young and foolish, I got into trouble with money. I made some bad enemies.' He gazed at Jason over his mug. 'This was before I found the Lord.'

Jason nodded. He'd not heard Jim talk about such times before.

'Geoff paid my debts for me. And when I broke my leg in three places and it wouldn't mend, he paid my bills until I could get fit enough to start earning again. If it hadn't been for Geoff I don't know what I'd have done. And there are dozens like me.'

'This is interesting, Jim, but can we get to the point?'

'This is the point. Geoff Wyatt was a good man and he was driven to an early grave by a great injustice. He was warned off racing, banned from every course and yard in the country, deprived of his lifeblood, and all because he owed a paltry fifteen thousand pounds.'

Jason didn't think fifteen thousand was necessarily paltry.

Jim caught the look on his face. 'Do you know how much money he lost to one bookmaker over the years? More than a million. And that same firm had him run out of racing for fifteen thousand. The firm had changed hands, passed from father to son. The father would never have been so vindictive but the son has a wallet for a heart.'

'Steve Armstrong.'

'That's him. And we've been hitting his business where it hurts, in a way he understands. He drove a man to take his own life and now he's paying for it.'

'So this is all just for revenge?'

'It's justice for a man who was a force for good in the world.'

Jason considered the shabby kitchen, the ancient grease-stained cooker and the rackety fridge that wheezed in the corner. He also thought of the extra five hundred pounds nestling in his back pocket thanks to Jim's little scheme.

'Do you mean to say you aren't doing this for the money?'

Jim looked shocked. 'I swear to you, in the name of the Almighty, that I have not taken a penny piece. I've not had a bet for thirty-three years and I shall never do so again.'

The same could not be said for Rose, but that was a separate matter.

'Whose idea was this?'

Jim could not keep a smirk of satisfaction from his face. 'Let's just say it was down to the Lord. Your good wife came to me for help and He gave me the idea – how to give a significant advantage to a horse. In the wrong hands, I knew it could be put to an evil purpose but I wanted it to be a force for good.'

Like stealing thousands of pounds from a man's business – but Jason let that pass. He was consumed by curiosity.

'Come on then, Jim, tell me. What exactly was this great idea?'

And he'd listened with grudging admiration as his uncle had revealed the secret.

So all he had to do now, and he'd hashed and rehashed the matter throughout the long night, was have it out with Rose.

Rob was in the office; Bella had left a pile of letters for him to sign. He'd told her to lie in – she'd been up half the night with Kathy, fretting.

As he worked he wondered what exactly had gone on – though, reading between the lines, it seemed pretty straightforward. Kathy had gone out for dinner with that toad Hal Cheviot who must have poured a gallon of booze down her throat in the hope of getting into her pants. And he'd succeeded – up to a point anyway – until Gary had burst in on the two of them and dragged her off, with Tomas's help.

It had been plain for months that Gary was mad about her, though Kathy was harder to read and Rob wasn't any kind of expert at gauging the romantic expectations of teenage girls. He never had been, even as a teenager himself. But Gary was an open book and Rob had also noticed the way he held his left hand last night as he'd helped Kathy into the house. Rob had seen the swelling. He wouldn't mind betting Hal Cheviot was wearing a swelling somewhere about his person this morning too. That thought was something to cheer a man up in troubled times.

He wasn't so confident that Gary's action would please Kathy, however. She was over eighteen and was entitled to romance who she wanted to, even if the recipient of her favours was the oily bastard who was trying to get his hands on Goldeneye.

No, scrub that thought. He kept forgetting that the situation had changed. Today was the day they had agreed with Steve to further discuss the matter of Goldie's birth. Not that there was much to discuss, just how they should come clean to the racing world. And once the true age of the horse was on the table, the interest of Hal Cheviot and the sheikh would disappear on the summer breeze.

Bella took a different view of the situation. As far as she was concerned, her daughter had foolishly put herself at risk and Gary had saved the day. She'd been appalled to discover her daughter on the doorstep, obviously the worse for wear, with her underwear stuffed in her handbag. But she'd stayed up with Kathy in the small hours when her daughter had begun to throw up. Rob pitied the third degree Kathy would be subjected to once she regained consciousness.

Jason fetched the morning tea, as he always did. Rose wasn't too perky first thing in the morning, whereas he was used to a lifetime of getting out of bed at cock crow to do horses, so it made sense.

As a rule, he'd leave her to come to in peace but not today. He waited for her to sit up and take the first sip.

'Last night is the end of it, Rose.'

Her expression didn't change, her face remained sleepy and serene, but her body seemed to freeze and her eyes grew just a bit wider. He had her attention.

'I got chapter and verse out of Jim,' he continued, 'and it's finished.'

'Oh.' She put her tea down carefully. 'I knew you were suspicious when you insisted on coming with me on Sunday.'

'I couldn't work out why you were so dead keen on going

to church every week. I thought you might be having an affair with Jim.'

Her face was a picture. It cheered him up no end.

'Oh, Jason, you didn't?'

But he wasn't going to be sidetracked. 'I've been into the safe and seen what's there. That's a powerful lot of money you've stolen.'

He could see her decide not to take issue with him over the rights and wrongs of snooping on her. Instead she said, 'I didn't want you involved. If it went wrong, I didn't want anyone pointing the finger at you. That's why I didn't tell you.'

He believed her. That's what Jim had said too – they wanted him left out of it. As if he could be.

There was one outstanding issue.

'What are you intending to do with the money?'

Rob was still in the foaling sheds when his mobile signalled. He had a text. 'Urgent. Look at your email and call me soonest. Steve.'

He headed back to the house. It must be something to do with Goldeneye. A draft letter to the Jockey Club maybe?

He booted up the computer and opened Outlook Express. The house seemed quiet. Both women must still be in bed.

Various messages downloaded into his inbox, including one from Steve. He opened it. There was no text, just a picture.

First he thought it was a piece of internet porn. Why had Steve sent him this? Then he looked closer.

A naked woman lay on a bed, her thighs white and flung wide. A man's back was in the foreground to the left as he bent over her, his hand on her breast. The girl was laughing.

It was Kathy.

Rob scrolled down. He was wrong – there *was* some text. It read: 'I've got much better ones than this.'

* * *

Rob made the call from up the hill. He couldn't risk being overheard by Bella or Kathy, not till he knew what this was about.

Steve picked up at once. His voice was ice cool.

'Just listen to me, all right? It won't help if you fly off the handle.'

Rob told himself that the words made sense even if what he most wanted to do in the world was ram them down his so-called friend's throat.

'You've seen the photo?' Steve said.

'Yes.'

'Listen carefully to what I'm going to say. I'm sure you know what this is about.'

Goldeneye. It had to be.

Steve's voice continued, tinny and creepy down the phone line. 'I've got a little round-robin email all set up. It goes to a select number of people I know in the sporting world – punters, journalists, a few key lads at racing yards. I won't bore you with all the details but it says something like, "Remember gorgeous Bella Browning, Britain's sexiest three-day-eventer? It turns out her daughter's just as much of an eyeful." And I've added a knock-out pic of Bella in her little shorts and T-shirt to the ones of Kathy enjoying herself last night.'

Rob was speechless. It was inconceivable that Steve was doing this.

'It's all a bit tabloid and tacky, I know,' continued the tinny voice, 'but I guarantee this'll be all over the net within twenty-four hours. Remember that girl who sent a sexy email to her boyfriend and he forwarded it to a few of his mates in the same firm? Or that Paris Hilton video – sexy blonde heiress having it off in a hotel? These things spread like forest fire. Your Kathy is about to be big news. Do you think she can deal with it?'

There were people in the world who could handle scandal on that scale, even some who'd parlay it into some kind of meal ticket. The reality TV freaks. Kathy was not one of them.

'You wouldn't do that to her.'

'Sorry, mate, you're wrong. But you don't need to worry. Provided you and Bella keep your trap shut about Goldeneye, Kathy will never become an internet superstar. Got it?'

Rob got it, all right.

By the time he returned to the house Bella was up. She looked tired and unhappy – and furious.

'We've got to call the police,' she said.

'Why?'

'Kathy's awake. She told me she thinks her drink was spiked last night.'

It made sense. That's how Steve must have got the photographs.

Bella's voice was insistent. 'She was deliberately drugged. I don't think she was raped but we've got to get her checked by a doctor. The police will know what to do.'

'Before you call them . . .' He hesitated, it was hard to know how to put it. 'Come and look at this.'

He showed her the photograph on the computer. Then he explained what Steve intended to do.

'But that's evidence!' she exclaimed, pointing at the screen. 'That proves he drugged her.'

'It proves he drugged her to you and me. But she doesn't look doped up, does she?'

'It's the truth.'

'People who look at this stuff on the internet don't care whether it's the truth or not. Do you want hundreds of thousands of them seeing photos of Kathy like that? This won't be some minor embarrassment she can shrug off.'

'So he just gets away with it?'

Rob didn't reply.

'Why did he do it anyway?'

'To force us to keep quiet about Goldeneye. If we say nothing about when the horse was born then these photographs remain secret.'

Bella shoulders sagged, the fury had gone. She looked at him miserably. 'God, I wish I'd never found that bloody disk. What fool cleans the underside of a drawer?'

'What do you mean?'

'That's where I found it. Taped to the underside of a kitchen drawer.'

'You never told me that.'

'I didn't think it was important.'

This was the first Rob had heard about it. 'Ivana had hidden it deliberately?'

'Yes. I thought it might be photos of her and some lover. You know, dirty ones.'

The irony wasn't lost on either of them but they weren't laughing.

Rob was sitting in the gloom of Kathy's bedroom, the thick curtains shutting out most of the daylight. He'd been there for ten minutes, watching her sleep, trying to quiet his raging thoughts. Most of all, wondering how to keep her safe from the prurient world outside. He'd agreed with Bella not to mention this new threat.

'Rob.'

He leaned forward so she could see his face and took hold of her small pale hand.

She squeezed his fingers. 'Thanks for saving me.'

'Gary's the one who saved you. He got you home last night, him and Tomas.'

'I know.'

Bella had told him Kathy remembered little of her experience, just of being at the racecourse restaurant with Steve and Hal. She knew nothing about what had happened in the hotel, or of being driven back to Rushmore.

Curious though he was, he didn't want to make her repeat herself. Not yet, anyway.

'Poor Gary.' She sounded as if she was about to drift off again.

'Gary's OK – he's just mad about you.'

'No. I mean about Ivana.'

'What about Ivana?' Rob stared at her pale face.

'He didn't mean to hurt her when he locked her in the stable with Cape Fear. It was just because he was angry with her.'

Her voice had got small. He gripped her hand tight and shook her arm. She could rest in a moment.

'Kathy, tell me exactly what you mean.'

She blinked at him, responding to the urgency in his tone. 'Oh. You don't know, do you?'

'No, but you're going to tell me right now. Then, I promise, I'll let you go back to sleep.'

Her face was insubstantial in the half light, almost merging into the white of the pillow. But her voice was firm as she began to speak.

Rob left Kathy and went downstairs; he had a call to make. This time he used the landline from the house; Bella was out with Chopsticks, not that it would have much mattered if she'd overheard.

'You pick your moments, don't you?' said Gwen when he finally got her to the phone. 'It's right in the middle of lunchtime service.'

'This won't take a moment, I swear, but it's really import- ant. It's about when Cape Fear attacked you and you had the wrong stable rubber in your pocket. Did you really never tell anyone?'

'To tell the truth, it was such a stupid mistake I kept quiet about it. But I was in a state because of the baby and everything so I told the father about it.'

'You mean the man who got you pregnant?'

'Yes. We had a big row about everything and I blamed him. If he hadn't been so foul to me I'd never have done anything so silly. Look, Rob, I've got to go. My supervisor is giving me poison looks.'

'Just tell me the father's name. Was it Tomas?'

'Tom? Of course not. He was just a mate.'

'So it was Steve.'

There was silence on the line. Had she gone? He could

hear the background murmur of voices and the clatter of cutlery.

Then she spoke again. 'I've got to go.'

And she hung up.

You think you know a person. You've seen him at every stage of his life, been side by side with him at school, on dates with girls, winning and losing at the races, even holding him up when his parents died. And he did the same for you. So you think you know him better than anyone else in the world. Your best friend.

Have you always been a fool where he's concerned?

Rob asked himself these questions as he sat in the stillness of Kathy's room, listening to the sound of her sleepy breathing.

She'd told him that someone had undone the gate that Gary had fastened to lock Ivana in. She knew that for sure because she remembered every lurid detail of running to Ivana's aid. Which was more than he did. For him, everything had passed in a blur, leaving just the agony of arriving too late and the sensation of standing in a sea of blood with the stench of the abattoir in his nostrils.

He remembered beating the horse back with the pole they kept outside the pen. You needed a weapon if you were going to spend time around Cape Fear. They called them mash poles in the yard because they were mostly used for mixing up horse feed. The pole was about the length of a baseball bat. Perfect for keeping a bad-tempered horse at arm's length and for giving him a whack if he stepped out of line.

Perfect, too, for cracking someone across the back of the head when they were looking the other way. Rob imagined it wouldn't be difficult to knock a slim girl like Ivana unconscious so you could lay her down and smash her head open on the concrete floor. Then put the stable rubber in her pocket and open the gate for Cape Fear.

It was possible for a person to commit such a crime if they had the determination and a good enough reason.

Even your best friend, who you thought you knew inside out.

Rob forced himself to think and not allow himself to be swayed by anger and the bitterness of betrayal.

Who stood to gain by Ivana's death?

A few days ago he would have thought, as Tomas had done, that Milos was the most likely suspect. He'd loved and lost and was unstable. If he couldn't have Ivana, then he'd make sure no one else had her. Ever.

But Milos had an alibi and new things had come to light. Like the disk of photos Ivana had kept taped to the underside of a kitchen drawer. The disk that proved Goldeneye was not a financial asset but a liability. And who most stood to lose by that information coming to light?

Rob also thought of the phone call he'd received from Ivana the night before she died. She'd told him she was leaving after work the next day and that they had to talk. She'd said there was something he ought to know and she'd tell him before she left. But she'd not had the chance.

Suppose that something was the secret of Goldeneye's birth? She'd been in charge of the stud while Rob was away, she would have known the truth. And she'd kept the proof hidden until she needed to cash it in. Had she used blackmail? How much had she asked Steve to pay her for her silence? The same amount, probably, as she would have requested from him in the interview that had not taken place. Ivana had been desperate for money to start a new life somewhere else.

But she never got the chance because Steve robbed her of life altogether.

Rob heard the sound of voices at the door. Bella was returning and she had Tomas by her side. Good timing.

He was wearing the same shirt as last night – you couldn't miss it – and Rob wondered where he'd spent the night. On second thoughts, he could guess.

Tomas had come to see how Kathy was doing. Bella took him upstairs to look in on her but he returned a couple of minutes later.

'She's sleeping. But she looks fine. I think she was very lucky.'

Not lucky enough, Rob thought, but he didn't want to talk about the photos. There was something else.

'I owe you an apology, Tomas. I didn't believe you when you said there was someone in the yard when Ivana died. Someone apart from Gary, that is.'

'So you know about Gary?'

'Kathy told me. But there's things you don't know.'

He explained about the pole in the stable. And the stable rubber in Ivana's pocket. And the disk of photos Ivana kept hidden which proved that Goldeneye was racing under false pretences.

Rob told him because Tomas was entitled to know how his sister had died.

Then he told him about the picture of Kathy on the computer and begged him to keep his knowledge to himself. Tomas agreed.

'What are you going to do about this?' he asked Rob.

That was the question.

'I don't know,' he said. And he didn't.

Rob spent the afternoon with the yearlings. Horses couldn't take time out from ordinary life when there was a crisis. They still needed brushing and feeding and mucking out, whatever the weather or the state of the world. It was one of the things that kept horse people sane, the routine that had to be adhered to, day in, day out. You couldn't bunk off and put your feet up when there were horses to do.

Should he go to the police? That was the issue. Tomas might distrust the authorities but he didn't. He'd expect the police to get to the bottom of Ivana's death and come up with the same answer he had done.

But it would take time. Steve had had long enough by now to dispose of any physical link to Ivana. He'd be a fool if he hadn't got rid of every item of clothing he'd been wearing that morning. And he was a tough guy. He was unlikely to wilt easily under a barrage of questions, especially when he'd had plenty of time to think about what he might say. He wouldn't be a simple nut to crack.

And in the time it took for these inquiries to go on, might Steve not have a moment to get to his computer and click an instruction or two? The instruction which would send his malicious email out into the world and ruin Kathy's life.

After he'd finished with the yearlings, Rob went to look over the mares. There were still plenty of chores to be done, and a lot to think about.

Was he just going to let Steve get away with murder? That couldn't be right.

But how could he throw Kathy to the dogs? It would destroy her – and Bella too.

Whatever course he chose seemed doomed.

By the end of the afternoon, Rob had a plan. It wasn't brilliant, hardly a plan at all, just a course of action. Something to do. He hated doing nothing.

He walked along the bridleway to Steve's house, turning over in his mind what he should say.

Really, he didn't want to say much at all. He just wanted to beat Steve to a pulp. Beat a full confession out of him and then hand him over to the police. But that was a path guaranteed to put himself in jail instead of the real offender.

He had only one advantage. Steve was not aware Rob knew he had murdered Ivana. He would think his only concern was to protect Kathy. If Rob swore faithfully never to reveal the truth about Goldeneye, might Steve destroy those photographs?

No, he wouldn't. The existence of the photographs was Steve's only guarantee that Rob and Bella would keep their mouths shut.

Unless he murdered them too.

That was pretty funny – until Rob pictured Steve smacking Ivana over the head with a mash pole.

He wouldn't be turning his back on his old friend, that was certain.

As he reached the end of the bridleway, the driveway in front of Steve's house came into view. A sprinkler played on the lawn and Steve's car was parked in the yard.

Rob stopped for a moment. He had to get this right. As he hesitated, he heard the sound of an engine.

A car was coming down the lane that ran parallel to the bridleway. It passed within feet of where Rob stood, obscured by the fringe of trees, and drove up to the front of the house. It swung round in an arc on the gravel and parked facing back down the drive – a dirty white Escort with a crumpled front bumper.

Rob watched Milos get out and ring the doorbell. He had a clear view of the front door as it swung open and Steve came into view. He was wearing a powder-blue shirt and linen trousers. He looked puzzled by his visitor, a man with a ponytail in a T-shirt and jeans.

Maybe it was the way Milos was standing – his right arm held behind his back as if he were hiding something – but Rob had a premonition. Milos was weird and unpredictable. A man obsessed by a dead woman – a woman Steve had killed. Rob had told Tomas about it and he wouldn't put it past Tomas to tell Milos.

'NO!' Rob shouted, running from the trees across the lane.

Steve turned to look at him as he sprinted towards the house, yelling as he came.

But Milos did not turn. He thrust his right arm upwards, light flashing for a split second on metal, before he buried it in Steve's chest.

Rob hurtled into Milos from behind before he could stab again. The pair of them crashed to the ground, Rob's arms encircling the Czech man, trying to hold down his knife hand. The impact sent the blade skittering across the gravel.

Milos rolled, pinning Rob beneath him. He was heavier and larger. Rob's right arm was free. He hit Milos in the face. For a second the Czech's grip relaxed and Rob heaved upwards, trying to free himself.

Steve was sitting on the ground, watching.

Rob called to him. 'Help me, Steve. Get him off me.'

Steve did not move.

Rob butted Milos in the face and the Czech fell back, his hands over his nose.

Rob pulled himself clear.

'Quick, Steve, call the police!'

But Steve sat paralysed.

It had been a mistake to turn away from Milos. Rob caught a glimpse of movement from the corner of his eye just before Milos kicked him in the head.

Rob was sprawling face down. He could taste metal and stones in his mouth. Close by a car engine started up, tyres squealed on the drive and the vehicle roared off. Gradually the engine noise receded till it was overtaken by the humming of bees and the whisper of wind in the trees.

Rob was conscious that he had to act – call an ambulance, get help, do something – but he was incapable of movement. As if trapped in a dream.

He forced himself to raise his head and saw that this was no dream.

Steve was now lying on his back, a necklace of blood across his throat to match the dark red puddle of his chest.

Rob stood shakily and bent over the man who had once been his friend. He could see that Steve was beyond help.

Behind the body, the door to the house stood open. He could call the emergency services from inside.

But he didn't. There was nothing that could be done for Steve now.

Standing in Steve's living room, Rob forced himself to think clearly of what would happen when the authorities arrived. They would go through Steve's life methodically and in detail. They would soon discover the contents of his laptop computer sitting on the desk in the corner. And what was inside the digital camera next to it.

Rob still had a chance to protect Kathy if he was quick.

The police were all over the place for days, interfering with the traffic into Rushmore Farm as they cordoned off the approach road which ran past Steve's house. But the major disruption was on the main highway three miles away where a car, a white Escort, had inexplicably careered off an empty road and smashed head on into the Victorian viaduct carrying rail traffic across the cutting.

Steve's stabbing was national news and a flock of crime reporters descended to pick over his bones, adding to the local confusion. For forty-eight hours they made hay with angles on the 'Bookie Bloodbath', speculating for the most part on an organised crime killing and rumours of business debts. As the co-owner of Steve's Classic-winning racehorse Goldeneye, Rob was pestered for a reaction. He restricted himself to stating that he was 'shocked', which was nothing less than the truth and placed him squarely in line with the rest of the racing industry.

After two days the police released a statement which breathed new life into the story. The deceased driver of the Escort was named as Milos Cerny, a stud farm hand who had once been engaged to Ivana, sister of the successful Flat jockey Tomas Jelinek, and a former girlfriend of Steve Armstrong's. The knife which had killed the bookie had been found on Milos's body. Even though Ivana had died in a stable accident three months previously, it appeared that Milos was sufficiently jealous of Steve to slay him on his doorstep and then deliberately kill himself in his car.

The reporters swiftly changed tack and wrote pieces about the love triangle that had led to tragedy. The police released photographs of the shrine to the dead girl that Milos had created in his flat and female columnists wrote at length about the power of earthly passion to transcend the grave.

Apart from the press there were many visitors to Rushmore. First there were uniformed police asking if anyone had seen anything on the evening of Steve's death. Rob thought he'd managed to avoid telling any direct lies, though his errors of omission had been considerable. There was no reason for him to admit his involvement. He was sure no one had seen him return to the yard along the bridleway. Later, a pair of plain-clothed detectives had arrived to satisfy their curiosity about Ivana's relationship to Steve. Their inquiries did not embrace the circumstances of her death.

In between these official visits, there were well-wishers, anxious neighbours and several locals keen to get as close as possible to the action without appearing ghoulish. Gary came as often as he could, given that he had a major work-load at the yard and regular appointments at the hospital to treat the chipped bone in his hand.

One person did not appear at all. Rob wondered whether to call Tomas, but what he had to say to him could not be said on the phone. You had to look a man in the eye when you asked if he had arranged a murder. After a day or two, he decided that Tomas's reticence was sensible. It was likely that the Czech jockey was steering clear for Rob's own good. Following his interview with the CID, which was humour-less and probing but, thankfully, some way off the mark, his gratitude for Tomas's reticence increased. The words 'accessory to murder' had an ugly ring and he would hate circumstances to be twisted so that they might apply to him.

Rob spent his time tending his horses and preparing a letter to the Jockey Club containing information which had just come to light about the birth of Goldeneye. All his plans to invest in the stud were on hold as he and Bella prepared to repay the prize money Goldie had accumulated so far. On paper, they had taken a big hit in the vastly reduced value of Goldie himself but Rob didn't care much about that. At least now they weren't faced with the prospect of losing him. He did not expect to see Hal Cheviot again and, if he did, he proposed to knock more teeth down his throat, just like Gary had done.

Rob's one real worry was that the police would come in search of Steve's laptop computer and digital camera. But even if they suspected these things existed, why would they look in Rob's cesspit?

He intended to install a horse-walker one day. And when

he laid the foundations, there were a couple of extra items he intended to bury.

The day he wrote to the Jockey Club about Goldeneye he felt relieved of a burden. Though he'd soon be poorer as a result, he felt much happier.

Kathy had been spending much of her time on the stud, with the mares in foal.

'Hey, Rob,' she said as she made them some coffee, 'I don't fancy another office job. Can I work here on the stud instead?'

'You mean I'm going to have to start paying you?'

'Aren't I worth it?'

Poorer but happier.

Kathy thought that Gary should have let her drive. His hand was taking time to mend; being a leftie, the one he used to change gears was the one he'd planted on Hal Cheviot's mouth. She liked to picture it: Gary's fist spreading the big lips all over that arrogant face – smack! It was a pity she hadn't been conscious to see it.

Ideally, she would have paid a visit to Black Vale Avenue on her own. But she'd not got round to collecting her car and, more significantly, she didn't fancy sticking her head in the lion's den without her protector. That said, she asked Gary to remain in the car outside.

He was reluctant because she'd been evasive about the purpose of her visit. But she couldn't tell him what it was, not just yet. By way of a compromise, she agreed to let him escort her to the front door then he could judge for himself if she was in any danger.

Kathy had arranged it so that they turned up during the next evening meeting at Hampton Waters. She wanted to catch the woman on her own and was rather banking on the barrel-shaped man being at the races. And if she interrupted a procession of women handing over money, she could cope with that. It would be like being caught red-handed, wouldn't it? However, she hoped that would not be the case – not now Gary was negotiating with Steve's estate to take over the bookmaking business.

The street seemed quiet. They sat in the car for five minutes to observe the comings and goings. There were none, except for an elderly woman exercising a sausage dog.

Gary drummed the fingers of his good hand on the steering wheel but he wasn't angry with her, she knew that. He was in love with her – not that he'd said so, but why else had he behaved the way he did when he'd saved her from Hal Cheviot? That was one good thing that had come out of this.

The woman at number 19 was just a handsome close up. There were a few lines and a thread of silver in the thick chestnut locks but she wore no make-up and her bones were those of a model.

Kathy had prepared her introduction and she was halfway through her speech, the bit about how she worked for the late Steve Armstrong and she had some questions relating to his business, when the woman invited her in. Excellent. She looked at Gary who said, without prompting, 'I'll wait for you in the car,' as instructed.

Rose – she'd introduced herself – ushered Kathy into a cramped front room with a naff patterned sofa and a huge old television that lived in a cabinet.

'I've seen your photograph in the *Racing Beacon*,' Rose said, 'with the horse that won the Prix Jacques Le Marois.'

Kathy explained her connection to Goldeneye.

'Lucky you,' said Rose.

But this wasn't the moment to discuss Goldie. Time to put her cards on the table.

'Look, this is a personal visit. And I'm not – well, Steve treated me very badly just before he died, so I no longer feel duty bound in any way.'

The woman was sitting next to her on the sofa. Her eyes were unblinking, her mouth full and soft. She looked kind but what was she thinking?

Kathy plunged on, aware that she might be turfed out on her ear any second. But she'd come this far and she had to know.

'When I was working for Steve I followed punters back to

this address. I'm positive they handed you money they'd won at his shops. There were dozens of them and they only bet on the first race at Hampton Waters.'

The woman's face hadn't changed. Her gaze was just as steady and she said nothing.

'Then I saw your husband, Mr Sidebottom, at the racecourse with a man who worked on the tractors, keeping the artificial surface in condition. He seemed to be in charge.'

The woman blinked, just once.

'I think you were fixing the races between you. And I know how.'

'I'm sorry, Kathy, I haven't offered you anything. Would you like a cup of tea?'

'No, thanks. I just want you to know that as far as I'm concerned the slate is wiped clean. But if you carry on I shall take my suspicions to the police.'

She would, too. Jerry would have a tough enough time taking on Fairweather's without being unfairly skinned at Hampton Waters.

Rose got up. 'I think I'll make a pot anyway. Perhaps young Gary outside would like a cup.'

'How do you know his name?'

'He's Charlie Moorehead's son, isn't he? I used to know Charlie quite well when my father was alive. Charlie trained for him at one time. Though almost everybody trained for Geoff Wyatt.'

Kathy had followed her into the kitchen.

She recognised the name Wyatt. There'd been a lot of talk at the time he died. She remembered now. The high-profile suicide. The perils of gambling. A modern day Rake's Progress some newspaper had called it. Her mother had read every word and said, 'Thank God I'm no longer married to your father.'

Unlike her hostess, Kathy imagined her face must be easily readable. Rose studied her closely and said, 'Yes, that Geoff Wyatt. He killed himself when Steve Armstrong had him warned off racing.' She poured boiling water into the teapot and set the kettle down with a bang. 'I'd be a hypocrite if I said I was sorry Steve was dead.'

So that explained the reason for Steve being the target of Rose's gambling scam. Revenge was a motive that Kathy could sympathise with.

Rose poured her a cup and Kathy took it gratefully.

'I hear,' Rose said, 'that Goldeneye is going to be stripped of the Two Thousand Guineas.'

Gosh, this woman was well informed. Rob's letter to the Jockey Club was not yet public knowledge.

'What's going to happen to Steve's half of the horse?' Rose asked.

'We're not sure. It belongs to his sisters as part of his estate. Rob thinks they'll want to sell anyway.'

'Maybe you can afford to buy him now.'

Kathy wasn't so sure about that. There'd been a lot of talk about finances in the light of their revised circumstances. Even at his reduced value, raising the money to buy Steve's share in Goldie looked beyond Rob and Bella, and though Charlie had now promised to contribute, they were still short.

'It doesn't look like it,' she said.

Rose said, 'I might be interested in a piece.'

Had she heard correctly? 'Really?'

'Provided he could race in my father's colours.'

Kathy was flabbergasted. Was this a genuine offer?

'Do you think,' Rose continued, 'that, provisionally speaking, your stepfather would be interested in having me as a partner in the horse?'

'I can't speak for him,' Kathy weighed her words, 'any more than I can speak for Steve's estate. But between you and me, it sounds good. Only . . .'

'Yes?'

'You haven't told me about Hampton Waters. I swear I won't say a word to anyone.'

'Of course you won't, dear, not if I'm thinking of entering into a partnership with you.'

So there it was, a bargain of sorts.

The tea was growing cold and they were still standing in the kitchen. It didn't matter.

Kathy couldn't wait any longer.

If it hadn't been for Gary going out of his way to cheer her up after all the recent dramas, she'd probably never have figured it out. He'd taken her to the beach at Redcar after a day's racing and she'd watched a group of kids running around on the sand. Then she'd made the connection.

She gazed steadily at Rose as she spoke. 'I think the groundsman specially prepared the track before the race meeting. He went round the inside lane with a heavy roller to compress the surface and make it hard. So any horse in that lane would have a huge advantage. Like running on a beach, there's a big difference between the wet sand and the soft dry sand.'

Rose said, 'Is that so?'

'Once the groundsman had rolled the inside track he then harrowed it lightly so it all looked the same. Then, after the first race, the whole track would be power-harrowed so it would go back to normal. That's why you only bet on the first race. And it's also why you only bet in races with one confirmed front-runner.' She beamed at Rose triumphantly. 'I'm right, aren't I?'

The other woman met her gaze and smiled.

'I hate to think of poor Gary sitting outside all this time. Why don't you fetch him so he can tell me all about Goldeneye?'

Kathy could see that this was all the answer she was going to get.

But it was enough.

She went to fetch Gary with a spring in her step.

Epilogue

Rob had never been to New York before and he felt a bit of a country bumpkin as the blue-coated bellman led the way into the hotel suite. Rob had booked it over the internet, conscious that in the current circumstances he had to watch the overheads, and had not expected much. To his surprise, the sitting room was huge. And through the window he glimpsed a sight that pushed buttons in his head, a silver fantasy of a skyscraper that he had seen many times on celluloid.

'That's . . .' he said, groping for the words.

'The Chrysler Building, sir.' The bellman had stowed their cases and was flicking on sidelights. 'You sure get a great view of the East Side from this window.'

Indeed you did. The bellman disappeared, pocketing his tip, leaving Rob to gawp like the tourist he was. He'd always imagined standing on the twenty-third floor of a Manhattan hotel overlooking the legendary city. And here he was, with an entry in the Breeders Cup Mile at Belmont Park tomorrow. Even if Goldie flopped, he promised himself a weekend to remember.

Rob should have been tense with worry. Goldeneye's race was a make-or-break occasion. Paying back the horse's prize money had swollen the overdraft to terrifying limits and he was still without a number-one stallion for next year's covering season – unless Goldie could pull off an impressive performance and fill the breach.

But Rob didn't care. He felt as if he'd been set free.

The Jockey Club had been decent about Goldeneye's registration. He'd faced up to them in Shaftesbury Avenue and come clean – as clean as he needed to be for their purposes. He explained that he'd been absent when the horse was born and the true birth circumstances had only come to light by chance, following the death of the head stable hand. His was an error of omission, rather than deception. They'd accepted that and he'd escaped censure. Though he'd expected a fine of some sort, the circumstances of Ivana and Steve's deaths seemed to have weighed in his favour.

The story had been played for all it was worth by the racing press. And the news that Rose Wyatt, daughter of the disgraced gambler and racing philanthropist Geoff Wyatt, had acquired a share in Goldeneye had kept it running. Even the mainstream papers had taken an interest and Rose had given interviews about the halcyon days when her father was a king of the turf. The fact that Goldeneye was now competing in the blue-and-gold silks of her father was given particular prominence. 'Even if Goldeneye comes last,' she told them, 'I shall be happy. Just seeing a horse run in my father's colours is what matters to me.'

In truth Goldeneye was likely to be outclassed in his first outing as a four-year-old. The Breeders Cup Mile was the top international mile race of the season and the entry included some fine animals, champion racehorses with impressive victories to their credit. Odalisque, the American filly who had landed last year's event, was in the field, as were the winners of other coveted races such as the Arlington Million and the Prix du Moulin. What's more, now Goldeneye was counted as four, he would be giving four pounds to the three-year-olds in the race.

It seemed to Rob that there was a real possibility Goldie might end up last.

Goldeneye's new management team had convened in the Mooreheads' living room the day after the Jockey Club had pronounced: Rob, Rose and Charlie. Rose was an unknown quantity to Rob but Charlie evidently knew her of old; he welcomed her like a long lost friend, with a kiss on both cheeks – the old bugger was certainly on the mend. As far as Rob was aware, her interest in the horse came through a chance meeting with Gary and Kathy. To be honest, he was more concerned that she was someone he could rub along with. He hadn't been entirely happy about the colours she insisted on but softened when her sentimental attachment was explained.

When they'd met, Rob had assumed they would just talk in general terms. But with the discovery of Goldeneye's real age his career was disappearing fast and they all wanted another run before the end of the season. Charlie had put the idea of the Breeders Cup on the table.

'I've only just been able to get up on the gallops and watch the horse at work. Gary told me how sharp he was but all the same I couldn't believe how he'd come on since I'd last seen him.'

Rob hadn't been convinced. His impulse was to protect Goldie. 'He'll be up against top runners. And he'll be giving lumps away to horses he was racing just the other week.'

Charlie shrugged. 'Name of the game, old son. Tomas says he's the fastest thing he's ever sat on.'

'With respect, Charlie, Tom hasn't ridden all that many good horses.'

'He's been riding a few recently. And he's a clever young man.'

Rob was aware of that. 'So Tom's in favour of this?'

'Hope you don't mind but I sounded him out.'

Rob thought about it. Tomas's opinion counted.

The Breeders Cup was the race Sheikh Al-Mazin had intended to groom Goldie for, so he must think the horse had a chance. Rob had heard that the sheikh had now bought Da Vinci, the winner of the Queen Elizabeth Stakes, with the Breeders Cup in mind. It would be nice to put one over on him.

Rose swayed the argument. 'Dad and I always went to the Breeders Cup, even if he didn't have runner.'

So here they all were, Goldie's new ownership team,

anticipating a memorable weekend – whatever took place on the track.

But there was one member of the Rushmore team who wasn't on the trip. Rob had offered to pay for Jacko.

The stable hand had been flabbergasted. 'Oh no, I couldn't,' he'd said.

'Why not? You've been involved with Goldie from the first, haven't you? From the very first.'

The significance of his words wasn't lost on Jacko. He might be slow but he wasn't dim. His pale eyes scrutinised Rob closely as he waited for what he might say next.

'You knew about Goldie, didn't you? You took a photo of him as a foal with Ivana.'

Rob had finally worked it out. The stable hand would have been at Rushmore that holiday, working odd mornings like always. And the shadow on the print, though unspecific, had been large.

'Why didn't you speak up, Jacko? Why didn't you tell me he was born in December?'

'I thought you knew. Anyway, Ivana asked me to keep it quiet. I've never said a word to no one.'

He certainly knew how to stay silent, Rob reflected. The irony was that if he'd spoken up, the girl he'd adored might still be alive.

'So what about New York? Are you coming with us?'

But Jacko had shaken his big head. 'If it's all the same to you, I'd rather stay here. I've seen New York on TV.'

So had Rob, but it didn't compare with the real thing.

'Hey.' Bella's voice breathed into his ear as her arms encircled his chest. 'What are you doing? I've been waiting for you next door.'

'What's next door?'

'The bedroom, stupid.'

The warmth of her body was seeping through the material of his shirt and he realised that she wasn't wearing a great deal.

He took his eyes off the skyline, incredible though it was. Some things were more important.

* * *

Tomas had often imagined riding in the States. He'd been sure it would happen one day and now that day had arrived, sooner than expected. He'd travelled out in time to acclimatise to the foreign working conditions. Here, the horses were all stabled in barns situated at the track and, rather than lasting for just a day or two, race meetings were seasonal, some going on for weeks at a time. It was certainly different to what he was used to in Europe.

Different did not mean worse, however, and he relished the opportunity to ride work on the racetrack itself. It gave him a chance to get used to the tight left-handed oval, common to all American venues. Though he couldn't duplicate the atmosphere of the meeting or the hurly-burly of a dozen thoroughbreds bunched around him, he could use his imagination. He'd seen the videos. And he'd ridden on the left-handed oval at Hampton Waters.

But this was different. This race was going to be the biggest test of his career.

Now, as he slotted Goldeneye into the starting gate, he was glad he had done his homework. It had been difficult to clear his head of the ballyhoo around him. The racecourse was packed and you could taste the racing fervour on the breeze. It could go to a new boy's head – and he felt like a new boy in this setting. For a moment, as he'd sat in the changing room listening to the murmur of the crowd outside, he'd wondered if he was out of his depth. Last time he'd ridden Goldeneye, the horse had been an acknowledged Classic winner, with the Two Thousand Guineas to his credit. Now Goldie had been stripped of his titles and exposed as a fraud. The horse had to start again from scratch, against the best milers in the world, carrying extra weight. Why on earth had he been so keen to expose the pair of them like this?

'What's up, mate?'

It was Ed Christie, his friend and housemate. Ed was on Odalisque, last year's winner, and was also riding the favourite for the four-million-dollar Classic later in the afternoon. If anyone ought to look stressed, it was Ed. Naturally, he looked as if he didn't have a care in the world.

'It's not like you, Tom,' he said. 'You're the bouncing Czech, remember?'

Tomas thought about it now as he waited for the last couple of horses to load. To the British lads in the field he was Bouncer, tough and resourceful in the saddle and one of them when the race was over. They'd seen him though the dark days after Ivana's death and, putting aside personal ambitions, they'd be thrilled for him to win if they couldn't pull it off themselves.

He'd just have to try his hardest, for the living and the dead.

The gate sprang open.

'How are you feeling, Rosie?'

Jason himself was a little uncomfortable. He'd been warned that the required dress code in the Belmont clubhouse was officially termed 'elegant'. He'd done his best but he'd never in his life aspired to elegance and he was conscious that his collar was gaping, sweat was pooling on his brow and the trousers of his only suit gripped his waist like a vice – he must have put on a few pounds since his wedding. He knew Rose had not married him for his looks but he hated the thought of showing her up.

'I feel fantastic,' his wife replied.

She looked it too, as he'd told her frequently since they'd left the hotel in the limo he'd laid on – well, it would be what she was used to with Geoff. Rose was loving every minute of being back at the top of the racing world and she seemed years younger. She'd knock 'em dead at the presentation, in his opinion. But he ought not to think like that. Forget about winning, just being here with her was good enough.

'I want to do something for Dad,' she'd said. 'I've not spent any of the money I've got from Steve Armstrong on me or you. I want to use it in Dad's memory.'

'You mean like a statue with his name on it?' he'd replied but that had been a pretty feeble joke.

In the end, in his opinion, she'd done just the right thing. She'd bought a piece of Armstrong's horse in Geoff's name. And there was no doubt in Jason's mind which part of the animal it was. Old Geoff – Geoff as he used to be – would have laughed like a drain to be memorialised in a horse's arse.

Goldeneye was drawn twelve out of thirteen runners, which placed him on the outside. It was reckoned to be a less than favourable draw but Tomas wasn't too concerned. It could get a bit rough on the inside in the early stages and in this position he'd stay out of trouble.

But he hadn't allowed for Goldie's sluggish start. The horse had been slow off the mark at Deauville where it had taken him a while to come to terms with the ground. Here he seemed to have gone to sleep waiting for the final runners to be loaded. The rest of the field had shot ahead and the pair were four lengths behind the field as they cut across to the inside to follow the rail.

Tomas told himself not to panic. Maybe Goldie just liked to come from the rear – it was what he did best.

Gary watched the race on one of the screens in the stand – it was the only way to see what was really going on.

'He's last,' he said, the words tumbling out on their own.

'Don't worry, son. It's where they are at the end that counts.'

Gary had heard his father say this hundreds of times and it irritated the hell out of him. But now it filled him with pleasure to hear that familiar voice rumble in his ear and his mother's retort, 'Oh, for God's sake, Charlie,' which accompanied it.

His mum and dad were here together, healthy and bickering. In the great scheme of things, it didn't matter where Goldeneye finished.

On the screen the horse was moving smoothly.

'He's catching them.' Kathy's fingers pressed hard into the back of his hand which she'd taken as the race began and pulled round her waist. Now she stood in front of him, the full length of her body leaning back against him. He could feel her quiver with excitement as Goldie overtook the back marker of the group ahead of him.

Gary's hand, the one that he'd damaged saving Kathy's honour, hurt like hell as she squeezed.

He didn't care.

They were well over halfway and Goldeneye had begun to work his way through the field. Tomas spotted a gap between the rail and the horse ahead and drove into the space. The other runner tried to veer back and shut him out. For fifteen yards they rode side by side, joined at the hip in a test of speed and strength. But Goldie wasn't going to be muscled out, he found a change of foot and spurted past.

Now they were boxed in. Tomas could feel the power surging through the animal beneath him but there was a wall of horses ahead and they had nowhere to go.

On her short acquaintance, Kathy loved everything about American racing. She liked the cry of 'It's post time' blown by a man in a red coat, the lightning rhythm of the on-track commentator's voice, the different vocabulary they used, like 'pole' for 'marker' and 'stretch' for 'straight', and all the other things that turned the familiar into New World strange.

She loved staying in New York, too. Rob had said that if Goldie won they should all extend their visit and paint the town. Kathy reckoned that sounded like heaven.

'Come on, Goldie!' she yelled.

Tomas was looking for a chink in the wall ahead. They were in the last quarter of the race now and fast running out of time. All he asked was a position to give Goldeneye a chance to show what he could do.

He nudged his mount to his right, looking for space on the outside but they were blocked off. He remembered his ride on Jack of Hearts at Leicester. There'd scarcely been an opening but he'd made one all the same. He'd just have to do it again.

He urged Goldie into the sliver of light between the two horses ahead. For a second it seemed that there was no way forward. Then his horse thrust his head into a channel that didn't appear to exist and barrelled into it.

To his left was Da Vinci, on his right Odalisque, the two favourites for the race. Whips cracked, hoofs thundered and Ed Christie's shout sounded in his ear, 'No you don't, you cheeky bastard!'

But the words were whipped away as Odalisque fell behind and Goldie raced alongside Da Vinci.

Tomas was damned if he was going to lose to the sheikh's horse. Even carrying the extra weight, they had to beat him. He wanted people to know that, barring an accident of a couple of days, Goldeneye was the quickest horse of his generation.

No one had told Goldie that he had been unmasked as an imposter, that his previous victories no longer counted in the record books and that his reputation was on the line. They didn't need to. Somewhere in Goldeneye, as in all champion horses, was the desire to empty the well of courage and stamina he carried within him.

Tomas hit him with the whip, not hard, more for encouragement; the animal needed no gee-ups or reminders. His instinct was to get to the line first and he simply followed it, with all the heart he could muster.

He's a flying machine, thought Tomas as they flew by the post. In first place.

There was pandemonium at the finishing line. The small British contingent had been following the story of Rose Wyatt's return to racing and Goldeneye's disgrace. What's more, many a sentimentally wagered dollar had just doubled in value. Here was a triumphant end to the best story of the week! The cheers rang loud and the lady herself was mobbed.

Jason beat a path through the crowd so Rose could get to the horse. His usually calm thoughts were all of a jumble. Just as well he wasn't an emotional man or he'd be blubbing by now.

Then, after Rose had congratulated the smiling jockey and fussed all over the horse and they'd set off for the after-race presentation, she'd reached out for him.

'Jason, come here.' She hooked an arm round his neck and kissed him on the mouth with passion. Kissed him like she'd never done before.

The crowd cheered even louder.

Kathy cheered along with everyone else. The sight of the middle-aged lovebirds only stiffened her own resolve.

Gary was surrounded by well-wishers. It was funny how many friends a winning trainer could acquire in the moments after victory. It was difficult for her to get close to him but that was OK. She'd have her turn over the next few days in the Big Apple.

Despite the crowd, she caught his eye and sent him a silent message of love.

It was about time.

Later, Rob slipped away from the celebrations and found Goldeneye in his stable. Pete was watching over him like a hawk but he stepped outside to give Rob some time with the horse on his own.

Goldie greeted him as he always did, with a gentle nod of his big brown head and an inquisitive nuzzle in the direction of Rob's jacket pocket. How come this son of the terrible Cape Fear had turned out to be so docile and friendly? Except where it counted, of course – on the racecourse.

On the day Rob had written to the Jockey Club he'd pulled down his father's old stud book and put a line through the entries he'd made under Goldeneye's name, erasing his entire racing record.

'The first thing I'm going to do when I get back,' he murmured to the horse, 'is put down that you're the winner of the Breeders Cup Mile. They'll never be able to take that off you, I promise.'

The horse blinked at him and shuffled his feet. He didn't care either way.